ABBOT LANE

JIM LAYEUX

ACKNOWLEDGEMENTS

First and foremost thanks are due to Linda Fitz, who not only made it possible for me to navigate the technical aspects of online resources and communication, but was instrumental in researching the shadowy world of anthrax and it's lethal properties. Couldn't have done it without you Linda! For proofreading and offering encouragement thanks are due to Maureen O' Donnell, Steve Paul Simms, Leslie Layeux, Edward Layeux, Melwood Cutlery, Jeff Barnes and Adam Chalmers.

And last but not least to AOS Publishing and my editors Michael Occhionero and Julia Bifulco.

For Gilbert, Mary, John and Edward Layeux

TABLE OF CONTENTS

PROLOGUE

Transcribed by Dr. Evelyn Lang Professor of Folklore, Ohio University. 'Kriel' (pronounced Krale) first appeared in a volume of ghost stories edited by Dr. Lang entitled 'The Haunted Lakes', Greer Press, Cleveland – 1936.1

Below is an extract of that account.

12 November, 1869.

The captain's spy-glass rendered the fog-shrouded cliffs along the Erie shoreline barely discernible. Overlooking the waves the grey visage of a fortress stood facing the pending onslaught. A fierce tempest descended upon the 'Katy' and the merchant ship was tossed about like kindling. Black water churned beneath her hull like froth in a witch's cauldron. Clinging to the guardrail first mate Peter Strand resigned himself to a watery grave. Shielding his face from the torrents he made out the blurred image of the captain on deck.

"All is lost Sir!" his words were vanquished by the gale.

Shouting louder he said, "Captain you have murdered your ship and crew!"

Pounded by the elements Damon Kriel wheeled about, "Silence! We'll weather this storm as we have the others!"

Struggling hand over hand along the rail toward a row of clattering buckets he shouted, "Every man on deck save the helmsmen! Have each take up a bucket and commence baling. We'll toss the spoils back into the face of the demon!"

"Captain!" pleaded his first mate. "We might save the ship if you'll give orders to arch toward the south shore out of the path of the storm!"

"Do as I say!"

Numbed by the furies and the captain's obsession Peter Strand retreated to fetch the crew.

'Amanda...'

The name slipped from the captain's lips like a feather.

As the storm bore down the frigid waters swept over Damon Kriel and his doomed crew.

CHAPTER

ONE

A mild breeze wafted through the Talleyrand Marine Terminal as the Florida sun cast wavering reflections over the water's surface. Seated on a bench the assassin had taken on the appearance of a longshoreman having a coffee break. Browsing a Jacksonville newspaper he placed it aside and sipped from a thermos cup. He adjusted his hardhat and cast rapid glances toward a rusty container ship berthed nearby. The 'Marie Atlantis' lay moored in the oily waters along Pier 7 for the better part of an hour. Beyond her stern tugboats were seen guiding larger vessels in and out of port. A dozen meters away a group of crane-operator's manoeuvred containers from stockpiles lining Marie's deck. Hoisted toward heaven the bins hung suspended, before being guided onto the backs of several flatbed trucks.

Pondering the directive informing him Dr. Azil Besserer, a treacherous microbiologist would appear as a senior crewman aboard the vessel - his instructions were blunt. Besserer was to be dispatched swiftly and discreetly. Without a sniper's perch the assassin was exposed – it would be necessary to follow the target. The encrypted message he'd received indicated Besserer would depart the ship flanked by a pair of crewmen carrying suitcases. Having Googled images of the doctor two were retrieved. The most recent was taken outside a tribunal court in A'biin a ten years earlier. The second was a student photograph decades old and irrelevant to his purposes. He studied the courthouse image and noted the fragile, tan-complected features topped with wisps of greying hair and committed it to memory. When the photo was taken Besserer had been forty-eight, he wondered how he might appear today and decided he'd look similar give or take a beard or moustache. The directive indicated he and his associates would be dressed alike: navy blue pea-coat, grey trousers, black shoes.

Waves lapped concrete buttressing the pier and gulls wheeled beneath a pristine sky. Their cries echoed as he considered his first assignment. Having spent his youth within the Temple, his studies were completed abroad before arriving in the US as a sleeper. Considered by his teachers to be outstanding in the art of stealth manoeuvre - he'd waited an eternity to be accessed. Meanwhile, he settled into the fabric of American life.

Following a dreary morning at the office, he set off to lounge alongside the pool attached to the Stanton Spa across the 59th St. Bridge in Queens, New York. Guiding the car through gridlock he relished the thought of plunging through water to purge his sins, while anticipating new ones. Upon arrival he basked in the company of several females and prepared to dive into the deep end, when his cellphone chimed. Excusing himself he hop-scotched barefoot across the burning patio stones towards the shade. Call-display on his devise revealed a blank screen.

"Hello."

A whiny screech erupted in his ear and his heart jumped. Remembering protocol he pressed 'record' as a medley of discordant noise was relayed to him from half a world away. There was a pause before the sound resumed, seconds later it ceased altogether. A look of consternation creased his brow and he noticed his trembling hand. Rousing himself he strode toward his poolside companions and slipped on flip-flops. He apologized for his sudden departure, stating he'd been summoned back to town on a work-related matter. Bowing toward the pout-feigning ladies he reassured them they were always on his mind. Briskly, he strode in the direction of the gentleman's change room and showered. He tossed his trunks and sunscreen into a shoulder bag and brushed his white shirt and matching slacks. Nodding at the attendant he strolled towards his convertible parked in the members area. Moments later he was racing along Queen's Boulevard into Manhattan proper. Shortly afterwards he entered his McDougal Street apartment and scoured the kitchen drawer for a pencil and paper. Seated at the table he withdrew his phone and accessed 'replay'. The riotous contents were transferred into coded visuals and appeared as hieroglyphics on the tiny display screen. He set about transcribing and jotted down reams of letters and numerals - erasing one and inserting another. The process repeated itself before the communique took on meaning in what amounted to a paragraph in his native writ. This was not the usual 'change-of-code' memo resulting from a compromised breach. Instead, he discovered he'd been issued his first assignment and was about to enter field operations on behalf of the SIAG.

Among the informed public the SIAG were known as the Intelligence division attached to A'biin, a tiny, oil-rich nation situated within the vast perimeters of the middle-east. In English the acronym stands for 'Soldiers of Infinite Ascendancy and God'.

The assassin had been employed as a literary curator within the New York Public Library system. Arriving in America years earlier as part of a student exchange program he appeared before NYPL Human Resource officials, bearing impeccable credentials awarded to him from the University of Bucharest in Romania. Documents specified his field of expertise lay in nineteenth-century literary research.

Answering each of their questions concisely he wondered if the deception would succeed. When he was hired as assistant curator in modern classics he was elated. Vetted by state officials who reported their findings back to Human Resources, results confirmed his qualifications. Placed on a salary of seventy thousand dollars annually, an abundance of paperwork was associated with the position. Allotted a third floor office within the 42nd Street main branch, he informed his handler of the development and settled into his new life. As agent-in-waiting he had no pressing responsibilities other than to show up for work and maintain a low profile. Meantime, months turned to years and still no wake-up call from overseas. Engaged in a rigorous fitness program at the gym it became apparent being a 'sleeper' was a never-ending waiting game.

In the months following his arrival in the US he lucked into the Greenwich Village apartment after charming a co-worker's mother, who was part owner of the building. Soon afterwards the cultural shock of America's wicked ways took hold. Indulging in his adopted country's livelier entertainments he found himself wavering in his commitment to the homeland. Keeping up appearances was a daunting experience. Schooled to present himself as a diligent citizen of whichever country he occupied, it was necessary to remain in character until the moment he entered the field.

He justified his frolicsome participation by reminding himself this was how people behaved in the West. One need only to refer to films, television and social media. If God-fearing America was guilty of fostering loose morals within a class system based on personal gain, none of it concerned the assassin who was practically an atheist. The evil he'd been cautioned against within the Temple was prevalent everywhere in the new world. If he had to endure Hell while maintaining cover - he'd give it his best shot. In a tireless effort to assimilate he was open to just about anything. Along the way cracks surfaced in the workplace. His attendance faltered and his flirtatious nature had been observed by several staff members.

The appearance of three men aboard the Marie Atlantis interrupted his ruminations. Obscured with caps and shades, the man in the middle bore a resemblance to the individual identified as Azil Besserer in the photograph. Emerging from a lower deck they paused at the railing before descending a ramp. Dressed alike each member of the trio carried a suitcase.

As the vessel rocked against rubber tires padding Pier 7, the assassin pulled his gloves tighter and rose from the bench. A whistle heralded the arrival of yet another cargo ship. To his right a row of storage facilities lined a transport route and he observed the trio approaching a customs terminal. An inspector glanced at their passports and waved them through. Continuing past offices belonging to JAXPORT (an abbreviation of Jacksonville Port Authority) the crowd thinned. The assassin produced bogus credentials and informed an inspector he was on break and going for a stroll. Once the gate was cleared he noticed the trio further down the boardwalk. They entered a driveway leading to a private warehouse. Sandwiched between his escorts the man in the middle appeared reticent as he was urged forward.

The assassin noticed a cluster of dockworkers assembled in anticipation of the latest arrival. Focused on the task at hand he considered the two men accompanying the target. Instructed to dispatch Besserer - if that meant his associates had to die, so be it. He strode up the driveway and noticed an SUV parked directly behind the facility. Advancing cautiously he peered around the corner and observed a rear door. Rapidly, he advanced and placed his ear to it and heard a clamour within. The door was unlocked and the possibility of a trap was considered. From beneath his longshoreman overalls he withdrew a semi-automatic fitted with a silencer. Daylight flooded the entrance as the threshold was forged. The door closed silently and the world faded to black. Extending his arm he inched forward allowing his eyes to adjust. A dim lighting fixture hung from the rafters and rows of stocked shelves receded into shadow. Traversing an aisle nearest the wall he noticed a workbench strewn with wrapping materials, and a motionless figure slumped in a chair. The assassin wondered if he was the unsuspecting dupe in a SIAG froshing ritual when something heavy landed on his shoulders. Knocked forcibly to the floor, he lost grip of his weapon and found himself on his back facing the pointed end of a dagger. Before the knife-wielder completed his thrust, the weapon was wrist-blocked and the assailant was gripped along both sides of his face. An extra second allowed time to exert a violent, bone-snapping twist of his opponent's head. The body rolled limply to one side and the pea-coat and grey trousers were observed.

There was another.

Retrieving the gun he rose and stopped cold in his tracks. The soft tread of a shoe was heard. Abruptly, a bullet from a silencer whizzed by overhead. Another struck a nearby support beam. The assassin hit the deck and determined the source of the shots. Seconds later he took aim and fired twice. Something collided with an object followed by silence. The assassin stole forward and discovered the shooter sprawled over a pump-dolly. In the faded light he noticed the startled expression in his dead eyes.

CLICK

The assassin was familiar with the sound of a .45 calibre levelled inches from his head.

From the dark recesses a nightmare voice gargled, "You're in the open put down your weapon."

The assassin sighed and placed his gun on the floor. Frisked from behind, a holstered revolver and sheathed knife were recovered. Shoved towards a stool he was instructed to sit. Obliging the request he cast a sidelong glance at Besserer slumped next to him.

"Unfortunately for you the doctor is very much alive," the odious voice resumed. "The effects of the administered drug should wear off by the time we conclude matters."

Staring into the void a chill ran down the prisoner's spine.

"How ironic," the speaker continued. "Both Dr. Besserer and yourself are of A'biinian extraction. Yet one of you is attempting to kill the other?"

When no response was forthcoming the host added, "A price must be paid - two of my assets are dead."

Unable to view the mute henchman lurking to the captive's rear his presence was felt nonetheless.

"I could be your handler for all you know?" the voice taunted. "A disappointed one to be sure."

Having walked into a trap on his first assignment the prisoner now had to endure a lecture.

"You're fortunate I'm not SIAG," the speaker persisted. "I understand they frown upon failure."

The hostage decided the vocal timbre emitting from his captor's throat was enhanced by a laryngectomy synthesizer.

Clearing his sinuses through the device his host declared, "For engaging in espionage and dispatching two men sentence will be pronounced swiftly! Any final words in your defence?

"No."

"I thought we were getting somewhere?" the speaker gurgled. "I assure you I represent neither the US, the SIAG nor any interest other than my own. That said we do share one thing in common. Care to guess what that is?"

"No."

"I'll tell you anyway a love of money."

"You're beneath contempt."

The prisoner was pistol-whipped along the side of his skull by the thug standing to his rear.

His host resumed with a question, "You've reaped a bountiful harvest living among us have you not?"

The hostage gazed into the dark and laughed. Expecting to be struck again he turned his face away.

"A display of defiance."the speaker mused.

The prisoner responded calmly, "If you're not SIAG how were you able to set me up."

His captor hesitated, "Several days ago your predecessor was apprehended. As he was being interrogated his phone was examined by experts. Among the retrieved data was the encrypted contact belonging to his replacement - that person was you. Your code was unravelled enabling me to establish contact in the guise of your overseas handler. I lured you here."

"You lie!"

The prisoner was pistol-whipped a second time.

"How else could I have contacted you?" his host queried. "Persuasive measures afforded your predecessor to reveal the basics of 'Discordant Word Formation' - a coded initiative developed by the SIAG, using sound variants and satellite technology. Once the process was made clear to code-breakers you were summoned with a wake-up call.

"You said you weren't affiliated"

"I retain connections."

The prisoner glanced at the microbiologist, "What of him?"

Laughter rippled through the voice apparatus like bubbling lava.

"Everyone knows Besserer is being hunted for offering his services to the highest bidder. His presence here is two-fold - he served as bait to lure you and I have further need of him. He was rotting in exile when his whereabouts was made known to me. I made an offer and he accepted. You witnessed him being smuggled into the country. His execution seemed an appropriate first directive to issue a novice SIAG agent like yourself."

The augmented breathing grew in intensity as the host slowly advanced.

"Once the SIAG discovered your predecessor had been apprehended he was terminated by means of an implant - similar to the one embedded in your own body Mr. Dante."

The name hung in the air like a shroud. His entire cover had been blown.

Peering into darkness the prisoner remarked, "I suppose you also know about the Playboy magazines under my bed?"

An abhorrent cackle erupted from the shadows.

Aware of movement to his rear the prisoner sat upright and felt the hair on his neck bristle.

"Once experts hacked into your file," the speaker resumed. "They were able to follow your trail backwards. Your entire history in this country is on record."

"You must be well-placed to have access to such expertise?"

"Perhaps. In any event I'm prepared to offer you an opportunity to work on my behalf. I need a professional in the field. You would profit greatly and continue to enjoy the benefits of life here in America. Under a new name and identity of course."

"Screw yourself."

Expecting to be struck again he was.

"You have an opportunity to free yourself from the bonds of the SIAG and live life as you truly desire Mr. Dante."

"Why me?"

"Because."

"Care to elaborate?"

"Five-hundred thousand dollars will be deposited into a Cayman account under whichever name you choose," the speaker extolled. "A portion of which is presently available to cover costs and living expenses. The rest will be withheld until our endeavour is complete in under a year's time."

Besserer stirred and raised his head. He blinked and went out again like a light.

"Right on cue," remarked their host.

The prisoner heard breathing to his rear and remained wary.

"It's my way or eternity Mr. Longshoreman. Choose!"

"What's expected of me?"

"The right answer."

"If I said I need time to consider?"

"That would be the wrong answer and you would die in an empty warehouse in Jacksonville."

With a killer breathing down his neck the prisoner nodded.

"What's that Mr. Dante?"

"Yes."

"Right answer."

The new recruit made no response.

"Tomorrow morning you'll meet with a surgeon. There's the matter of removing the deadly tracking device embedded in your bones."

Nodding toward his subordinate the man retrieved a syringe laced with enough eszopiclone to knock out a horse. He jabbed the needle into the neck of the recruit causing him to slump over instantly.

"Gather any devices," the voice rippled. "See to it the prisoner is X-rayed at the Jacksonville clinic we discussed. Results must be ready by morning."

Starting toward the rear of the facility the gurgling sound subsided.

The recruit was gripped about the waist and flung over the tall man's shoulder.

"This way," he muttered hauling his load out back and placing him in the rear compartment of the SUV.

Moments later he returned carrying Besserer.

Both were spread alongside one another and a blanket was tossed over both men. The passenger remained concealed by tinted glass in the rear seat.

As they departed the warehouse the dead were left for the JAXPORT authorities to dispense with.

JUNE – TEN MONTHS LATER

Sunlight sprayed the windshield as the Chevy swung onto Alta Vista and slowed to a crawl. Lowering his visor the driver brought the car to a standstill behind a stream of idling automobiles. Seated at the wheel Jesse Carlton frowned and adjusted his shades. Downtown was typically clogged and Friday's were worst. Every parking space within a mile was occupied. He'd planned on walking but procrastinated. Drumming his fingers on the steering wheel he glanced about for Carterelli's, a popular Italian restaurant located along that stretch. Up ahead a vehicle signalled its intention to pull from the curb. Opposite the median a madman prepared to make a u-turn hoping to secure the spot. Encouraged by the chorus of horns riding his ass the driver hesitated at the last moment.

"*Patience,*" Jesse whispered as he drew ahead of the desired space. Signalling, he reversed and navigated the car into the tight expanse until his tires aligned with the sidewalk.

"*Voila,*" he muttered inching forward and switching off the engine.

He purchased two hours on the meter and crossed an intersection towards an array of retail shops and restaurants. Despite a sagging US economy the town of Lantern Falls prospered. Nestled along the Lake Erie shoreline in northern Ohio; bistros and cafes resided a stone's throw from the corporate field offices towering over exquisite, century-old homes. Long time residents still lamented the loss of their picturesque town.

The previous week Lee Tondar, a history professor at the Grissim Institute texted Jesse an invitation requesting the young man join he and his wife for dinner Friday evening. Having met the professor on only one occasion the request was puzzling. However, it wasn't every day offers came his way and he graciously accepted. Grissim was situated less than a mile north of town. The campus was set among clusters of cedar trees overlooking the lake. In weathered splendour it's centrepiece remained Sentinel Hall. The antiquated structure loomed over the south shore on an never-ending watch.

The preceding summer Jesse was hired by the county to fill potholes for six scorching hot weeks. Straddling the running board of a tar and gravel truck he shovelled muck with a crew of second generation east Asians. On sweltering afternoons they'd toss him bottled water from a cooler and invite him to join them in the shade. Despite being an outsider his efforts earned him the camaraderie of his sweating mates. On the heels of that job he spent three weeks working as an apprentice in offices belonging to the town's only newspaper, the Lantern Falls Observer. Writing bylines the job paid less than his work with the road crew, regardless it was a Godsend for someone preparing to enter the field.

More than one hundred and twenty Print Media students were enrolled at the Institute. Most returned to their out-of-state residences during breaks. Jesse was among a handful who remained in Lantern Falls year round and his prospects this summer looked brighter. The managing editor of the Observer offered him a two-month residency commencing the first day of July. The job would bolster means of covering tuition and rent.

His encounter with Lee Tondar followed a staging of Edward Albee's play 'Whose Afraid of Virginia Woolfe', produced by a touring company out of Detroit. Accompanied by his wife, Lee appeared backstage after the show offering congratulations to cast and crew. Jesse was present with his girlfriend, Shawna Del Ray. It was she who'd lobbied the Arts Committee to book the show. Gathered 'round a punch-bowel pleasantries were exchanged before the group eventually drifted apart. As the greenroom filled the professor escaped leaving his wife to bask in the artistic reverie.

In realms of Print Media and Modern History, Grissim is one of several post-secondary institutions celebrated for achievement's in either vocation. In a world of social networking and cable news, the Institute stubbornly retains Print Media at the core of its curriculum. Broadcast media is left to larger universities. Most predicted doom for an Institute featuring specialized offerings – instead, both program's continue to flourish. Their success is due to Marion Benton, who for more than three decades functioned as college Dean. Approaching her seventy-fifth year many of Ms. Benton's former pupils remain devoted. Among numerous tasks she oversees Hillgram Hall, an antiquated playhouse which serves as a lecture hall and occasional performance space. In addition to the Albee play dozens of productions have been mounted on it's thrust stage over the years, including several home-grown offerings.

Jesse's extracurricular activities included contributing to the student newspaper 'Medusa's Tattler'. He commits himself to a daily regimen of exercise, including thrice-weekly martial art's instruction offered by a colleague at a downtown gym. Upon his arrival at Grissim he expected to find a physical education program in place, instead he discovered formal classes were non-existent. Organized sports initiatives had been discontinued a generation earlier a result of cost-saving measures. Students were encouraged to put together informal teams and have a go at one another on the sod opposite Abbot Lane.

Having kept the Tondar's waiting Jesse quickened his pace. A block further he paused outside of Caterelli's and entered the softly-lit establishment. An aroma of spices and pasta struck him like a tsunami and he took his place behind several patrons waiting to be seated. When his turn arrived he gave his name to the hostess and watched her strike it from a reservation list. She scooped up a menu and smiled, "Your friends are this way Mr. Carlton."

Mediterranean-style music mingled with a buzz of conversation as Jesse was led towards his destination. In a snug alcove a man and woman were seated beneath the glow of a Tiffany lamp. Placing his menu on their table the hostess said, "Enjoy.

A silver-haired gentleman of average height who Jesse recognized instantly as Lee Tondar, rose with his arm extended. The young man returned the gesture and was motioned toward a vacant seat.

"Make yourself comfortable son. We're delighted you could join us."

While on their feet the professor turned to the woman seated next to him, "Dot you remember Jesse Carlton - Jesse, my wife Dorothy."

"How are you Jesse!" she welcomed heartily.

"Fine," the young man replied. "And yourself?"

"Wonderful."

Dorothy Tondar was an attractive, middle-aged woman whose brown hair was coiffed neatly above her shoulders. Slightly heavier than her husband she dressed impeccably and bore a radiant smile.

Jesse took his seat and remarked, "You may recall we were introduced..."

"Following the Albee play," Dorothy interjected. "A delightful production - one you had a hand in I believe?"

"Only as an audience member," replied their guest. "The woman I accompanied brought the production to the attention of the Arts Committee."

Gazing across at his host Jesse said, "How are you Sir?"

"We're not on campus son, please call me Lee."

"Lee it is."

The older man cleared his throat, "When we spoke after the play you mentioned you'd done some work at the Observer. Dot reads everything they print. She also reads most of the articles published in the student newspaper."

"Oh oh," the young man responded. "Actually, I've only had one piece appear in the Observer. Last August I covered the War of 1812 reenactment by the lake. In fact I start a summer job at the paper in a week. Perhaps I'll cover the event again."

Lee pressed the issue, "You're returning to the Observer?"

"Until classes resume."

Their waiter greeted the new arrival and offered to take orders. The Tondar's requested a bottle of house wine; an Italian red and the trio settled on Caesar salad followed by a pizza layered with mozzarella cheese and vegetables. The waiter jotted down their orders and disappeared.

"Any other plans?" Lee inquired.

Jesse mentioned he intended to visit family in Windsor, Ontario before the job commenced.

The professor hesitated, "Whenever I chat with Print Media students a shared concern is often raised. I'd be interested to hear your take son?"

"Certainly."

Leaning over the table he asked if Jesse perceived a threat to his vocation, with the advent of social media and a thousand-channel universe?

"To put it succinctly how do you size up the future of print journalism?"

The young man pondered the question, "I'm told new tabloids pop up frequently in supermarkets."

Lee grinned, "A refreshing viewpoint."

While the pair conversed Dorothy sized up their guest's age and concluded he was twenty-two, which proved correct. The robust student stood approximately six feet, three inches with his shoes on. His dark eyes matched the colour of his hair which was combed back to reveal a pleasing face.

When the opportunity arose, Dorothy inquired about his past and discovered he'd taken a year off after completing high school. Travelling the country, he did odd jobs and spent time in both Canada and Mexico before returning home to Toledo, Ohio. He applied for enrolment at Grissim and was accepted, afterwards he found lodgings in Lantern Falls. To help cover entrance fees his mother and grandfather chipped in.

The wine arrived accompanied by salad. Ten minutes later their waiter placed the main course before them and served piping hot slices using a spatula. When he departed Lee filled their glasses and the trio toasted. Once the pizza cooled they dug in.

Savouring the taste Jesse said, "Delicious!"

"Best this side of the Mediterranean," the professor confirmed. "It's strictly a hands-off-the-slice affair - unless one wishes to wear melted cheese on one's lap."

"Really Lee," his wife scolded.

Encouraged to help himself Jesse gripped the spatula and manoeuvred a second slice onto his plate.

"Pity they don't deliver..." Dorothy lamented.

She reconsidered the remark, "Perhaps it's best."

As the meal progressed the trio chatted among themselves. The Tondar's inquired about Jesse's off-campus living arrangements and learned he rented a basement bachelor in the suburbs. The cost of tuition was discussed and they all agreed it was in the nation's interest to invest in affordable post-secondary education.

Without warning Lee's fork landed with a clatter on his plate. Erupting into a seismic coughing fit, Dorothy reacted instantly by slapping him on the back until the coughs subsided. She quietly explained her husband's outbreak was not a reaction to the meal they were enjoying.

"Lee suffers from an ongoing respiratory condition," she asserted.

Rubbing her husband's back she inquired if he'd taken his medication.

"I did I'll be fine."

The professor's eyes were watery and his normally pallid complexion was a hue of crimson brought on by the ordeal. Retrieving a napkin he dabbed at the corners of his mouth.

"We'll take a stroll and get some air," Dorothy offered. "It's a lovely evening."

A final slice remained and Jesse's host's insisted he have it stating they needed room for apple crisp and coffee. Their guest remarked he hadn't been so stuffed since Thanksgiving and agreed a walk was in order.

"If you need a lift home afterwards I'm happy to oblige," Jesse added.

"Nonsense," the professor replied withdrawing his wallet. "We're seven blocks away and a walk does wonders, especially after downing a bottle of Italy's finest. Thank you just the same."

Lee left a generous tip for the superb meal and service. Having genuinely enjoyed himself Jesse thanked the Tondar's for the invitation.

"The pleasure was ours," Dorothy responded. "Let's do it again sometime!"

Outside Carterelli's the sidewalks were busier than they'd been on arrival. An accelerating motorcycle was heard along with a steady procession of cars and pedestrian traffic. Despite the bustle it was a perfect evening for a stroll. They sauntered along the crowded walkway and crossed at the lights. Their pace slowed as Dorothy paused to admire a host of summer fashions displayed in a storefront window. Breathlessly she whispered, "They're gorgeous!"

She placed a wrist through her husband's arm and said sweetly, "Darling, I must have a peek I won't be long."

Without awaiting a response she joined another woman admiring the display and the pair were soon pointing out the finer details. To avoid the pedestrian onslaught Lee motioned the young man towards the edge of the curb. He thrust his hands in his pockets and returned to the subject of summer employment.

Above the fray he said, "When I was your age our generation followed an urge to hit the road during summer breaks in the same manner you did."

His companion agreed, "I'm glad I travelled, but there was never enough time or money."

Wrinkles creased the older man's brow and Jesse was concerned he might succumb to another coughing fit.

Instead he said, "Son, I wonder if you might..."

"Yoo-hoo Darling!"

Standing alongside her friend Dorothy waved from the display window, "Just a quick dash inside. I'll only be a jiff."

As the ladies made their way a commotion occurred.

A man running at terrific speed charged towards the pair, as they were about to enter the boutique. Several feet away a couple were nearly bowled over by the suddenness of the assault. With dazzling precision the runner cut between Dorothy and the other woman, snagging their purses and vanishing around the corner. Jesse took off in pursuit, meanwhile Lee rushed to the aid of his wife and her friend. A startled onlooker was on her phone punching 911. Both women were guided toward a nearby bench and Lee assured them the police had been summoned. He placed an arm about his distressed wife and told her everything would be done to recover their stolen purses.

"We'll need to give a statement," he added.

He rose and gave Dorothy's companion a reassuring smile and kissed his wife gently on the forehead, "You're safe here I'll fetch Jesse and return."

Dorothy brought a crumpled tissue to her nose and nodded.

The street the assailant fled down was a less travelled artery. Jesse managed to round the corner in time to see the man charge down an alley lodged between two antiquated buildings. The passage ended in a littered back lot with trashcans and a rusted pick-up without wheels or windows. Lamplight receded into shadow as Jesse maintained pursuit. The runner entered the lot and tossed the stolen article's to a waiting confederate. Turning to face his pursuer the thief paused long enough to size up his adversary. Meanwhile, Jesse noticed a short, well-built male in his twenties. Wearing a sleeveless black t-shirt, track pants and runners; a toque was pulled over his forehead and a bandana concealed his face. By the tell-tale body language and his agility, Jesse determined the man possessed an understanding of martial arts.

The thief lunged forward striking him on the side of his jaw in a blur of motion. As Jesse staggered backward a fist slammed into his gut folding him over like a pillow. Blood dripped from the corner of his mouth as he attempted to get his bearings. Glancing up he saw his opponent sailing through the air with his legs splayed, ready to make contact with his upper torso. Jesse crouched low and caught him with an elbow shot to the side of his skull – which sent him to the pavement with his light's extinguished. Turning about he observed the second masked-marvel advancing. Like his slumbering consort, he sported a handkerchief over his features and was attired head to toe in black. Unlike his colleague he was built like a brick shit-house. Jesse was caught off guard with a left-hook followed by rapid-fire thrusts to his midriff. Buckling over the student landed upon the pavement with the wind knocked from his sails. The brawny mug decided it was time to finish the job and moved towards his fallen adversary. As he reached down to grasp him - a split-second was all Jesse needed to wrap his legs about the man's thick neck. Applying all his strength Jesse brought his upwardly mobile fist crashing into the thug's temple, and watched him fall face-forward into oblivion.

Lee managed to pursue his dinner guest down the alley and paused along the periphery of the back lot. Having witnessed the confrontation it's outcome was determined in under ninety seconds.

"I'm glad you chose to remain off to the side professor."

"I wasn't aware my presence had registered," the older man replied breathlessly. "Things appeared over before they began."

"Tell that to my jaw."

Panting heavily Lee closed his eyes.

Jesse brushed off grime accumulated during the altercation and stood between both sprawled figures.

"These guys are professionals why would they pass time snatching purses?

"Desperation?" Lee offered tentatively.

"You okay?" Jesse inquired.

"I will be."

While the professor caught his breath Jesse informed him the stolen purses were on the hood of the nearby wreck. He gestured towards the derelict vehicle.

"I suggest we leave both article's untouched until the police arrive."

"Sound advice," Lee responded.

Jesse proceeded to unmask and re-mask his unconscious assailants. Both were unfamiliar and he found no ID or weapons.

He apologized for taking liberties, "I'm curious by nature."

Lee understood perfectly.

The young man stood up, "Mrs. Tondar and the other lady - how are they?"

"They're unharmed I should get back."

"Of course."

"We'd best be prepared to answer a few questions."

Both men stood in the decrepit back lot as siren's wailed to a halt opposite the alleyway. Beams of light zigzagged as silhouettes of policemen cast elongated shadows upon the brick walls.

Lee turned to his companion, "Before we were interrupted I was about to ask if you'd mind swinging by my office Sunday morning - say around eleven. There's something I'd like to discuss with you."

Jesse considered the request, "Sure."

"Good I'll meet you in the lobby of Sentinel Hall."

A voice resounded from the alleyway, "Drop all weapons and raise your hands!"

Several uniformed officers entered the area with their sidearm's drawn. A flashlight was directed towards the sprawled figures lying on the pavement. The officer in charge instructed the older man and his dishevelled friend to turn about and face the wall. With their legs spread they were thoroughly frisked. Having given his name and and occupation, Lee informed the officer his wife and her friend had their purses snatched. He further stated his young friend pursued the thief, unaware an accomplice was waiting.

The officer glanced at the unconscious men stretched before him.

"Frankly Mr. Tondar I'm surprised to find a professor from a distinguished college amid such unsavoury surroundings."

Lee shook his head ruefully and stated he had every intention of informing the police.

"You both could have been killed," the cop persisted.

Lee had to concur.

Jessie's statement mirrored his companion's, otherwise he remained silent.

Once identities and contact numbers were established, the pair were released and informed they might be called pending further investigation. At the crime scene Dorothy and her friend, along with several eyewitnesses had given statements. The purses belonging to both women were returned with their contents intact. The police concluded preliminaries and set off toward the station with their battered cargo in tow. Dorothy exchanged email addresses with her fellow victim and they hugged. Once she returned to her husband's side they were able to resume their walk - finally.

"The nerve!" she exclaimed. "Such a brazen attack with all these people about."

She shuddered, "If I'd seen him coming I would've shoved my purse right in his kisser..."

Lee noticed his wife was still rather stressed and decided to hold off mentioning the event's which unfolded at the dark end of the alley. Gradually, they drew up alongside Jesse's parked vehicle.

"Until Sunday morning then?"

"Until Sunday morning," Jesse replied as cheerfully as possible.

Once farewells were exchanged the Tondar's departed. Jesse removed a thirty-dollar parking infraction from beneath the wiper and shoved it in his pocket. Seated in the driver's seat he massaged his jaw and contemplated the events of the past hour. Leaning forward he started the engine and swung onto Alta Vista. Ten minutes later he entered his basement apartment and crashed.

———————

TWO

TEN MONTHS EARLIER - SEPTEMBER

The surgeon was summoned by means of an encrypted text directive. An hour later he secured the parlour door and entered a twin garage attached to his lavish residence. An overhead light fixture revealed two vehicles. The nearest was a streamlined Mercedes Benz; the other would carry him to his clandestine rendezvous. He entered the box-shaped delivery truck and glanced in the mirror where he noticed a rogue hair jutting out. Moistening his forefinger he applied it to the strand until it lay flush with his scalp. Along both sides of the vehicle the words Semic Furniture were emblazoned. A fully-operational emergency room was concealed within the delivery truck. If pulled over he'd been instructed to hand over a card, requiring the authority to contact the listing engraved along it's surface. Once initiated the card would be returned and the truck waved along.

The driver was Dr. Peter Ivan, principal surgeon at an exclusive clinic he'd founded in the wealthy Atlanta enclave known as Tuxedo Park. Dr. Ivan considered himself a patriot first and a successful physician after the fact. He played a small but vital role in keeping his country safe from the evils of a foreign, religious mindset. In the capacity of 'surgeon-on-call' he'd been recruited as an asset two years earlier by a mysterious entity within the National Security Agency. The surgeon's area of operations extended from North Carolina as far south as the Everglades. On this assignment he was expected to journey to a place called Acres Road, nine miles west of Jacksonville, Florida.

Easing the truck from the garage he guided it down the driveway and disappeared along a tree-shaded avenue. The gate secured automatically and his neighbours wouldn't have given the matter a second thought. Furniture deliveries were routine in that neighbourhood.

Funding for the Mobile Emergency Room or 'MER' as the surgeon referred to it, was provided by the Agency at a cost of five hundred thousand dollars. The money was spent modifying and refitting the truck with state-of-the-art equipment and the latest medical accessories. A custom engine purred beneath the hood as the driver manoeuvred the vehicle through morning traffic onto Interstate 75.

Since his recruitment Dr. Ivan hadn't exactly been overwhelmed with cloak and dagger intrigue. Occasionally, a text would arrive and he'd find himself dashing off to one safe-house or another where a quick patch-up or his medical opinion was required. Afterwards, he'd vacate the premises and return to his civilian practice or the golf course. In short, Dr. Ivan had yet to perform a life-saving operation on some tortured field-agent who'd stumbled in from the cold. After two years service he'd been issued fewer than a half-dozen assignments. No wonder he felt jaded. There was an upside however, his salary provided by the American taxpayer was considerable.

Cool air streamed from the dashboard grid as he rounded the turnpike merging with I 75. He applied pressure to the peddle as, 'We Are The Champions Of The World' blared from speakers.

The surgeon considered his private practice which employed three doctors, four nurses, and one very busy receptionist. Presently, he spent less than three hours per week hovering over an operating table at the urging of his A-list clientele. Other patients were received by subordinates. In addition to his Tuxedo Park estate, he owned a rambling country home in West Virginia and held property in Barbados. Income earned as an Intelligence asset was merely a perk. America was at war and the surgeon was nothing if not a vigilant homeland defender. He felt kinship with the medics of yore bearing a Red Cross, while dashing into the face of machine-gun fire to aid a fallen soldier. His was a cross he bore proudly.

Longing for action he felt a strange foreboding about this latest assignment. On the upside the rendezvous was less than five hours away. However, encrypted directive's were usually accompanied with ID known only to himself and his handler. In this instance the entry was nonexistent. Regardless, the message was streamed via an Agency channel. Perhaps his services had been conveyed to a colleague.

He approached Jacksonville and turned onto a county lane before bringing the truck to a standstill. Relieving himself he returned to the MER and accessed GPS coordinates. Directions indicated Acres Road intersected with Highway 8 the route he'd been travelling. The location struck him as odd as previous assignment's were routinely conducted within nondescript suburban homes. He returned to the highway and slowed as Acres Road loomed. Signalling onto the deserted stretch he found his destination. A driveway led to an abode where a tall white male was observed waving in his direction. The individual sported a plaid shirt, jeans and boots. The surgeon wasn't fooled nohow. This was no ordinary hayseed, likely he was keeper of the safe-house.

The truck was motioned around to the rear of the dwelling.

With that accomplished the driver exited the front seat and strode to the rear of the MER. Twin doors sprang open revealing the emergency compartment in it's pristine glory. The surgeon extended a hand to his host who returned the gesture without giving a name. He excused himself and reentered the house to fetch the patient.

Dr. Ivan understood the 'need-to-know' aspects of clandestine affairs.

Glancing about his desolate surroundings he observed a billboard sign indicating the entire region was slated for development as a housing project.

A twin-step walk-up attached to the rear of the MER was released and he climbed within. While his host was occupied he donned a disposable smock and glanced over the sanitized interior of the compartment. The confines were roughly five yards lengthwise and eight-and-a-half feet across. It accommodated an operating table which functioned as a recovery bed. Intravenous equipment hung from a nearby rack alongside an anaesthesia mask. An oxygen tank was harnessed next to a chrome cabinet encased in shatterproof glass. Within it an array of gleaming instrument's were displayed. Pills and medications were refrigerated or secured in cabinets. Attached to the interior chassis was a monitor equipped with a magnifying screen and adjustable lighting. It represented the latest in enhancement technology.

Only a nurse was missing - in war sacrifices had to be made.

Dr. Ivan wondered what was keeping the keeper? As if on cue the man appeared behind a gurney. Leaping from the MER, the surgeon assisted transferring the sedated patient into the compartment and onto the operating table. His relative youth was noted and he observed the purplish bruises along the side of his head. Vital signs were all stable.

The keeper vanished a second time and reemerged an instant later clutching a brown dossier. He bounded into the compartment and stood alongside the visual monitor. A series of slides were withdrawn and he urged the surgeon to access the device. The slides were placed on an illuminated glass surface and the magnification was adjusted. Four images were showcased from various angles. Each highlighted a lower portion of the patient's left ankle.

Withdrawing a pen from his breast pocket the keeper guided the tip towards a specific point.

"See it?"

Squinting at the enhanced image the surgeon slipped on glasses and noticed a tiny article buried deep within the talus bone.

"I see something," he responded.

"If you look carefully you will notice a slight protrusion on the object."

The surgeon focused. "Yes I see it."

"That is a GPS tracking implant," confirmed the keeper.

The surgeon was startled to learn an implant could be so microscopic. It would deceive most scanning apparatuses such as those found in airports and courtrooms.

"Can you remove it?"

Viewing the implant from different angles Dr. Ivan thought perhaps his ship had truly come in. Despite his host's accent he sensed a tangible weightiness surrounding the assignment and was no longer ambiguous.

He made an exaggerated show of study, "Hmm...yes it's clearly apparent now."

"This man is a US operative who was abducted by enemies of the State," the keeper remarked. "He was drugged and implanted with this device so our adversaries could access secrets. The implant is a threat to National Security."

The surgeon bristled and pondered the insidious minds who'd conceived such a plot, without considering his own side practised similar deception.

"I'll remove the article," he asserted. "It'll involve laser surgery and a period of recuperation, but the job will get done."

The tall man smiled, "I knew I could rely on you."

Donning a mask and protective glasses the surgeon prepared the patient. With his head poised a foot and a half over the lower-left ankle, he dug directly into the bone with a laser knife. Cutting around the implant he glanced repeatedly at a monitor to view the readings. Loaded with sedatives the patient's breathing remained consistent throughout the ordeal. In under twenty minutes the sinister device was removed with needle-nosed tweezers. The surgeon displayed the tiny, blood-soaked article to his guest. It was carefully rinsed and laid on a tray to bear scrutiny beneath a zoom lens.

The keeper gazed at the monitor and remarked, "Not only is this gadget designed to track. It kills it's host when they are of no further use. Had we been unable to dislodge it the latter would have occurred."

He retrieved the object and placed it within the folds of a handkerchief.

Once the talus bone fissures had been tended to and the skin incision's closed, Dr. Ivan removed his gloves and rinsed his hands thoroughly. His host was handed a sealed bottle of painkillers and informed the patient would need several days recuperation.

"His ankle will ache and he'll have a slight limp. However, he'll soon regain his stride."

The surgeon assisted placing the patient back on the gurney and transferring him into the safe-house.

"He'll recoup here and be properly ministered," the keeper asserted

Once the transfer was underway and the stretcher was about to be wheeled inside the man said, "I'll manage from here. I wonder if you'd mind waiting while I jot down a brief account of today's procedure?"

"Not at all."

The tall stranger reentered the dwelling hauling his load.

Dr. Ivan tossed his gloves and smock into a toxic-waste container and rinsed his hands a second time. Bandages and cleansing solvents were returned to their rightful place. He stepped from the MER as his associate emerged from the house. The surgeon was handed a sheet of paper detailing the operation.

"Paperwork...." the keeper sighed.

"Tell me about it," the patriotic healer replied reviewing the document.

He passed it back, "Without getting technical that's basically what transpired."

"Thank you," the man remarked placing the sheet in his dossier.

Sounding more informal he added, " I must go into Jacksonville on an errand. I know its an imposition but may I beg a lift from you. My vehicle is in storage."

He nodded towards an attached garage, "I have a suspicion it's being monitored in town by prying eyes."

The surgeon was extended a knowing glance.

Dr. Ivan understood perfectly and responded with an unreserved, "Yes".

Living among shadows was probably all the poor bugger understood.

"Thank you."

"Let me know when you're ready to leave?"

"I'm ready now."

"Then we're off."

Fastening the twin-steps to a harness he secured the rear doors and trudged around to the driver's mount. Climbing behind the wheel the surgeon discovered his passenger already buckled in. The engine started and he manoeuvred the truck onto Acres Road while his companion indicated the quickest route into Jacksonville. Complying with directions the driver strained to see something other than farmland. Decidedly uncomfortable the surgeon tried to think of something to say.

Reluctant to turn on the radio lest it clash with whatever the passenger had on his mind he finally remarked, "You must find it isolating out here?"

"Yes."

The sun was low and dark clouds lingered in the east. The route appeared to be taking longer than implied with no sign of civilization in sight. The driver shuffled restlessly while his passenger muttered something about expected rain. Abruptly, he leaned forward and pointed toward a crossroad post with a handmade sign nailed to it. In bold letters 'Fresh Cabbage' was scribbled. An arrow pointed down a side road towards a stall.

"Cabbage!" the keeper declared. "I could bake rolls and feed the patient and myself properly."

He turned to the driver, "Stop I implore you."

Apologizing for the outburst he said, "It's rare to find fresh produce anywhere in this county. Most farms are owned by the state and ship directly to market. May I take a moment and purchase enough for a few meals? Microwave dinners get tiresome."

Cabbage harvest was in earnest and the fields were bountiful. With some reluctance Dr. Ivan swung onto a dirt road and gazed toward the distant stall.

"Thank you," his grateful passenger sighed. "This won't take long."

The truck approached the rickety stand and the driver considered the odd location. Being a retail operation it should have been on the road best travelled. He also wondered why no one was tending the stall.

Two days later the farmer who maintained the property noticed an unusual number of crows hovering above a corner acre. On closer inspection he was horrified to discover the partially devoured remains of a human being. The unfortunate individual had been the subject of the crow's appetite. Once the state police arrived the farmer was informed the man had been shot twice in the head at close range. No trace of a weapon or vehicle was recovered at the scene. A considerable amount of rain had accumulated. Clues revealing how the victim got there and which way his killer or killers vanished were washed away in the downpour. It was up to forensics now. The bewildered farmer was never considered a suspect and was informed the victim had been one of Atlanta's leading surgeons.

A dozen miles away a break and enter was reported in a vacant home up for sale. The B&E occurred around the same time as the cabbage-patch killing. The house was deserted with the exception of several blankets nailed haphazardly over the interior windows.

TEN MONTHS LATER - JUNE

The label attached to the shrink wrap indicated the sandwich was three days old. It tumbled from the vending machine like trash down a garbage chute. A thin layer of chopped egg held two slices of stale white bread together with the strength of industrial glue. Yanking both slices apart it's buyer peered inside. Mixed with a smidgen of mayonnaise; the egg hadn't even been properly boiled. Orange splotches of yoke instead of the desired yellow were in evidence everywhere. He was able to sight the indentation marks left by the fork on the egg whites, where it was purportedly chopped. He cussed himself for forgetting his lunch and stuffed the travesty in his shirt pocket.

Seated in the lunchroom surrounded by card tables and folding chairs Ray Pearson glanced about his surroundings. A trio of vending machines lined a wall next to the counter. One contained soft drinks, another dispensed snacks - the third was the dreaded sandwich machine. Craving sustenance Ray noticed the middle machine stocked donuts wrapped in cellophane. He fumbled for change and happened to whiff the untouched sandwich and decided to forgo the snack. He reached for his thermos and poured coffee instead. It's fragrant aroma scented the stagnant air.

To his immediate left two of Ray's lab-room colleagues were speaking heatedly in Somali. Debating the upheavals back home occasional flare-ups sometimes occurred. Most of the time they got on fine. Across from them a middle-aged female was reading a paperback and sipping diet cola. Her lunch routine rarely altered - pasta and vegetables in a plastic container stored in the lunchroom refrigerator.

Taking in his surroundings Ray recalled the space as it had been when it was a real cafeteria. Staffed by a catering firm contracted to serve hot meals to more than one hundred employees - clattering dishes, chatter and cash register girls were recalled. Over the ensuing years the building's interior was restructured to create more work space. The cafeteria was reduced to its present size, soft lighting fixtures were refitted with harsh fluorescent and vending machines replaced the caterers.

A soft-spoken aboriginal male of average height and weight Ray dressed casually in a work shirt, pressed jeans and runners. Entering middle-age his passive features revealed traces of a smile at the corners of his mouth. Remarkably, he'd worked at that same location since leaving high school twenty-six years earlier. Businesses operating out of the facility had either gone belly-up or merged with larger firms, leading to layoffs and outright closures. Throughout it all, Ray was fortunate to weather a succession of on-site employment. When one company folded he was often hired by the next. A job might last three months or three years depending on the fly-by-night employers. Out to make a quick buck these hucksters at least provided Ray with a steady paycheck.

Residing on the second floor of a rooming house, Ray shared bathroom and kitchen accommodations and slept on a sofa next to his coffee table. Surrounded by a dresser, books and a guitar, he rose at eight each morning and commuted to work by means of the Detroit Transit System. As the bus wound through the industrial streets east of the Southfield Expressway, he stared vacantly from the window. Seeking to improve his lot he'd enrolled in an advanced computer course two nights a week. The program required a nine-month commitment and if successfully completed, he'd be in a position to apply for higher wages within the manufacturing sector.

While attending night school he'd met an attractive black emigre from Puerto Rico named Gloria Mayorga. She worked box office matinee's at a downtown movie theatre and attended Graphic Art's classes in the evenings. Following months of courtship, Ray started spending weekends at her apartment where she enjoyed his easy-going manner. With a regimen of work and school-related activities keeping both occupied, they struggled to remain above the poverty line.

Abruptly aware his colleagues had departed the lunchroom, Ray roused himself and made his way along the corridor towards Lab D. An office and restrooms appeared along his right. Opposite them a row of identical labs merged with a shipping room at the end of the hall.

Technicians were discouraged from interacting with those working in other labs. Mealtimes and breaks were scheduled thirty-minutes apart by management. Ray and his lunchroom companions made up the team assigned to Lab D. With the exception of himself his mates could barely speak English. In a pantomimed ritual of gestures and shrugs they managed to communicate among themselves. With Ojibwe blood flowing through his veins Ray related easily with his marginalized comrades.

Sentra Avenue was situated among one of Detroit's most industrialized regions. The artery was lined with weather-beaten factories, warehouses, auto-body shops and even hosted a strip club. Ray's current employer Electron Era was located along the stretch south of Pappas Place – a modest diner operated by Tal Pappas. The burly short-order cook served up meals to satisfy the appetites of plant workers, truckers, cab-drivers and cops all of whom frequented his establishment. Closed weekends his doors opened at six am until three pm workdays.

In order to make the looming week more bearable Ray occasionally treated himself to one of Tal's Monday breakfast special's. During one visit the conversation rolled around to Ray's employer.

"Thought you said they cut the night shift where you are, Ray?"

"They never initiated one," the patron replied dipping toast in his eggs. "Won't be surprised if day shift ends up on the chopping block neither."

"Kinda strange," Tal resumed. "Ever since they rebooted operations there's been a stream of nighttime activity. Workers takin' breaks outside, a van comin' and goin' at all hours."

Ray frowned and speared a home fry, "There's a night watchman on duty."

"Screw him!" Tal responded dismissively. "Harry Flotsin's a dork. He's in here all the time and claims to know everything. Tells me to mind my own business!"

The cook tossed a towel over his shoulder and approached the counter. Despite the diner being empty he lowered his voice, "I lease the middle floor of this joint to storage holders and live on the third."

He leaned in close, "From there I can spot an alley cat at two hundred yards. Not much to look at I grant ya. Quiet as a tomb at night 'cept for the diesel's rolling off the overpass and the activity surrounding your place."

Tal paused as two city workers entered.

"Be right with you fellas."

Touching up Ray's coffee he quietly concluded, "All I'm sayin' is if there's no night shift, someone's getting paid overtime."

"Well it isn't me," his customer remarked wiping crumbs from his shirt.

Tal chuckled and replaced the coffee pot.

He turned to the new arrivals, "What can I get you gentlemen?"

Downing his coffee Ray fished out his wallet and left ten dollars on the counter, "Gotta run Tal, keep the change."

"Later," the cook called out cracking a pair of eggs over the grill.

Decades earlier Silicon Valleys sprang up in virtually every industrial centre of North America. The emerging sector allowed small manufacturers to start lines of production they hoped would expand. If microchip technology peeked during the mid-nineteen seventies - it limped with overkill by the early eighties. The bubble finally burst in the wake of cheaper productivity from Asian markets. Finding it difficult to compete North American firms were often left high and dry. Workers found themselves with a pink slip and an unwanted vacation.

From the mid-1980's onward digital technology represented a second coming. Products ranging from computers to home entertainment systems were being scooped off the shelves. Inevitably, this was followed by a lull as the digital market overwhelmed itself. Electron Era entered the fray during the latter part of this recess period. Leasing the Sentra Avenue building, the new tenants initiated a period of on-site renovation lasting several weeks. By August a job notice appeared in a community newspaper and a small quota of position's were filled. Ray learned they were hiring and established contact. Requested to bring his resume along for an interview he was hired on merit of his experience in low-tech manufacturing. He left his job at a car-wash and commenced working in mid-September, as the plant delved into modest production.

The 'lab technician' tag attached to his position sounded loftier than the reality. Ray's latest assignment was a variant of others which came before. A few interesting challenges had livened the drudgery over the years. At one point he was being groomed as a foreman, however before that occurred the firm in question was absorbed by a multinational entity and everyone was fired. Inevitably, the enterprise pulled up stakes and relocated to Mexico where labour was cheap.

Once Electron Era initiated operations they informed employees they were taking a cautious approach. In prosperous times round-the-clock production was essential, presently that wasn't the case. As far as Ray could tell the fledgling company maintained a skeleton crew. He'd counted fourteen heads when their supervisor, Jackson Bell assembled staff in the lunchroom two days before Christmas. Cans of no-name soda pop and a family-size bag of Cheesies were on the counter next to a roll of paper towels. Other than one's lab-mates no one knew the next person. Within minutes the party was over with the puzzled worker's being prodded back to their respective labs by their generous overseer.

———————————

Each lab had a captain accountable if delays occurred. Naturally, the position wasn't enhanced with a salary increase. Ray was appointed the post because he spoke English. The routine they followed was simple:

A technician retrieves a tray from a pushcart labelled 'incoming'. Each tray contains ninety digital-circuit sheets the size and weight of a postcard. Utilizing needle-nosed tweezers the sheet's are dipped individually into a cleansing solvent and placed under a hot-lamp for several seconds to dry. Afterwards, they're returned to a tray labelled 'clean' and deposited onto a pushcart marked 'outgoing'. With the cart fully loaded it's shuttled through to the shipping room via a 3' X 3' hatch. Each worker is expected to process a dozen trays per shift totalling eleven hundred sheets. Despite the eye-searing repetitiveness of the task, Ray and his gallant crew stayed ahead of the procedure.

Hunched over an incoming tray one morning he came across several dozen defective sheets. The stained product was placed at random among it's pristine neighbours and would have gone undetected, had their handler not been alert. Picking up a wall-phone he dialed Jackson Bell and received no response. If the supervisor had a cell number Ray didn't know it. This was the second time in as many weeks an incident of this nature occurred. The previous week he'd picked out several ravaged samples and sought out the foreman. He was found in the lobby chatting with the daytime guard and informed of the problem.

Bell waved off the discrepancy and declared, "We'll recall the damaged product and replace it at no cost to the buyer."

He cast the security guard a glance.

"Leave a report on my desk," he informed Ray. "I'll get the shipping guy to pick out further defects."

"But the shipping guy won't know what to look for," Ray insisted. "The sheets are inserted into grooves sideways. The damage can't be observed from that angle."

Bell merely nodded at Ray's logic and suggested they return to Lab D and retrieve the contaminated sheets.

The incident repeated itself and once more Ray went looking for Bell.

He entered the front lobby and was confronted by the same security guard, a man named Wicker. Seated at a desk he glanced up from behind a trio of monitors.

"Yep."

Ray said was looking for Mr. Bell regarding a work related matter.

"Haven't seen him," the guard responded. "Likely he's bogged down with paperwork somewhere."

"He's not in his office."

"I said somewhere."

Wicker's eyes narrowed, "Shouldn't you be at your work-station?"

"I'm looking for the supervisor regarding damaged product!" Ray's voice had taken on an edge.

The guard eyeballed him, "You were here bitchin' 'bout the same thing last week. Got issues use the inter-office phone."

"I did no answer."

Wicker leaned forward, "Your name's Pearson ain't it? It's on yer' pass. If I see Mr. Bell I'll say you were askin'...alright!"

Ray's pass was pinned to the shirt he wore beneath his smock and wasn't visible. Wicker rose and glared at him, "Alright!"

Much as he hated to admit it this clown was actually preferable to his night-time counterpart. Ray wasn't the only veteran at that facility, Harry Flotsin had been employed onsite even longer. Ray's first encounter with the portly watchman had been twenty-five years earlier, when both worked night-shift for Norenco; a firm manufacturing components for ghetto-blasters and Walkman radios.

The company disappeared long ago, however Ray recalled nights when he and his mates - mostly Blacks and Hispanics from the inner city, would arrive for work to find Harry sitting on his butt eyeing them with contempt. If a supervisor arrived his manner reversed entirely. Among a flurry of greetings he'd usher them through the lobby like visiting royalty.

One frigid winter night a 'dipshit' - Harry's term for shift workers, stood outside smoking beyond an allotted break. In response to the offence Harry ambled across the floor and secured the doors, leaving the poor wretch exposed to the brutal Michigan winter. The shivering worker pounded the heavy glass, meanwhile Harry sauntered back to his desk and feigned a yawn. Toting a walkie-talkie he eventually strode back and released the latch. The enraged employee charged forth, meanwhile Harry placed his finger over the emergency button attached to the communication devise and reminded the frozen labourer who held the upper hand. Not giving a shit the worker lashed out and the police were summoned. Harry wound up with a fat lip, meanwhile the provoked employee was fired and charged with assault.

A rumour circulated alleging Harry had applied to become a police officer. Evidently, he'd been rejected outright after giving a series of questionable responses during his first and only interview. Facing a panel of veteran law enforcement officials he was queried on matter's involving race relations, firearms and gang violence. Harry's answers were perplexing to say the least. When asked whether officers should discharge their weapons if uncertain a suspect is armed Harry nodded enthusiastically, "Get them before they get you!"

A female panel member glanced up, "I beg your pardon?"

Without missing a beat Harry stated it was high time the cops kicked some serious butt and cleaned up the rabble.

When issues pertaining to race and sexual orientation were raised, the panel sat stunned as Harry rattled off slurs and made reference to the 'tarts and homos' littering the streets. On the subject of gang-related violence he addressed one of the panellists, who happened to be black as 'you people'.

In the end it was decided Harry wasn't the recruit the Detroit PD was seeking at that time or any other.

"Their loss," he muttered crumpling the rejection slip he'd received in the mail.

Harry believed he would've looked smashing in a cop uniform. What other calling afforded him due respect? The military? Cool outfits but the rigours of service were unsuited to his lifestyle. Parking enforcement officer? No thanks somebody might hit him. Lifeguard? Not much uniform there - besides he couldn't swim.

Reluctantly, Harry returned to the ranks of Security Official.

It was Ray Pearson's good fortune his old nemesis maintained night watch where no lowly dipshits were around to dump on.

Ray departed the lobby and felt Cal Wicker's salamander eyes on his back.

Smoky orange Plexiglas lined the left side of the corridor and sturdy partitions separated each lab. He paused as an idea took shape. All material's delivered to Ray and company were shuttled through a hatchway on a cart from Lab C. Strips of rubber draped both sides of the hatch, preventing visual contact and allowing the flow of product to continue. He wondered if folks in the neighbouring lab had an explanation for the defective sheets. Contact was forbidden between technicians from other labs so he had no idea who worked next door. Management justified this stringent policy by stating discourse was counterproductive. Security cameras were mounted along the corridor, while others were angled towards doors leading to and from the building. In his many years of labouring onsite Ray had never witnessed such precautions. Security measures verged on paranoia. The plant processed digital components for inclusion in home entertainment appliances. Did management believe they'd be targeted for industrial espionage? It seemed unlikely a bulk-parts manufacturer shipping to bargain-basement wholesalers - would have the world's spy agencies tripping over themselves to get at their technical assets.

Ray stood before Lab C and reminded himself the issue was work-related. If he was discovered in a lab other than his own it had to do with the quality of product. Aware the door was locked from within, he peered through the Plexiglas and knocked. Four faces glanced up from seemingly familiar tasks. The lab captain rose and strode reluctantly toward the door. His eyes shifted from the visitor's face to the sample of the defect. Ray gestured for the man to open the door so he could explain. The captain turned to his bewildered colleagues and shrugged. The door was unlocked and Ray was confronted by a middle-aged Asian male with bright, intelligent eyes.

"You're not management!" he whispered. "We could get fired for this."

"Sorry to bother," Ray said apologetically. "I'm in the lab next door. We've been receiving damaged goods from you guys."

The captain replaced his glasses and glanced at the sample, "May I see that?"

Ray was admitted and he noticed two female technicians of Hispanic origin. The fourth was a Caucasian male who appeared to be in his mid-seventies.

"Yes," sighed the captain turning the stained article over. "We've come across lots of this stuff lately. You would've received more had we not picked out most of it. The damaged product you received must have slipped by us." He glanced at the others and cleared his throat.

"Did you notify the supervisor?" Ray inquired.

"Absolutely, I informed Mr. Bell the instant we started receiving this crap. I was instructed to leave the rejects for him. We do but still it keeps coming."

Ray recalled Bell's indifference when he brought the matter to the supervisor's attention.

The lab captain studied his guest, "I know the cause of the damage."

Caught up in his surroundings wrinkles formed along Ray's brow.

"Overly cleansed and recycled..." the man continued. "This sheet has been rinsed to the point of obliteration. Solvents and acids have destroyed the digital hardware on it's surface with a prolonged cleansing procedure."

Ray caught gist of what was being implied, "You're saying it's been dipped to death!"

"That's what I'm suggesting."

"But the product only needs to be cleaned once at the end of the process. That's our job in Lab D."

"It's what we do here," the other replied. "This sheet has been cleansed hundreds of times, which is why surface ravages have appeared. The carnage is happening more frequently."

Ray studied the expressions of those around him and noticed the familiar solvents and procurement instruments.

"We assumed you guys were engaged in a different part of the process."

A feeling of nausea overwhelmed him. Apologizing to the captain and his team for the intrusion, he retrieved the sample and departed. Instead of returning to his lab, he backtracked in the direction of Lab B and peered through the glass. Three technicians were within, one observed him and brought it to the attention of her colleagues. Ray could scent the familiar cleansing solvents. Further on he came to the first lab and noticed four technicians going through similar procedures.

Retracing his steps he strode past Lab D and was observed briefly by his crew. His chest tightened as he paused before the shipping room. Perhaps someone within could shed light on what was going on. Knocking firmly he received no response and pounded a second time.

His throat was parched and the rancid odour of the egg sandwich made him queasy. He felt a chill and needed a washroom. Abruptly, the door was unlocked from within.

KLACK

"It's open," a voice bellowed from the opposite side. "Light switch is on the right."

Wondering why the lights weren't on already Ray grasped the handle and entered. Confronted with a black void he fumbled for the switch and heard shuffling feet. An instant later he felt a blow to the side of his skull and slipped into darkness.

———————

THREE

TEN MONTHS EARLIER – SEPTEMBER

At approximately 1 pm Atlanta time a man paused on a crowded sidewalk to relieve the pain in his left ankle. Toting bottled water he withdrew a vial of painkillers and popped two tablets. He set off again retaining a visible limp.

Carl Kristy he muttered.

The code-name was crafted for him by his handler. He'd been informed of it by the pistol-whipping sadist who served as his chaperone. The moniker had a Christian ring to it which took some getting used to. Resuming his laboured trek Kristy dodged a multitude of suits and skirts. Unable to recall the deadly tracking device extracted from his ankle he was grateful nonetheless.

Having cultivated the demeanour of continental charmer and world traveller, he'd been instructed by thespian's within the Temple and became a formidable actor. The thesis of their art was never to overplay a role. It was a lesson he struggled to overcome.

A sharp pain shot up his leg and he hesitated. Walking was essential if he was to make a full recovery. He paused to caress the bandaged scar and glanced at his destination a dozen meters distant. Once inside the lobby of the Stafford Hotel he entered a pharmacy. Browsing magazines he picked out a current issue of Time, as a tall, tan-complected man drew alongside. Eye contact was established and the man departed the store. Kristy counted to ten and limped off in the same direction. The person he followed was the same henchman who'd roughed him up in a Jacksonville warehouse days before. The man was a constant presence as Kristy recovered from his ordeal beneath the knife.

The pair drew up separately before a pair of elevators. Kristy tried to forget the Jacksonville debacle and prepped himself for his first real chat with it's architect. He would've preferred more time to recuperate, however his benefactor felt otherwise. The previous morning he'd struggled to get out of bed. As the day progressed he was able to achieve more of a natural gait. Deemed fit enough to meet with the boss his overseer allowed him a stroll before the meeting commenced. Aware he was being observed Kristy and gave him the slip purely to amuse himself. His training enabled him to mimic dialect's wherever he found himself. Fluent in several languages English had become his second tongue.

Having not been formerly introduced to his roughneck escort, he decided to furnish him with a name in the same manner one had been crafted for him. Over the course of their acquaintance his chaperone's only spoken words were, 'this way' and 'follow me' .

An elevator appeared and they rose to the thirty-first floor. As the doors whisked apart his guide gestured with an outstretched arm, "This way."

Room numbers were displayed as they entered a softly-lit corridor. Drawing up before Suite 3110 his escort rapped in measured intervals. A buzz emitted and Kristy was motioned across the threshold. Adjusting his eyes to the gloom he was guided towards a chair in the centre of a living room. An envelope lay alongside a glass of ice-water on an end table. Seating himself Kristy crossed his legs and kept the sore ankle leg off the floor. An oval-shaped pool of light shrouded by darkness was observed. The effect was rendered by draping a towel over a lampshade and setting it on the floor. His paymaster sat before him in silhouette with the curtains drawn. The outline of a brimmed fedora and shades were visible on the head of the mystery man.

"Welcome Mr. Kristy," the voice rippled. "Kindly refer to me as Sir."

Kristy's chest tightened and he nodded.

"Do you fancy your latest code-name?"

"It suits me fine Sir."

"I hoped you'd like it."

The voice-disguising device he used had been conceived by journalists so 'star witnesses' could appear on television. Anonymously, these guest's would expose others in return for cash. The subject is placed in silhouette while their natural speaking voice is fed through a synthesizer, giving it a gargling, slightly demonic timber.

Abruptly, a name for Kristy's cryptic handler surfaced. The face facing him had no face - not one which could be discerned. Christened 'the Face' the recruit had no intention of uttering the name to his face - he preferred living. Cordially, he remained Sir.

The outline of his host staring back silently unnerved Kristy.

"I trust your operation went well?" the voice bubbled.

"Other than a receding limp I get about. Thank you for arranging the extraction."

The Face nodded, "You'll grow accustomed to the dim lighting and vocal hyperbole. Under normal circumstances a conference table would suffice. Due to the nature of this operation discretion must be exercised."

"Of course."

Kristy sipped water and feigned a look of intent.

"Shall we get down to business?" inquired his host.

"By all means".

"I take it the 'brief' you were provided with during recuperation was reviewed."

"It was."

"In addition to our Detroit venture you'll recall much of it dealt with an individual named William Penther."

"I studied his file."

"Mr. Penther and his followers are indispensable, especially with regards to Detroit."

"I understand."

"Presently, three of his closest disciple's maintain the electronics plant mentioned in the brief. To stem the tide of immigration ripping the nation asunder, Penther believes they're the vanguard of an Aryan movement designed to incite a race war. Because of their conviction he and his men were successfully recruited by V."

He nodded towards the individual who stood to Kristy's rear.

"In fact it was V who initiated the operation by following my directives. This includes leasing the Detroit compound and felicitating Azil Besserer's entry into this country. You'll recall he was smuggled in the day we both became acquainted. Because V has been responsible for laying so much groundwork I'm recalling him. Further efforts in the field would make him too visible a target. Instead, I'm replacing him with you."

Seated in the dark with a lopsided grin Kristy managed to say, "So I'm to be a target for whatever you're planning?"

"V is wanted by the authorities you are not!" the Face responded forcefully. "That's an advantage not available to my associate."

Kristy held his tongue.

"As my field operative you'll make certain a flow of cash and directives are made accessible to Penther - who in turn passes them onto Jackson Bell, foreman of the Detroit installation. Adding to the illusion of legitimacy, Mr. Bell has filled more than a dozen positions with worker's churning out bogus product. Those job's will expire upon completion of our project. An atrium exists beneath the plant - wherein a decontamination chamber has been installed alongside a small lab. A steel basin has been inserted into an excavated pit to facilitate development of Besserer's weapon."

That morning Kristy received a statement from the Cayman National Bank on his returned cellphone. It arrived in the form of an onscreen pop-up. The receipt indicated one hundred thousand dollars had been deposited into a freshly opened account - under the name Karl Kristy.

The silhouette seated before him was granted his full attention.

"While recovering from your operation Dr. Besserer was flown to Detroit and installed within our compound. Production of his formula is about to proceed so you'll follow directives as effectively as your predecessor did. Your first assignment will be to acquaint yourself with Mr. Penther at his rural retreat in Indiana. V has smoothed the way on your behalf."

When Besserer's weapon was referenced Kristy bristled. As agent-in-waiting he'd been frequently updated with regards to the fugitive doctor and his doomsday formula. The SIAG referred to his weapon as 'Airborne Cataclysm' or AC. Originally concocted by a colleague of Besserer's working out of the same government laboratory; that individual was found dead of apparent suicide. Once the SIAG turned their attention toward Besserer, he'd vanished taking samples of the formula with him.

"The weapon will take roughly nine months for its potential to be realized," resumed the Face.

"And I'm to monitor its progress?"

"That task will be handled by men working alongside the doctor. In addition to your courier duties - you'll observe the activities of an Intelligence analyst mentioned in your brief."

"You're referring to the Ohio professor?"

"Lee Tondar," the Face responded. "He serves on faculty of the Grissim Institute where his position is two-fold. On one hand he's a history professor - on the other he's a seasoned spy. You'll conduct campus surveillance. I want photos and license plate numbers of after-hours visitors frequenting Sentinel Hall, the building Tondar retains an office and lectures in. I expect reports following each watch."

With measured calmness the Face added, "Your SIAG predecessor was murdered by your own people due to his treachery. On this side of the pond we do business in a similar manner - without implants naturally. Please remember that."

"I shall," Kristy responded.

Pain shot up his leg and silence fell over Suite 3110.

It was broken when he remarked, "My brief states renovations conducted within the compound were carried out by two contractors. Do they pose a risk?"

"A pertinent question?" remarked his host. "Contractor's were necessary to facilitate the atrium. They erected a wall and blasted out a portion of the ground floor. V set-up partitions to create a living space on the lower level where a washroom and a storage area previously existed. Penther's men pitched in and installed a prefab decontamination chamber and showers inside the atrium. A ground floor shipping room and labs were left intact by the former tenant. We added security cameras and staff afterwards."

"And the contractors?" Kristy persisted.

"When work in the atrium was complete both men were paid in cash by Jackson Bell. That same evening their van collided with a retaining wall on a Detroit overpass and vaulted over the guardrail. Sadly, neither the driver nor his partner survived."

Kristy felt the presence of V lurking behind him and decided not to pursue the matter.

"Don't leave without taking the envelope," the Face gurgled. "You'll find directives printed in the coded-dialect you've hopefully studied."

Once the meeting concluded Kristy reached for the envelope and rose to his feet. References directed towards his mute chaperone indicated the man was given a name after all. As with the Face a more interesting pseudonym materialized.

"This way," the man repeated and the name stuck.

———————————

TEN MONTHS LATER – JUNE

Framed photographs lining the mantel reflected sunlight streaming through bay windows. The single-bedroom unit was home to Lee and Dorothy Tondar. Situated on the ninth floor of a condominium in downtown Lantern Falls, the photos displayed were taken over the course of many years. A few were captured while the couple resided in Florida, others highlighted Dorothy as an attractive young art student in Maine. Several featured Lee long before he'd met his wife. One revealed him as a pallid seven-year-old suffering from tuberculosis. The illness persisted until he was twelve when it miraculously disappeared. In another he and a high-school chum waved at the camera as they bit into candy apples on Coney Island. Only three photographs chronicled him during his formative years. Two were group shots taken while he served in the Marines, a third showed him as a freshman at Princeton following his discharge.

Lee grew up in a modest bungalow on the outskirts of Baltimore, Maryland. His father Harold worked with the Defence Department as an engineer during the emerging years of the Cold War. In wake of Sputnik he participated in designs for America's first space satellites. To provide a post-secondary education for his children, he accepted contract work on behalf of several private engineering firms. Lee's mother Helen worked as an administrator at a nearby high school. Lee and an older sister Shelly were raised in a caring environment befitting a middle-class family of the era. Their parents remained together until Helen passed away of cancer at the age of seventy-one. Shelly and her husband moved into the family residence to care for Harold until his own passing several years later. Both parent's worked hard to ensure their children might benefit when they were no longer around.

At school Lee was dubbed a 'brain-boy'. His interests revolved around history, science and art - passion's not shared by his jock-oriented peers. Because TB carried lingering effects Lee shied away from the football grid. Track and Field was mandatory and a source humiliation for the young man. As final pick among competing teams, the ordeal came down to Lee sitting on the sidelines while cheerleader's shouted 'rah-rah' at his mates. Ironically, he became an enthusiastic college football supporter later in life.

At Princeton Lee showed remarkable integrity in both History and Communications, so much so the university extended him a scholarship during his sophomore year. After receiving his Bachelor of Arts he entertained the notion of teaching at college level. Opting for tenure as a history professor at a local Maryland college; he was abruptly recruited into the NSA's fledgling Signals Intelligence Division (SIGINT), by the Dean of Modern History at Princeton. Whisked off to a facility in Delaware, he entered into an intense program involving code-breaking, encryption and signals study. Ten months later he was packed off to Maine where he was assigned to teach history at Ealing, a mid-sized college on the fringes of Bangor.

During his first term at that posting a friend introduced him to a pretty arts student named Dorothy Rush. Enrolled in her final year and living in-residence, Dorothy was as boisterous and cheerful as Lee was withdrawn and introspective. Despite occasional dissent their opposing dispositions clicked. Both enjoyed travelling, reading and spending nights together. The following year they were married and took up residence in a rented apartment, where Dorothy experienced issues with infertility. The diagnosis prevented the couple from having children. When Lee relinquished his teaching position to accept contract work on behalf of the government, Dorothy went with the flow. Vague about his professional life Lee's first assignment involved analysis of photograph's taken by U2 spy planes along a spectrum of global hot spots. It was his success in encryption which secured him a place in SIGINT at clearance level, during the waning years of the Cold War. Working out of Maryland HQ, Lee was made station-chief of an Intelligence outpost sequestered within of the campus of Billings University near Fort Lauderdale. At Billings he supervised a team of young cipher clerks assigned to intercept data from satellites orbiting the Gulf Coast and Caribbean.

With the cold war ebbing the Agency decided to splinter part of its operational apparatus. By 1990 bold new advancements in satellite transmission were being deployed. The heaven's were littered with orbiting canisters and twinkling circulars. It became apparent some of these devices were actually spy satellites, engaged in transmitting coded content from adversaries working against US interests. Lee recalled a time when only three man-made object's circled the globe, Sputnik, Canada's Alouette and American Explorer 1, which launched from Cape Canaveral in 1958. Telstar, the world's first communication satellite ascended from the same launchpad in 1962.

When the Tondar's arrived in Fort Lauderdale they rented a townhouse nearby Billings in the Central Beach region. From their deck the Atlantic Ocean was sighted in the hazy distance.

Abruptly, Lee was sent to Portugal.

It was necessary the Agency monitor Russian relays nearer the source - without standing on their doorstep. With an ocean separating both superpowers, a signals-retrieval expert was needed to establish a suitable European location for pristine reception. To allow SIGINT greater capability in disseminating Russian Intelligence, Lee spent several months scouring the Portuguese countryside for sites offering clear reception. With her husband overseas, Dorothy remained in Fort Lauderdale immersing herself in cultural events and charity work.

Lee was recalled as scores of new gizmos cleared the atmosphere at orbital levels. The sheer volume of circling canisters strained SIGINT to the max, leaving little time to decipher crucial Terra-based transmissions. With the Berlin Wall down Russia's nuclear arsenal remained a concern. The US faced the added threat of mid-east terrorist organizations attacking American targets and those of her allies. Subsequently, it was decided a new agency with links to the NSA be created. It was hoped this splinter outfit would ease the burden of encryption personnel. Suspect relay's would continue to be referred to SIGINT if further scrutiny was warranted. The fledgling offshoot was christened the Universal Communications Agency or UCOMA. Their headquarters would occupy an entire floor of the National Security Agency building in Maryland.

While stationed in Portugal Lee encountered his share of intrigue normally associated with being a field agent. In the guise of a Boston investor contemplating becoming a shareholder in a Lisbon development initiative, he travelled the length and breadth of the country. Wherever clear points of reception were identified, he'd record the coordinates along lines of latitude and longitude and pass them onto SIGINT officials.

Trailed by what he believed were Portuguese police his stalker's turned out to be two KGB agents curious about his activities. Suspecting the American had a hidden agenda, the pair were directed to move in and extract information. As Lee prepared to return to the States one gained entry to his rooming house in the city of Guarda. The individual never got beyond the front stoop. While in Florida, Lee - the unlikely athlete - took up a rigorous study of Jujitsu and managed to enhance his defensive skills significantly. As the intruder started up a flight of stairs, a sleight-of-hand caught him at the base of his neck. Bound and gagged inside the quarters his assailant, Lee frisked the prisoner and recovered a semi-automatic and a passport. As the enemy agent struggled with his binds, his American counterpart sat in a chair with a silencer-affixed automatic levelled at his head.

Removing the man's gag Lee whispered, "You've been following me...why?"

When no response was forthcoming a bullet grazed the top of the man's head and buried itself in a dilapidated wall facing an alley. Flinching, the man responded in poor English he was a private investigator assigned to tail him. He stated the identity of his client needed to be withheld in accordance with his profession.

A second bullet removed several hairs from his scalp and he conceded to being a Russian operative.

Lee inquired about his associate?

"He is merely a point man awaiting word from me you have been interviewed.

"You mean interrogated and possibly executed.

"No I swear!"

Lee left him bound in a closet and slipped out of the rooming house and the country.

The Agency remained preoccupied with the 'pristine reception' initiative and Lee was shuttled off to Norway in the middle of winter. Posing as a Canadian architect studying nineteenth-century Nordic design, he spent his first night in the scenic town of Lillehammer. A week later his rented vehicle was rear-ended along a deserted stretch by a trio of Russian agents. Forced into their van at gunpoint he was frisked and his gun and fake ID were confiscated. Informed he'd be taken to a safe-house outside Oslo for interrogation, a three-hour journey ensued before they drew alongside a suburban transit station. Instructed to depart the van silently, they strode toward a second vehicle where Lee noticed the platform packed with commuters. One of his abductor's led the way, two others flanked him. As he was motioned forward their weapon's were concealed beneath bulky overcoats.

Abruptly, Lee bolted in front of a slow-moving bus and just missed being struck. He dodged among the crowd and bounded onto a separate platform, sprinting toward a bus headed for downtown Oslo. One of the abductor's caught sight of him and charged forward. Lee paused to retrieve a tiny device from the hem of his sock and tossed it. The object struck pavement and plumes of odourless black smoke discharged triggering alarms. People reacted and began running for shelter. Lee made it aboard the coach as it's doors whisked shut. Staring back at the mayhem he wiped sweat from his brow and found a vacant seat.

Next day he was back in America.

While stationed abroad Lee's name along with several others, had been bantered about as a possible first Director to helm UCOMA. An unnamed source made a case against him stating he was too valuable in the field. Weary of overseas assignments, Lee informed his superiors he desired to remain stateside to spend more time with his wife. The same source then suggested Lee would better suit the fledgling Agency, someplace where he and his wife could ease into retirement.

In the end Lee was passed over for the position of UCOMA director.

Shortly afterwards the Tondar's arrived in Lantern Falls, where Lee accepted the role of station chief servicing a covert outpost in Northern Ohio. On the upside, Royston Adams was appointed UCOMA's first director. Adams was hardly the warrior envisioned by some decision makers as befitting the Director's chair. Those folks would've preferred Nelson Seymore-Johns to head the new division. Johns, a no-nonsense Admiral also failed in his bid for the job. He would later assume the loftier rank of CIA Deputy Director. Naturally, politics reared its head regarding aspirants vying for becoming UCOMA chief. None had been more supportive of Lee Tondar's candidacy than the newly anointed Director himself. In run-ups to the nomination Adams spoke persuasively of Lee's gifts, insisting he offered the agency a lifetime of clandestine experience along a spectrum of Intelligence gathering.

Lee stood on the escarpment overlooking Lake Erie and pondered his first few years at Grissim. He marvelled at the pristine satellite reception those coordinates provided. The Institute was in good standing and the posting allowed him to resume his earlier calling as a history professor. The lakeside setting was situated next to the tourist-friendly town of Lantern Falls where a vibrant cultural scene flourished. The local playhouse offered a year-round program, which Dorothy Tondar was eager to become involved with.

In accepting the Ohio position Lee maintained a busy timetable.

Saddled with the responsibility of manning a spy station; his teaching duties amounted to several lectures per week in addition to tutoring and essay grading. The faculty he joined was headed by Marion Benton whose staff consisted of younger men and women, who surmised Lee's tenure was mostly ceremonial. Not slighted at being removed from the hub of activity in Maryland, the Tondar's attempted to cultivate a healthier lifestyle in their advancing years.

With a requisition sheet forwarded to the office of UCOMA Director Adams, Lee set about refitting the Information Retrieval Installation (IRI) with state-of-the-art data-retrieving technology. The gear was installed covertly within Sentinel Hall by NSA technicians in place of older systems. Satellite dishes were upgraded and Lee began disseminating incoming transmission's almost immediately. His 'overhead-region' (that portion of sky existing along a series of coordinates), included most of the lower Great Lakes with parts of Canada and the mid-west overlapping. Alliances were forged with neighbouring UCOMA stations, various levels of Ohio authority and the Canadian Security Intelligence Service. With a covert presence dating back to the War of 1812, the 'Hall' fostered OSS and NSA code-breakers over the course of two World Wars and one very long cold war.

Lee managed his academic responsibilities dutifully, meanwhile technology continued to engulf the skies. Trolling reams of data he passed scrambled relays onto SIGINT, while unravelling a percentage of suspect signals himself. His old champion Royston Adams suggested Lee take on a rookie analyst to assist him. Instead, Lee preferred to recruit a Grissim student he believed well suited to communications. The idea of grooming an aid rather than engaging a preppy specialist from the Agency's talent pool took precedence.

Intelligence dissemination is considered tedious by most practitioners. Highly automated it requires data-tracking and assessment on a daily basis. Orbiting objects are scanned by sensitive, Terra-based retrieval dishes to determine content. A satellite transmitting a cable television signal is automatically scanned. If nothing unusual is detected it proceeds unfettered through the overhead region. Should an article display a scrambled relay or awkward signal Lee attempts encryption. If he's unsuccessful the information is passed onto to SIGINT and subjected to their vast resources.

Despite a gift for exposing suspect signals Lee became buried in a deluge of data and was forced to take action.

———————

FOUR

Lee's choice for recruitment was a young man he'd become acquainted with through an extracurricular activity for students and faculty alike. Calling themselves the SETI Club the group met once a week in an empty classroom. Equipped with laptops each participant was assigned a sliver of the universe to scan for signs of life. SETI (the Search For Extraterrestrial Intelligence), provided amateur enthusiasts an online resource in surveying the celestial skies for traces of alien existence. Afterwards, the group would adjourn to the campus watering hole 'the Bag' where finding's were discussed over drinks. So far nothing had been retrieved in terms of a wave from space, however all remained hopeful.

Lee Tondar attended several gatherings and took note of a cheerful genius named Stuart Tuppins. The young man's ambition had yet to be defined, however he showed great promise in areas of digital communication. He bore an alluring laugh and his bespectacled features were crowned with a mane of tousled, brown hair. Lee learned the young man spent his evenings honing in on garbled frequencies, courtesy of a satellite dish mounted outside his dorm room window. Intrigued, he approached the lad and discovered he was completing his final semester. They exchanged ideas on modern communications and became friends. When Stuart graduated he remained in Lantern Falls and became Lee's 'asset'.

Swearing a 'Secrets Act' stating allegiance to God and Country, Stuart embarked upon an extensive study of code-breaking under Lee's tutelage. Inside of two years he'd become as gifted an analyst as his seasoned mentor. Relegated comfortable if somewhat cramped quarters within Control (a name Stu adopted instead of the sterile sounding IRI), his assistance allowed Lee to process incoming data more rapidly. As far as faculty members and students were concerned, Stuart was hired as a professor's assistant under Lee's auspices.

Billions of signals passed over the Grissim station annually.

A better than average ratio of success had been established since Stu's recruitment. Suspect relays highlighted onscreen in yellow were disseminated by UCOMA personnel. Stuart succeeded in breaking a series of potentially damaging signals, initiated by an organized crime family out of Cleveland. Deploying rubber rafts and using disposable phones, teams of smugglers were guided across the St. Lawrence River into Canada at night bearing shipment's of firearms and contraband. Stuart gathered evidence and brought the matter to Lee, who informed the Bureau of Tobacco and Firearms. On another occasion Stu managed to disrupt the efforts of a Muslim extremist, attempting to radicalize bored high-school kids via a podcast streamed out of Akron, Ohio.

Over the course of his apprenticeship Stuart managed to impress not only his boss, but the higher-ups in Maryland. Inevitably, he received an offer from SIGINT to join their ranks. Encouraged by Lee to accept the posting, the professor again had to reject Royston Adams entreaty to provide him an assistant. Sighing audibly into the receiver, Director Adams reminded him the request could be made mandatory. In the end Lee had his way, Adams only stipulation was his choice be thoroughly vetted by NSA security prior to their recruitment.

Stuart remained in close contact with his mentor following his transfer to Maryland. Though affiliated both serviced different agencies. One of Stuart's responsibilities at SIGINT involved posting daily 'feeds' to UCOMA station's throughout the country. The briefs informed personnel what regions to monitor closely, which objects had reentered orbit and what space junk had tumbled from the heavens. Stu paid special attention to anything involving his former workplace and noticed Grissim came up short on a series of daily briefs. In lieu of the oversight he withdrew his phone and invited the Tondar's to join him as his guest's in Baltimore over the coming weekend. The invitation was gratefully accepted and plans were set in motion.

Over Stuart's objection his ex-boss intended to book a room at a downtown hotel.

"I have a fully furnished guest room Lee!"

"Son in addition to the pleasure of seeing you, these out-of-town excursions provide an amorous interlude for two old timers like Dorothy and myself."

Silence resonated at the other end, "I guess...?"

Lee struck a compromise, "Tell you what we'll spend Friday night at your place and Saturday at a hotel, deal?"

"Deal! I'll meet you at Baltimore-Washington Airport Friday afternoon. Text me your arrival time and gate number."

Dorothy arranged to spend Friday night in Baltimore with a female chum from college. As their flight touched down the woman welcomed the couple and invited Dorothy on a shopping excursion.

Stuart caught up with Lee in the airport lobby, "Where's Dot?"

"She's with a friend," the older man explained. "She said to assure you she'll be joining us tomorrow."

They departed the airport in Stu's Ford Explorer and stopped for Chinese take-out before returning to his condo in midtown Baltimore. Lee viewed the city from the balcony as it stretched toward the Atlantic. Stuart dished chow mien and vegetables onto separate plates, double-checking the portions. He chatted non-stop from the kitchen and set the meals down on a dining room table. Pouring two glasses of red wine Lee was motioned toward a chair.

Stuart raised his glass, "I picked a scrumptious pot roast out for tomorrow's dinner. I insist Dorothy partake."

"She wouldn't miss it."

Digging into their food Lee noticed lines had formed along his host's brow.

"What is it Stu?"

The young man glanced up, "You're being kept out of the loop on portion's of updates forwarded to UCOMA stations, Lee."

His guest frowned and suggested it was likely an oversight.

Stuart shook his head, "These appear to be deliberate omissions affecting the Grissim station alone. All other outposts received completed briefs."

"Please continue."

Admitting Grissim communiques received his full attention the young man stated, "That's how I noticed the exclusions."

"You're a good spy, Stu."

"Thank you."

Lee listened as his former recruit recalled his observations.

"By observing download's forwarded to other stations Grissim came up short by comparison."

"So what's being withheld?"

"Two omissions were apparent," his host remarked. "One referenced a scrambled SIAG transmission streamed to Chicago. Another concerned a domestic terrorist by the name of William Penther - remember him?"

Lee thought for a moment. "Wasn't he the militiaman imprisoned for attempting to blow up a federal building in Memphis?"

"The same," Stuart responded. "Now why would someone withhold that information from you?"

"Good question."

The young man agreed.

Lee assured his friend he'd look into the matter.

When their meal concluded they retired to the balcony. Stuart topped their wine glasses and less pressing issues were discussed. As midnight approached Lee bid his jovial host good-night and retired to the spare bedroom. Pulling the sheets to his chin he considered Stuart's revelation. Next morning he contacted Royston Adams along a secured frequency. Without mentioning Stu he asked why certain updates his station received appeared incomplete. The UCOMA Director sounded surprised to learn Grissim feeds had come up short. He assured Lee he'd make inquiries.

"SIGINT has received a surplus amount of signals laced with disinformation. Subsequently, select transmission's have been systematically deleted. That might explain the exclusions?"

"Perhaps."

"I'll follow up and get back."

"Thanks Royston."

Sipping coffee on the balcony with his host Lee mentioned his chat with the Director.

"With Adams on the case someone is bound to cough up an explanation," Stuart remarked.

"Are all briefs stored in Agency data-banks?" Lee inquired.

"They're held there for a period of time and eventually destroyed as a security precaution. I initiated a search for the Grissim feeds and discovered they'd been deleted."

"Damn!"

"Relevant transcripts might exist on file at other U stations."

"Meaning...?"

"I could contact a neighbouring outpost and request they forward a printout matching the incomplete feed's you received. I'll be discreet and explain a mistake occurred at my end."

"Doesn't sound very ethical?"

"It isn't."

"Can you do it?"

"I can try."

A heavy fog descended over the distant eastern seaboard.

Stuart agreed to compile whatever information he could regarding the oversight and forward it covertly to Lee. The results might prove insightful.

Dorothy arrived by cab late Saturday afternoon and the trio gradually settled down to a wonderful pot-roast dinner. The evening was spent laughing and reminiscing while jazz streamed from the stereo. At ten Lee summoned a taxi to take he and Dorothy to their hotel. Escorting the couple down to the lobby Stuart inquired again if they'd prefer to spend the night.

Lee winked and Dorothy grinned as they entered the rear of the cab.

"I understand?" Stuart nodded. "See you tomorrow at noon."

The following day they met for brunch at an outdoor cafe along the Inner Harbour district. Afterwards, some sightseeing was undertaken with Stu serving as guide. Their host was embraced by both Tondar's who bid farewell until the next time. Hailing a cab they retrieved their luggage from the hotel and made the return flight to Cleveland. Lee's VW Beetle was waiting in the passenger parking lot once they touched down. Forty minutes later they crossed the Lantern Falls city limits.

———————

Waking from a dreamless state of slumber Jesse glanced at the digital clock next to his bed. Sitting bolt upright he realized he'd overslept. It was 10:30 Sunday morning - the alarm was supposed to have roused him at nine. For years he'd pummelled the contraption mercilessly, now it was paying him back. He made a mental note to add a new alarm clock to his innovatory of necessary items. His meeting with Lee Tondar was in under an hour. Rising sluggishly he ran a hand through his hair.

Following the events of Friday evening with the Tondar's, most of Saturday was spent working out at the gym. He bought groceries and did a load of laundry. His basement unit was situated along a residential street on the fringes of Lantern Falls. The house was owned by a retired electrician and his wife. The only time he saw them was the first of the month when rent was due. Jesse did the math and concluded living in town was more affordable than residing on campus. His bachelor unit served as a living room, bedroom and kitchenette rolled into one. A tiny bathroom stood apart. While preparing to enter his final year at the Institute he felt the cramped quarters closing in.

Sunday mornings were reserved for sleeping in yet here he was showering and rushing to keep an appointment. The mirror revealed a tinge of purple visible on his chin. He was grateful the bruises sustained during the purse-snatching incident had receded. With eight days to go until his gig at the Observer commenced he reviewed his itinerary: Monday was shopping day - pants, shirts, socks...an alarm clock. Also gifts would be purchased for his mother and grandfather, whom he intended to visit Tuesday in Windsor. Emma Carlton was a social worker residing in Toledo; routinely she would visit her father affectionately known as Gramps. Allotted his living room couch, a sleeping bag on the carpeted floor was assigned to her son. When schedules jibed, Jesse would retrieve his mother in Toledo and together they'd surprise Gramps with a visit.

Raised among modest surroundings Jesse enjoyed a happy upbringing. His father was rarely mentioned and the subject was avoided. Without sibling companionship he relied on his imagination. While Emma struggled to keep up her son never lacked for decent thrift-shop clothing. Following his fourth birthday the pair settled into a two-bedroom apartment in downtown Toledo. The new residence was a step up from their former dwelling and remained Jesse's home for the next fourteen years. He attended elementary and secondary schools where friendships were forged. A public library was several blocks away and Jesse spent endless hours browsing the shelves. At night he read until he fell asleep. A smile registered while recalling those long-ago nights.

Friday, he'd return to Lantern Falls where dinner was slated with his on again/off again girlfriend, Shawna Delray.

Gillian Burke gazed from the kitchen window without seeing. She was unable to hear the drone of her neighbour's buzz-saw as it sliced excess hedge foliage dividing their properties.

"Why not stay an extra day Tom?" she said over her shoulder. "I'll be at the gym all afternoon. Steve and Samantha would enjoy your company."

"Actually, Sammy and I are spending time at Pioneer Village," her husband corrected. "You're welcome to join us, Dad?"

Slapping her forehead Gillian muttered, "Pioneer Village I forgot you guys were going."

"Come with us Tom!" Sammy weighed in.

Thomas Burke had flown up from St Louis Friday to spend the weekend with his son Steve, his daughter-in-law Gillian and their eight-year-old daughter Samantha.

"I'd love to stay but I've got back therapy in the morning. It's free for seniors on Monday's I'd better not pass it up."

He rubbed his shoulder and glanced across at Steve, "I'll take you up on that trip to Antique Town another time."

"That's Pioneer Village dad. It's old you'd like it."

Noting the sarcasm Tom winked at his granddaughter, "Know what Sammy?"

"What?"

"You and your comedian daddy here are lucky people. If that brunch your mom concocted wasn't the best this side of the Rockies – dang me."

Samantha giggled, "He said it again."

"Said what?" queried her dad.

"Dang me. Tom says it lots."

A quizzical look crossed the older man's features, "Well I..."

"Samantha, you should be sensitive about the different ways people express themselves," her mother cautioned.

Sammy viewed her grandfather more as a buddy than a relation. A notion Tom encouraged.

"Dang me sounds cool," remarked the eight-year-old. "What's it mean Tom?"

He pondered the question, "Don't likely know may been a song..."

"You've used that expression since I was Sammy's age," Steve remarked. "It's from another time and place..."

"Let's not get into that bygone-era stuff," his father replied defensively. "I'm alive and kicking and doing fine thank you very much."

"You're doing better than fine," Gillian insisted. "If we're half as fit as you when we're your age - we'll live to be a hundred."

She forced a smile and returned her gaze to the window.

Their twin-story home was located in a residential section of Evanston north of Chicago. Steve spent most days pounding out column's for a variety of financial publications. Reports lay strewn about the desk and floor of his study. Despite the backlog he always made time for his wife and daughter. On summer weekends they'd go to Lincoln Park or the beach. Skating became part of the ritual during winters. On cold, damp days they'd go to a movie or watch one at home.

The previous evening Gillian arranged to drive her in-law to O'Hare Airport, where Tom's flight to St. Louis was scheduled to depart at noon.

"That affords me time to get to the gym where a tennis tournament is slated," she added.

"Sammy you'd better bid Tom so-long," Steve urged his daughter with less than an hour remaining. "He has to leave shortly if his flight is to be met."

Scooping the last pancake from a plate Samantha gripped the syrup bottle and drenched it. She glanced up, "Guess I should have asked if anyone wanted it first. Anyone want it?"

"Great time to ask," replied her dad.

"Sorry."

Tom smiled and rose from the table. "I'm so stuffed I'll need to be carried to the car."

"Dang me!" Sammy exclaimed.

"I heard that!" her grandfather responded.

Gillian was still at the window when Steve strode up behind and placed his arms about her waist, "You get ready darling I'll take over here."

"Thank you," she whispered.

Turning about her moist eyes and sombre expression startled him. Quietly, he asked what was wrong. She shifted her gaze and went to fetch her things.

Meanwhile, the elder Burke recalled the first time he'd set eyes on his future daughter-in-law. It was nine years earlier and he took an immediate liking to her. Now in her late twenties Gillian retained her dark-toned beauty. Shiny black hair cascaded past her shoulders and she bore a cover girl smile. Her trim form and dark eyes combined to create a stunning image.

She met Steve while he completed his master's degree in Economics at the University of Chicago. Following a seven-month courtship Gillian accepted his proposal of marriage and the course of their lives was set in motion. Tom was delighted when a granddaughter arrived, shortly thereafter the new parent's mortgaged the home they currently occupied.

Gillian was upstairs as the Burke clan strode the path to the driveway. Steve carried his father's suitcase and his wife's car keys. Once the luggage was in the trunk of the Hyundai, Sammy took her grandfather's hand and shook it like good buddies do. Gillian appeared at the front entrance wearing a track outfit with her purse slung over her shoulder. She toted a hefty gym bag and paused to shut the door.

Steve rushed to assist and noticed his wife's vacant expression.

"You sure you're OK, " he whispered.

"I'm fine," she responded distractedly. "I should've got brunch off to an earlier start so your father wasn't rushed."

Lowering her voice she added, "It's also that time of the month"

"Dad's flight isn't for another fifty minutes."

Without receiving a response he asked, "What's with the extra baggage...?"

"I'm donating some old gym clothes to the fitness centre."

The blank expression returned until Samantha ran up and clasped her mother's hand. Gillian leaned over and kissed the child on both cheeks. Staring intently she whispered, "You be patient with dad and know mommy loves you very much."

Steve noticed his wife's welling tears. He'd never witnessed a display of emotion over a few hours parting.

"You up to driving?" he asked.

"I'm fine," she said wiping aside a tear.

She glanced at her father-in-law. "I'm only sorry the weekend is over and Tom has to head home."

"That makes two of us," Sammy piped in. "After you drop Tom off why not come back and join us Mom?"

"I'd love to sweetheart but there's a tournament today and I'm needed."

The surrounding neighbourhood was typically suburban. Evergreen's cast shadows over manicured lawns adorned with hedges and gardens. Houses were set back from the street and a scent of charcoal and flowers permeated the air.

Gillian placed her head on her husband's chest. "I love you," she whispered.

Her lips rose and she kissed him gently.

Withdrawing sunglasses she was handed the car keys. In the driver's seat she buckled up and Tom followed suit on the passenger side. The vehicle backed slowly down the drive as husband and daughter stood off to the side waving.

Gliding down the highway in the direction of the airport Tom listed the ways Samantha had matured. Gillian nodded silently and responded at appropriate intervals. With one hand on the steering wheel she wiped the moistness from beneath her shades.

Tom cast a sidelong glance, "Everything okay Gillian?"

"I'm fine," she sniffed. "A bit tired that's all."

She swung into the massive airport and guided the car towards a parking area and an available space. Tom wondered why his daughter-in-law appeared distracted but was reluctant to probe. The family knew little of Gillian's existence prior to meeting Steve. She claimed to have been born in Egypt and educated in Europe. Due to her father's business interests she travelled extensively with her parents and an older sister. Tired of being shuttled about, she fell out with her family and settled in America to study Civic Planning at the University of Chicago. A framed photograph shows Gillian at two years of age alongside her parents and sister.

Tom knew too well the fragility of family life. His own wife left him while the boys were still in high school. As parents they could no longer communicate. Having met someone she could talk to she departed – it was as simple as that. Following the breakup the boys stayed with Tom and visited their mother twice a month on weekends. Presently, Steve's brother Carson lived near their dad in St. Louis.

Gillian switched off the engine, "When you're up later this summer I hope you'll stay longer than two days, Tom. Your granddaughter will insist upon it."

"I won't let the little lady down."

They exited the car and strolled to the rear. Tom retrieved his suitcase and accepted Gillian's offer to escort him to the Terminal 2 loading gate. He'd made the Chicago trip dozens of times. Regardless, airports confounded him with their ever-changing departure and arrival times and various checkpoints.

Squinting against the sun Gillian remarked, "Let's get you cleared."

Abruptly, a turbulent wind whipped across the expanse of the parking lot forcing the elder Burke several steps backward. Holding her own Gillian grasped his free hand as the gust's descended. Accompanied by a cacophony of jet-propelled noise, dust-devils whirled in a frenzy as the giant bird winged low overhead. They entered the terminal and Gillian's phone chimed. The display screen was blank and she pressed some digits before replacing the device. Immediately, they resumed their course towards the proper gate.

Her phone vibrated a second time. The number belonged to Steve's landline.

"Sorry to bug you mom!" Samantha announced. "Is Tom there? Can I speak to him? I forgot to tell him something."

Dealing with noise distractions and crowds Sammy's mom relied, "He's here sweetie - make it brief OK?" Her heart broke as the words departed her mouth, "I love you..."

She handed the phone over, "It's your biggest fan."

Gripping the phone Tom listened intently, "No I won't forget..."

An airline attendant interrupted, "Tickets please?"

Passenger's were being directed towards a series of metal detectors and TSA security officers.

"They're ready to board," Gillian prompted. "Got your ticket?"

"Have to run young lady," Tom said into the receiver. "See you in August."

Rummaging his pockets he fumbled for the return stub. Finding the envelope he passed it to the official who handed back a receipt.

Gillian drew her father-in-law aside and embraced him firmly.

"Sammy was reminding me not to forget my photo album when I'm up next," he remarked. "There's some snapshots of Steve when he was her age."

He smiled at his daughter-in-law, "You take care now I'll see you soon."

Without responding she kissed his cheek and vanished among the crowd. Tom grasped his suitcase and strolled through an airport scanner without issue. He deposited his luggage and made his way to the tarmac. While waiting to board a voice boomed over the speaker system.

"Attention passengers bound for St. Louis, Oklahoma City and Dallas aboard Flight 122. Please be advised a forty-minute delay is in effect while a technical matter is tended to. We regret the inconvenience and assure ticket holders we'll be underway shortly."

Amid a chorus of groans the brazen voice repeated the message.

Tom shrugged and decided to take a stroll. He reached into his pocket for the receipt and discovered it next to Gillian's cellphone.

"Damn!"

With a forty minute delay he decided to head to the parking lot and Gillian's car. Likely, she'd discovered her phone missing and would attempt to retrieve it. He punched Steve's number on the devise and received a voice-mail response. Explaining why he called he stated he'd try again later. In the parking lot he discovered the Hyundai where Gillian left it. He scribbled a note on his ticket envelope and placed it beneath her wiper. Afterwards, he returned to the terminal and decided to have her paged. An information booth was on the ground level and he requested the attendant page his daughter-in-law. The young man inquired if that person was lost.

"No," Tom replied. "I was using her phone and mistakenly placed it in my pocket at a departure gate. I'm sure she'd like it returned."

The attendant needed to clear the matter with his supervisor and pressed a button to explain the situation.

"Can do," he remarked when the call concluded. "May I have your name and the name of the relation?"

Moments later the message was broadcast throughout the various terminals. The announcement indicated a relative was waiting at the Terminal 2 information booth.

Ten minutes later there was no sign of Gillian. Tom spoke to the attendant and said he'd check back and made another trip to the parking lot. He found her vehicle with the note still attached. Inside the terminal he was informed his daughter-in-law failed to show.

"If she returns please have her contact her family."

"Will do Mr. Burke."

Walking the length of the terminal Tom attempted to pick her face out from the rush of commuters. He rode up one escalator and down another surveying ticket lines and scanning retail shops on two levels.

Meantime, he had a flight to catch!

Twenty minutes later his plane departed the runway. Gazing down at the rippling waters of Lake Michigan he turned Gillian's phone over in his hand and stared passively into the blue.

"Dang me".

———————

FIVE

Lee Tondar grasped the railing and followed the staircase up a flight towards the marble expanse of the lobby. Erected during the War of 1812, Sentinel Hall served as part of a front line of defence against aggression from the north. The conflict between British and American forces two centuries earlier, resulted in several such fortresses being erected along the south shore of the lower lakes. The citadel overlooking Lake Erie bore resemblance to a Gothic castle with it's rectangular grey facade. Over a century the Hall morphed into an array of lecture halls and classrooms belonging to the Modern History Department serving the Grissim Institute.

Legend surrounding the Hall had taken on a life of its own with it's folklore being liberally embellished as it passed from generation to generation. One well-documented tale added much to its notoriety. Midway through the nineteenth century the fort was vacated by the Yankee army, who'd come to terms with their northerly neighbours and found new incentives further south. Within a month the abandoned fortress was converted into a brothel by several industrious ladies who provided sailors, trappers, and traders with an assortment of food, drink, and merriment in return for a nominal fee. Raucously unimpeded these endeavours carried on for more than a dozen years until the residents of Lantern, (as the town was then known) asserted themselves and exorcised the ladies and their grizzled patrons from their midst. Following their ouster the community initiated plans to turn the former garrison - and bordello, into the town's first real schoolhouse. In 1897 a theatre was erected funded by a wealthy philanthropist named Roland Abbott. In return for his support he stipulated both Sentinel Hall and the theatre be used as institutes for learning. Over the ensuing years other buildings were added until it evolved into the renowned college it became. Abbot Lane, an artery running the width of the campus was bestowed in honour of Mr. Abbot. The Institute itself had been named after Victor Grissim, a civic engineer and first mayor of Lantern. It was he more than anyone who lured investors from New York and Chicago, to the scenic local set upon the bluffs overlooking Lake Erie.

In honour of the defenders who once occupied the fortress, Mayor Grissim imparted the name Sentinel Hall upon her. The structure retained its ominous grey shell, replete with rooftop turrets along her twin-story structure. Patrician columns stood stanchion on either side of the entrance facing away from the lake. They served as a reminder to the quiet dignity of her military heritage.

The interior altered dramatically befitting the whims of faculty members and students who once resided there. The 'Hall' segued into its present form following the end of the Great War. Lecture halls and classrooms were furbished. Windows were installed allowing natural light to penetrate its chambers. More recently a museum was established in the lobby. During the Great Depression portions of the cellar underwent changes. Alteration's occurred covertly when staff and students were on summer break. To this day sections of the basement remain unknown to all but a select few.

Sunlight streamed through an arched window as Lee Tondar arrived at the top of the stairwell. A uniformed officer emerged from the security booth, "Good Morning Sir."

Panting audibly the professor replied, "Morning Sasha."

He glanced up at an antiquated clock bearing Roman numerals, "I have an interview with a young chap named Jesse Carlton. Please ID him and buzz me when he arrives?"

"I shall," the official responded.

Retracing his steps the professor entered the sanctum below.

Traffic along Windover Road was quiet that Sunday morning. Seagulls encircled the bluffs adding a sense of motion to the excursion. Falls Valley rolled away to his right as Jesse guided the Chevy in a northerly direction. Sweeping down from the Grissim campus the valley extended south nearly a kilometre and ended along the northern edge of town. Interspersed with bike paths and decorative gardens it's single drawback were the power lines streaming the length of the valley. Hydro made certain overhead cables were placed a safe distance from the trails and recreational areas below. A man-made waterfall was the valley's chief attraction, it's significance had been the inspiration behind the community's expanded namesake. For nearly a century the town was known simply as Lantern. During the mid-1950's when the waterfall was erected, citizens voted to go with the more tourist-friendly moniker, Lantern Falls.

The waterfall itself was a dwarf when compared with Niagara - her monolithic neighbour to the east. Constructed to service aspects of the region's hydro needs, its most popular function was as a tourist attraction. Tumbling in a white rage over granite rock it's actual height was not more than fifty feet. The source was a man-made reservoir situated behind the falls, where lake water was continually pumped and recycled. At the foot of the waterfall visitors could feel the spray overwhelm them on hot summer days. Picnic tables were available along with ample parking. Food trucks were present on weekends and holidays and public washrooms could be accessed until 10 pm.

Jesse swung onto Edgewater Drive leading into the campus proper. He cruised past several buildings and turned left onto Abbot Lane. Bringing the car to a standstill he sat gazing at Sentinel Hall. Overcome with a lonesomeness he was used to seeing students dashing from one place to another. June waned and a ghostly aura lingered as the 'Hall' loomed against a backdrop of water and sky. Aware of it's heritage he'd marvelled at it's imposing facade ever since arriving at Grissim. The building housed the Modern History department - Media students attended a more contemporary facility on campus. Jesse pressed lightly on the gas and advanced until he came to a half-crescent situated before the antiquated structure. Securing a parking spot he switched off the engine and brushed lint from his shirt, before departed the vehicle. The scent of fresh water struck him instantly. He approached the steps leading toward the front entrance and heard gulls crying opposite the fortress. Satellite dishes were mounted to overhead turret's Between either column he bounded up the steps towards a pair of broad oak doors. An intercom was accessed and he noticed surveillance cameras focused in his direction.

A woman's voice emitted from the speaker, "Name please?"

"Jesse Carlton."

"And the nature of your visit?"

"I have an eleven o'clock appointment with Professor Tondar."

A buzzer sounded and he entered.

An expansive lobby spread before him and he recalled the historical display's encased in glass and mounted on bases. A security booth was situated along his right. Behind transparent walls a uniformed guard greeted him.

"Mr. Carlton?"

"That's correct."

"May I see some identification?"

"Certainly."

He withdrew his wallet and passed his driver's license and student ID through an exchange panel. Once the document's were reviewed they were handed back.

"If you'll sign the register I'll let the professor know you're here."

Jesse logged his name and arrival time while she spoke into the receiver. Placing the pen aside he was informed the professor was on his way.

While waiting he browsed the wonders of the lobby museum. Framed portraits included Abraham Lincoln, Mahatma Gandhi, Sarah Bernhardt, Franklin and Eleanor Roosevelt, Elvis, Orville and Wilbur Wright, Martin Luther King, Madame Curie, Charles Dickens, the Kennedy brothers, Marconi, the Beatles among others. All were exhibited in recognition of contribution's made over the past two centuries. Among the artifacts a bronze globe was mounted within a sturdy cast-iron frame. Along it's base the year 1800 AD was etched indicating how the world's geography appeared at that time - and how it had changed since. Restored black and white photographs of the Great Lakes region and its inhabitant's hung on partitions. Several images were taken more than one hundred and fifty years earlier. Among them was a photograph dated before the turn of the last century. The grainy portrait depicted a group of sombre loggers pausing at their labour as the camera captured the moment forever. Replicas of the first diesel engine, Henry Ford's debut automobile, the Titanic, Sputnik, an Apollo capsule and the International Space Station were mounted behind glass. A photo of Alexander Graham Bell hung alongside displays of the first wire-service, telephone and cell device.

Jesse glanced over his shoulder and noticed the guard pecking away at a keyboard. He had a gut feeling of regimented professionalism. The woman had been cordial, however an undercurrent of protocol was apparent. He was certain she was observing him yet could discern no trace of it.

Due to the marble floor and high ceiling the lobby bore a distinct echo and footsteps were heard ascending from the lower depths. They paused briefly and finally Lee Tondar appeared at the top of the stairs and noticed Jesse before a display case. He strode briskly across the floor and offered the young man a firm handshake. Thanking his guest for coming he invited him to follow.

"I hope you've recovered from our Friday evening ordeal," Lee remarked. "My wife is taking the incident far better than I."

"She's a brave woman," Jesse replied. "Her attack was brazen and cowardly."

The professor nodded but made no reply.

At the bottom of the stairs they entered a dimly-lit corridor. Footsteps echoed and they paused before a thick wooden door on their left. Engraved in bold inscription were the words:

LEE TONDAR: MODERN HISTORY.

Embedded in the wall alongside the door was a keypad and Lee inserted a card and accessed entry. Jesse observed surveillance camera's pointed both directions along the corridor. Motioned inside the office he was directed toward a seat opposite a cluttered desk. Diplomas and certificates hung along one wall. Bookshelves overwhelmed with files and periodicals lined another. No windows were evidenced, instead light radiated from the glow of a reading lamp set upon the professor's desk.

Jesse's host pointed to a frosty carafe, "There's ice water if your dry."

"Thank you," the other replied pouring water and drawing up the chair.

Seating himself at his desk the professor glanced briefly at some notes, removed his glasses and looked up.

"I'll get right to the point son," he said in earnest. "One of my unofficial duties here at the Institute is to act as a scout. In a manner similar to a sporting franchise I look out for talent. The qualities I seek in young people include intelligence, skill, physical prowess, and moral conviction."

He placed his notes aside and went off-script.

"The invitation to dinner Friday must have appeared strange coming from someone you'd met on only one occasion?"

Jesse shuffled in his seat and said he enjoyed the meal and company immensely, despite what later occurred.

The professor nodded, "In addition to being an instructor at this Institute, my other responsibility is to serve as an Intelligence analyst and recruiting officer for a branch of the US government."

The young man appeared perplexed and leaned forward.

"I was recruited into the ranks of the service after completing my master's degree at Princeton," the professor resumed. "I was twenty-three a year older than you are now."

He coughed into his fist.

"I've invited you here with a job offer," he continued. "The position would commence immediately."

A look of surprise registered on Jesse's face.

"I'm not going to recite any of that serve your country crap," the professor insisted. "Except to say the situation our nation faces is critical."

The young man sat stationary as Lee pressed ahead.

"Obviously, I can't go into detail without your full cooperation. But if you'll allow me I'll quickly brief you."

The professor leaned over his desk.

"There is reason to believe a highly placed official within US Intelligence is hellbent on destruction. The identity of this person remains a mystery, however his or her intent is clear. It appears this individual is preparing to launch a massive strike somewhere in the American mid-west. It would involve individuals who may or may not be linked to terrorist organizations abroad. Such an attack would provoke a nuclear response by the US in retaliation of such a calamity. The end result would eradicate the alleged enemy, meanwhile countless lives would be lost here at home. The scenario could also incite a global holy war."

Allowing the words to linger the professor focused on his guest.

Jesse considered the implications of what he was hearing, "Why are you telling me this, Sir?"

Without missing a beat the older man responded, "Because I'm asking for your help. The likelihood of a major strike is plausible. Without proof analysts find it difficult to believe such a plot could be unleashed by one of their own. Ranking Intelligence official's are constantly under scrutiny, subsequently most believe a perpetrator would've been exposed. Security service's continually monitor terrorist activities here and abroad, real and perceived threats are closely observed. This person isn't a mole working on behalf of a hostile adversary - more likely he's a fanatical patriot. One who would allow scores of fellow countrymen to perish in order to advance their own malignant doctrine."

Still reeling Jesse managed to say, "You're suggesting the government doesn't believe one of their own could be involved, however you say otherwise?"

"Basically."

The young man released a gust of air and leaned back.

The professor observed his reaction and explained further.

"Ten months ago a SIAG operative was taken into custody by US authorities. I'll refer to this individual as ONE. During his interrogation ONE claimed his would-be successor had been activated - not by the SIAG, but by someone buried within the ranks of US Intelligence. A day later ONE was found dead - liquidated by an implant. The Agency suspects the same devise was removed from his replacement to prevent that person from falling victim. It's my belief the successor is working on behalf of this deceitful insider. ONE made several revealing statements while under interrogation. Before being apprehended he claimed a tall Latin man approached him with an offer of recruitment. Rejecting his proposal ONE was informed a 'strike of considerable magnitude' would occur somewhere in the American mid-west within a year. The man further stated the SIAG would be responsible.

With his cover blown and capture pending ONE beat a hasty retreat for the airport and the first flight out of the country. While hailing a cab Federal agents swooped down and charged him with espionage. With his death its safe to assume the SIAG would've changed all existing codes, and placed assassins on the trail of their wayward sleeper. Unfortunately, the name of the dead man's interrogator remains classified."

Jesse sat dumbstruck staring at the floor.

"I'm a media student with no experience in such matters," he murmured.

"You're an informed and capable young man."

"I'm grateful for the praise but this is way out of my league."

Lee rounded out his narrative, "By a process of elimination the rogue behind this threat can be exposed."

The young man frowned, "Without access to relevant files how can that be achieved?"

"Certain resources are available to me. In the meantime this station will do everything in it's power to prevent a catastrophe - which is why I need someone in the field. By deploying cloak and dagger methodology I intend to rout this person out. That's where you would come in."

"This station ...?"

Lee gestured about the room, "You've noticed the excessive security precautions."

The young man had noticed.

"Whatever your decision I request you sign a confidentiality agreement. Basically, it states this conversation never took place and you have no knowledge of Intelligence activities conducted out of this institution."

The professor hesitated, "I would never have asked you here had I not trusted you, son."

He slid a sheet of paper across the desk and Jesse read the statement. He signed it and passed it back.

"If the government doesn't believe a provocateur is among them wouldn't their security agencies disagree," Jesse asserted. "Presumably, it was they who interrogated the dead man?"

"The agencies involved maintain the late SIAG operative's statements were subterfuge and disinformation - a point likely encouraged by the renegade."

Jesse sat stone-faced until the professor interrupted his thoughts.

"I hope you'll take a few days to consider my request. There's more to say, however I think you appreciate the urgency."

The young man glanced up, "I'll be out of town a few days visiting family. I'm due back Friday."

"Fine!" Lee responded. "Why don't we meet here same time Saturday morning."

The student rose slowly to his feet. Without further ado the professor escorted him upstairs, where Jesse barely noticed the museum artifacts as he departed the hall. Guiding the Chevy onto Abbot Lane, he glanced in the mirror and noticed Lee Tondar at the top of the steps observing his departure.

———————

It was mid-morning when Emma Carlton reentered her father's residence. She noticed her son sprawled along the sofa focused on nothing in particular. Once the door closed he was roused from his trance-like state.

"Thought you'd be sleeping? " Emma remarked. "You're on vacation."

"I slept great Ma..."

"Your infectious energy was barely containable when you were here in March – why so sullen?"

Emma had been up since the break of dawn and had already run several errands. Entering a tiny kitchen area she placed some grocery items and her purse on the counter and turned to face her son.

"Is there something I should know Jesse?"

Having returned from his morning jog the lad's sweatshirt was moist and clung to his upper body. He'd been unusually subdued since his arrival two days prior.

Receiving no response Emma turned her attention to placing away the groceries.

"You say something Ma?"

"Nope I like talking to myself."

Jesse apologized, "I'm sorry I was daydreaming."

"Which girl is it this time?"

"Knew you'd say that."

"Well..."

Emma Carlton was a small, attractive woman in her mid-forties with an easy smile and dark eyes. Her raven hair was tinged with silver and curled above her shoulders. She wore little makeup and managed to keep herself trim. Attired in a summer skirt and sandals she dressed for what was shaping up to be a gorgeous day. When a situation warranted counsel Jesse turned to her - presently that wasn't an option.

"There's no women issues," he sighed. "Matter of fact there's no woman."

"What about Shawna?"

"I left her after she left me."

Emma stared at him quizzically.

"She's a sweetheart Ma I just feel it's coming to an end. Different paths and everything."

He hesitated, "Actually, I was thinking about my pending job. Along with spending another summer in Lantern Falls."

"Serious stuff," his mother jested. "So instead of proofreading copy you see yourself lying on a beach in the company of a woman - make that plural, sipping cold drinks and getting bad sunburns."

"Yes."

Emma reentered the living room, "You'll survive summer. Besides, this is your final year in Lantern Falls, unless of course you're offered a full-time position at the newspaper."

"You're optimistic remember I study print journalism - something akin to becoming town crier."

"That's nonsense Jesse and you know it. When people want sound bites they turn on TV. When they want the real deal they read a newspaper. That will never change."

"Then why have so many presses folded?"

"You forget all the new publications cropping up on newsstands."

"After the others fail."

Emma released a sigh.

Jesse hoped the topic served as a decoy for what was truly on his mind. He trailed his mother into the kitchen and poured orange juice.

"So you won't say what's troubling you?" Emma persisted.

"Nothing's troubling me," he lied.

"You've never brooded like this."

Jesse was silent while his mother headed back toward the sofa. Snagging a pillow she made a motion of tossing it in his direction.

"You wouldn't dare..."

"I would."

As she was about to throw the cushion he laughed through his nose.

"That's rude Jesse!"

Allowing the pillow to fall to the floor she added, "Do you snort like that when you're on a date!"

"I snort louder."

Grinning mischievously he exited the kitchen and scooped the pillow from the carpet and gave his mother a peck on the cheek, "Where's Gramps?"

"He's in the courtyard. Why don't you join him I'll bring out tea."

Jesse could barely recall his present journey up to Gramps place. Windsor resided on the Canadian side of the US border along a lateral line directly north of Lantern Falls. The rugged Erie shoreline provided ideal conditions for vineyards and cornfields to flourish. Visits had always been a source of revitalization. On this occasion weightier matters plagued him. Routine concerns such as rent, tuition and a shrinking relationship with his girlfriend, were off the radar. A week earlier nothing had been more pressing than getting his laundry done.

In the courtyard Jesse noticed his grandfather reclining on a lawn chair. In reality Gramps was Francis Carlton, a retired machine-shop worker who'd been employed thirty-eight years with the Ford Motor Company in Windsor.

Sliding into the lawn-chair next to his Jesse said, "Sleep well Gramps?

"Yep."

"Emma's on the way with tea."

Despite the balmy June weather the National Hockey League was still in session. The Stanley Cup final was two days hence.

Unfortunately, for Gramps his beloved Detroit Red Wings had been knocked out of the running.

"So whose it going to be Toronto or Dallas?"

Three years earlier a stroke had befallen his grandfather leaving his speech and hearing impaired. His wit remained sharp however, "W…Wings are out! I don't give a flying puck who w…wins."

"Right."

Emma arrived carrying a tray and placed it on a nearby table, "I've put a chicken in the oven, we'll have a sumptuous meal this evening."

"Yea!" Jesse piped in.

He turned to the older man, "Tea Gramps?"

"S…sure."

Pouring cup's of Earl Grey, Jesse passed them over and filled one for himself.

"Gramps was just saying he doesn't care who wins the Stanley Cup on account of Detroit being shut out."

"He'll change his tune once the puck drops," his daughter remarked. "Or go with whoever doesn't score first."

Enjoying the controversy Gramps sat there grinning. Emma drew a chair opposite him and raised her voice, "Jesse is heading back to Lantern Falls tomorrow around one."

Gramps shot the young man an inquisitive look, "Congrats, how much you w…win?"

Mother and son exchanged glances, "Not won dad Jesse has to leave by one o'clock tomorrow."

"Wings didn't win neither. Hell with 'em!"

Emma blinked, "Don't worry I'll be staying a day or two longer just to pester you."

"W…whose worried?"

Once Gramps nodded off mother and son chatted quietly. Gradually, Jesse's eyelids grew heavy and he began to fade. For two nights running he'd lain awake until three or four am with the same thought in his mind. Sleeping on the floor had never posed a problem until now.

"Lie back and rest honey," Emma whispered as her son drifted off.

That evening the family enjoyed a scrumptious roast chicken meal around the dinner table. Following apple pie and tea Gramps bid goodnight and retreated to his room. Once the dishes were rinsed, mother and son reminisced quietly while cable news droned in the background. Two hours later Emma switched off the television set and offered the sofa to her son. Jesse wouldn't dream of it and in his exhausted state a bed of nails would've sufficed. With both father and son sleeping soundly Emma lay awake in the dark.

Friday morning Jesse awoke later than usual and packed his things. After he showered Gramps emerged from the bedroom rubbing his eyes. Emma was in the kitchen scrambling eggs and frying bacon. Jesse pitched in and prepared toast and coffee.

So far he'd made no decision regarding Lee Tondar's request. Nevertheless, plenty of thought had gone into the matter.

Emma was stirring creamy egg contents into a frying pan.

"I know you're keeping something from me, Jesse. Now before you get defensive I want to say I understand. There are some things we can't share – even with our mothers."

She dried her hands and stood on her toes to kiss his cheek. "If you need to talk call me."

"I will," he said returning the kiss and embracing her.

In the parking lot Jesse tossed his bag in the trunk and got behind the wheel. Plenty of sunshine and a light breeze filled the air. Emma stood alongside her father with her arms folded. Her son rolled down the window, "I'll be thinking of you Gramps - by the way I know who you're rooting for."

"Do not!"

"Do too."

"F...fat chance."

Leaning gently on the horn Jesse glided backwards onto a side street and headed off in the direction of the bridge. He felt sluggish despite having a good night's rest. Approaching the border crossing a sea of automobiles and rigs converged into relegated lanes - each determined to traverse the mighty Ambassador Bridge. Four-hundred million dollars worth of trade made it's way across the mammoth structure each day, making it one of the busiest border crossings on earth. Seated idly in the driver's seat Jesse peered through the smog towards a second bridge. Named in honour of Gordie Howe who led Gramps beloved Detroit Red Wings to such heights - the structure was far from being realized.

The Ambassador remained a marvel of twentieth-century engineering. Linking the US with Canada it became a pain in the ass for everyone concerned. The world had changed dramatically over the course of nearly three decades. Following 9/11 observers watched as a field of force was thrown around America's borders. Armed guards quadrupled at every crossing. Passports were required of tourists and business execs alike - including every facet of the import/export industry. Customs agent's sat behind surveillance modules as vehicles were scanned and probed with an array of sophisticated gadgetry. Meanwhile, dogs strained at their leashes sniffing for contraband and firearms.

It was argued the beefed up security was having it's desired effect. There had been no incidents of terrorists being apprehended at the bridge with intent to commit heinous acts against US civilians or institutions. The government claimed terrorist activity had been greatly thwarted with the inception of the Department of Homeland Security.

It could also argued that before the costly build-up of national isolation, no one had been convicted of engaging in acts of terrorism or sabotage at the Detroit/Windsor crossing. A roll-call of drug traffickers, illegal immigrants and smugglers made up the bulk of arrests. Meantime, diplomatic bickering continued between both countries. It reached it's zenith a decade earlier when the US accused Canada of harbouring terrorists, then turning a blind eye to their activities. Canadian official's denied the charge emphatically. Having shared an overlapping history for more than two centuries, both nations held much in common and remained foremost trading partners and allies.

Jesse released a frustrated expletive and raised his forehead from the steering wheel. In forty minutes he'd moved the length of perhaps a dozen cars, and still a line of automobiles stretched before him. In the hazy distance he could barely made out the customs terminal. His passport and ID lay on the passenger seat next to an empty water bottle. Swallowing was difficult because of his parched throat and he visualized a washroom. With lines forming outside a public utility Jesse figured the bottle might come in handy. He wasn't alone in his frustration. Beyond a wire fence in the idling truck lanes, a trucker climbed from his rig and strode towards an overstuffed trashcan and placed a well-directed boot to its midriff. The force sent the can spiralling along it's rim where it crashed to the pavement. Contents were strewn everywhere and his action elicited an explosion of honking horns from his trucker colleagues. In less then a minute a pair of armed guards were on him. As the trucker was escorted from Jesse's sight-lines a third official occupied his drivers seat. Once truck lanes finally moved the rig was guided slowly forward. Ten minutes later the can-kicker was back hurling obscenities over his shoulder. A scrunched-up ball of paper was visible in his right hand suggesting he'd been fined for the trashcan assault. As his movements were monitored his trucker compatriot's honked in a show of support. Even regular commuters demonstrated solidarity by slapping their vehicles and beeping horns.

Attending border guards appeared indifferent. It was a routine day.

No wonder they carried guns.

Having not slept properly for two nights out of three, Jesse found himself overwhelmed with fatigue and reclined in the driver's seat.

Back on the highway a road sign indicated Cleveland was fast approaching.

Cleveland!

There were no plans to travel further east than necessary. Evidently, he'd overshot the Lantern Falls turnoff.

A frosted water bottle lay unopened on the passenger seat and he no longer needed a restroom. Apparently, he'd pulled over en route but couldn't recall?

Cleveland went by in a flash and another sign indicated he was several miles west of Valelle.

Valelle? What in hell is that!

A purple skyline loomed in the distance and cattle grazed next to an abandoned amusement park. It was the same palisade Emma had taken him to as a child, abruptly it segued into his old public library. At the entrance Lee Tondar sported a trench-coat and fedora. A bandana covered the lower part of his face and he twirled a baton. Along the highway a mule idled by with Dean Benton seated side-saddle blowing blues harmonica. A flash occurred and the earth shifted beneath Jesse's tires. A sonic boom resounded as if two planets collided. Glancing toward the city a column of fire rose to heaven. It fanned into an encompassing cloud and rained red embers and ash over the landscape.

Something dark and foreboding stood upon the burning hillside. Suddenly, it was very near. Translucent rags flowed beneath a slicker hat revealing a featureless face. Luminous eyes were focused upon him and he was unable to look away.

Abruptly it was gone.

An atomic gust shattered the windshield and the vehicle was tossed into the air.

A car horn sounded.

Ma ...Gramps!

Wide awake Jesse found himself trembling and noticed cars inching forward up ahead. To his rear they were laying on their horns.

Twenty minutes later he presented documentation and was waved over to the US side. Deprived of sleep and challenged by indecision he decided he'd descended into a type of catatonic nightmare. A feverish chill coursed through his being as he visualized the spectre gazing over the desolate landscape.

Cruising the Interstate he pulled into a service station and used the restroom. He purchased water, refuelled then made straight for home.

———————————

SIX

The sealed envelope was discovered fourteen months before by William Penther. It was inserted beneath the crack of his door by an anonymous courier. The person was elusive enough to avoid alarms, scanners, doberman pincers and an armed bodyguard. The typewritten content's revealed the sender admired Mr. Penther's efforts to defend patriotism against an onslaught of Government regulation and foreigners. It stated the author was a wealthy businessman with numerous resources at his disposal. The sender planned to mount his own offensive, wherein policy-makers would be informed refugees of all stripes were no longer welcome in his homeland. He added the plan would be greatly enhanced with Mr. Penther's participation.

To prove his earnestness the envelope contained fifty unmarked one-hundred dollar bills. The sender hoped Mr. Penther would consider his offer and view it as an opportunity to resume the struggle to bring America to her senses - unimpeded by financial restrictions. The final paragraph read, 'If you are willing to become part of this campaign, you will meet with my associate at the Blythe Park fountain in Fort Wayne seven days hence at 2 pm. The contact will introduce himself as V. He'll be wearing sunglasses and a denim jacket.'

The note was signed Sir.

Penther's first impulse was to burn the letter and put his property on high alert. Instead, he said nothing to his assistant and allowed the dogs to continue sleeping behind the lodge. He'd heard from kooks before - perhaps this person was genuine? An opportunity like this might never come his way again. The IRS were closing in on accumulated back-taxes and revenue was needed to maintain the lodge and grounds. Penther kept the letter close to his chest while he pondered the matter and decided to meet with the sender's representative. The five thousand dollar advance would be avowed only if he accepted the offer. While fondling the cash he reread the note a dozen times. Once the money was divided he would take half and give a thousand to the lawyer assisting him with his IRS woes. The rest would be divvied among his disciples.

His bodyguard Aldo Dopple was frying eggs in the kitchen of their rural Indiana compound. A week had passed and Penther informed him he was driving to Fort Wayne to meet with a gunrunner acquaintance.

"I need to broker a transfer," he said seating himself at the table.

"You mean I don't go?" Dopple responded.

His boss frowned, "I need you here in the event the Feds pay a visit. If they show I want you to act polite and tell them I'm looking into a job prospect. Got it?"

"Sure," muttered the disappointed subordinate.

"I'll be back this evening."

Penther arrived in Fort Wayne behind the wheel of a dark green minivan. Scheduled to meet with the letter-writer's associate, he parked and ventured across Blythe Park in the direction of the fountain. The faces of those seated about it's circumference were hastily observed, meanwhile preschoolers squealed each time a geyser of water erupted from the fountain's spout. Mothers basked in the sunshine while observing their brood. The lunchtime crowd had mostly dispersed, leaving Penther room to breathe and it took only a moment to identify the person described in the letter. An olive-complected man wearing shades stood facing him opposite the fountain. Over six feet and trim he appeared muscular beneath a denim jacket.

The man approached and said softly, "Mr. Penther?"

"You talking to me?"

"I am V."

"Thought you might be."

The contact motioned him towards the fountain and they seated themselves.

"Your journey was pleasant?" he inquired revealing traces of an accent.

"It was alright."

The individual nodded.

"It is our hope you will enlist in our cause."

"And what cause is that?"

"Sir will have to fill in the blanks."

He lowered his voice, "I can assure you our work adheres to the principals of patriot's like yourself."

"That much was outlined in the letter."

"You would be generously compensated," V added. "The endeavour would involve a small team hand-picked by yourself for a period lasting up to a year."

Guarded in his responses Penther mumbled an arrangement might be possible.

"If Sir thought you unreliable he would never have made the offer."

A group of school children traipsed by accompanied by their teacher.

"I take it this initiative was ongoing before I was considered," Penther remarked.

"That is correct."

"The letter implied I would continue efforts my way and not under the direction of another."

"I'm sorry if the message was misconstrued Mr. Penther. A plan is already in effect - our goals remain the same, however."

Penther held his tongue.

"Should you agree to become involved your men will operate within a secret facility. You remain on the outside as courier."

"Courier!"

"I am one myself we serve as lifelines in this venture. This entails the transference of funds and directives to those on the operational end. The success of this operation relies on your most trusted subordinates. Your involvement keeps personnel to a minimum"

Penther looked the other way and remained silent.

"This is too vague," he finally said. "Nothing you've said explains a plan."

"Everything will be outlined if you choose to join us."

The militia leader fixed his gaze on the pavement.

"Yes."

"You will accept our offer?"

The militiaman nodded in affirmation.

"Sir will be delighted!"

"When will I receive details?"

"You shall hear from me by the weekend."

The emissary rose, "It has been a pleasure Mr. Penther."

He departed leaving the lodge-owner as much in the dark as he'd been upon arrival.

Over the coming weeks meetings were held between both men. The first took place in a Fort Wayne coffee shop where Penther informed V, three of his most trusted followers had enlisted. Aldo Dopple rounded the number off at four. He and his bodyguard would remain in the field, while the others were to be installed within the lower depths of an electronics plant in Detroit.

With V supervising the men were put to task erecting partitions to create a temporary living space. Appliances were installed in a makeshift mess room. Beside a preexisting washroom sleeping quarters were established. The accommodation included bunks, a television and a card table. The space would host it's tenant's for roughly one year. A microbiologist was slated to arrive making a total of four residents. Allotted a storage room as his quarters, Dr. Bezzerer was afforded the luxury of privacy.

Two contractors were hired to blast out a portion of the basement ceiling, creating a twin-floor work area dubbed 'the atrium'. Metal doors were installed to seal the spacious room off from the rest of the lower-level. The contractors had been informed toxic chemicals were to be used, subsequently they were instructed to install a made-to-assemble decontamination chamber within the atrium. Nearby, a circular vat of steel roughly ten feet in diameter, had been inserted into the concrete floor and underlying soil. The burrowed cavity would be drained of waste and transferred weekly to a landfill. Once the contractors completed their tasks they were to be paid in cash.

The longest-serving member of Penther's rag-tag militia was placed in charge of plant operations in V's absence. Jackson Bell had a background as an electrician.

Inside of three months two significant event's occurred.

Azil Besserer was installed within the compound and Carl Kristy had been brought on board to replace V as courier. The departing middleman informed the others, it was necessary for him to focus on separate aspects of their campaign. They were assured his replacement had been personally selected by Sir. The move was harshly criticized by Penther - things ran like clockwork why mess with it! Conceding the inevitable, the militia leader still believed he might achieve something greater than he could on his own. Those conniving thieves in Washington would tremble once their message reverberated.

PRESENT

A fine mist hovered over the parking lot attached to the Lone Star Steakhouse in suburban Fort Wayne. Easing the minivan into a vacated space, Penther killed the engine and stared at the traffic taillights cast reflections on the rain-drenched pavement as cars whisked by. He made it a point to arrive before a scheduled appointment as an intuitive precaution. Reconnaissance was imperative for a patriot defender who trusted nobody.

Standing at roughly 5' 8" William Penther appeared taller to his disciples - who would've followed him to hell and back. When not attired in camouflage fatigues he dressed simply and inconspicuously. For his meeting with Carl Kristy he wore a windbreaker, trousers and work boots. His cropped brown hair was parted neatly above facial features which defied expression. Prison psychiatrist's interpreted his introspective and voyeuristic nature as anti-social and possibly psychotic. Penther would stare back coldly and state they were in error.

The Lone Star was a modest eatery located along the main drag leading into Fort Wayne from the airport. The property owned by Penther was an hour's drive west. Gaudy fast-food outlets and box stores littered the landscape as evening descended. With no sign of Kristy his lips tightened. Despite harbouring a mistrust of his handler he was always on time for an exchange.

Ten months earlier when Carl Kristy first appeared at the lodge a pair of salivating doberman's were there to greet him. He mounted the steps and was met by Aldo Dopple who levelled a rifle at his head. V's successor informed the bodyguard he was there to introduce himself. Dopple curled his lips and ushered him into the parlour. Their guest stood facing Penther and passed him an envelope. It contained encrypted information and a photograph confirming his identity. Browsing the document Penther motioned him to a table and both men sat facing each other. Kristy remarked it had been a privilege to be associated with Sir. He pledged to transfer funds and directives in the same dutiful manner as had his predecessor.

Penther instructed Aldo to tail their new bag-man and discovered he'd booked himself into a motel outside of Ellery - a dozen kilometres from their lodge. The following day a first exchange was conducted and transactions went smoothly. Penther continued to harbour doubts and considered the possibility the venture was an elaborate set-up mounted by the Feds, who intended to snare him and his boys in a sting. Profiled as a domestic terrorist Penther was used to being observed.

During that first meeting Aldo listened mindlessly as conversation between both men lurched forward awkwardly. Over the next few days Kristy asserted his anti-government credibility by claiming the country was better off during frontier times. The idea of giving money to Washington would've induced gut-wrenching laughter he insisted. Listening impassively Penther agreed with everything expressed by their guest. He'd been telling his followers the same thing for years which made him even more suspicious. Despite V's assurances he suspected their visitor was a federal plant. Penther decided to put him to the test and gave instructions to have him ambushed. Kristy made known his intention to hike up to the lodge for their next meeting. Navigating the Yokum Trail he was knocked unconscious from behind with the butt end of a rifle. When he came to he found himself bound to a tree. Confronted by his attacker whose veiled voice was audible beneath a balaclava Aldo slurred, "This is private property dickhead!"

Obscured by foliage a dozen meters away the lodge owner monitored Kristy's reactions as he struggled to undo his binds. The hiker swore he was simply visiting acquaintances at Rykles Clearing.

"So you say!" his assailant responded.

Tethered at the wrists and ankles the former SIAG sleeper could easily have unravelled his binds and dispatched the insufferable wretch who'd bashed his head. In the role of courier serving the same master, such action would've undone the fragile relationship existing between himself and the militia leader.

Aldo made himself scarce leaving his victim secured to a tree. The feeling of being observed persisted and Kristy faked struggling to free himself. Without an audience it would've taken seconds.

When nothing came of the ambush Penther decided to give his new handler the benefit of doubt. The following morning he paid a visit to Kristy's motel room and admitted it was he who'd masterminded the assault. Feigning surprise Kristy issued forth a tirade of curses. He sat on the edge of the bed and grudgingly admitted he could understand Penther's precaution.

"I had to be certain," the lodge owner muttered. "Undercover agents are continually attempting infiltration. I instructed Aldo to give you the once-over and told him to lay off the rough stuff."

Kristy brought his hand to his head and admitted the injury was superficial. He intended to drive to the lodge the following morning to reconvene their aborted meeting. Keeping his promise he arrived at eight and took his place opposite Penther. The flow of conversation between both men was less guarded and each contributed with regard's to pick-ups, drop-offs and rendezvous points.

Having studied his host's file Kristy drew his own conclusions. The Face had provided him with documents drawn from police records, newspaper clippings and intelligence briefs. They detailed Penther's nefarious activities, including expounding hate on behalf of several racist organizations. There were the gun-running and para-military exercises he'd conducted. During his incarceration for plotting an attack on a Federal building, an appraisal appeared in a publication calling itself Defiance! The article highlighted Penther's struggle on behalf of decent white folk and presented a glowing two-page profile. A contrary piece published in an Indianapolis weekly, recalled how scores of former recruits had distanced themselves from the militiaman's entourage of super-patriots.

During their meeting the location's for future conferences were finalized and contact procedure was established. Before adjourning Kristy handed over several disposable phones, which included proper encryption codes. Aware Penther loathed alcohol he managed to abstain over the course of their summit. Despite the reverence the militiaman held for his adoptive father, Strom Rykles he considered drunks little more then dependent cockroaches.

Back in real time outside the Lone Star Steakhouse, Penther tried to quell the uneasiness he felt whenever he met with Carl Kristy.

On a separate front inquiries were being made regarding the whereabouts of several men associated with the militia leader. Penther shrugged off queries and said he hadn't heard from any of them since being sent up river. Former supporters either languished in prison or had drifted.

In the skies over Fort Wayne's International Airport, a Cessna commissioned by Carl Kristy was cleared to land and it's sole passenger debarked carrying a briefcase. He emerged from the main terminal and hailed a cab. Directions were given and they set off for the steakhouse.

With only minutes remaining until their nine pm rendezvous there was still no sign of Kristy. The handler was usually punctual and Penther wondered if something had gone wrong.

Abruptly, a taxi whisked into the parking lot and braked to a halt. Kristy emerged from the rear seat and made his way toward the restaurant entrance. Attired in a trim-fitting dark suit and tie, his hair was combed back and his cuff-links glistened. He projected an air of confidence.

Penther emerged from his vehicle and strode toward the entrance. His footsteps echoed and Kristy spun about. When he noticed who it was he extended his right arm, "How goes it buddy!"

"Alright. "

"Great!"

Highlighting perfect teeth Kristy motioned him forward, "Let's see what's on the menu and get caught up."

Inside the establishment a table was requested apart from other patrons. Once they were seated Kristy's benevolence underwent a shift and something other than the rakish businessman emerged. Penther was always startled by his handler's deft change of character.

From a zippered pocket, the militiaman withdrew a chrome cylinder the size of a flashlight battery and passed it under the table. Kristy unlocked his briefcase and placed it within. Unobserved by patrons he withdrew a similar canister and passed it back. The entire transaction lasted only seconds.

Kristy made small talk about how effectively his pilot managed the unruly slipstreams at 5000 feet. Abruptly, a waitress arrived with menus.

"Anything to drink gentlemen?"

Turning on the charm Kristy remarked, "Perhaps a glass of wine. Can you recommend a vintage?"

"We only have the house brand Sir."

"That would be fine."

It was the first time he had consumed alcohol in Penther's presence.

"And for you sir?" she inquired of the unsmiling customer.

"Water."

"Okey dokey," she remarked and dashed off.

Kristy frowned, "Your sunny disposition is bound to draw unwarranted attention Mr. Penther."

His companion made no response.

The waitress returned with their beverages, "Ready to order gentlemen?"

Kristy glanced at the menu, "I'll go with number three well done."

Penther nodded, "Same - make mine rare."

Jotting down their order's she thanked them and departed

Kristy lowered his voice and stared across the table, "What's on your mind?"

The dinner rush had abated and nearby tables were unoccupied.

"There was trouble at the plant," Penther muttered.

"Go on?"

"Bell informed me a lab captain started making inquiries."

"And the nature of his inquiries?"

"He quizzed a technician in another lab about the recycling process."

"What is this worker's name?"

"Ray Pearson he's been employed at that site for years."

"What occurred exactly?"

"Wicker and Bell took him down they had no option. No one saw a thing."

"Where is he now?"

"Locked in a janitor's room on the lower level."

Kristy stared into his glass.

"The police came around," Penther resumed. "They asked some questions and wanted to see the lab where Pearson worked. They interviewed his crew but their English is bad. Bell cooperated fully."

"And the other lab?"

"They weren't questioned."

"Does Bell believe the police are suspect?"

"He told them Pearson appeared agitated and disappeared sometime after lunch without explanation. A girlfriend made contact inquiring about Pearson's whereabouts. It was she who alerted the police."

Kristy glared across the table, "With all that surveillance gear were your 'boys' snoozing!"

Penther stared back icily, "Wicker spoke with Pearson in the lobby. He was looking for Bell and going on about damaged product. Wicker said he'd inform the supervisor and suggested he return to his lab. Instead, Pearson entered a lab next to his own and likely put two and two together. His movements were monitored and the supervisor was summoned. Pearson entered the shipping room and they took him down."

"You're sure this guy is secured?"

"Yes."

"Police get missing person's reports all the time. Hopefully, they won't suspect a thing until our business there concludes over the coming days."

"And the other lab...?"

"Do nothing," Kristy responded. "Once the plant is vacated Wicker can cut a permanent severance deal with members of both labs. Meantime, we forge ahead."

The waitress arrived with their steaks. She placed them on the table and returned with a basket of rolls, "There you are fellas."

When she departed Kristy said, "What of Besserer?"

"He claims to be ahead of schedule."

"Claims?"

Slicing into his beef Penther shrugged.

"The good doctor dislikes your lads intensely," Kristy remarked.

Gripping his fork Penther glanced up, "Who gives a shit what that A'biinian puke thinks. For months he's looked down his nose at my team, while drawing a fortune from your paymaster."

Kristy took exception and leaned forward, "That 'puke' is key to the success of this venture. Your associate's are paid handsomely for their efforts. I suggest you tell them not to engage Dr. Besserer in anything other than the task at hand or a price will be paid."

Penther wiped HP sauce from his mouth, "What in hell is that supposed to mean!"

"Just what it implies," Kristy responded. "If Besserer is antagonized further your men will be penalized financially - as decreed by Sir."

Holding his temper in check Penther stabbed at his potatoes.

"I urge you to remind your followers not to lose sight of the objective," Kristy advised. "We need to stay the course and ignore the doctor's arrogance – at least for the time being."

Penther sniffed and shoved his plate aside.

Buttering a roll Kristy resumed, "You'll liaison with Jackson Bell a final time and provide him with the directives I've issued you. The fund's necessary to see the Detroit operation through to its conclusion await withdrawal. I'll make certain Besserer's final report is received by V, who will pass it along Sir. That gentleman will determine the precise time we're to unite at Rykles Clearing. When that occurs we'll witness the efficiency of the doctor's weapon from a distance."

With the meeting over Kristy rose and retrieved his briefcase, "I'll be in touch."

At the counter he paid their bill then rejoined his dour companion in the parking lot for the sake of appearances. Parting company the militiaman climbed into his van and disappeared along the rain-swept boulevard.

Meanwhile, his handler caught a cab back to the airport.

———————

Corporal Soo stood alongside the security station in the lobby of Sentinel Hall discussing the weather with her replacement Dennis Drake. The burly guard's shaved head gleamed beneath lights highlighting artifact's making up the lobby museum. Removing his jacket, he straightened his tie and recounted a dilemma his parent's currently faced. Having retired to Florida they found themselves with nothing to do.

"I'd have no problem finding things to do," remarked his supervisor.

"Nor would I," agreed her colleague.

While he pondered the matter his boss said, "You've been with us a month now Dennis, what's your verdict on the Ohio posting?"

"I like it," he replied. "It's more laid back than the Beltway."

Before assuming his current assignment Dennis had been stationed along Pennsylvania Avenue in DC for a two-year stint.

Sasha Soo detailed her own first impressions, "The view from here is stunning. The bluffs, the passing freighters, Sentinel Hall. I enjoy taking turns about the grounds during my shifts."

"Got that one right."

"On clear nights lights can be observed winking along the Canadian side. Have you noticed?"

"I have indeed," he replied. "You can almost touch them."

She smiled, "I've completed the staff holiday schedule for July and August. You're down for the ten days you requested."

"Thank you."

Relatively new to the post herself the Corporal intended to cover shifts without bringing in replacements. Bidding Dennis adieu until she reported back for duty twelve hours hence, Sasha adjusted her purse and started toward the lobby doors. The sun was low and the Institute grounds lay in shadow as she emerged into the open air. Residing temporarily on campus, Sasha occupied a dorm on the fourth floor of the seven-story Residence building. Unable to secure suitable lodgings in town on short notice, Professor Tondar arranged accommodation on her behalf. Being late April a number of student unit's had become available. Her quarters consisted of a washroom, sleeping space and kitchenette. In her spare time she sought new digs in town.

Stationed at Fort Jackson in Columbia, South Carolina for three gruelling years, Sasha relished the responsibility of command. At twenty-three she assumed the rank of Corporal. The lithe Asian female fit comfortably into a regimented lifestyle and had immersed herself in Military Intelligence. During her final year in South Carolina, an external matter surfaced making life intolerable. Fortunately, her superior's were aware of the situation and did the proper thing. An opening for chief security officer at Grissim became available and she was offered the position. Ripe for a challenge Sasha jumped at the opportunity. She arrived at her new posting in advance of Dennis and another recruit named Sean Drummond. Both were in their early twenties and secured lodgings in town. Between the three of them vigil over Sentinel Hall was maintained in twelve-hour rotations, alternating on weekends. Their unit was part of a larger elite which proved lethal if provoked by unkind adversaries. From the get-go a quiet respect flowed between the Corporal and her team.

The path between Sentinel Hall and the Residence building wound its way along a manicured hedge lining the courtyard. Traces moonlight penetrated wisps of drifting clouds overhead. Lamps illuminating the trail were extinguished during holidays to conserve energy. Sasha scolded herself for having forgotten her flashlight and used the light from her phone to distinguish the outline of the path.

A soft tread was heard and she spun about.

Peering through darkness she noticed nothing unusual. With a palm on her sidearm she resumed course at a brisker pace. From the corner of her eye she detected movement behind a hedgerow. She turned and withdrew her weapon.

"Show yourself," she demanded.

There was no response.

Leaves rustled as she journeyed the path. Arriving at the Residence building she entered the lobby and accessed the stairwell. Inside her unit the door was secured and she kept the lights off. Peering between shuttered blinds toward the courtyard below, nothing appeared out of the ordinary. She changed into panamas and opted to shower in the morning. Double checking the door lock she slipped beneath the covers and placed her weapon under the pillow.

CHAPTER

SEVEN

With regards to her first assignment Taras had only the scantiest intelligence the SIAG were able to provide.

Ten months earlier a sleeper code-named Ulsar had been turned by an enemy of A'biin. The tracking implant in his body was removed within hours of his defection. Had he been truly dead his GPS would have flat-lined - instead it vanished completely. Prior to his disappearance Ulsar's predecessor had been apprehended. The harried agent texted a communique to his overseas handler, stating he'd been approached to work on behalf of a ranking US Intelligence figure for a large sum of money. Before he could flee he was taken into custody and led off to an interrogation chamber. A chilling final entry in correspondence with his handler, revealed the person who tried to recruit him, mentioned a SIAG weapon of mass destruction was being constructed somewhere in the American heartland.

Months after those events unfolded Taras considered the plight of the doomed operative and his AWOL replacement. Her handler - a man named Heron, related that before Ulsar abdicated, he made trips to upstate Massachusetts. GPS also confirmed he'd been spending weekends in Cambridge, before returning to his job as library researcher in Manhattan. Sighted in the company of a female student attending Harvard, no trace of that person had been observed since. In hindsight a succession of women had been observed in his company. On more than one occasion he was told he'd be recalled, if he persisted to violate protocol with his rakish antics. Contrary to western spy mythology such endeavours are deemed toxic within Intelligence procedure - especially among the SIAG.

Ulsar's signal was tracked en route to Jacksonville, Florida. It registered for several hours at coordinates matching those of the city's marine terminal. Granted leverage the SIAG attempted to trace his movements to determine intention. The following day his signal vanished west of Jacksonville. It was determined the device embedded in his ankle had been removed.

Before his disappearing act the SIAG requested the identity of the Cambridge woman. Ulsar confirmed he had indeed met a Harvard student nicknamed 'Candle' and insisted it was all quite innocent.

This was the one thread Taras had to go on.

She intended to hunt him by way of his girlfriend assuming there was only the one. Establishing contact with Harvard University's registry office, she asked if she could acquire a list of students who'd abandoned their studies the previous fall. She stated a missing family member was being sought. The information couldn't be revealed over the phone and she began her quest, by making the fourteen-hour drive east in a rented vehicle. Arriving in Boston she checked into a hotel under an assumed name and produced corroborating ID. The next morning was spent at the printers duplicating a truant officer's identification card and assigning a fictitious name to it. The replica was copied from a life-size image obtained on the internet. Attaching a photograph of herself, she had the card laminated and hoped it would suffice.

That evening she dined alone in a Thai restaurant before returning to her room overlooking the Charles River. From her window she gazed at the city lights and wept. With overwhelming heartache she struggled to obliterate the past. It was hopeless trying to bury her heart.

The following morning she showered and dressed. Ordering a light breakfast of grapefruit and toast she planned her agenda. Clutching her suitcase she rode an elevator down to the underground car-park and stored it in the trunk of her vehicle. Wearing a blouse, matching slacks and low heels she reentered the lobby. Despite the conservative attire, she looked striking with her hair drawn back in a pony-tail. On the sidewalk she lowered her sunglasses and hailed a cab. While they made their way across the bridge toward Cambridge, the driver was instructed to drop her off nearby the administration office's attached to Harvard. Despite the obstacles in obtaining personal information; her task was made more challenging not knowing the name of her quarry.

At an intersection bordering Harvard Square, she handed the driver fare and a tip and departed. She stood before a series of imposing structures, dating back two centuries and asked a passerby to direct her to the administrative buildings at University Hall. Following directions she came to an ornately decorated edifice. Upon entry she approached an information desk and asked the gentleman on duty where she might find the enrolment office.

"We don't deal with enrolment here, Madam," he replied. " Registration gets underway at the start of August. You may submit an online application if you wish."

Taras smiled pleasantly and presented her truancy officer card, "I'm making an inquiry regarding a missing student."

The attendant glanced at the ID, "I suggest you contact the Registrars Office. I'll give you the number and extension. Call first if there's no response try the Office of Finance - it's within walking distance. I'll give you that address as well."

He scribbled down the information and passed it over.

"Thank you."

Outside Taras found a phone booth and contacted the Registrars Office. A voice-message informed callers the office would re-open the first week of August. Replacing the receiver she was directed toward the Office of Finance. A lobby directory was surveyed and she found the appropriate department. It was up two flights and she joined a small line. When her turn arrived she was redirected to the third floor. When she finally accessed the correct office she noticed two staffers tapping away at keyboards.

"May I be of assistance?" inquired the nearest who rose and walked toward the counter.

"Possibly," Taras replied.

She withdrew the forged truancy card and introduced herself as a probation officer. Drawing a name from thin air she said she was looking for Sarah Verch.

"It's likely an alias used while she attended Harvard. We believe she dropped out sometime last fall and vanished. Her family is distraught. My supervisor has asked me to pinpoint the time of her departure and her most recent address."

Glancing at the ID the clerk asked for more information.

"Agency files suggest Ms. Verch may have been enrolled in a General Arts program. I was hoping departure records for the period in question might indicate something."

The woman considered her request.

"We concern ourselves mostly with tuition and are informed in advance if a student won't be returning. I may be able to retrieve a file with the names of women who chose not to return due to maternity issues, work - things of that nature." She returned to her desk and said over her shoulder, "You're aware personal addresses remain confidential."

"I understand. Thank you."

Minutes later the woman handed over a single page print-out, "I'm afraid you'll have to peruse the information at the counter and return the page once it's been reviewed."

Taras nodded, "Would it be alright if I jotted down contact numbers or email addresses, which prove pertinent to our inquiry?"

"I don't see a problem."

"Thank you."

Alone at the counter Taras scanned the list. References to academic standings, tuition and home addresses were stored on a separate file unavailable to her. Due to Harvard's renown, contact listings appeared under several area codes. In total less than a dozen entries applied. Rapidly, she scribbled down the names and contacts and returned the notebook to her purse. She thanked the receptionist graciously for her cooperation.

"You're welcome," the woman replied retrieving the print-out. "I hope you find who you're looking for."

"So do I."

Back in her hotel room Taras circled four Boston area-code numbers, the rest were out-of-town listings. Several entries were accompanied with email addresses only. She decided to start with them and make phone calls later. Departing the hotel she strolled three blocks and entered a cybercafe. She took a seat before an available computer and opened a Yahoo email account. Messages were typed to five recipients. The text stated she was writing on behalf of a student group, working in conjunction with the Faculty of Arts and Sciences at Harvard. She inquired if the individual was considering re-enrolment for the fall semester. Awaiting possible replies she uploaded a detailed map of Boston and ordered juice and a sandwich. Over the course of ninety minutes two recipient's responded. The first stated she was presently employed and had no plans to return to school. The second wouldn't be attending for financial reasons.

Having clocked in three hours computer time no further messages were received. Taras closed the account and squared up at the cash register. Back at the hotel she rode an elevator down to parking and stashed her purse in the car trunk. Afterwards, she approached the front desk and requested to speak with the hotel operator. Directed towards a woman wearing a headset, Taras explained she was a hotel guest and said her purse had been misplaced or stolen at a conference she attended. Her phone and credit cards were lost, however she kept funds in the event of such emergencies.

"May I deposit a hundred dollars and use my hotel room extension to make several out-of-town calls?" the patron politely inquired.

The operator said it was policy to use credit cards for such transactions. In light of the situation she agreed to make an exception.

Placing five twenty dollar bills on the counter Taras scribbled down her room number and assumed name, "I'll return later thanks so much."

Back in her room she picked up the receiver and listened to the dial tone. If the line was monitored, none of the tell-tale signs were apparent. She withdrew the list and first contacted local phone numbers. Introducing herself as a representative of a student group associated with the FAS at Harvard, she inquired about Fall enrolment. The first response was curt and to the point. The woman stated she was too busy rearing twins to return. Another said she'd maxed-out her student loan and couldn't afford tuition. The next was answered by a machine and she decided to try later. A male voice responded to her final local dispatch. Following some unwelcome innuendo on his part, Taras repeated her request to speak with Nicole - the woman whose number she'd contacted. Abruptly, he yelled to someone in another room. When Nicole finally spoke she said it would be wonderful to complete her degree, but the slob she lived with spent all her savings on liquor. Taras hesitated and said she was sorry. When the call ended she scratched the name from the list.

The female voice at the other end of her first long-distance call had an edge to it. After Taras recited her student-group spiel, the hostile respondent wanted to know who'd given her number away and who the caller was.

Taras apologized for interrupting at a bad time.

"All the time will be bad for you if you contact me again bitch!

Placing the receiver down the caller's instinct suggested her target had been identified. The paranoia was tangible across the miles. Listed as Kari Ellstone, the tiny matter of not knowing where she resided persisted. Taras reminded herself she was seeking Kari's *former* address in order to find Ulsar.

That evening Taras paid her hotel bill and was refunded ninety-eight dollars for the brief long-distance call to Ms. Ellstone. She drove across town and booked herself into a second hotel, leaving the car in it's underground accommodation. The following morning she returned to the Office of Finance at Harvard, and spoke with the clerk who'd been so helpful the previous day. Reciting a story conceived an hour earlier, she mentioned her office had determined the identity of the student they sought and established phone contact.

"She's in a dire way and threatened to kill herself," the imparted the truancy officer. "The police have been alerted but are unable to determine her whereabouts."

"Gracious me…," the woman murmured.

Concern was etched on the visitor's features, "I wonder if you could identify the address matching the student's name. It would help enormously."

"I'm really not supposed to," the clerk whispered.

She glanced towards her preoccupied colleague and sighed, "I'll see what I can do."

With the student's name scribbled on paper she returned to her desk and tapped a keyboard. While this occurred Taras glanced toward the hall. She was uncomfortable returning to the same location two days running. On the way up a male security guard took a second look. Fortunately, his gaze appeared to be one of admiration.

The clerk returned to the counter and handed over the address.

"I'm sorry to have put you to so much trouble," Taras conceded. "I promise not to again."

The woman smiled, "I hope it all works out."

Twenty minutes later a taxi delivered Taras to the address the clerk had scribbled down. The subject's former residence was situated in a prosperous area of Boston known as Roxbury. Attired in a summer dress and sandals, Taras tossed her hair back and approached the brown-brick dwelling. She heard music emitting from a side entrance and rang the doorbell. A young woman sporting braids and blue overalls responded.

"I'm sorry to disturb you," the caller stated. "I'm looking for Kari Ellstone?"

The scent of cannabis lingered and a man stripped to the waist appeared.

"She's been gone more than a six months now," the woman responded.

Disappointment registered on the stranger's face.

"I've attempted to contact Kari by phone. Her number is no longer in service. I'm a visiting relative, this address is my last recourse."

"As I said she's gone."

"Do you have any idea where she can be reached? It regards an urgent family matter."

The young man chuckled, "Likely involves millions."

The comment implied Kari came from a privileged background.

"It's very important," their visitor reiterated.

The young woman thought for a moment, "When Kari left Harvard and moved out she said she'd return every few weeks to retrieve mail. Initially, she did. After a spell she informed us she was moving upstate. That's the last we saw of her."

"Is there anything else you remember?" prompted their guest.

"Shortly after moving out she phoned," the woman recalled. "She was anxious about an envelope posted to this address. She described it as one of those padded jobbers. I checked to see if it was here - it was. She gave me a forwarding address and requested I send it to her."

"Do you have the address?"

"It was six months ago. I don't think so.

"Please try to remember."

"It was a post-box number."

"Can you recall a city or town?"

"I recall her telling me not give out the address."

"Please. This involves a family crisis."

The young man interjected, "It was some Cove east of Rockport along the coast."

"Thank you!"

"You're welcome."

"Would you happen to have a recent photograph of her?"

"Why would you want that?" the girl inquired. "You're a relation - you ought to know what she looks like."

"Unfortunately, the snapshots I possess are years old."

"Afraid we don't have any."

Taras thanked them both and took her leave.

"Say howdy if you see her," the shirtless man called out.

"I shall."

The screen door closed and the couple withdrew.

Rockport...

Repeating the name Taras walked several blocks before hailing a cab. At the hotel she purchased a map of Massachusetts in the gift shop. Back in her room she spread it out and located Rockport along the northern tip of the state. Twenty miles east lay the town of Halton's Cove.

Kari Ellstone was a runaway from a well-off family. Her mother was a successful Park Avenue art dealer, her father and grandfather had made their fortunes on Wall Street. A young woman of average height and weight, Kari's fair complexion was framed with auburn curls. Passionate whenever something struck her fancy, she remained indifferent to most things in life. Growing up in Queens, New York, she'd graduated high school with above average grades before rapidly losing her virginity. A brother seven years her senior lived in Norway and rarely kept touch.

During her eighteenth summer a restless anxiety gripped her. Out of the blue she and a girlfriend followed a cow-punk band to Dallas, where Kari became involved with the bass player and lived with him for three weeks in a Deep Elum flophouse. Around this time an assortment of drugs became available along with requisite intakes of alcohol. Following a brief period of experimentation Kari grew bored and caught a flight back to New York.

To her parents disgust she decided not to enter university and chose instead to drift from one thing to another. She joined Poetry and Monsters - a group of wild-eyed artisans who moved between Greenwich Village, Cambridge, and Philadelphia, staging dramatic readings at open stages and coffeehouses. Weary of passing the hat and sleeping on floors Kari turned next to environmental causes. Involving herself in a northeastern replenishing initiative, she helped organizers revitalize acres of forests damaged by fire. The endeavour was thrilling at first. She spent weeks hiking the woods bordering Vermont and became involved with a hairy young radical, who arrived with only the shirt on his back. Due to his constant snoring and less than inspired harmonica blowing, their union soon played itself out. The adventure finally ended when the black flies drove her back to Queens.

Kari's folks were greatly relieved when she decided to attend Harvard. With family connections and better than average grades, she was ushered into Classical Arts at the renowned institution. Rather than live on campus she chose to rent accommodations at a house in Roxbury, maintained by acquaintances from her Poetry And Monster days. For nine weeks she appeared content. Classes were effortless - it was simply a matter of attending lectures and making certain assignment's were submitted on time. Lying alone in her room she wondered if she'd made the right choice.

Toward the end of October she was sipping cider at the Cellar Bistro on Concord Avenue. At a nearby table she overheard an engaging debate being waged. Glancing in that direction she noticed a man seated opposite a younger couple. They seemed enraptured by their companion, who was well dressed and exceedingly handsome. He bore a lightly tanned complexion and appeared to be in his late twenties. As their laughter resounded it was apparent he had a wonderful sense of humour. Occasionally, their conversation reverted to English. During one such interval the man made reference to Norway. He noticed Kari observing him and smiled. Seizing the opportunity she said, "I heard you mention Norway. My brother lives in Oslo."

"Does he really!" the man exclaimed. "I have been to Oslo myself. An old and beautiful city."

"So I'm told," she replied. "Perhaps I'll visit one day."

"You should," he responded. "Would you care to join us. We were discussing Europe and our adventures there."

She hesitated then reached for her cider. Crossing the floor she sat next to the gentleman and introduction's were made. The couple opposite her were from Saudi Arabia. Both were engaged in post-graduate work at Harvard. The man seated next to her offered his hand and introduced himself as Nickolas Dante, "Or Nicky if you prefer."

"Pleased to meet you, Nicky. I'm Kari if you prefer."

Sipping beverages they boasted of their wanderings. Kari recalled a number of exotic trips she'd taken with her parents when she was young. Unfortunately, most had faded from memory.

"A pity," Nickolas remarked.

"Yes," she agreed. "I'm older and more appreciative now. Hopefully, the opportunity will present itself again - without my folks of course."

She finished her drink and said it was time to go. Nickolas rose to his feet and asked if she would meet with him again. Consenting to his request she said, "Present location, same time Friday - that work for you?"

"I'll see you then."

When they met Nickolas suggested an Indian restaurant he frequented over on Mt. Auburn Street and they set off on foot. Guided to a table their waiter lit a candle and said he'd return. Scouring the menu they decided on curried lamb, white rice and wine. Without delving into her background Kari talked a bit about herself. She mentioned Harvard and spoke of her involvement with an environmental collective over the summer. Listening intently her dinner partner appeared intrigued. When she asked about him he said he was a freelance author from Cairo, "I have been commissioned to write a series of chapters for inclusion in a book being published back home."

She inquired about the subject and was told it dealt with peace initiatives existing between middle-east nations and the West.

Flashing a quizzical smile she said, "You don't reside in the greater Boston area do you?"

"I'm afraid not. In my spare time I enjoy driving south along I 95 and hooking up with friends here in town. Its rather isolated where I am."

"I see."

Shadows played on his bronze features and his flesh radiated in the flickering light.

"Candle..." he murmured.

"I'm sorry...?"

"Forgive me...I'm drawn to candles. They're warm and bright as are you."

"Why thank you."

He lowered his voice, "Candle shall be your nickname. Do you object?"

Kari laughed, "If it pleases you."

She steered the conversation in a different direction, "So what are your immediate plans Nickolas - I mean Nicky?"

He leaned back, "I've rented a bungalow upstate and plan to complete my assignment before the deadline expires - which was months ago."

She laughed, "Your English is excellent."

"I studied the language back home with dreams of visiting the West one day."

"How long will you remain in America?"

"Until the work gets done."

"Are you married?"

Leaning forward he smiled, "I wondered when you'd ask."

Flushing she replied, "Well...?"

"My life is an open book," he responded. "And you?"

"I haven't given the matter much thought."

Over the coming weeks they met Friday evenings and remained together until Sunday, when both returned to their duties. As autumn turned to gold, they attended local theatre productions and strolled arm in arm along sidewalks strewn with leaves. Sipping wine on Cambridge patios, a taxi would be summoned to whisk them to a hotel room Nicky had reserved in advance. Kari would've happily invited her Egyptian prince to her Roxbury digs – if only to show him off. She decided he'd be less than thrilled crowded around an ash strewn coffee table, in the company of several reefer-toking motormouths spilling beer and screaming along to AC/DC.

During one of their walks Nicky informed her he'd be away for several weeks. His publishing deadline loomed and he had yet to assemble a final draft.

"It will be difficult not seeing you," he confided. "But if things don't get done I'll be forced to head home."

Kari was devastated. She assumed they would follow the same routine indefinitely.

"Do you have a yard?"

"Yes, why do you ask?"

"Then allow me to join you," she pleaded. "While you work I'll grow tomatoes and do some sketching. I'm a decent cook and can offer clerical services - I type seventy words per minute."

Taking her hand in his own Nickolas smiled, "It's early November and there are your studies. You told me you were determined to see the school year through."

"What we have matters more."

"I'll only be gone three or four weeks."

Wiping aside a tear she said, "I'm going on twenty and have my whole life to attend classes. I'm self-sufficient financially – you won't have to provide for me." Her voice trembled, "I only wish to make you happy, Nick."

Dante was silent and closed his eyes. Finally he said, "My retreat isn't so bad, you might even grow to like it."

She squeezed him and buried her face in his chest. He placed his hands on her shoulders and stood at arm's length. "You understand my job involves intermittent travel. Interviews have yet to be conducted. There will be stretches you'll be entirely alone."

He allowed the words to settle.

"That will give me time to dig a garden and find a kitty," she sniffed. "You don't have allergies to cats do you?"

"No."

"Good. I'll have company when you're away."

"Then let us proceed," he said. "I'll need a week possibly longer to wrap up a few things. I'll keep in touch. Once I return we'll journey up the coast together."

"I'll miss you every minute."

They embraced and he whispered softly, "Promise me you'll resume your studies at a later date."

"I promise."

Nine months after that exchange took place Taras found herself merging onto a two-lane highway off Interstate 95. Approaching the coastal town of Halton's Cove, the Atlantic Ocean straddled her along the right and she breathed the salt-water air. Breeze ruffled her hair and a smile had formed along her lips. Several discreet inquiries would lead directly to Candle.

From early September until the final weeks of April, those attending Grissim congregated at 'the Bag'. The student-run lounge was situated on the ground level of the Commons Building. It opened at seven each morning and offered an assortment of teas, coffees, juices and muffins. During evenings from six to eleven - midnight on weekends, beer and wine was served. Artwork created by Grissim students adorned the walls, while jazz and country-blues resonated from overhead speakers. The space afforded patrons an opportunity to chat comfortably. Pupil's belonging to both history and media fraternities would gather in clusters. The tribes occasionally mingled if romance blossomed between individual's from either camp. The Bag remained dark from the first week of May until students returned from summer break. In the interim Charley's Hideaway, a restaurant/bar located downtown served as a meeting place for young people.

The previous summer Jesse Carlton was introduced to a fellow media student he'd recognized from the lecture hall. Seated with mutual friends, Shawna Delray was one of several students who remained in town following final exams. Leasing a one-bedroom apartment in a house belonging to a female cleric employed at the Institute, Shawna's decision to tarry year 'round rather than return to Winfield, Kansas and her father was resolute. This was the second summer she'd stayed away. Having returned home the previous Christmas, she remained for three days before hightailing it back to Ohio. Her father spent the entire time before a TV drinking whisky and doting on his latest flame. As for old friends most had fled town. There was another reason Shawna chose to remain in the Falls. For the past year she'd been involved with Jesse Carlton.

Following his return from the Windsor excursion, the two met outside the Shadowlands Cinema for a prearranged movie date. Afterwards, they strolled to Charley's where the feature was usually discussed. This evening was different. Rattled by his apparent out-of-body experience at the border crossing that day, Jesse appeared distracted. Seated across from Shawna she noticed him staring blindly into space.

"What's up Jesse?"

Silence lingered until he sputtered, "I'm sorry...the drive back from Windsor was unsettling."

"It's not that far."

"No."

"How are your mother and grandfather?"

"They're fine. Thanks for asking."

"I remember you said your granddad was a character."

"He sure is."

"Did you enjoy the film?"

"It was alright."

Shawna looked perplexed, "Usually you have a lot to say."

"I'm a little out of it."

A waitress arrived and Shawna requested a BLT. Jesse ordered the same and asked for a jug of beer and two mugs.

Shawna was an alluring young woman who took her studies seriously. Initially, their relationship involved chatting with friends at the Bag. Eventually, it grew into something more and they became lovers. Both enjoyed discussing world events, listening to music and jogging. During seasonal weather they'd picnic in Falls Valley by the waterfall. Afterwards, the night would be spent at either his place or hers. Over the course of several months the relationship began to sour. If he didn't phone - she wouldn't and so forth. Encounters on campus became icy affairs until things gradually smoothed over.

"We should have chosen history!" Jesse stated abruptly. "At least there's an afterlife, one can always teach."

Shawna had heard it all before, "I enjoy what I'm studying."

"That's nice."

"So why did you choose Print Media then?"

"I figured it was up my alley."

Shawna leaned over the table, "What is it you want, Jesse?"

"That's a loaded question."

"I'm sorry," she sighed.

"No I'm sorry," he apologized. "I'm just not as certain about things as you are."

"You're always implying the newspaper industry is toast," she responded. "That's bullshit!"

"That's not what I meant."

"By informing people and posing questions – it's important Jesse!"

"In a peripheral way."

"Peripheral!" she repeated. "To convey events while attempting to put things into perspective is vital."

Shawna was committed. There was something of Jessie's mother in her.

The waitress arrived with a pitcher of beer and two frosted mugs. She returned shortly with their sandwiches. An awkward silence hung in the air once she departed. Jesse filled their glasses while Shawna nibbled at her sandwich.

"So what did you think of the film?" he asked.

Wiping a spec of mayo from the corner of her mouth she said, "I've already forgotten it. I'm tired of onscreen explosions. I relate better to psychological drama."

Jesse nodded and touched up his glass, "I envy you. You're focused and have a goal."

"I like to think so."

"I've decided," he muttered assertively.

"Decided what?"

"Sorry I'm blithering..."

Wishing she was back at the Shadowlands watching other peoples lives unravel, instead of her own Shawna remained silent.

Jesse asked if she planned to remain the summer in Lantern Falls?

Staring across the table at the man she'd been in love with she said, "I'm leaving Grissim."

"What!"

"I'm going to New York."

"I had no idea?"

"I wasn't certain either until now."

Grasping her napkin she whispered, "It's funny all along I assumed it would be you heading off to the big city - and the reverse turns out to be true. Life is like that sometimes."

Jesse was speechless.

"I received an offer from a friend who works at the Daily News," she resumed. "It's a gopher's job, but a foot in the door. I'll see what happens."

"What about your final year at the Institute?"

"Ms. Benson assures me I'll be able to secure night school placement in Manhattan to complete third-year requirements."

"When are you leaving?"

"Soon as I find accommodation."

Rising from the table she started for the door while Jesse settled up. Outside they walked in silence. A bus drew up to a stop and Shawna turned to face the young man, "I hope the future's good to you Jesse. Take care."

Kissing him on the cheek she was gone.

———————

EIGHT

Next morning Jesse awoke with a hollow feeling in his gut. Gazing from the window he observed his sorry reflection and shuffled off to the washroom. Attempting to process what Shawna had imparted to him the previous evening he showered and made coffee. Afterwards, he slumped before his laptop and focused on the pending meeting with Lee Tondar.

Global events constituted a significant part of what was to be his intended profession. His knowledge of A'biin and her security counterpart, the SIAG was superficial at best. Typing A'biin into a search box he hoped to learn more about America's diminutive adversary, than what was reported in soundbites. A government sponsored website was uploaded and he reviewed the nation's recent history, which included the discovery of oil-rich deposits beneath her desert sands a century earlier. The nation's devotion to the Muslim faith was cited. Names of provinces and cities featured prominently, along with an overview of it's capital, Siana. The primer concluded with a flowery tribute to A'biin's new leader, Amet D'han.

He cleared the page and typed in the acronym SIAG. Instantly, the words 'Soldiers of Infinite Ascendancy and God' appeared at the top of the screen. Hoping to find a succinct, unbiased account of the clandestine network, he scrolled to see what was available. Like her Israeli counterpart Mossad, the SIAG were an effective often ruthless Intelligence organization. Most blogs and websites offered existing information. For instance, it was known the SIAG were governed by a four-man directorate whose agent's spanned the globe. Those making up this quadrangle of power were referred to as the 'Wise Men'. Under their watch the SIAG remained committed to the nation's sovereignty, both internationally and among her mid-east rivals. Until recently

A'biin had been controlled by fundamentalist's within the country's ruling elite. With the ascension of a more moderate governing entity, leniency towards citizens rights and a willingness to negotiate with the West were extended. The SIAG itself had been restructured with control given over to a far-sighted centrist leadership The move infuriated secular hard-liners who'd been relegated to the sidelines following D'han's rise to power.

Much of the data amounted to press releases. A number of bloggers, including several right-leaning US think tanks took pot-shots demonizing the spy network - even in its more moderate incarnation. Revealingly, one scribe wrote the SIAG were known by no one least of all themselves.

Jesse downed the remains of his coffee and switched off the laptop. Scurrying out to the car, he found himself cruising north along Windover Road in the direction of the Institute. Signalling right he entered the campus and swung onto Abbot Lane. He noticed Lee Tondar on a courtyard path tossing bread crumbs to a cluster of pigeons. Jesse parked in a visitor's spot and approached the professor.

"I thought I'd meet you in the courtyard," the older man remarked. "Its a perfect morning for a stroll."

A squirrel scurried by and bolted up a tree. Seagulls circled high overhead.

"It's remarkably quiet this time of year," the professor observed.

"I noticed the same last week," replied his guest.

"You mentioned visiting relatives?"

"I spent time with my mother and grandfather in Windsor."

"Ah..."

Lee drew to a stop and faced the young man, "Have you considered my request Jesse?"

"Yes. I've decided to accept."

The professor's taunt lips appeared to waver, "I'm indebted to you son."

Placing a hand on the young man's shoulder he said, "Let's return to Control. There's much to discuss."

"Control?"

"I'll explain."

They made their way toward Sentinel Hall. Entering the lobby Jesse was introduced to a security official named Dennis Drake. The marble floor echoed as they skirted the museum exhibits in the direction of the stairwell. Lee spoke softly, "Dennis is part of a three-member security team supervised by Corporal Soo, whom you met previously. Having undergone several years Intelligence training in her own right, she has access to the space you're about to enter. If something were to happen to me or anyone manning this station the Corporal assumes command."

Once more Jesse found himself outside the professor's office. The door was accessed and he was ushered through. Taking the same seat he'd occupied earlier, Lee sat at his desk and focused on the young man.

"You feel certain you've made the right decision?"

"Yes," Jesse replied. "I've given the matter plenty of thought."

"On the surface it'll appear you're employed as my temporary assistant," Lee stated. "There's plenty of paperwork associated with being the only faculty member on campus over summer. An assistant will seem warranted."

Jesse nodded and remained silent.

The professor paused to glance at his notes, "That brings us to your summer job at the Observer. The opportunity will have to be forfeited Jesse. I hope you won't come to regret that decision."

"Once word is out dozens of candidates will vie for the position," replied the young man.

"I would imagine."

"I'll inform the managing editor I'm unable to accept the job due to unforeseen circumstances."

"You wouldn't be lying."

Lee resumed his narrative, "As professor's assistant you'll be placed on a weekly salary of two-hundred and seventy dollars - not including outside expenses. As for being enrolled in Media rather than Modern History - its a moot point. Neither pursuit is essential. The position is clerical and involves mostly filing and retrieving. The fact you live here year round and study at this facility, makes you a logical candidate for shuffling papers and scrolling files. It's purely cover."

Unlocking the top drawer of his desk Lee withdrew a tiny remote, "You inquired about Control."

He swivelled in his seat and aimed the device at the rear wall. Applying pressure with his thumb, a hum resonated and the wall whisked silently from left to right before vanishing entirely. Startled, Jesse leaned forward and found himself peering into a clandestine chamber the size of an operating room. Along the right side was a door, otherwise the only point of entry was through Lee's office.

Motioning his apprentice forward the older man remarked, "This is Control. It's official title is Information Retrieval Installation or IRI. All forms of overhead signals are intercepted and disseminated here."

"Overhead signals?"

"Correct. I work on behalf of a National Security Agency splinter operation known as UCOMA – the acronym stands for Universal

Communication Agency. At least seventeen security agencies represent the US. I belong to a more recent offering. In an age where satellite technology dominates orbital and sub-orbital space, UCOMA has become a necessary player. The mother ship remains the NSA and SIGINT in particular. UCOMA serves as an independent affiliate focused primarily on man-made orbiting objects."

Along one wall a digitally illuminated sky map was mounted. Thousands of tiny green dots rotated around a blue ball in slow motion. Lee indicated each dot represented an object orbiting earth. "Every article is scanned before being uploaded into data-banks for dissemination. Each UCOMA station focuses on a different portion of firmament referred to as an overhead region."

Lee pointed towards a monitor highlighting several images. "Orbital debris and space junk," he remarked. "Objects which have run their course and are destined to burn up in the atmosphere."

Hard drives with glowing pilot lights indicated everything was operational. Clocks set at international times were mounted giving the chamber an aura of a newsroom. The professor singled out a lone computer, "This is for reference use. A-Space and similar networking sites can be downloaded here."

He paused, "Until a year ago I had an assistant named Stuart Tuppins. Stu was a Modern History student with a rare gift for communications. When he graduated I recruited him to assist me here in the IRI. Eventually, his talent was recognized by several NSA big-wigs and he was admitted into the ranks of SIGINT as an encryption analyst. He'd been with me nearly three years."

"How do you maintain all of this and still manage to teach?" Jesse inquired.

Lee considered the question, "I've been involved in academic postings and Intelligence analysis for more than three decades. Since being transferred to this Institute my scholastic responsibilities entail one lecture per weekday - with additional time devoted to paperwork and essay grading. Academic aspects of my job are routine, maintaining this station constitutes more time." He glanced about, "I'll enlighten you to the wonders of this technology at a more opportune time."

Guiding him to the door Jesse had observed earlier the professor said, "I'll show you your quarters."

"You mean I'm to reside here!"

"Naturally. You'll live in-residence at no cost. The field assignments you'll embark upon, necessitate your being readily available."

He grasped the doorknob and ushered Jesse into a narrow passageway. Along either side, several doors were ajar with lights on for his benefit. To their immediate left was a kitchen. Opposite that a storage room. Along the same side was the bathroom replete with a toilet, shower and sink. Across from it were a pair of identical living quarters. Jesse's was nearest and he peeked inside. Whenever work demanded his full attention Lee occupied the room next to it. Each space contained a bed, closet and dresser. Desks were furnished with a chair and reading lamp. Despite a lack of natural light the arrangement was more than suffice. The storage room down the hall would accommodate Jesse's weights and exercise-gear.

They made their way back through Control and reentered Lee's office. The professor sat at his desk and coughed into a handkerchief as Jesse sat facing him. Unlocking a drawer the older man withdrew a file-folder. A sheet of paper was produced and placed before the recruit.

"Please review the document, son. If you agree with what's outlined kindly sign the bottom. It relates to your being hired as an agency asset."

"Sounds sinister?"

"Many things will appear so."

Perusing the contents Jesse added his name.

"When am I expected to move in?"

"Immediately. There's little time."

Lee withdrew a flash-drive from the folder and slid it across the desk.

"This is not to leave Control," he informed the young man. "It's contents deal with the SIAG and how that organization relates to our investigation."

Jesse reached for the memory stick and held it in his palm.

"Do you have many personal belongings?" inquired the professor. "I'm happy to assist you move."

"I have few possessions," the student replied. "My apartment was furnished. There's some clothes, books, weights and my car - that's about it. I can move everything in a single trip. I'll touch base with my landlord and let him know I'm leaving. Last month's rent was paid in advance."

"Good," responded the professor. "Once you're set up we'll discuss aspects of your job. You'll be briefed by Corporal Soo at nine am tomorrow regarding security matters pertaining to this station. She will issue you the relevant passes and codes. Once that's been carried out I'll show you an alternate point of entry leading to and from these chambers."

Jesse couldn't recall seeing another way out during his tour.

"More on that later," Lee concluded

The young man fixated on the clandestine fantasy room beyond his host's shoulders.

"Is everything alright son?"

"I suppose so," Jesse replied pensively. "Life truly is stranger than fiction."

"If you only knew."

Beams of sunlight penetrated the dense woods of rural Indiana. Dew shimmered on wavering leaves alongside the Yokum Trail, as it wound north toward Rykles Clearing. The remote stretch was surrounded by vast forests, interrupted by an occasional creek or marsh. Further east dozens of pristine lakes permeated a landscape born of glaciers, during the Pleistocene Ice Age. On that bright July morning Special Agent Jake Gill of the Indianapolis branch of the FBI, downed the remains of his coffee he'd purchased while refuelling in Lafayette. With the window down he extended his left arm and allowed the breeze to surge up his sleeve. Aware the land he traversed was owned by the infamous William Penther; GPS indicated the militiaman's lodge was several miles ahead at the end of the line. At one time Penther's property hosted scores of super-patriots, training to participate in attacks upon government institutions. Undergoing hours of regimented drills, recruit's thrilled to the hunt in the landowner's abundant woodlands. Their leader was well known to the FBI. Released from Terre Haught penitentiary eighteen months earlier, Penther served seven of ten years for his involvement in a failed domestic strike he'd purportedly masterminded.

Having never met the lodge owner agent Gill was acquainted with him nonetheless. He'd spent weeks scouring files pertaining to the Indiana militiaman. Inexplicably, the Bureau had given Penther considerable leverage since his release. There had been the obligatory surveillance manoeuvrings involving mail and wiretaps - most of which had been discontinued. Informant's kept occasional tabs, otherwise he was on his own. Evidently, officials concluded Penther's involvement with anti-government initiatives had ceased. They believed he was more concerned retaining his real-estate holdings willed to him by his adoptive father. Disciples who'd gravitated toward his isolationist manifesto had all but dispersed. Penther appeared content going on hunting excursions or visiting outdoor-themed box stores around the greater Detroit area. The Bureau decided Penther's endeavours were of little consequence and loosened his leash from the tether of the law.

The militia leader wasn't the only person of interest to Gill. He desired to speak with Penther's sidekick – a man named Aldo Dopple. The agent intended to question both about the disappearance of three former militia members who'd been among Penther's most rabid followers.

Jake's friend and fellow FBI agent Ronny Mills had also vanished. Ronny was closely associated with the Penther file. News of Mills disappearance was announced within weeks of Dopple's release from prison. Jake had never partnered with Mills, although both attended the same high school before enrolling at the Academy. Stationed out of the Indianapolis branch office they became fast friends. The previous fall Jake attended a barbecue in the company of Ronny, his wife and their six-year-old boy. Beneath the verdant limbs of an oak tree Ronny pulled his friend aside and admitted his suspicion's regarding Penther's coming and goings. Assigned to monitor the reformed militiaman, he managed to consistently evade Mills among the suburbs of Detroit. On another occasion Ronny waited hours for Penther to emerge from a shopping mall. The following week at the same mall he trailed him on foot. He noticed his target exiting a door at the rear of the mall and entering a taxi. When his findings were reported Ronny's superiors suggested Penther's movements were consistent with a man adjusting to life on the outside.

When Ronny vanished the Bureau assured his distraught wife they were taking his whereabouts seriously. Both Penther and Aldo were interviewed as persons of interest, but denied any knowledge in the matter. Jake brought his missing friend's suspicions to the attention of his own superior, who agreed to obtain a search warrant allowing examination of Penther's premises. When they came up empty the Bureau allowed the pair to slip from their radar and sought answers elsewhere.

Jake guided the vehicle between strands of pine and evergreen. He rounded a bend and noticed an open field along his right. The clearing hosted a farmhouse and stable. As the pastoral setting passed from view more trees appeared. The pavement turned to gravel and he drove several kilometres until a second clearing hove in view. Tethered to the grid of a power generator, a pair of doberman's cocked their heads and sprang to their feet. Within the lodge Aldo reacted to the beasts and triggered alarms. Parting the blinds he noticed a car turn into the dusty lot where their minivan was parked. A burly man in his forties emerged and started toward the steps leading up to the front door of the lodge.

Penther switched off the ground alarms and entered the parlour.

"You expectin' anyone?" Aldo asked.

"Nope."

Wiping his face with his sleeve Dopple muttered, "Don't care shit about the law, but I know a lawman when I see one - an' I'm seein' one now."

Penther crossed toward a laptop lying open on the counter and placed it out of sight. In it's place he withdrew a sportsman's catalogue and flipped to a random page. Aldo draped his shirt over a pistol holstered about his waist and strode to the door.

Gill smiled and presented his badge, "I'd like to speak with William Penther."

Dopple grunted and motioned him inside then retreated to a nearby couch. On the facing wall Gill observed a pair of crisscrossed Winchester rifle's above the mounted head of a grizzly. Aldo shoved a stick of gum into his mouth as the agent closed the door behind him.

Sporting a lumber jacket and boots Gill stared at the man behind the counter and introduced himself.

The lodge owner nodded.

"I'm correct in assuming you're William Penther?"

"I suspect you know that already."

"Actually I do," Gill admitted. "I prefer making a positive identification regardless."

The dogs railed out back as the agent glanced at the grinning miscreant sprawled along the couch.

"And who might this gentleman be?" he asked knowing full well.

"Name's Aldo Dopple," the bodyguard responded. "If I can help mister cop jus' holler."

Gill smiled and returned his gaze to the man behind the counter.

"Reason I'm here Mr. Penther regards several missing individuals."

The agent retrieved a pad from his pocket.

Aware he was conducting an unauthorized investigation and would likely face repercussions, Gill was determined to uncover what became of his missing colleague and the others.

"These individuals were reportedly acquaintances of yours," resumed their visitor. "I'd like to run a few names by you and your companion."

"Suit yourself," Penther replied.

Gill knew the names by heart but hesitated deliberately.

"Lets see," he muttered referring to his notes. "Jackson Bell, Samuel Wicker, Cal Train."

He glanced up at the lodge owner, "Know anything of their whereabouts?"

"Haven't seen nor' heard from any of them in more than a year."

Gill placed the pad away and thrust both hands in his pockets. He gazed about the rustic cabin interior and nodded at the array of guns adorning the walls. Meanwhile, Dopple cleared a mouthful of phlegm and let loose with an ear-shattering snort. Ignoring the indecency Gill said, "The disappearance of these people was reported ten months ago. Alarms have sounded in certain quarters."

"Like the man says we ain't seen 'em," Aldo piped in.

Turning toward the buzzard-like face the agent said, "I don't recall addressing you sonny boy."

The bodyguard glared back while Penther stared straight ahead expressionless.

Finally the lawman said, "Mind if I have a look around?"

Dopple rose but was motioned to stand down by his boss.

"Go right ahead," Penther responded.

A portion of the counter top was raised and Gill was ushered through. Following a narrow hall into the depths of a living area, he was trailed closely by both men. Peering into a pair of bedrooms and a washroom he entered the kitchen.

"I'd like take a turn about the grounds if I may?"

"Follow me," the landowner murmured guiding him onto a rear deck.

Beyond the railing the famished doberman's strained at their leashes. Penther cursed and they were temporarily silenced. Descending the steps onto the grounds Gill gave wide berth around the drooling canine's. He started across the dry grass and strode the periphery of the woods. When he returned to the deck he noticed the path leading toward the bunker. Obscured by trees, it had been searched weeks earlier by federal agents and nothing of relevance was uncovered.

With the lodge occupant's eyes upon him the seasoned FBI man felt his skin crawl.

"Bet there's some fine game 'round these parts?" he remarked.

"Deer, bear, rabbits..." the landowner responded.

"That so?"

Spitting over the railing Dopple said, "You ain't tasted nothin' till you tasted raw bear."

Gill smiled but made no reply. Escorted by his host's he reentered the lodge and paused at the kitchen table where a long-gun lay on it's surface.

"I've seen these in photographs," he remarked. "I forget what they're called?"

"It's a German Mauser," Penther stated. "Aldo collects rarities."

"Nice."

With their attention diverted Gill dropped a tiny listening device down a crack between the fridge and kitchen wall. Returning to the parlour he withdrew a card from his pocket, "If anything comes up I can be reached at this number."

Penther took the card without looking at it.

The agent turned to depart and nodded at Dopple. The dishevelled bodyguard glared back like a demented Jack O' Lantern. Gill descended the steps and entered his vehicle. As he backed onto the Yokum Trail the dog's kicked up dirt at the rear of the dwelling.

———————

Lee Tondar was within Control scanning reams of incoming data. Abruptly, his phone vibrated signalling an incoming text. Only two people were privy to that frequency - his former associate Stuart Tuppins and the Grissim security chief. The message was from Stu.

Ensconced within NSA HQ, the young analyst noticed Lee was again shortchanged regarding briefs forwarded to UCOMA stations via the Signals Intelligence Division. Outposts were entitled to receive *full* updates - including the one based out of the Grissim Institute. The crucial 'feeds' alerted UCOMA personnel what objects and signals to observe with regards to relays, space junk and other vital data.

Lee adjusted his glasses and read the text, *'Finally met a woman who enjoys my company. Could be serious?'*

Something was in the wind.

He contacted his travel agent and booked a round-trip flight to Baltimore at noon the following day. Unfortunately, for Stu there was no woman - the geek factor tended to intrude. Hopes of romance sprang eternal and provided the young man and his former boss an effective 'heads up' code.

Since his transfer Stuart did what many single professionals do when time affords. He hung out at the bar. The Dale & Holler was a British themed beer and wings establishment located along Baltimore's Inner Harbor. The classic rock was good, the food was better and plenty of pretty women frequented the place. Due to the nature of Stu's work visual monitor's made him feel secure. Subsequently, his bar stool faced several mounted TV screens.

The '*finally met a woman*' text was the third of it's kind messaged by Stu after leaving Grissim. The first was sent a month after he assumed the Maryland posting. It concerned the interrogation and death of a SIAG operative in US custody. The information was passed to all UCOMA stations but withheld from Lee. A second omission regarded a scrambled SIAG relay streamed to Evanston, Illinois. Now a third 'oversight' had occurred and the professor arranged to meet with Stu at the Dale and Holler.

He contacted Corporal Soo and requested they talk straight away. Seated opposite each other in the professor's office Lee mentioned he had to leave town briefly. Jesse Carlton would be on hand Monday at 9am to take up official residence. Sasha was instructed to issue him the relevant passes and codes.

"I gave the lad a hasty tour of the IRI and living quarters," he indicated, "Perhaps you might offer him a more detailed briefing."

Sasha had been responsible for vetting the muscular new recruit. Nothing inflammatory was unearthed, no run-ins with the law or questionable associations were on record.

Having met with his security chief Lee drove home to spend a quiet evening with Dorothy. They enjoyed a home cooked meal and lounged together on the sofa where he fell fast asleep. Over supper Lee informed his wife Stuart requested his presence in Baltimore. It regarded an urgent work-related matter and he would return next evening. Sensing a certain anxiety Dorothy decided not to broach the matter.

The following morning he departed Hopkins International and landed at Baltimore/Washington Airport roughly ninety-minutes later. Departing the terminal he hailed a cab and was conducted to the Inner Harbor district. Dressed in a manner befitting a tourist he sported a brightly colored shirt, cap and shades. On arrival he paid the driver and strolled toward the rendezvous point on foot. Exquisite shops bristled with business and he stopped for iced tea and a sandwich. Resuming his course he pondered Stu's message. Perhaps something was revealed from the composite brief he'd assembled.

It was nearly four when Lee entered the Dale and Holler. He made his way through the venue amid throngs of young people. Patrons stood about sipping drinks in anticipation of catching others staring back. The music was overwhelming and every seat was occupied. It was Sunday afternoon and Lee wondered what Saturday night was like.

He noticed his former apprentice at the bar and approached from behind.

"This seat taken?"

The young man jerked and spun about, "Geez, you nearly gave me a seizure!"

"Blame it on the music," Lee shouted.

Stuart frowned, "I had to chase a dozen women away to secure you a stool."

"Call them back!"

"Too late."

Accepting the seat Lee viewed his surroundings.

"We're okay here," Stuart assured him. "No one can hear a thing."

"I've noticed."

A woman tending bar asked the new arrival what beverage he desired.

"Light ale will be fine."

On a first-name basis with the bartender Stu requested she make it a pint and put it on his tab.

Once his beer was served Lee leaned in, "The place is jammed!"

"Weekends are always busy," Stu replied.

Lee noticed his companion dressed in office attire.

"You put in time today?"

"We've been busy."

Stuart wore contact lenses and looked somewhat trimmer about the waist. His tie was loose and a jacket was draped over the backrest of his stool. The 'weight thing' remained a concern. He kept discovering new ways to keep off the pounds. The latest was an exercise video he attempted to emulate. Stretched along a carpet in front of his TV, he was prompted by a trio of shapely female fitness gurus. When things stalled he blamed his genes.

"So what's up?" Lee inquired.

Leaning in Stu said, "A week ago a phone was turned over to the FBI branch office in St. Louis by an older gentleman. He stated it belonged to his daughter-in-law who had been reported missing. Evidently, she'd driven him to O' Hare in Chicago for his return flight to Missouri. The woman was slated to participate in a badminton tournament at a local gym that afternoon. When the Feds inquired they discovered no match was scheduled. Her phone wound up in her stepdad's possession in the confusion of boarding his plane. In compliance with the FBI he turned over the device. Analyst's discovered an undecipherable irregularity stored within it's database.

Believing it was cryptic the readout's were sent to us. We have yet to crack the entire code, however some startling discoveries were made."

A trio of women sporting halter-tops and shorts squeezed up to the bar next to Lee. Vying for the bartender's attention they were unable to decide what to order. Transaction's lasted nearly five minutes.

"You hungry Lee?"

"I'm fine you go ahead."

"No thanks beer is fattening enough," Stu sighed.

Lee stifled a cough and took a deep breath. Stuart was well-acquainted with his friend's asthmatic condition, "I hope you brought your puffer along?"

"I did please continue."

A look of concern registered and the young man resumed. "Anyway, we discovered something the Feebies overlooked. Cross-referencing the cellular readouts on the woman's phone through SIGINT storage banks, a source was recovered. It was a code we'd cracked months ago. Here's the bitchin' part Lee. It appears the missing woman was contacted by way of Siana."

"Interesting," the professor mused.

"It gets better. Prior to the woman's vanishing act an outgoing call was made from her phone to Harvard University. Now I ask you what would connect an incoming SIAG signal with an outgoing call to Harvard?"

"You'd be surprised."

"I knew you'd say that."

"Who's the woman?"

"Gillian Burke. She's married to a financial columnist. They have an eight-year-old daughter and own a home in Evanston. Her past is sketchy. According to her immediate family she entered the country as an exchange student a decade ago, after arriving from Spain. She met her husband while attending the University of Chicago. With their marriage pending she remained in the US."

Lee shot his friend a glance, "You suspect she's a sleeper?"

"Fits the profile. We have a dead SIAG agent who needs replacing. Naturally, they'd wait awhile before someone was accessed."

"Where's her family?"

"Sequestered in protective custody in Chicago."

Lee backtracked, "Do you have any knowledge of who interrogated the deceased SIAG operative?"

"I'm way out of the loop on that one."

"Of course."

"It would be helpful to know," Stuart agreed.

"I have a source at Langley who might assist."

"Langley! Those guys refer to SIGINT staffers as crypto-cockroaches. Not nice at all."

"I'm sure you have some choice pseudonyms for them?"

"More than a dozen and counting."

Lee smiled, "Anything else which might pertain?"

Stuart thought for a moment then shook his head, "More will be revealed once we crack the rest of the gibberish stored on Mrs. Burke's readouts. By the way I uploaded the results of those 'briefs' printouts we discussed during your previous visit. I sent them off to you this morning. By matching Grissim's deficient 'feeds' with materials submitted by the U station in Kalamazoo, results confirm what we suspected. Text me when you've had a chance to review the findings."

"I'll follow up first thing."

Stuart toasted his companion, "Here's to the unravelling."

Clinking his friend's glass Lee sipped and remarked, "As usual you've been an enormous help."

Both men spent time chatting. Stuart mentioned how nice it was to see Dorothy during their recent visit. He promised to drive back to the Falls for a weekend in the near future. Lee decided not to mention Jesse Carlton. The decision wasn't due to any resentment Stu might harbor. On the contrary, his former aid would've been delighted to hear Lee no longer had to bear the workload alone. If that arrangement worked out Stuart would be informed.

Both men embraced before parting. Stuart decided to remain behind for a final pint and promised to keep in touch. As Lee squeezed through the crowd Deep Purple kicked things up a notch with 'Highway Star' cranked to eleven. Exiting the bar he hailed a cab to the airport and his flight home. With the sun sinking low in the west he considered what passed between Stuart and himself. He pondered the missing woman. Did her disappearance fit into the scenario of an alleged heartland terror attack?

Ten minutes later he paid the driver and entered an airport terminal. Waiting to board his flight he planned his agenda.

NINE

As Agent Gill's car disappeared along the Yokum Trail his departure was observed from the parlor window by William Penther. Sprawled upon the couch Aldo scratched himself and muttered, "If that FBI puke had a search warrant, he might've checked the bunker and seen our stuff packed and ready to go. It would've been the last thing he ever saw."

Penther wheeled about with a look of fury in his eyes. He strode to the sofa he dragged the frazzled bodyguard by his collar and threw him violently against the wall. The lodge owner brought a hand to his ear pantomiming someone listening in and shoved Aldo toward the counter. Retrieving a pen and paper Penther scrawled, *SEARCH THE PARLOR FOR BUGS - I'LL TAKE THE REAR. DON'T SAY A WORD!* Dopple stared wide-eyed as his boss retreated toward the living area and began rummaging the bedrooms. It would've been easy for Gill to place a listening device. Gradually, Aldo emerged from the parlor and gestured to imply he couldn't find a thing. Penther motioned for him to keep searching. Once the washroom and bedroom's were scoured the militiaman entered the kitchen. He shoved the stove aside and found nothing. Standing on a chair he scanned the shelves and observed no trace of a miniature transmitter. Dragging the refrigerator forward he peered into the crevice. Along the baseboard his sharp eyes detected a tiny object no larger than the head of a screw. Retrieving the article he stared at it intently and allowed it to slip from his fingers. With the heel of his boot he ground it into the linoleum floor then scooped up the mangled object. Placing it on the kitchen table he gripped the German Mauser.

Loitering in the parlor Aldo never knew what struck him. As he turned Penther swung the butt end of the rifle into his gut. Dopple covered his head as the enraged lodge owner placed the weapon aside and shoved him toward the kitchen. Snagging the crushed listening device he hastened Dopple through the rear door onto the deck. The dogs recoiled as they descended the steps onto the grounds where Penther glowered at the shrinking bodyguard.

"Maggot! The Feds plant a bug on my premises and you decide to tell them we're planning a vacation!"

Clutching his stomach Aldo stared back terrified, "I...I wasn't thinkin'."

"You never think you mindless sub-human. Gill likely heard everything and will be back with others."

"Sorry Bill," Dopple moaned.

Penther was muttering through clenched teeth, "We can't afford to get popped at this late stage so here's what you're gonna do. Take the van from behind the bunker and intercept Gill before he reaches the highway. Make him disappear. Got that!"

A wry grin formed along Aldo's lips.

"You know what to do," resumed his master. "Gill will report what was recorded the minute he arrives back in Indianapolis. He'll be able to back his claim with the acoustic evidence in his possession. To ensure that doesn't occur you'll overtake him and do what you have to do. Any recordings found on his person or in the vehicle must be destroyed. Meantime, I'll make a thorough sweep of the lodge."

Dopple bounded up the steps and entered the lodge. Moments later he reappeared armed with a Beretta 9 millimetre holstered beneath army-surplus fatigues. In his right hand he carried a hammer, in the other he toted a zip-lock bag containing raw ground beef. Outlining an assault tactic they'd deployed years before, Penther recalled the manoeuvre and nodded affirmation. Aldo trod onto the crusty ground and unleashed Boot, the swiftest of either dog. Scenting raw meat it's willingness to cooperate intensified tenfold. Club, the neglected beast showed frustration by issuing forth a series of whines. Only one dog was needed to participate in Dopple's scheme. Flanked by the hungry animal they started towards a rusted Econoline parked behind the bunker. Aldo slid the door aside and stashed the hammer then ushered Boot within. He stored the meat in the glove compartment and started the engine. Fuelled by adrenaline the driver steered the van up an incline and cruised past the lodge. He swung onto the Yokum Trail while Penther watched from the deck. Dust rose as the vehicle slipped from sight. Reentering the kitchen, the lodge owner emerged moments later with an offering of meat and water for the slighted beast.

Agent Gill slowed his vehicle and beheld the grazing field he'd witnessed on the way up. Replete with horses and a stable, the property included a twin-story home. A 'For Sale' sign hung at an angle from a fence post. Abruptly, the road segued from dirt to asphalt and more woods appeared. Focused on the winding curves, Gill wondered how such idyllic splendour co-existed alongside Penther's sinister compound. He shuddered recalling his maniacal associate gloating as he departed the lodge. Easing up on the gas he brought the car to a standstill along the side of the road. In his haste he forgot to access the transmitter attached to his car radio where a receiver would capture the lodge signal. Depending on the surrounding terrain it carried a transmission range of roughly fifty miles. With the engine running he switched on a synchronized recorder and heard a stream of static.

Damn.

Adjusting the tuner he listened intently - nothing. Likely, the planted device had been discovered. He would've placed others but his movements were closely monitored.

The disappointed agent needed to relieve himself. He glanced in the mirror as a weather-beaten van entered the frame and disappeared around a bend up ahead. His guard went up when he realized the driver's visor was down despite an overcast sky.

Drizzle turned to rain as Gill stepped hurriedly from the vehicle to conduct his business. He returned to the car determined to make tracks. Shifting into gear he set off along the paved portion of the road with his foot a little heavier on the pedal. The blur of an animal charged across the damp pavement directly in front of him. He braked hard and the car skidded onto the side of the road at sixty miles an hour. Cranking the steering wheel, the left side of the vehicle departed the ground and toppled onto its side. Grinding metal was heard as the car slammed forcefully into a tree. With the engine smouldering the car lay reeling on its roof. Meanwhile, Gill was pinned upside down between the steering wheel and backrest. The agent's seat-belt had snapped on impact and his neck was broken. His head impacted the windshield with such force the glass shattered. His breathing was laboured and his eyelids fluttered. Blood dripped from both sides of his mouth.

Aldo Dopple emerged from the trees a dozen yards distant and approached the wreck. The hammer he wielded would ensure the FBI man's fate was properly administered. Leaning alongside the upturned car he peered through broken glass at the dying man. His vacant stare was observed and Aldo smelled gasoline. Backing a safe distance away the car rocked violently, as flames sprang from beneath the hood and engulfed the vehicle. Dopple retrieved Boot devouring the remains of his snack. A shredded zip-lock bag covered with greasy residue lay nearby. Scooping it from the ground he cleared any evidence of their presence there. Rain would wash away other tell-tale signs. With dog in tow Aldo strode the curvature of the road and drew alongside the van. Licking his chops Boot was motioned within. Aldo placed the hammer beneath the drivers seat and climbed behind the wheel. The recorded evidence Penther alluded to was reduced to ashes among the charred remains of the fiery crash.

Having anticipated the precise moment the agent's car rounded the bend to within ten feet of their position, Aldo flung the meat across the road and released the dog. Gill's car went into a tailspin and wound up on it's side. The ruse had proved successful in the past. Authorities would conclude the driver was in too much of a hurry along a damp, winding stretch and assume the obvious. It was known the Yokum Trail was treacherous to driver's with a heavy foot. Investigators would be informed Gill had paid an unauthorized visit to the lodge, where an amicable chat occurred before the agent departed.

Rain intensified as Aldo turned over his engine. He switched on the wipers and poked his head out the window to make certain no other vehicles were in the vicinity. With the way clear, he made a sharp U-turn and drove past the smoking wreck in the direction of the lodge. Upon arrival he returned the van to it's place of concealment and retrieved the hammer - along with the remnants of Boot's supper. While the doberman bolted ahead Aldo strode purposefully towards their dwelling. He clamoured upon the deck and flashed a wry grin at Penther, as his boss emerged from the rear door. Without waiting to be asked Dopple described what occurred.

"You're certain nothing incriminating was left behind?" the landowner insisted.

"Nothin' the rain won't take care of. Didn't even have to use the hammer - the guy was dead before the engine exploded. Guess he tried to avoid hitting a critter."

Penther allowed himself a rare smile.

Aldo entered the lodge and stashed his weapons. He flushed the zip-lock bag down the toilet and prepared a ham sandwich in the kitchen. Penther withdrew the disabled listening device from his pocket and tossed it from the deck with all the force he could muster.

———————————

The journey north from Boston had been pleasant. A pale sky contrasted brilliantly with the chill waters of the North Atlantic. Sailboats were observed on the horizon and gulls wheeled in the salty air. If she could share one moment of it with...

"NO!"

Gripping the steering wheel tighter her pained expression personified a look of helplessness. She'd attempted to suppress the past in a manner taught to her within the temple. Like a demon provocateur, memories continued to wreak havoc on her vulnerability. It was forbidden to allow former associations to intrude. Lives were dependent upon how she carried out her directive. Vanquishing all but the task at hand she continued along Highway 110 in the direction of Halton's Cove. Twenty minutes later a fast-food outlet and motel appeared along the outskirts. The clock on her dashboard registered 11:15 am. Pressing further into the community she observed the 40 mile speed limit. Homes with trimmed lawns and tidy hedges lined a main thoroughfare. It felt like Sunday on a weekday as she halted at an intersection. Beyond the median stood a Presbyterian church. A block further a shopping mall was situated across from the post office. Likely, the plaza was the only one in town and seemed a good place to make inquiries concerning Ms. Ellstone.

Jutting into Ipswich Bay like a hitch-hiker's thumb Halton's Cove was situated along a peninsula. To the east lay the Atlantic Ocean, the rest of the country sprawled west. She signalled and entered the parking lot of the mall and noticed plenty of vacant spaces. Saltwater was scented as she departed the vehicle. Dressed in accordance with that of a concerned relation, she was attired in a beige dress, white blouse and low heels. Placing away her sunglasses she strode towards the mall entrance. Upon entry she frowned, it might have been any shopping concourse in North America. A supermarket and pharmacy stood opposite each other. She began her quest at the latter and strode toward the prescription counter at the rear.

Addressing the pharmacist she said, "Sorry to bother you. I'm up from Boston seeking a lost relation. Her name is Kari Ellstone. Would the name ring a bell?"

The woman smiled, "I'm here five days a week and assure you I've never heard the name. Try the police station dear its a little further east. Adam's behind the desk tell him Gracie sent you."

"Thank you," Taras replied.

The last place she wanted to visit was a police station.

Her next stop was a licensed restaurant separate from the food court. Speaking with a waitress she repeated her story and apologized for not having a current photograph, "Does the name Kari Ellstone sound familiar? She's twenty years old."

"Afraid not."

"Is there anyone on staff I might ask?"

"Harold's in the kitchen - he's the day-cook. He don't see no one and we don't let him – he scares 'em."

Taras smiled and thanked the woman.

Repeating her query at the supermarket and several retail shops she received similar responses.

Departing the mall she strode to her car and noticed the post office. *Of course.*

The tiny matter of extracting confidential information persisted. It would be Harvard all over again, except the post office was a government agency and would prove more challenging. Crossing at the intersection she entered the building and fell in line behind a lone customer. Two wickets stood facing her, one attended by a bespectacled young man - the other by a middle-aged woman. When the latter became available the gentleman in front of her made his way in that direction.

"May I help you here Ma'am," offered the male clerk.

"Thank you."

Approaching the counter she recited her story of a runaway niece and apologized for not having a recent photograph, "The poor dear was never around long enough to have her photo updated."

The young man displayed a toothy grin, "Does your relation live in the area?"

"Evidently."

"And the name again...?"

"Kari Ellstone," she repeated. "Her first name is spelled with a K."

"I'll check," the clerk replied tapping a keyboard.

While he browsed his client managed a grateful smile.

"Based on what you've told me Ma'am, I recall a woman in her early twenties dropping by to retrieve an occasional parcel or envelope. I've served her from time to time, she has a post office box." He indicated several rows of silver boxes lining a rear wall.

"Would you have anything on file - an address or contact number?"

"There may be ma'am but it's confidential and I'm bound by restrictions."

He sounded genuinely regretful.

"I understand."

She prepared to make a more persuasive pitch when the clerk said.

"Being a visitor you may want to take in the Stinson Line. It runs toward the coast off Route 27 north of town. It's a stark and beautiful landscape with only a smattering of homes. The view of the ocean is spellbinding."

"Thank you I shall."

Arriving back at her vehicle she departed the mall and trailed a school bus for half a mile. She accessed GPS and turned north in the direction of Route 27. Several kilometres later a crossroad sign indicated the Stinson Line. Signalling right she reduced her speed and kept her eyes open for signs of habitation. The helpful postal clerk had been able to obtain Kari Ellstone's listing and conveyed the general location without giving away the address.

Only a smattering of homes...

Ulsar's precious 'Candle' was beginning to burn brighter.

Taras surmised the subject of her quest resided in one of the homes along that isolated stretch. The landscape was indeed stark. Amid acreages of brown grass an occasional Berkshire tree tilted away from the sea. Grey rock jutted from forlorn fields. Children frolicked in the front yard of one of the abodes. Taras took notice of the dark houses (homes whose occupant's appeared to be away), some had garages making it difficult to discern whether anyone was present. A paved road called Rowans Drive brought an end to the Stinson Line. For the second time that day the mighty Atlantic unravelled before her eyes and Taras paused to offer a silent prayer. Moments later she swung the car about and started back. Her destination was the motel she'd observed on the outskirts of town. Having identified seven dwelling's along either side of the Stinson Line, the subject of her quest would be revealed by a process of elimination.

It was going on two pm when Taras checked into the Oceanside Motel. Afterwards, she sampled the appetizing seafood at a local family restaurant. Back in her room she showered and slept soundly for six hours. Rising and splashing water on her face she slipped into a dark pullover, black jeans and Doc Marten boots. With her hair bound in a ponytail, she looped a belt-purse around her waist and sheathed an ankle dagger beneath her cuffs. Departing the motel she drove north towards the Stinson Line. As darkness fell the road appeared foreboding. The first home was brightly lit from within and two cars were parked out front. A flickering television was observed through the blinds of a second dwelling. The residence where children had played out front stood opposite it. At this hour they'd be snug in their beds. A smile registered on the driver's face and faded quickly. Along her left a trio of homes were situated next to each other. Two were occupied and a third was dark. The split-level in the middle had a trailer parked in the driveway.

Allowing her headlights to guide the way Taras continued for roughly a kilometre. Along the left house number seven hove in view. The home featured an attached garage and was entirely dark. Accessing a driveway she switched off the engine and strode toward the front entrance. The parlor window had it's curtains drawn. Erected on a basement foundation - a neglected garden featured prominently. Mounting the steps Taras knocked and waited. When no one responded she rang the bell.

Nothing.

She returned to her car and decided to drop in on the neighbours. Backtracking, she parked adjacent to the three homes and exited the driver's side. Approaching the first she knocked lightly. The porch lights lit up and a man appeared with a brown puppy muzzling his ankle.

"Scram Monty," he scolded.

Catching sight of the brunette on his front stoop he blinked.

"Sorry to trouble you," the woman remarked.

"No trouble."

"I'm looking for a young lady roughly twenty years old named Kari Ellstone. She resides somewhere in the area."

Scooping up the pup the man said, "Afraid it's just the wife, me and Montague here."

Taras smiled and asked if he knew anyone who might fit the age description?

"Can't say. Don't get around much anymore."

Thanking him she withdrew.

Next door was the split-level with a trailer outside. Pressing the buzzer a middle-aged woman responded. Taras repeated her story and the occupant appeared thoughtful.

"I believe a young lady lives up the road."

Nodding in the direction of the coast she added, "Use to maintain an attractive garden but it's withered now. Saw her in town the other day."

Touche...

Taras expressed her gratitude and returned to the vehicle. She made a U-turn and headed back in the direction of the darkened bungalow. Bringing the rented car to within fifty yards she parked along the shoulder and switched off the engine. The rest of the way was made on foot and she paused alongside the garage to observe her surroundings. Beyond the forsaken garden the door would've posed no obstacle. Instead, she mounted the steps and pressed the doorbell a second time - again no response. Someone was within she felt it in her bones. Consolidating a plan she strode back to the road. Abruptly, the sound of an approaching automobile was heard. Along an incline leading from the coast a pair of headlights appeared. The car veered by at an accelerated rate and nearly grazed her vehicle parked meters away. Between whoops and whistles, a pair of teenage boys leaned from open windows hurling innuendo. Above their guffaws the driver leaned on the horn. They sped toward Route 27 where their taillights swerved gradually from sight.

'*Nice,*' murmured Taras.

Focusing on the matter at hand, she bolted into a field along her right and started back toward Ms. Ellstone's not-so-vacant abode. The terrain appeared moor-like minus the bogs and quagmires. Certain the lady of the house would make a run for it; before that occurred she intended to extract information. Stealthily, she approached the rear wall and crouched beneath a window screen and heard breathing overhead! With her arms splayed tightly against the bricks, Taras determined the occupant was surveying her property. Footsteps retreated and the sound of scraping hangers was heard. Evidently, someone was preparing a quick departure.

A cat meowed and a female voice muttered, "Shut up."

Following a prolonged silence Taras dashed around to the side of the abode. She stopped short of the driveway and heard a car engine turning over. Apparently, an entrance led from the house into the garage. The retractable door rose automatically and a vehicle faced the road. As it started forward, Taras placed a dagger between her teeth and moved into position on her stomach. Gripping the hilt she reached out and slashed the right rear tire as it lumbered from the garage. The car lurched down the drive with the wheel hissing like a serpent. The beleaguered automobile swung onto the road and scraping metal was heard grinding through rubber. In a vain attempt to manoeuvre the vehicle forward, the driver panicked and applied pressure to the pedal. Taras prayed the hot-rodders wouldn't stage a comeback. Meantime, the disabled car veered onto the shoulder and came to a standstill. Immediately, the driver's door flung open and a woman emerged. Staggering forward she tripped and fell. As she struggled to rise she felt the presence of someone nearby.

"Hello Kari."

Gasping for breath the waylaid driver scuttled backward on all fours. As the stranger advanced the felled woman screamed for help. Sound carried in the open and she needed to be silenced.

Taras offered her hand and spoke soothingly, "I'd like to talk."

As Kari prepared to bolt an upthrust to the jaw stilled her and she went limp. Borne securely, she was placed along the rear seat of the impaired vehicle. Assuming the driver's mantle, Taras shifted into reverse and heard the wheels scrape away from the shoulder. The car had to be returned to the driveway lest attention was drawn. As the tire rim grated into asphalt she feared the axle might give away, however the transfer was completed successfully and she switched off the engine.

Turning to her unconscious passenger she slipped a purse from off her shoulder. It's contents were examined and a phone and keys were removed. Taras pocketed the items and emerged from the driver's side and circled the vehicle. The limp woman was withdrawn from the backseat and carried gently into the garage. Once the automated door closed Taras adjusted her eyes and observed a side entrance. From the depths a cat meowed and she wondered if it had been fed. She entered the abode and an overhead light revealed a kitchen. Beyond that was a parlor and Kari was laid along the sofa. Taras noticed a flashlight on the coffee table and retrieved it before extinguishing the kitchen light. Twine was discovered beneath the kitchen sink. In the event Kari screamed or attempted flight, her wrists and ankles were bound and her mouth was gagged with fabric. A tray of cat chow sat next to a water bowl in the hall. The kitty had been fed but chose to remain in hiding.

Gripping the flashlight Taras slipped out the back door and circled the house before emerging along the Stinson Line. Her car was fetched and she parked behind Kari's then reentered the dwelling. While the occupant napped a search was conducted on the main floor and cellar, where nothing of relevance was found. Running cold water over a facecloth, Taras reentered the parlor and stood the flashlight on end. It provided minimal illumination as the gag was removed and the moistened facecloth was applied to Kari's forehead. Her eyelids fluttered and she sat bolt upright observing someone in shadow. Her limbs were bound and she recoiled along the couch.

"How are you feeling?"

The speaker was a beautiful woman.

"Who are you!"

"It doesn't matter."

"Why am I tied up!"

Drawing up a chair Taras stared across the coffee table, "Are you Kari Ellstone?"

"None of your goddamn business - let me go!"

"So you can run away again?"

"Who the hell are you!"

The intruder rose and entered the kitchen. She returned with a tissue box and placed several sheaves between the trembling woman's fingers.

"I'm sorry your chin is sore. It was necessary."

"Bitch!"

"Is this your place Kari?"

"No!"

"Why do you reside here then?"

"It belongs to my boyfriend!"

"Where is he?"

"He's due back any moment.

"Right..."

"What do you want with me!"

"Information. If you're truthful you'll be released. If not it may go hard."

The prisoner glared at the woman.

"It's not about you, Kari. It's about your boyfriend. We know him by different names. They're one and the same. Relate the name you know him by and describe him to me?"

"Untie me first."

"Certainly. But just the wrists."

Reaching down the stranger withdrew a dagger from an ankle sheath. She leaned over and slit the binds as the former Harvard student shuddered.

Once the knife was replaced her captor said, "Please answer the question?"

Kari muttered Nickolas Dante's name.

"You one of his lovers?" she added sardonically.

"Hardly," the woman laughed. "There's reason to believe your partner is involved in some questionable dealings. Lives may be at risk - we wish to prevent that."

"Who's we!" the prisoner stated indignantly. "If you're a cop or a government type show me ID?"

"You could say I'm a secret agent," replied her interrogator. "I can't identify myself or I wouldn't be a secret. Describe Nickolas Dante to me."

"Why!"

"It's confidential. Answer the question."

"My answer is confidential!"

The stranger rose from her chair.

Swallowing hard Kari murmured, "He's roughly five foot ten, olive-skinned, dark-hair, good-looking." Glancing up she remarked, "Sound familiar?"

"Where is he?"

"I wouldn't know?"

"Where is he Ms. Ellstone!" There was an edge to the stranger's voice.

"I never know!" she cried. "I haven't seen Nicky in almost two weeks."

"Why is that?"

"He used to leave here three or four days at most. Later his trips became longer with fewer phone calls. I maintain this place with only the cat for company."

"Are there work-related responsibilities you administer on his behalf?"

"No," she responded. "Aside from keeping up an appearance of domesticity I run a few errands."

"Errands?"

"Picking up supplies in town, visiting the post office - routine stuff."

"What did Mr. Dante say his business was?"

"He's a freelance journalist from Cairo researching a book. The draft was supposed to be completed months ago. He said he leased this place to finish the project and mentioned his publishing deadline had been extended. Beyond that I know nothing."

Bowing her head Kari began to rock back and forth.

"Is he flush with funds?"

"He isn't concerned with money. He uses cash, prepaid credit cards and disposable phones for everything."

"Nicholas gave you the nickname 'Candle'."

A cloud passed over the young woman's features. It was a mixture of fond remembrance and hostility.

"How would you know that!"

"I know."

"Lots of people have nicknames. He gave me that one and I allowed him to use it."

"There are no services you provide Mr. Dante other than maintaining his house, feeding the cat and running errands?"

"What are you implying!"

"I'm implying you may not be telling the truth. It's possible you're more involved with Nicky's work than you admit. What about the post office visits?"

"Is that a crime! Once or twice a month he'd call from God knows where and ask if I'd retrieve an envelope or parcel. He claimed they were from his publishing representative here in the States."

"Do you remember the name of the representative?"

The young woman considered the question. "Orchard and Sons - something like that."

"Do you recall where the deliveries were sent from?"

"Different places...Atlanta, Baltimore..."

"When did you last visit the post office?"

"Three weeks ago I picked up a package. He retrieved it days later during a brief visit home."

"When he's here what do you do?"

"That's none of your business."

"Did he do much writing?"

Kari appeared apprehensive, "No."

"Curious, a writer not writing after having spent so much time researching. Not to mention leasing a retreat for that purpose?"

Sounding despondent Kari muttered, "He does most of his work on a laptop in motel rooms. He planed to complete a final draft here."

Taras held up the key ring extracted from her purse, "I assume one of these fits the post-office box. What is the number?"

"If I told you Nicky would kill me."

"Nicky will kill you anyway."

Kari stared back horrified, "What!"

It was apparent the young woman knew nothing. She was an innocent caught up in a broad deception.

"Has Nickolas Dante ever struck you, Kari."

Instead of responding she nodded.

"If he's never here and hurts you when he is - why do you stay?"

She blew a strand of hair from her face, "He slapped me once when I threatened to leave. He hasn't struck me since and says he needs me."

"What's the post box number?"

"Piss off."

The sound of steel scraping the rim of a scabbard encouraged a response.

"Box 121 the key is smudged with blue."

Pocketing the article and unravelling twine, Taras made a motion to bind the woman's wrists a second time.

"What are you doing? I told you everything!"

The stranger's smile was reassuring, "I believe you. I'd like to have a final look around. When I'm done I'll leave."

With Kari's wrists secured the secret agent reentered the bedroom. Clothes were folded inside drawers or arranged neatly in a closet. A utility bill addressed to her, but evidently always paid by Nickolas Dante, lay on top of the dresser.

Kari was staring vacantly at the wall when the visitor returned to the living room.

"I'll depart now," the woman remarked. "I urge you to do the same. You were doing just that when I arrived. Its possible Mr. Dante suspects you know more than you should. Find somewhere safe and lay low. This will eventually pass."

Kari wondered how the woman possessed knowledge of Nickolas Dante's activities. She even knew her nickname! Either she was a jealous lover or the government spook she claimed to be.

As if her mind was being read the intruder brought a gloved forefinger to her lips.

"I have your cellphone," she whispered. "You have no transportation or communication available to you. When I've put enough miles between myself and Halton's Cove, I'll contact the local authorities and inform them of a stranded woman at this address. Once they arrive, I suggest you state you were accosted and bound by someone wearing a pullover toque, seeking money and items of value. The less you reveal the quicker you'll be free of this place."

Taras reentered the kitchen and emerged with bottled water from the refrigerator. Acknowledging, Kari's less than trustworthy demeanour, the bottle was placed between her tethered hands so she could remove the cap with her teeth. She managed to bring it to her parched lips as stranger spoke softly, "Seek safe harbor Kari."

It was well after midnight when her key ring was placed upon the coffee table - minus the post box key. Withdrawing a roll of cash from her belt purse, the intruder peeled off eight one-hundred dollar bills and placed them under a corner of the carpet in plain view of Ms. Ellstone.

"That's for the damaged tire, the phone and bus fare out of town."

Kari was exhausted and offered little resistance as her mouth was gagged a final time. From the depths of the house a cat meowed. Taras never did catch sight of the creature.

"I'm certain the kitty will emerge once I've departed," she said.

When Kari glanced up the woman was gone.

In the driveway a car backed away and headed off in the direction of the Route 27. As the engine faded the young woman bowed her head and wept.

———————

TEN

The Vista was situated along East Fayette Street in downtown Baltimore. Seated at a bench nearby the intersection of Beaufort and Fayette, Richard Valamar sported a beige windbreaker with an Orioles baseball cap pulled over his brow. As he prepared to move into position he glanced at his wristwatch. The high-end condominium featured an early twentieth-century architectural design which distinguished it from her neighbours. Having cased the site the previous evening Valamar witnessed his target arriving home at roughly eight-thirty. This jibed with information given to him by Sir. Reconnaissance indicated the building's watchman concluded his shift at seven pm, after which security duties were relinquished to an automated system until the following morning.

At precisely 8:15 pm Valmar crossed at the intersection. Like thousands of city dwellers he was out enjoying a stroll. Thrusting his hands in his pockets he shuffled past the ramp leading toward an underground car park attached to the Vista. Not a single vehicle had entered or departed in more than twenty minutes. Adjusting his shades and made his way a half-block further before turning back. Abruptly a sports car emerged from below. Rather than ducking down the ramp in plain view of the driver, he waited for a more opportune moment to present itself.

A convertible slowed and signalled onto the ramp. It's driver appeared more concerned avoiding pedestrians than observing who was in her rear-view mirror. The passerby seized the moment. While the woman aimed her remote toward at the garage entrance, Valamar sauntered leisurely onto the ramp from the sidewalk. Meantime, the driver entered the underground and rounded a bend toward a lower level. With Valamar out of her sight-lines he entered the subterranean car park. Numbers indicated two levels existed beneath the one he trod. A sniper's nest needed to be established. Avoiding camera's focused on the entrance and drive-thru areas - the parking space assigned to his target might've been on any one of three levels. Subsequently, he situated himself nearby the entrance where a kill-shot could be rendered as the target drove by his position.

Reference material provided to him by Sir suggested the individual adhered to a routine timetable. He departed Fort Meade at roughly six each evening travelling forty minutes to his favourite eatery along the Inner Harbor. Depending on traffic he was usually seated at the bar inside of three quarters of an hour. Following two pints, some light conversation and a meal he'd depart, arriving home at approximately eight-thirty.

Hunkered behind a minivan in a shadowy corner of the underground, Valamar's perch afforded a clear view of the entrance. Removing a Rugar semi-automatic from the lining of his jacket, he fitted a silencer to it.

Several blocks away Stuart Tuppins paused at a traffic light. He was considering Lee Tondar and pondered his friend's well-being. The Grissim professor appeared frailer during recent visit's and his cough had worsened. Within Maryland Intelligence circles along the beltway, Lee's methodical diligence was highly regarded. It was hard to grasp how someone of his standing had been kept out of the loop regarding a disputed terror file. Normally, his advice would've been eagerly sought. Convinced a rogue element was at play within the upper ranks of the NSA, Stuart kept his suspicion's in check.

Savouring fond memories of working alongside his mentor Stu hung a left onto East Fayette. He signalled right onto a ramp leading into his car park and aimed a remote at the door. With the way clear he guided the Explorer toward a reserved spot along the main level. With briefcase in hand he departed the driver's side as a beep confirmed his vehicle's secured status. Moving toward the elevators something reverberated. It sounded as if someone spat twice in rapid succession.

The bunker was approached from off a beaten track. Brushing mosquitoes aside, William Penther entered a code on a keypad and a hum resonated. The locks unhinged and he applied his shoulder to the door and stepped across the threshold. Originally commissioned by his late guardian Strom Rykles during the height of the cold war, the walls of the bomb-shelter were camouflaged green and brown. It's rectangular structure consisted of a storage cellar and ground floor. The dark green roof angled downwards from a crest, so rain, snow and radioactive fallout wouldn't accumulate. An inch of solid steel encased layers of concrete, mortar and insulation. Naturally, no windows existed. It's dimensions were equal to that of a single-car garage. The area surrounding the bunker was monitored from within by hidden cameras. Placed strategically about Rykles Clearing, the nearby woods and upper regions of the Yokum Trail were afforded scrutiny.

Decades earlier old man Rykles had stocked the bunker with caches of firearms and cases of whisky. Crates of tinned goods, beef jerky, water and oatmeal made up the rest of the inventory. Penther maintained this tradition minus the whisky. Quantities of non-perishables and first-aid supplies were stored alongside firearms, ammunition and explosives. Security devices and online access were upgraded and a new septic tank was installed. Utilizing underground cables attached to the lodge fifty meters distant, a generator powered the facility. The bunker stood as a shrine to the old man.

Penther's recent incarceration had little to do with the gun-running activities he'd been associated with. Prosecutors believed he was the principal architect behind a failed attempt to blow up a federal building in Memphis a decade earlier. The 'Isolationist Army' a militia outfit founded by Penther was implicated in the aborted attack. Its leader was well-known to law enforcement officials as a leading figure among anti-government forces, based out of the American heartland. Despite this nothing of significance could be pinned on him. The Isolationist Army was a splinter group who'd severed ties with an Indiana State Rights organization, Penther accused of being federal spies. Droves of impressionable young men descended upon the militia leader's property and began spreading his gospel of government robber-barons siphoning taxes, while allowing foreigners to infest the republic. With the aid of a superb legal team Penther's prison sentence - along with those of several followers had been reduced. Given the gravity of the charges observers were outraged. If the Memphis attack had succeeded it's effects would have been catastrophic. Were it not for the effort's of an undercover operative who'd infiltrated the ranks of the militia, hundreds of innocents would have perished. Ammonium Nitrate, a powerful explosive substance was discovered in the possession of a Penther disciple. The ingredients were identical to those used in the foiled Memphis attack.

At forty-four years of age Penther emerged from prison an even more embittered man. He loathed the federal government and its agencies - especially the IRS. He despised assemblies, regulations, congressmen, senators and Washington DC in particular. Regardless, he managed to convince almost everyone his agenda of expounding hate had been renounced. That he was intent on leading a quiet life.

As the day of reckoning approached he found himself waxing nostalgic.

Given up by a teenage mother he never knew, young Bill was raised in an Indianapolis orphanage and adopted at age seven, along with another boy a year older named Garrett. Their surrogate father, Strom Merrill Rykles was a sixty-nine year old timber baron, who owned several hundred acres of prime woodland in central Indiana. Each spring dozens of itinerant workers were hired to cut and haul timber down to mills along the Wabash River until winter set in. Acquaintances recall Strom was once engaged with a desire to marry and raise kids - preferably boys. Following a courtship which lasted three years the woman left him for another man. Old timers in Ellery remember her concealing bruises behind scarves and shades when she ventured to town. Her departure vanquished Strom's visions of domesticity forever. In more than forty years he never pursued another woman.

Once the boys became teenagers they were integrated into the ranks of the hired help, allowing the old man to conserve payroll funds. This was fine with Bill who felt right at home. There was the cabin Strom built years before on two acres of open land he called Rykles Clearing. The surrounding woods were ripe for the hunt. Who could ask for more?

One summer while Bill was relaxing during a break he overheard one of the loggers discuss the bunker. The hand recalled his uncle saying Strom sold twenty-five acres of his beloved land for the sum of nine-thousand dollars, to erect the bomb shelter. When Bill heard this he was stunned. Nothing mattered more to the old man than his property. He later discovered the story was true. In 1958 Rykles contracted a construction firm in Chicago to build the bunker and defended his action by stating, "What good's land if the commies start rainin' atom-bombs down on it."

Television was in its infancy by the time Strom turned twenty-three. He despised the medium and boasted he'd never own one. However, something he'd inadvertently witnessed on the box managed to scare the shit out of him. On a clunky RCA Victor mounted above a bar in Ellery, a news item impacted him with the force of a sledgehammer and ultimately drove him to near-bankruptcy. TV networks and movie theatres at the time were airing government-sponsored films simulating nuclear attacks. As America's paranoia barometer was rising, viewers were subjected to appalling images of houses being reduced to particles after being blown away in a gust of atomic fall-out. Sirens wailed as school children ducked beneath desks with hands clasped over their heads, in an attempt to save themselves.

The gentle townsfolk of Ellery were forced to endure animated displays of Strom's indignation. This usually occurred Saturday's when he went to town to quench his thirst and vent. One afternoon as Hank Williams streamed from a Wurlitzer, Rykles informed everyone present he was erecting a bomb shelter. More inebriated than usual he started bellowing dire warnings, laced with obscenities at the assembled patronage. He informed them they'd be dead within months if they didn't commence to building bunkers of their own.

"You'd best not be comin' roun' mine," he slurred.

The unsteady timber baron rose to his feet, "Jus you wait 'till the Reds start hurlin' thermonuclear shells down on yer lily-livered arses. You'll come runnin' my way an I'll be waitin' with a shotgun aimed at each n' ever' one of yer ugly mugs."

One wintry night inside the cabin Rykles sat at the kitchen table, refilling his whisky glass and talking candidly about his long association with the Ku Klux Klan. Both lads were hardly surprised by the admission. Standing quietly at the sink rinsing dishes Garrett was repulsed but held his tongue. Meanwhile, the younger of the two appeared enraptured.

"I joined with the Klan when I was a lad of twelve," recalled the old man. "My pappy took me to gatherings up on Tanner Hill. I stayed with 'em 'till the late sixties when they busted up and scattered. Still keep my robe folded neat in the bunker cellar."

His features soured and he slammed his glass down on the table surface.

"The Klan turned yeller!" he shouted. "Now ya got yer niggras, chinks 'n wetbacks 'everwhere. We'll show 'em one day won't we laddies?"

Garrett ignored the remark.

The old man belched and his head loped onto his chest. Raising his chin he refocused on Bill, "I said we'll drag 'em through the gates of hell won't we laddie!"

"Yes sir."

After viewing the atomic bomb newsreel, Rykles business interest's took a back seat as he became more obsessed with the communist menace marching his way. Stockpiled weapons and ammunition accumulated inside the bunker. Dwindling finances gradually took their toll. His bookkeeper advised him he'd end up bankrupt or behind bars, if he didn't sell off a significant portion of land to repay years of mounting back-taxes. Competition from rivals in the timber sector strained Strom's lax performance in the marketplace. He blamed his financial woes on the commies in Washington and withdrew from reality. Sighting 'pinkos' everywhere, he severed contact with acquaintances in Ellery and told his boys the town had turned red. He refused to talk civilly to anyone except young Bill. Employees were fired if Strom suspected them of being government plants. One worker was terminated for having the gall to suggest the bunker would be useless in the face of a nuclear attack. As he explained it, oxygen tanks stored within the bunker afforded six to eight weeks life-support. Whereas, the radiation outside might persist for years. The math spoke for itself.

Following gruelling days brandishing axes and buzz-saws in the bush, the boys languished on the cabin veranda in the evenings. As the old man lit a smoke and began banging back whisky, Garrett was ordered to fetch lemonade. Rocking back and forth Strom expounded on his worldview as his charges listened quietly on the stoop. Bill remained enamoured with what he was hearing. Meanwhile, Garrett's eyes were focused above the treetops.

"I hope ya might be listenin' lad?" Strom muttered fixing the older boy with a fierce glare.

The drunker he became the more he regaled them with talk about white folk going the way of the dinosaur. He blamed everyone – Abraham Lincoln, the United Nations, people on radio and TV, the pansies in New York and California. Having never learned to read or write, newspaper and book publishers remained exempt. He blamed the government and the Internal Revenue Service mostly. The boys were informed his own pappy died when he was twenty-two, leaving the land and timber business to him. He added the IRS had been robbing him blind ever since.

"I ain't givin' them thievin' sumbitches a nickel!" he proclaimed.

The logic appeared sound to Bill.

"They ought to be payin' me!" the old man slobbered. "I supply 'em raw materials to make toilet paper an' their negra slums an' they wanna foreclose me!"

On a related front their surrogate father had no intention of enrolling his boys in school. They taught lies there. Instead, they cut timber while other kids received an education.

One morning Garrett asked their literate cook Sam Jenkins to teach him the alphabet and some basic arithmetic. He offered to pay him from the pittance Strom gave him for a week's toil in the bush. The kindly cook refused payment and set about instructing the boy behind a workman's tent in the Clearing for an hour each evening. When the old man learned of Garrett's extracurricular treachery, he directed his fury at both the bewildered cook and the boy. Rather than discontinuing the exercises, Rykles insisted his other charge be included in the 'learnin'.

A rig-driver named Peter Ducanti offered to take the boys to the Annual Summer Fair in Indianapolis, provided Strom loaned him one of his run-down automobiles. Needing time to himself the old man consented and insisted both lads accompany the driver in an ancient Oldsmobile. As they drove south Bill sat sullenly in the rear seat, meanwhile Garrett chatted up front with Ducanti like they were best pals. The younger sibling hated crowds and despised the incessant noise. He didn't much care for furry animals either - except when he hunted and ate them. Staring at white bumpkins mingling with niggers wasn't his idea of recreation. Most of all he missed the old man. Yet here he was in the back seat listening to a pair of wimps yak about nothing. He thought about the cabin and Clearing. It was mid-morning and Strom was likely sauced by now. Bill was concerned about the old man's alcohol dependency and blamed the government agencies closing in on him.

Leaning forward he told the driver to kill the music emitting from the dashboard radio. Ducanti nodded and turned the volume lower.

"Turn it off!" roared the backseat passenger.

Garrett frowned and reached forward to extinguish the sound.

The riled occupant sat glaring out the rear window. Meanwhile, the pair up front gazed ahead in stony silence. When it was determined their intemperate passenger slept they quietly resumed their chat. Bill peeked from one eye and noticed his so-called brother casting rapid glances over his shoulder and heard Ducanti curse the old man.

"Once he's left the car," the driver whispered.

Arriving at their destination Ducanti circled the area for a place to park. Once a spot was secured Bill declined to participate in the fairground excursion and chose to stay put. He was disgusted with his companions and pissed at the old man for insisting he go along. Over the past year Bill had grown apart from his adoptive sibling. Garrett appeared charmed with the outside world. The tinny transistor radio and comic book's he kept stashed beneath his bunk delighted him. His hatred of Rykles was obvious. Garrett's compassion for the old man was irreparably ruptured, when he asked to attend a real school and was slapped about and docked a week's pay for entertaining the notion.

Garrett and Ducanti explored the fairground attractions while Bill lay sulking along the rear seat of the sweltering automobile. An hour later his stomach growled suggesting nourishment was necessary. He stepped from the vehicle and started towards a row of snack trucks. Withdrawing a bill he purchased a hamburger and soda intending to eat back in the car. The urge to find a washroom dawned suddenly. The attendant pointed out a crowded boardwalk where several portables were situated. Gripping his lunch Bill grudgingly took his place behind a line of fair-goers. Next time he would pee beside the car.

Once his business concluded he strode toward the parking area and discovered the Oldsmobile was gone. He froze and jumped when a horn sounded. Whirling about he noticed a four-door sedan with its windows rolled down.

"Forget your car buddy?" the driver inquired.

"No," Bill responded haltingly.

"Good 'cause I'd like to park right about where your standing."

"I had a car...?"

"Really! That's nice."

"It was here."

Bill gestured toward the ground.

"Ah...keyword 'was'. What *was* the make?" taunted the driver as guffaws emanated from the rear seat.

"An Oldsmobile."

"Hmmm...Can't say I seen it."

He turned to his companion's, "You seen it?"

More laughter.

"Sounds to me like you missed your ride lil' buddy."

Bill stood with his burger and drink in hand. Turning about he started away and glanced over his shoulder as the sedan assumed the vacated spot. Four older teenagers emerged and he sat along a curb and placed his meal aside. He locked both arms about his knees and buried his head. The hunger pangs he'd experienced earlier dissipated, however he ate regardless. Deciding to initiate a search for the car's occupants he entered the fairgrounds proper. Throngs of visitors were dodged and he surveyed the crowds both inside and out of several exhibit buildings.

A thought suddenly struck him!

What if Garrett and Ducanti left him behind deliberately?

He recalled the driver saying 'Once he's left the car.'

Was his departure from the Oldsmobile their cue to bolt?

For the next forty minutes he continued his search without success and decided to contact the old man. Finding a pay-phone he placed a collect call and waited. On the eighth ring he received a response.

"You were supposed to stick with Garrett!" Rykles shouted when informed about what occurred.

"He rode off with the driver, " Bill responded.

"The hell you say?"

"I used the washroom when I got back the car was gone. I looked everywhere for them."

Cussing out loud the old man threatened to hang Ducanti.

"Wait next to the fairground entrance," Rykles instructed. "I'll get someone and pick you up. Meantime, keep lookout for them two!"

Bill waited outside the fairground gates until the old man appeared. With his head poking out the passenger side of a rusted pickup, he climbed unsteadily from the vehicle and ushered the youngster into the front seat. Squeezed between Strom and a driver named Crawly, the stench of whisky on the old man's breath was as foul as his mood. Regardless, he managed to obtain directions to the nearest police precinct and a short while later they parked outside.

It was late afternoon when Bill and the old man left the truck in Crawly's hands and entered the station. Following a brief interval an officer escorted them to the desk of the acting sergeant. The official had heard of Strom's misadventures from numerous sources. Politely, he urged the boy to state the facts. As Bill recounted event's the old man stood off to one side fuming. His shaky demeanour had been fuelled along the way with the mickey stuffed in his jacket lining.

"This weren't no random accident!" Strom railed. "It's a kidnap attempt by IRS agents - with Ducanti on their payroll."

With each slurred syllable his voice rose.

Having jotted down Bill's statement, the sergeant assured them they'd be notified pending word on the disappearance of the pair. Rykles objected to any delays as one of the attending officers confiscated the mickey he'd unknowingly withdrawn.

Strom reacted predictably, "Gimme, Gimme!"

They were escorted from the building and Crawly had the passenger door open. With the trio crammed up front they beat a hasty departure for Rykles Clearing. Less than twelve hours later the Indianapolis Police Department were in contact with the timber baron. He was informed a person identified as simply Garrett, had been located and was presently registered with the Children's Aid Society at an undisclosed location across the state line. The youngster made claims of physical and psychological abuse while in the care of one Strom Rykles, and charges might be pending. The car used in the incident was recovered at a supermarket parking lot and awaited retrieval at the owner's discretion. The driver Peter Ducanti was nowhere to be found.

Over the next few years things went from bad to worse for the old man. On the upside, Garrett decided not to press charges against the pathetic creature who'd been his guardian. Strom remained incensed by his accusation's and swore legal retribution. According to Garrett's statement, Ducanti stated he planned on leaving Rykle's employ citing the racist insults being consistently hurled his way. Concerned for the older brother's well-being Ducanti suggested he run away. By offering to escort both lads to the fair a plan was devised. With Bill occupied the other two would hijack the Oldsmobile and depart the fairgrounds. Ducanti would transfer Garrett across the state line and deliver him to a CAS crisis centre. Afterwards, the vehicle would be discarded and Ducanti would make himself scarce.

After these events transpired, federal agents swooped down and reclaimed more than one hundred and sixty acres of Rykles land, in lieu of hundreds of thousands of dollars in accumulated back taxes. With his affairs in shambles Rykles livelihood came crashing to a halt. All hands were terminated and the heavy-duty saws and accessories were sold off. The last to go were a pair of flat-bed transport trucks. Living his final days surrounded by twenty acres of retained land, Bill did his best to attend to the frail figure withering away from liver disease within their decrepit cabin. Shortly after Bill's nineteenth birthday Rykles succumbed. What remained of the landowner's estate was willed to the young man in a terse and ominous note dictated to a county physician:

I, Strom Merrill Rykles leave my land and everything I own to my only heir, William Penther Rykles. Guard what's yours laddie. You'll know what to do.

The will was witnessed by a county coroner summoned to Strom's bedside when the end was near. Bill arranged for the old man's cremation and scattered his ashes about the Clearing. While attending these duties he pondered his own fate. With the timber days gone forever it was necessary to generate income to maintain land taxes.

Bill reverted to his original surname with no disrespect intended towards his late adoptive father. Government forces had rendered the Rykles name toxic; he needed to start from a clean slate. From here on in he was William Penther.

The old man never trusted banks. Following his death Penther was rummaging through supplies in the bunker cellar and came across three-hundred thousand dollars. The cash was stored in boxes labelled 'Beef Jerky'. Dumbstruck, he wondered if the money had been left for him or if Strom had simply forgotten about it. Suspecting the former he sat down on a crate and steadied himself. The lumber baron had been frugal throughout his entire life. In addition to not paying taxes it was implied he hoarded profits. Honouring his guardian's lifelong struggle, Penther intended to withhold informing the IRS or anyone about his generous inheritance.

'Guard what's yours laddie. You'll know what to do.'

The novice landowner decided a portion of funds would be used to initiate a small militia. Its immediate aim would be to 'discourage' landed immigrants from settling in the region. Another order of business was to reinvest in his property. In order to prevent people from suspecting his good fortune it was necessary to turn a profit. He decided the surrounding woods would make an excellent sportsman's paradise. Game abounded and hunting licenses were acquired as easily as the season was long. Fascinated with guns Penther erected a rifle range in the Clearing. Charging a nominal fee, gun owners could indulge themselves in target practice or hunt along twenty acres of unfettered woodland. The endeavour also provided an opportunity for the landowner to recruit fellow compatriots into his personal army.

By the time he was thirty Penther had become a regional hero. The hunting grounds and firing range at Rykles Clearing, were a popular draw among a closely knit group of enthusiasts. Penther sank part of his inheritance into restoring the cabin, now referred to as a lodge. Work was contracted out to grateful locals who'd become enamoured with his generosity – and his causes. Coats of enamel were layered onto the log exterior and the entire structure was insulated. A deck and parlor were added and a new roof was installed.

The clients Penther attracted were mostly frustrated young men who were bitter at the ineffectiveness of State's Rights organizations. They drifted in from towns like Chattleburg and Feather Lake, several hailed from neighbouring states such as Michigan and Ohio. These were men with time on their hands and an axe to grind. They were the son's of factory workers, farmers and merchants who struggled to hold onto their properties and businesses. Incensed at the widespread loss of manufacturing jobs, they lacked the skills and education to compete and were ignored at every level by their government representatives.

Huddled within the lodge at the end of the Yokum Trail, they listened as it's owner bluntly assessed the dark forces poisoning their communities.

The militia leader began trafficking guns and munitions wholesale from suppliers in Chicago and Detroit. Residuals from the sale of such weapons was marginally profitable. By offering his services Penther was further able to entice young men to join his movement. Recruits found in him a father figure - someone they could rally behind with conviction. As he shared his anti-government musings an inner circle formed. They consolidated plans to unleash a series of event's which would reverberate around the country.

Beyond the parlour window wind rustled the limbs of trees. Penther took it as a sign the old man was pleased.

———————

ELEVEN

Along the right side of the Sentinel Hall lobby a security station offered a view of the museum and stairwell leading toward the lower sanctum. Within its transparent confines monitors displayed interior and exterior images of the Grissim campus. On a counter-top desk an in-house phone was visible next to a laptop and reading lamp. A coffeemaker and microwave resided on a shelf above the mini-fridge. Nearby, a restricted washroom was situated along the perimeter of the lobby.

Inside the booth Corporal Soo sat tapping away at a keyboard. Sean Drummond, a member of her detail was due to report early for duty affording her time to brief Mr. Carlton. The recruit was slated for a nine am briefing. Charged with issuing him the necessary codes and passes enabling access to the IRI; Sasha was instructed to answer any questions he might have regarding his new lodgings.

A monitor highlighted her replacement's arrival in his parking spot outside. Drummond ascended the steps and was buzzed through. His footsteps echoed and he focused on an antiquated clock mounted on a marble column.

"Right on time," he declared jovially.

Glancing up from her work his superior smiled and slid aside a window panel.

Sean Drummond was a robust black man whose physique was evident beneath his immaculately pressed uniform.

"Thanks for coming in," Sasha remarked. "Coffee tastes better than usual."

The guard raised his drive-thru mug, "I came prepared chief."

"Is ours really that bad?"

The sentry cleared his throat and changed the subject.

"Seems a trifle early in summer for someone to receive an academic posting," he said referencing the Corporal's meeting with Jesse.

"You would think so," Sasha replied.

Slipping on her jacket she said, "I'm stepping out for some air Sean. Our guest should be arriving shortly."

"Gotcha boss."

Sasha departed the lobby and took in her surroundings. Cries of gulls were heard above the deserted grounds. Given the rigorous training she'd endured while stationed at Fort Jackson; nothing prepares one for the unexpected. Scarred physically and emotionally by her deceased tormentor, she wondered if her judgment had been impaired by the experience. Was it possible she only *thought* she was being followed the other night? While residing in South Carolina she met weekly with a support group consisting of women who'd survived similar crisis. It helped to talk about her ordeal within a collective environment. Currently, that option was unavailable.

The turbulent waters and stark beauty of Lake Erie aroused a certain fearlessness within her. Abruptly, a light-brown Chevy swung onto Abbot Lane and proceeded towards the Hall. Turning rapidly about she reentered the lobby.

Jesse parked his vehicle in a visitor's spot. He emerged from the driver's side and withdrew two large duffle bags from the trunk. The contents amounted to everything he owned. Strewn along the rear seat lay an assortment of body-building gear and accessories. He decided to retrieve them later and mounted the steps. At the top a voice reverberated through the intercom.

"Welcome Mr. Carlton please proceed."

The voice belonged to the security chief he'd been introduced to previously. Nodding for the benefit of the cameras - a massive door swung open and a brawny guard offered assistance. Jesse thanked him and said he'd manage. Ushered into the lobby he noticed Corporal Soo next to the security station. He approached and offered greetings.

"Hope you weren't startled by the intercom," the official remarked.

"Sounds like a drive-in root-beer stand."

Jesse's response brought a smile to the male sentry and elicited nothing from his boss. The new arrival glanced from one uniform to the next as Sasha made introductions.

"Jesse this is Sean Drummond. Sean meet Jesse Carlton. He'll be assisting the professor this summer."

The guard saluted.

The student appeared perplexed and turned to the Corporal, "Do I return the gesture?"

Drummond chuckled and fielded the question. "When we deal with associates of persons we serve its a courtesy."

"Or you can just call me Jesse," offered the professor's assistant.

"Jesse," the guard repeated and they shook hands.

Glancing at her watch the Corporal intervened, "It's nine o'clock. We'll initiate the briefing in the professor's office. Allow me to assist with your baggage?"

"I'm fine thanks."

"As you wish."

Jesse retrieved his luggage and accompanied the Corporal toward the stairwell. Arriving before the professor's office the security chief initiated entry procedure. When they were within, Sasha took her place behind the desk and switched on a reading lamp. Unlocking a drawer she withdrew an envelope with Jesse's name on it and motioned him toward a seat. He placed his bags aside and sat down.

Sasha glanced across the desk, "A background check was conducted with regards to your assisting the professor. No glitches were apparent and further scrutiny is unwarranted."

She passed over the envelope, "This concerns security protocol. Once you've reviewed the contents I'll answer any questions you may have."

Jesse noticed her aversion to eye contact and wondered if she was like that with everyone? During their initial meeting a regimented professionalism had been brought to bear. Military posturing was one thing, however her conduct befitted her rank as security chief. It was difficult not to notice the attractive Asian woman who exemplified such officialdom. A hue of gold created by the desk lamp gave her features a sculpted appearance. Clipped bangs aligned perfectly with trimmed eyebrows. Subtle streaks of red highlighted her jet black hair. During their first encounter Jesse glimpsed a brief smile - the effect enhanced her admirable features immeasurably. Despite the holster about her waist the uniform clung to her form like a glove.

Jesse withdrew two sheets from the envelope and noticed the first was another secrecy document requiring his signature. Bending towards the light he perused the text and signed at the bottom. The second sheet revealed a code of some sort. It's sequence consisted of four digits and three letters scrambled haphazardly together. Other items included a pass allowing entry into the professor's office and a tiny remote, identical to the one Lee used to access the clandestine chamber referred to as an IRI. A disposable phone concluded inventory.

"With regards to the remote," explained the Corporal. "By applying thumb pressure you'll be able to access the IRI. To gain admission into this office the code must be entered along with the entry pass. Finally, the phone is to be used only as backup. A secured device will be issued to you by the professor at a later date. If you'll take a moment to scrutinize the code I'll put your memory to the test."

Complying with her request Jesse focused on the numbers and letters and closed his eyes. When they opened again the security chief said, "Follow me."

They stood in the corridor with the fortified door barring the way and his instructor looking on. Jesse entered the code and swiped his pass. A click was heard and he accessed the door.

"Please try to remember the sequence," the Corporal urged as they reentered the office. Reclaiming their seats she added, "It's imperative both the pass and remote remain in a secure place. They're to be utilized by you and you alone."

"Of course."

She gathered the signed forms and placed them away.

"Well?" she said.

"Um...well what?"

"You have the remote..."

"The remote? Right...!"

He retrieved the device and aimed it at the rear wall.

"Press firmly," she advised.

The wall panel whisked to one side and the chamber magically appeared. Monitors were operational as streams of data scrolled across screens. Shouldering his bags Jesse rose and crossed into the retrieval facility. Sasha followed and motioned him in the direction of the living area. Entering the narrow passageway the recruit placed his baggage inside his quarters. He rejoined the Corporal and they explored the kitchen and culinary accoutrements.

"You'll stock up on food supplies according to your schedule," she informed him.

"I hadn't thought that far ahead," he admitted.

They returned to the hallway and Sasha made reference to the quarter's next to his own. "When occasion warrants the professor spends his nights here. Lately, the trend has become more frequent."

Pointing out the storage room she said, "The code you memorized allows entry into this space as well. More about that later."

She gestured toward the washroom, "No pass necessary. Washroom and bedrooms are secured from within."

Turning to face him she remarked, "I hope the accommodations meet with your approval Mr. Carlton?"

He peered into his quarters, "I'll get back to you on that."

"Please do because nothing else is available."

"The living arrangements are fine Corporal."

"Good," she responded. "I'm available to assist if you have belongings."

"I have a few items in the car and can manage."

"Fine."

They paused before the storage room and she gestured toward the keypad, "Kindly access."

"Certainly."

Rummaging his pockets he withdrew the pass and repeated the code procedure. Gaining entry he felt for a switch and the dark room flooded with light. Corporal Soo followed and pointed out a series of shelving units. Stock included first-aid supplies, light bulbs, batteries, bathroom articles and a variety of non-perishables.

"All the basics," Jesse remarked.

"Pretty much."

Abruptly, a buzzing sound shattered the calm! The security chief sprinted into the hallway and reentered the IRI. Once the source was identified she applied her finger to a mute button on a touchscreen and the sound subsided. Peering over her shoulder Jesse noticed lines of onscreen symbols repeating themselves.

"This workstation is Grissim's link with UCOMA HQ," she informed him. "The message will play out until the professor responds to it. The sound we heard alerts staff to crucial updates. If a crisis occurs a siren is deployed."

"UCOMA headquarters is within the NSA building in Maryland I understand?"

"That's correct."

Sasha withdrew her phone and entered a link.

"How are things Sean?"

She paused momentarily then replied, "Good. I'll be about five minutes."

They returned to the professor's office and seated themselves.

"That concludes our briefing Mr. Carlton. Any questions?"

"Please call me Jesse."

"Jesse."

Curious he asked, "Other than Professor Tondar, yourself and your security team, who else knows about the arrangement down here?"

The security chief hesitated, "I can't respond to that fully. Select officials at both the NSA and UCOMA have knowledge. Dean Benton is aware of course. A while back the professor had an assistant. Barring an emergency even my staff is forbidden entry into these chambers. They're here to protect a government installation administered by the professor. That's all they need to know."

"Lee mentioned another exit?"

The security chief frowned, "You've barely started and want out?"

"I mean a fire escape or something."

Traces of a smile formed and Sasha caught herself, "There's another way. I'll leave that for the professor to explain."

"Then we're good," Jesse declared. "Thank you for the tour and briefing."

"It's my duty."

An awkward silence ensued.

"I have work waiting," she finally said. "The professor is due to arrive any time now."

Jesse smiled.

Securing the desk drawer Corporal Soo departed leaving him cut off from the world. He reentered the IRI and aimed his remote - rapidly the wall panel slid shut. Within his quarters, he retrieved a laptop from a duffle bag and reviewed the flash-drive Lee issued him regarding the SIAG. Additional content concerned an individual named William Penther.

Gradually, he drifted off to a place where a ragged figure stood above a shattered highway. Roused by the sound of shuffling footsteps; coughs echoed along the hall as Jesse rummaged his bags for slippers. It was mid-afternoon when he strode into the kitchen.

Lee Tondar stood over a coffeemaker and smiled as the young man entered.

"Hope I didn't startle you," he said. "This being your first day and all."

The recruit rubbed his eyes, "Its time I was up."

"I'm told your meeting with Sasha went well. I'm sorry I was unavailable."

"She was very helpful."

Lee gestured toward a chair."

"There's been a small breakthrough," he remarked. "A friend revealed some startling information."

Jesse took a seat and gave the older man his attention.

"Because of a misplaced cellphone we have knowledge of a recently deployed SIAG operative. Her target is likely the individual turned by our rogue."

Lee's narrative about a doomed SIAG agent and his turncoat replacement was recalled.

"Lets take ten minutes then meet in my office," Lee suggested. "I'd like to discuss your first assignment."

Jesse returned to his room and emptied both duffle bags. He placed his clothes away and lined the dresser top with books. Anxious to hear about his maiden undertaking he strode through the IRI and entered the professor's office. Lee was sifting through papers as the young man sat opposite him.

Peering over his glasses the professor remarked, "As my agent its imperative you remain secret. Your task will require the use of disguises and effects. The more convincing the deception, the more success you'll have in procuring information."

Jesse was perplexed but held his tongue.

"It's certain this station was deliberately kept out of the loop regarding vital updates from SIGINT," the professor confirmed. "The omission's are directly related to our renegade. For obvious reasons I'm reluctant to deal with the Agency. However, I've broached the matter with the UCOMA Director. Hopefully, something will be uncovered regarding these oversights."

"Do these exclusions extend to other UCOMA stations?"

"Just ours."

"I'd say that isn't good."

"I'd say I agree."

Lee paused, "I'm flying to Chicago to conduct some interviews."

"When?"

"Tomorrow morning."

"And myself?"

"You'll depart for Indiana in a few days and observe the movements of William Penther. His profile is included on the flash-drive you were issued?"

Jesse nodded.

"Most of the information was lifted from FBI source material and press clippings. It's relevant to note more than one Federal agent assigned to the Penther file has gone missing or turned up dead. You're to proceed with caution. This man is dangerous and has killers at his disposal. GPS coordinates matching his lodge and those of the nearest town Ellery, are stored on the flash drive. He resides in an isolated area referred to by locals as Rykles Clearing. Oddly, several of Penther's most devout followers have vanished. They may have gone to ground fearing retaliation from the militia leader. An FBI special agent named Jake Gill was recently found dead - the result of a freak car accident several kilometres south of Penther's dwelling. He'd been conducting an unauthorized investigation into the disappearance of a fellow agent."

Lee paused to glance at his notes, "I'd like to know if Penther remains confined to his property or if he's absent for lengths of time. It would be interesting to note who surrounds him, other than a right-hand man named Aldo Dopple."

Recalling the name from the profile Jesse raised an eyebrow.

"With regards to extracting information," Lee continued. "If an associate of Penther's is alone and vulnerable the application of physical discomfort might apply. Nothing life-threatening of course. A frightful display of theatrics would benefit enormously. This can only be carried out if the odds are overwhelmingly in your favour. Otherwise, avoid direct contact and simply observe."

Jesse had a hundred questions but settled for three.

"Sir?"

"Please call me Lee."

"Lee. Can you expand on what you mean by physical discomfort? Also what kind of theatrics are you suggesting? Lastly, how long would I be expected to observe the situation in Indiana?"

The professor leaned back contemplating each question.

"Physical discomfort implies anything short of murder unless its in self-defence. Fearful theatrics means scaring the shit out of an adversary so information is volunteered willingly. This can be carried out by deploying ghoulish disguises and other deceptions - techniques as old as the spy game itself. Euphemisms such as 'cloak and dagger', 'skulduggery' and 'spooks' have long been associated with our profession. As for the length of your stay, I suggest long enough to establish a pattern regarding Mr. Penther's comings and goings. Four to six days might tell us something."

"With regards to disguises what did you have in mind?"

The professor smiled, "The question should be what does Jesse have in mind? Surprise me son."

"Sir...I mean Lee. To be burdened with anything other than shades and a baseball cap on a surveillance operation seems at odds with the intent of a stake-out. Isn't the idea to remain concealed?"

Lee glanced up from his desk, "By applying strategies of fear at it's most base level information can be obtained. Humans are a superstitious lot. Consider the absence of a 13th floor in high-rises or an unwillingness to walk beneath ladders."

He stopped short and returned to the matter at hand, "Once you're in Indiana you'll make subtle inquiries in town by day and observe at night."

"How long will you be in Chicago?"

"Only one day. The FBI are providing protective custody for the family of the alleged SIAG female. I wish to speak with them and return to Lantern Falls the same evening. Meantime, I hope you'll consider disguise options. Additionally, we don't want a trail leading back to Grissim. When you begin your assignment you'll rent a vehicle here in town under an assumed name. Upon arrival in Ellery you'll secure a motel room. Rykles Clearing is roughly a dozen kilometres north of town. All transactions will be undertaken using cash or prepaid credit cards."

The professor glanced at his watch and slid a second flash-drive across the desk. "This concerns Indiana please review it. I'll field any questions you have afterwards?"

"I'm sure I'll have a few."

"I'm sure you will."

Lee rose to his feet.

"Before we conclude allow me to show you an alternate means of entry into this outpost."

Jesse retrieved the memory stick and they strode toward their living quarters.

"Two centuries ago our troops thought of everything," related the professor. "This included how to re-position themselves should the enemy reduce their fortress to cinders by cannon fire, or attempt to forge the lake in an outright assault."

They paused before the storage room and Lee accessed entry. Switching on the light Jesse was motioned to follow. The pair drew up behind a stocked shelving unit. Leaning over the professor placed his pass flush against a chink in the floor. Automatically, a 4' by 4' portion of the concrete surface descended on metal brackets. A faint glow was observed below. The slab formed the first of several steps leading toward the depths.

"The pass you were issued is required here as well," Lee stated. "Forty-watt lighting fixtures are triggered automatically. Things will appear faint at first so you may want to bring a flashlight. For now we'll make our way without one. Permit me to lead."

Cautiously, Lee placed his right foot on the first step and began his descent. Jesse followed and a dank passageway was revealed at the bottom. The walls had been blasted from sheer granite and were moist.

The ceiling was shored up with timber and steel braces. Jesse peered into the gloom to determine the tunnel's end. Once they'd forged the passage the young man observed nothing but more granite.

Facing the barrier Lee murmured, "Allow your eyes to follow my forefinger and you'll notice a copper object resembling the head of a nail."

In the faded light Jesse squinted at the embedded article.

"By applying my pass to it's surface a scan affords departure," Lee instructed. "A similar inlay outside offers reentry."

He placed his pass over the object and stepped sideways. Abruptly, a six foot arch of stone slid rearwards on twin rails. A row of artificial cedar trees obscured the opening and eclipsed the lake. Lee stepped from the tunnel onto a ridge roughly two yards wide followed by Jesse. The elder pointed toward a copper scan embedded outside the entrance. Applying his pass the door whisked forward blending seamlessly its surroundings. They made their way roughly a dozen yards and drew alongside a parking area attached to the rear of Hillgram Hall. Shielded by fake trees furnished by NSA engineers, Lee parted some branches aside showcasing the view Lake Erie provided. If vessels were sighted the pair remained obscured and couldn't be detected - even through binoculars. Aside from seagulls they were the only other lifeforms. The craggy shoreline was visible a hundred feet below. Sailing crafts steered clear fearing reefs and angry whitecaps.

Jesse had witnessed the view countless times but never from such a vantage point.

The grandeur of the lake stretched before them and the wind began to stir.

"So this is how I access my bedroom?"

Lee drew a long breath and exhaled, "The surface of the cliff is off-limits to students, faculty and the general public. The way can be trying under harsh conditions."

Staring at the surf below Jesse nodded.

"It takes roughly five minutes to traverse the tunnel and path linking the IRI with the parking lot," resumed the professor. "The passage was upgraded by engineers before my arrival at Grissim. Excavated during the War of 1812, it was restructured a century later at the start of the Great War. It's been maintained by the Agency ever since."

They stepped over a guardrail onto the parking lot and a gust of wind nearly bowled them over.

Lee raised his voice, "This is where you'll leave your car. Less attention will be drawn parking here."

Dark clouds were moving rapidly in their direction. The lake appeared turbulent and receded into grey. The wind velocity increased and the air grew moist. Turning toward his apprentice Lee advised they start back. They wound their way along the reclining path towards the point of reentry and Jesse was requested to initiate access into the tunnel. He withdrew his pass and placed it over the copper scanner and the door retracted instantly. When they were within he applied the card to the interior scanner and watched the granite door shimmy back into place.

They traversed the tunnel toward the steps on opposite side and reentered the storage room. Lee placed his card over the chink and they watched the topmost step become one with the floor.

"Remarkable," the young man muttered. "Is the surface of the cliff monitored?"

"A camera focuses on the lake but not on the bluffs. The parking lot behind the theatre is scrutinized onscreen and security personnel observe the area while making their rounds."

They returned to the office where Lee unlocked a drawer and withdrew several documents. He placed them inside his briefcase and glanced at Jesse, "If you need to touch base I can be reached through Corporal Soo. Once I return you'll be issued a secured phone."

"Good luck in Chicago."

"Thanks."

After the older man departed Jesse returned to his quarters and sat on the edge of the bed. He fell backward and tumbled into a black vortex. When he awoke he glanced about for a window - forgetting where he was.

He retrieved the flash-drive and inserted it into his laptop.

Indiana...

It took all of thirty seconds for Kristy to gain entry into the Commons Building - he was getting rusty. In his Temple days such tasks were accomplished in half that time. Regardless, thirty seconds was still okay. Since mid-October he'd been engaged in bi-monthly surveillance rituals at Grissim. Each stake-out lasted between twelve to twenty-four hours. This was to be his final go-round. Having breached the grounds earlier that morning the area was scanned using an LI – 3 ultra-violet heat and light sensor. The hand-held device displayed amazing accuracy in identifying security lasers. As for surveillance cameras he relied on instinct.

Having landed at Cleveland's Hopkins International Airport two hours earlier, the forty minute drive to Lantern Falls was made in a rented automobile he parked in town. Recalling his first visit to the Institute, he remembered scouring rooms along the third floor of the Commons Building, seeking an observation perch offering a clear view of Sentinel Hall. He found the ideal spot in an abandoned clerical office which remained his lair for the better part of eight months. With school in session surveillance was conducted after-hours. During summer the Institute lay dormant for the most part.

During his first watch he sequestered himself behind shuttered blinds with a zoom-lens camera looped about his neck. Studying a photograph of Lee Tondar he glanced across at Sentinel Hall and experienced a sudden chill. Inexplicably, the fortress appeared to dissolve in the surrounding mist. Brushing off the incident he decided a draft from an open window had been the source of his shivers. As for the vanishing citadel - the fog was thick along that shoreline.

Among the directive's issued to him by the Face the bi-monthly Grissim vigil's remained consistent. The reports Kristy delivered to his paymaster indicated the professor followed a routine timetable. Anyone visiting Sentinel Hall after hours was captured on camera and license plate numbers were recorded.

On Kristy's final watch the chief security officer was relieved by one of two burly guards. Both were recent additions to their posts. The female who'd taken command during the waning days of March was Asian. Through binoculars she appeared alluringly attractive. He later discovered she resided on the fourth floor of the Residence Building.

Kristy considered the Grissim assignment meaningless. Evidently, the Face disagreed having deemed the aging professor a threat.

Once the woman's replacement arrived a brown Chevrolet appeared. The male driver emerged and withdrew two bags from the trunk. The individual looked unfamiliar. Kristy snagged two photographs and jotted down his license plate number. One snapshot captured the driver, while the other featured his vehicle. The driver image revealed a physically imposing young man in his early to mid-twenties.

An hour later the replacement guard emerged from Sentinel Hall and drove off. Kristy considered his brief shift, when abruptly the professor's Volkswagen turned onto Abbot Lane and drew to a stop before the grey structure. Lee Tondar climbed from the driver's side and entered the building.

As these event's unfolded the former SIAG sleeper, sipped bottled water and munched raisins. Fortunately, a washroom was available in the room next to the one he occupied. Aside from what he'd observed and had on camera, nothing further transpired. Concluding his watch, he secured his backpack and departed the building the same way he'd entered. Scanning the corridor and campus grounds with the LI – 3, he remained mindful of cameras.

Stealthily, he retreated towards town by way of Falls Valley.

TWELVE

Taras checked out of the Oceanside Motel a few hours after her encounter with Kari Ellstone. The post office had just opened and she was grateful the young clerk who'd been so helpful the previous day wasn't on duty. She withdrew the key matching P.O. Box 121 and discovered the compartment empty. Dismayed there was nothing to indicate Ulsar's whereabouts she remained pragmatic and decided it was best to depart town quickly. Climbing behind the wheel of her rental she bid Halton's Cove farewell.

Merging onto I 95 she considered her life in America. She had prayed every night the coded-dispatch from Siana would never arrive. When it did she was bound by blood and honour to serve her oath. She maintained a daily agenda of rigorous exercise and was physically prepared but emotionally unqualified. It had taken years to forge a Western identity - now she was forced to revert overnight. Hailing from a nation of under seven million souls, the strip malls and fast food of her adopted country were a long way from home. The array of entertainment remained as overwhelming now as it had on her arrival. Both nations were joined at the hip on one account, however. Within their respective borders wealth and poverty lived side by side.

For over two centuries regional and economic disparity had strained the fabric of America. Differences ran deeper than anyone dared admit. Having adopted a broader outlook, her own nation's mistrust of the US persisted. Dependent upon fossil fuels excavated from beneath A'biin's desert sands anti-American sentiment ran high. Within the palaces of Siana official's remained cautiously optimistic. Following the moderate leanings of their new leader Amet D'han, overtures had been extended toward the West. D'han had successfully severed ties with the sectarian regime who'd held sway over the nation's affairs for centuries.

Taras had been indoctrinated into the Temple of the SIAG at age eight with the blessings of her parents. Representing the security arm of the nation, the Soldiers of Infinite Ascendancy and God proved adept in matters of Intelligence gathering and defensive strategy. Following a series of upheavals, the old guard were replaced by representatives of D'han's more liberal directorate. At the opposite end a small but potent contingent plotted to seize back power. If diplomatic resolve between A'biin and the West failed, recent successes could be undermined by remnants of the old order.

Change was in the wind, however.

A'biin had appointed it's first UN ambassador establishing a global dialogue. Significant reforms were implemented in realms of Faith, amendments which would've been considered heresy several years earlier. Despite the progress certain customs remained unchanged. Religion is instilled into each A'biinian newborn - in the same manner Jesus Christ is throughout the Christian world. During indoctrination SIAG recruit's are continually reminded the West lies upon a precipice of moral and economic collapse.

The Temple lay to the east of Siana. Young men were reared within a similar compound miles away. Teras adopted English and Spanish as second and third language requisites. Mathematics, applied sciences, and world history were studied at length. Faith remained part of the ritual, with prayer and meditation taking up twenty minutes at the beginning and end of each day. Strength and speed were instilled. Pupils were instructed by Masters in Jujitsu and other forms of martial arts. Participants studied acting techniques with emphases on body-language and accents - motivation took care of itself. Screenings of Hollywood films and television were featured as students were confronted with the superficial nature of Western culture. Subjected to the latest musical trends they concealed their love of the form beneath grim expressions.

Firearms of all designs were scrutinized. Target practice involving assault rifles and semi-automatic weapons took up three hours each day. Over time Taras became a formidable sharpshooter. However, it was her uncanny ability with a dagger which took precedence. She considered the weapon more effective than guns and honed her craft for hours on end. Clips and ammunition hindered progress and were better suited to military operations. Without physical impediment she was able to conceal three blades on her person at any given time.

Explosives were deconstructed, everything from assembling Molotov cocktails to an understanding of nuclear weaponry bore scrutiny. Hand grenades, homemade ammonium nitrate bombs and landmines were rigged and deployed.

Following years of study Taras and eleven other females entered the ranks of the SIAG.

On a psychological level the women were taught how not to love. Sexual endeavours were permitted only as a tactical component in the challenges ahead. Depending on circumstances, marriage was encouraged so long as it served as a mechanism for deep-cover. Where outright lust was concerned agents were recalled and their careers terminated, if those boundaries were breached.

Shortly after Taras turned eighteen a young man bearing the physique of an Olympian was admitted to her quarters, by an emissary who quickly withdrew. The youthful stranger's arrival had been foretold to her by one of the wise men. The elder explained it was part of a natural design. Within her sanctum she gazed upon the young man's bronze profile. They held hands and smiles were exchanged. In the wavering candlelight it was understood what would pass between them. Removing their garments they embraced tenderly, their flesh responding to the other's gentle caresses as passionate love prevailed.

When morning dawned the young man departed never to return. As wondrous as the sensation had been, Taras compartmentalized the experience and returned to playing with knives and guns. Not so easily forgotten was the event which sidelined her for nine months. Eventually, she gave birth to a beautiful brown-eyed boy and had her heart broken, as the child was whisked away to be reared by adoptive parents representing the state. The wise men believed strength lay not only in training, but within the genes. Having her child snatched up hardened her heart profoundly.

Observed favourably by Temple instructors, preparations were set in motion for Taras to establish a 'background profile' abroad. Her teacher, a man named Heron, was appointed her handler. A respectful relationship existed between the pair and she was briefed in great detail. Granted three weeks rest and relaxation at a state retreat in the southern interior, she spent afternoons hiking and swimming. At night she studied maps and read up on Spanish and American history. In an effort to hone her language skills she listened to voice recordings before nodding off to sleep.

When Taras returned to Siana her move to the continent got underway. She was provided with fake passports and a Spanish identity. With enough funds to cover living expenses she enrolled at Miguel Del Institute in Barcelona, and was billeted with a middle-aged couple residing nearby the campus. The pair were generously reimbursed for the hospitality they extended toward the student they treated like a daughter. Immersing herself in an 'Urban Infrastructure' program offered by the Institute Taras maintained excellent grades. After two years she graciously bid her Spanish family adios and set sail for New York. With her passport and documentation in order, she cleared customs and stepped onto US soil carrying two suitcases. Boarding a Greyhound bus for Chicago she intended to resume 'Urban Planning' studies at the university and prepare for life as a sleeper agent.

She settled into a furnished flat within a rambling Victorian brownstone in Old Town and met a graduate student at a building restoration fundraiser. Introducing himself as Steven Burke, she gave her name as Gillian Armand and the pair became involved in a lengthy courtship. One month before her twenty-first birthday they were married. A year later a baby girl arrived. After much debate about what to name her Steven's father suggested Samantha. The couple pooled their resources and mortgaged a home in the Chicago suburb of Evanston.

Taras drew up alongside a service station payphone off the highway. She withdrew the sheriff's number in Halton's Cove and fed some coins into the dispenser. A voice responded and she explained she'd been walking her dog along the Stinson Line and heard a series of alarming banging noises, emitting from one of the homes on that stretch. She gave the dispatcher the address and urged him to send someone then hung up. Back in the car she resumed a southerly course along I 95. Doubts continued to nag her with regards to Kari Ellstone's well-being.

Before embarking on her quest to hunt down the young woman's lover, she retrieved a parcel delivered by an asset to a drop-box in Chicago. It's content's included identification supporting several different versions of herself. Funds were provided to last eight weeks. If she failed to terminate the wayward sleeper she'd likely be recalled. Thoughts of returning to Siana after a dozen years away and a botched first assignment were inconceivable – so was the notion of defecting and spending her life in shadows. She had hoped Kari's responses would've shed light on the exact whereabouts of her target.

At a drive-through parking lot she Googled 'Orchard and Sons'. Nothing resembling that name was listed anywhere under US publishing. So much for Ulsar's probable handler? Despite the inherent danger, Candle's flame would hopefully draw Nickolas Dante.

Taras would be waiting.

On a separate matter she conceded the cover belonging to Gillian Burke had been blown wide open. By now the authorities were on the lookout for the person she had once been. She cursed her sloppiness regarding the cellphone kerfuffle at O'Hara - aware of the incriminating evidence stored on the device. The data was encrypted but would soon be exposed and the outgoing call to Harvard would be followed up. If only Samantha had called five minutes earlier.

Sammy...

Purging the torment from her heart she focused upon the road. With her task in upstate Massachusetts concluded; wherever Kari journeyed her ex was sure to follow. Crossing the state line Taras continued toward Manhattan. Forging the Koch Bridge she entered the borough of Queens, where Kari's parents resided. Her profile suggested the Ellstone estate was a likely destination.

Fitted with a new identity Taras was now Leah Rogers, a prospective retailer scouting locations for a clothing boutique. Attired in heels and a bright summer dress she looked the part.

She removed Ulsar's photograph and studied it closely. The old familiarity persisted.

Having reviewed the flash-drive issued to him by Lee Tondar, the recruit was afforded detailed insight into William Penther. The account was both fascinating and disturbing. Jesse switched off the laptop and initiated a book hunting expedition. Departing Sentinel Hall he drove to the Public Library and discovered the title he sought was unavailable. He approached the front desk and inquired about 'The Haunted Lakes', stating the volume contained several regional ghost stories. The librarian lowered her glasses and typed in the title.

"You're in luck," she said. "It's been out of print for years, but was reissued under the name 'Legends of the Lakes' by another publisher." She glanced up, "Unfortunately, we haven't received our copy yet."

Jesse hedged, "Do you know anyone who might carry the title?"

"Historical societies may have received copies," she replied. "Its tourist season so bookshops in Cleveland or Toledo might have them in stock? I suggest calling ahead to make certain."

"I take it Lantern Falls doesn't have a historical society?"

The woman removed her glasses and sighed, "With the wealth of history surrounding this region you'd think so. Unfortunately, that's not the case. I wish I could be more help."

"You've been very kind," Jesse replied. "I'll try Maxim's Book Cellar."

"Check out Salinger's over on Pina Street while you're at it."

"I shall."

Walking several blocks Jesse entered Maxim's. The shop stocked mostly paperback fiction and non-fiction. The book was unavailable. Ten minutes later he entered Salinger's and made the same inquiry. With assistance from a staffer they searched the appropriate shelves without success. On the sidewalk Jesse withdrew his phone and contacted information. When an operator responded he requested a listing for the Toledo Historical Society and was eventually linked.

Jesse mentioned he was looking to purchase a book entitled `Legends of the Lakes'. Informed copies were available, he recalled the location being on the ground level of the Tourism and Recreation building in downtown Toledo. He thanked the man and said he'd swing by. Retrieving his car at the library he glanced at the gas gauge. The tank was half full as he pulled from the curb and made for the highway. In under an hour the book had been purchased and he was cruising Interstate 90 eastward.

Back in the Falls he signalled onto Abbot Lane and recalled Lee's request to park behind the theatre. He brought the Chevy to a halt and backed onto Edgewater Drive, accessing a lane encircling Hillgram Hall. He parked in a spot overlooking the lake and departed the Chevy with book in hand. Several air-ducts and a fire escape were visible along the rear facade of the rust-coloured playhouse. It's exterior contrasted sharply with the grey shell of Sentinel Hall a little further along the shoreline. Jesse decided to broach the clandestine entry route and approached the path concealed by cedar trees. Following the recline he placed his pass over the copper scan and the granite door repelled backwards. The procedure was repeated within and the archway resealed itself. Straddling the passage he emerged inside the storage room. He placed his pass on the chink and watched the steps ascend.

Jesse reentered his quarters and placed the book aside. He changed into track pants and runners before departing the IRI, via the front lobby. Waving at Sean inside the security station, he jogged the length of Falls Valley several times. Wiping sweat from his neck and brow, he returned to their quarters, where he showered and fixed a cheese and lettuce sandwich. Relaxing in his room he reacquainted himself with the ghost he recalled so vividly from his youth. He stared at the revised paperback edition and wondered if the tale would resonate as powerfully as it once did. The cover featured a computer-generated image depicting a fog-shrouded ship upon eerie green waters. He preferred the dust-jacket illustration on the old hardback anthology. It rendered a cloaked spectre gliding over dark waters with it's arms extended.

Jesse flipped the pages and was relieved to find the manuscript as he remembered it. In addition to the 1936 copyright; the forward by Dr. Evelyn Lang who was responsible for transcribing the original was still intact. Eight stories were indexed. Each derived from original narratives based upon oral tradition. The tales were loose accounts of supernatural occurrences, involving inhabitants who existed within the perimeters of the Great Lakes region. Collected from sources in neighbouring states and provinces; pioneer and indigenous folklore accounted for at least three accounts. Each story was accompanied with a trio of black and white sketches placed throughout the text. The illustration's accompanying Jesse's choice entitled 'Kriel', depicted the young protagonist Damon Kriel locked in an embrace with his bride-to-be. The next revealed a merchant ship with it's stern raised toward heaven, as it was ravaged by a ferocious gale. Finally, there was the chilling depiction of Captain Kriel as a ghostly entity gazing over the perturbed waters of Lake Erie.

Jesse was startled to discover Kriel's image was similar to that of the spectral figure he'd envisioned on the burning hillside, following his return from Windsor. He read the first paragraph and was transported back to the apartment he and Emma shared in Toledo.

Adjusting his lamp he set about rereading.

———————

Azil Besserer was a solemn olive-skinned man whose moist brown eyes blinked continually behind silver-rimmed glasses. He'd been lured to America after being whisked from a 'pressing situation' abroad. Among the lowlifes he was forced to endure he kept to himself. The toothy grin he once displayed was a rare sight under present circumstances. Easily antagonized he was prone to erupt into tangents at perceived threats. Provocation usually flowed from the lips of Cal Wicker, one of the neanderthals assigned to their clandestine project.

During his formative years equations and bacterium quantities occupied Dr. Besserer's mind. Once the prospect of wealth entered his consciousness, he displayed great willingness to appease well-to-do clients who sought his services. Over eight intolerable months he plotted retirement and an exulted life of luxury. Sequestered within an industrial prison he dreamed of the fortune awaiting him in accumulated Swiss bank deposits, care of his elusive paymaster.

On the second day of each month Azil was afforded an opportunity to feed change into a payphone, in order to confirm his deposited earnings. Establishing contact with a banking representative in Zurich, he was assured his instalments continued to increase his balance. Afterwards, he'd be escorted back to the compound to resume his duties. Knowing little of the motive behind Sir's operation, Besserer sensed dread for the citizens of Detroit.

His infamous concoction was referred to as 'Airborne Cataclysm' or AC. He described it as an aerosol enhanced Anthrax isolate, whose origin's dated back to a Soviet-era bio-weapons program. Following an accidental release inside a Soviet biological weapons complex in 1979, the isolate purportedly caused collateral infections and deaths. Besserer claimed to have applied a technique of transfecting the Anthrax with two plasmids, designed to greatly increase virulence of the pathological bacteria. He selected the most aerosol stable spore variants and devised a unique delivery system.

That evening a final batch of AC was to be stockpiled within the steel-encased pit hosting the leaden polystyrene cubes. Once the operation concluded, participants would depart the compound and the weapon would be released by remote from a distance. Triggered by relay, gas-induced flames discharge the contents by melting the polystyrene coating and rendering the poison active. While this occurs, the lid enclosing the pit retracts and the mutant strain is jettisoned through a blasted-out portion of the ceiling. Industrial fans encircling the cavity ensure the corrupt agent renders the area toxic.

"Why take time injecting Styrofoam cubes?" Jackson Bell argued. "Why not simply deploy the anthrax straight out?"

Besserer sighed and stated such methods afforded minimal effectiveness. An immense volume of the fatal cubes ensures widespread dispersal of the payload. A significant portion of the city would become uninhabitable. Anthrax spores can stabilize and remain infectious for years. Cleanup would be an arduous task.

Azil's situation within the lower-level of Electron Era had become intolerable. Fresh air was obtained only on designated breaks at the rear of the building after sundown. The dreary view afforded a panorama of abandoned warehouses and factories. A vacant lot pockmarked with weeds divided the compound from her derelict neighbours. Sick of the dreadful frozen dinners he subsisted on; the most distressing aspects were the tormentors surrounding him.

The microbiologist knew something of prison. Back home he'd been accused of treason and spent several years in a maximum security facility in Siana. Charged with selling secrets to dubious foreign buyers

Besserer denied all charges. He insisted he'd been drugged and framed by enemies of the state. When the new Directorate assumed power they chose to stay Besserer's lifetime sentence without appeal. With insider help he was afforded means of escape in exchange for favours. A month later he found himself living in uncomfortable exile on the Continent. Commissioned by his terrorist liberators to produce vials of AC in a pharmaceutical laboratory, while awaiting a face-altering operation; he was contacted by his current employer. Sir arranged his escape from the fortified lab and had him smuggled into the US and sequestered in a dank cellar.

Azil desired to drink expensive wine and debate frivolous matters with like-minded individuals. He envisioned iced-tea on a tropical terrace delivered by a bowing manservant. Glancing about his abhorrent surroundings he counted the minutes until freedom beckoned.

Entering the decontamination chamber within the atrium, he removed his shoes and donned a protective suit. A final batch of cubes needed to be injected and stored in the pit. Clean-up and sterilization took roughly twenty minutes. Surfaces were swabbed with mentholated spirit and Formalin was added as a disinfectant. Ultra-violet lamps kept the area sterile when personnel were absent. On this final occasion none of it would be necessary.

Azil recalled his arrival the previous fall. Weeks were spent training Bell, Train and Wicker to deal safely with pathogenic bacteria and sterilization procedure. Aware of the dangers they paid close attention. Infected syringes and tubes were discarded into hazmat containers to be buried behind the building. Protective suits and headgear were stored within the decontamination chamber.

Besserer's quarters was a storage room situated just outside the atrium. It contained a single bed, a battered dresser and a radio he kept tuned to a classical music station. News and world events depressed him to no end. Crossword puzzle books were stacked next to his bed. To his dismay the washroom and mess area were shared with the others. When the bathroom was unoccupied the sink was used for laundry purposes. The entire lair conveyed the appearance of a military-style barrack. Natural light was gleaned during chaperoned breaks and Besserer's monthly payphone visits. Meals were prepared while the others slept. Afterwards, he dined alone in his quarters accompanied by Bach, Beethoven and Mozart.

Burdened by the awkward hazard suit he entered the prefabricated lab and approached the incubator. Removing a flask of

AC, the hyper-virulent Anthrax isolate was treated to an effective spore inducing formula. Besserer placed the flask in a containment hood and proceeded to purify and concentrate the substance, for injection into polystyrene cubes. Two micrometers of AC were deposited into their weightless encasement's. Each contained roughly 50,000 spores - more than the known lethal dose.

A digital clock indicated 6:30 pm. He planned to work another hour before calling it quits. The following morning would be spent packing raw materials into the protective carrying case he'd arrived with. A final check of cables and detonation frequencies would be undertaken. Jackson Bell intended to attach explosive charges around the periphery of the atrium ceiling. With the weapon operational Besserer's departure from Electron Era couldn't come soon enough.

As senior biologist within a SIAG research lab years before, significant inroads into biological warfare were made. Attaining clearance at the highest level; the crimes he'd been charged with systematically ended Besserer's career. In response to his interrogators he maintained he'd been drugged, but was able to omit critical data.. Prosecutors argued how information could be omitted while under the influence of mind-altering drugs. Speaking gibberish before the assembled tribunal he was sentenced to life for high-treason. Following his dramatic escape involving a mail truck, he found himself in Europe preparing to undergo the face-changing operation at a secluded clinic. Word arrived via an emissary that a wealthy American sought his services. Correspondence ensued and details were thrashed out. A short while later Besserer was smuggled into America for a period lasting up to one year. Over that time five million dollars would be deposited into his Zurich account in monthly instalments.

"Not a word to anyone," warned the emissary.

"Of course."

The face surgery could wait.

———————

THIRTEEN

The idea of donning a disguise nagged him most.

Sprawled along the bed Jesse reminded himself why he'd offered to assist the professor. As a journalism student he'd become little more than a restless observer. Sports and reading had been passions throughout his teenage years – the NFL was something more than a gleam in his eye. Aside from tossing the ball on the grass bordering Abbott Lane, he'd been away from the grid for more than two years. The prospect of reentry into the game was possible, however at the ripe age of twenty-two he'd be required to attend a learning institution with a football franchise - and accomplish it without the benefit of a scholarship or money.

Leaning back on the pillow he contemplated Lee Tondar's insistence upon concealment. The professor emphasized the seriousness of their endeavour, so why the gimmick? Disguising oneself ran counter to the idea of working undercover. The very act was bound to draw attention. Jesse could assist in a variety of ways - surveillance, field-work, research. Yet Lee was insistent he shield his features like a Klansman; in what was termed a 'cloak and dagger strategy of fear'. Having made the decision to step into the deep end of an apparent real-world crisis, he decided to confront the professor and urge him to reconsider the veiled aspect of his assignment. Placing the matter aside he continued re-reading the beleaguered saga of Damon Kriel.

7 November 1869

A northerly wind billowed off the lake stirring dead leaves along the grounds of the vast estate. Securing his horse Damon Kriel strode from the stables toward the rambling homestead belonging to the Brill family of Campton County, New York. As he approached Amanda Brill rushed out to greet him, kissing his lips passionately. Motioning him inside she took his riding cloak and draped it on a rack. He was escorted to the dining room and guided toward a seat opposite her own. Once greetings were exchanged with most of those present, Damon winked at Amanda who radiated gold in the flickering candlelight

Abruptly, their attention shifted to the solemn figure seated at the head of the table. Avoiding eye contact Ephraim Brill cleared his throat. Heads were bowed as he recited the following words: "God in heaven we humbly beg you to accept our gratitude for the bounty you provide - even as we walk among sinners. Amen."

The others blinked.

Grace had been recited by him thousand of times but never with the added words, 'even as we walk among sinners.' The phrase implied they were sinner's as a result of the company they kept. The elder Brill glanced around the table and made the sign of the cross. He retrieved a silver spoon from the assembled finery and dipped it in the bowl set before him. Raising it partway he blew on the contents, before bringing it to his thin lips. On cue the others followed. Ephraim's gaze shifted from the appetizer and settled upon the young man invited at the behest of his daughter. Through narrow slits etched into dark recesses Brill peered down his long nose. The unsettling image was enhanced by sinewy strands of grey hair shimmering in light of the candelabra. Staring icily at their dinner guest the patriarch refocused on his soup, while a manservant and maid stood to his rear in silence.

To Ephraim's right sat his eldest Peter, a buoyant gentleman of twenty-one studying law at Harvard in Massachusetts. Baby fat and peach fuzz were still evident on his features. Across from him sat poor, distracted Lucille, mother of Katherine Brill - Ephraim's dearly departed wife. Amanda was seated next to her brother. Graced with sparkling blue eyes and a bright smile, golden locks framed her features like a bonnet. A year younger than Peter, it was she who'd prevailed upon him to make the journey home, to serve as a buffer against the possible wrath of their father. In Ephraim's eyes Amanda represented the last vestiges of his life's companion. Beloved Katherine lived forever in her. Known as a taskmaster of unyielding temperament, Ephraim had been widowed seven years. His disposition had grown more severe since his wife's passing.

Across from Amanda sat the devil.

Damon shuffled in his seat and decided his best recourse was to try to be at ease.

Ephraim Brill was among the wealthiest landowners residing in Upper New York State. One of six children born to impoverished Dutch parents; the family boarded an overcrowded sailing vessel bound for the New World decades earlier. Following a perilous ocean crossing they set foot on American soil and found lodgings among the poorer quarters of Buffalo, New York. Employment was found in the textile sweatshops, where Ephraim's parents and siblings spent their lives in the service of others. Rejecting a life of servitude he made his fortune with wits and an iron will. Ephraim taught himself the language of business and studied the markets. He learned to invest large sums of money and borrowed heavily. Over time his investment's profited. Acreages of land purchased during lean times, paid off thrice-fold once demand returned.

Land abounded in those days and rich, fertile soil stretched toward the horizon.

Over time Ephraim secured several thousand acres of prime real estate. In the ensuing years his advice was sought by financiers in Manhattan and Albany, including the State Assembly. In his own community he was named Commissioner of Regional Farmers, a logical choice since most of the farmland was his. He provided funds to establish the Campton County Sheriffs Office and served as its first chairman.

Ephraim's children enjoyed a strict yet privileged upbringing - private schools, a nanny, tailored clothing, travel. Katherine had been a doting mother whom the children ran to for council or a sympathetic ear. Even at that time their father was a pious and rigid disciplinarian. Insistent his children receive the highest grades, he would berate them if they fell below expectations. Tutored in graces afforded their station they were rarely able to let their guard down.

Following their mother's untimely death from cancer, Peter completed lower school and was sent east to Harvard. He missed his sister but cherished his new found freedom. Ephraim's intention for Amanda were decidedly different. She would remain with him indefinitely. Eventually, she would marry a wealthy and worthy suitor and settle into a lavish cottage on her father's estate. It became apparent she was bound to spend the rest of her existence under the joyless watch of her father, attached to a husband she could never love.

The notion Ephraim's wishes would be challenged by a street-reveller posing as a dinner guest was laughable. Incidents of debauchery and hooliganism were reported to Brill. It was his word which determined judgment passed to perpetrators of crimes. Where Damon was concerned he kept close tabs. One New Years Eve in

Syracuse he came across young Kriel with a pair of barmaids clinging to his coattails. He and his rabble had engaged local's outside a tavern by singing bawdy songs, fuelled by endless pitchers of ale. Observing the crowd revelling in the deviant's dark carnival, Brill climbed on a makeshift pulpit and began hurling blasphemy at the sinner and his wretched companions.

On another occasion, one not witnessed by Ephraim, but reported nonetheless. An informer mentioned Damon had been involved in a waterfront brawl in Rochester. Evidently, he was defending a wench's honour before a trio of rowdy sailors and took on all three. When the fight concluded, he wavered unsteadily over their unconscious forms and toasted them in song. Mounting his horse he tumbled from the opposite side and lay there in a heap.

The Chairman circled the account in his little book.

Along with Ephraim and his brood, the Kriel clan were also of Dutch extraction and resided in Campton County. Damon's parents were among the wealthy few who owned an estate with vast land reserves attached. His father Simon had made his fortune in shipping. Establishing trade routes among settlement's dotting the shores of the Lower Great Lakes, he became the region's first shipping magnate. Simon played a significant role in local affairs as did Brill senior. Damon's mother Sybil was a committed philanthropist, while older sister Caroline taught school.

Ephraim loathed the Kriel's and considered them shallow and decadent. Swayed by the latest trends emanating from the Continent, they were like royalty with a commoner's touch. It wasn't simply fashion which installed his contempt. Their library included partisan journals and manifestos from godless nations, whose sole intent was to subvert God's will. Influenced by European scholars and free-thinkers, Simon Kriel would inject their treasonous musings into town hall meetings. In Ephraim's view gullible travellers like the Kriel's were likely glad-handled by foreign minds of insidious intent.

Frustration was mounting among farmers who claimed their earnings were being siphoned off by Brill's accountants in lieu of unpaid rent and taxes. The debts were no fault of their own - there had been lengthy droughts. Meantime, Simon Kriel's notion of a union infiltrated the peasant classes and they began voicing collective concerns. It was one more reason Ephraim despised the young man seated at his dining room table.

Tension in the room was thick enough to cut with a knife. Its effect was aided by the diminishing daylight. Between laced curtains the setting sun allowed the candelabra to cast lengthy shadows along the tablecloth.

Peter was first to break the silence, "I must say the weather here is damp. It's actually quite balmy in Cambridge."

Aware her brother was attempting to diffuse an awkward situation, Amanda suspected Damon was wishing he were anywhere else. Lucille nodded repeatedly and kept asking what day it was.

"I think Cambridge has made you balmy dear brother," Amanda replied melting the frost with her laughter. "I can't imagine what you do in your spare time?"

Peter cast a sidelong glance, "You'd be surprised how much progress I've made as an athlete."

He gazed across at Damon, "I had no yearning to engage myself in anything sporting until I went east. People here abhor games. Have you an interest in competitive sports Damon?"

"I run the track occasionally does that count?"

"Indeed it would!" Peter replied raising his glass. "Running requires great physical effort."

Servants were laying out a main course of roast turkey, scalloped potatoes and crusty bread. Afterwards, glasses were replenished.

"Amanda tells me you're a merchant sailor and a ship's captain to boot," Peter resumed. He smiled at his sister, "I'm glad you were able to join us, Damon. I believe you and my sister would make an ideal couple."

A fist slammed along the surface of the table with such force drinks and finery were sent flying. Food and drink spattered the tablecloth and laps of those present. Servants responded by scooping the spoils from the floor. A maid guided bewildered Lucille from the room.

Ephraim was seething as he stared down his son and spewed, "Don't ever imply the notion of such an alliance in my presence."

Peter pushed his chair back, "I simply suggested they would make a..."

"And don't let me hear you speaking like a fop beneath this roof. You're taught to behave like a lawyer not a lily-livered dandy. Keep up that line of talk and I'll pull you from that school."

"I am what I am!"

"A Brill is what you are!" the old man thundered. "Start acting like one."

Retrieving broken glass from off the floor Amanda glared up at her elder, "You ought to be ashamed of yourself for allowing prejudice to overwhelm these proceedings. You're a hypocrite, father! You insist we display etiquette and look how monstrously you behave."

Brushing her words aside the old man resumed his tirade.

"You've had the upbringing most people only dream of and you want to throw your life away for the likes of ... that!"

He gestured in Damon's direction.

"Now see here father...," Peter interjected.

Damon cleared his throat and cautioned him.

Exasperated, the older sibling rose and departed the room.

Apologizing for her father's conduct Amanda slipped a shawl about her shoulders and went to look in on Lucille. Several minutes were spent gently rocking the older woman. The maid was requested to bring a plate of thinly sliced meat, potatoes and a cup of tea. Once the meal arrived, Amanda sat next to her grandmother and patiently spoon fed her. Afterwards, Lucille was assisted to bed and her pillow and blankets were adjusted. Departing the room, Amanda made her way toward the front entrance and slipped into the brisk night air. She pulled her shawl tighter and lowered her head.

Damon found himself alone in the dining room with Ephraim Brill. It had been his intent all along – minus the bad table manners. Arranging the occasion had been an ordeal for Amanda. She'd pleaded with her father to extend Damon a dinner invitation. After weeks of requests the elder Brill yielded. In light of what just transpired asking for his daughter's hand seemed redundant. Damon believed in formalities, however, if the old man refused they'd elope.

Plans evolved over a fortnight. With the wheels in motion the lovers intended to wed eight days hence at a secret rendezvous. Amanda posted a letter informing her brother of the pending marriage and again solicited his presence. Before Damon could utter his vow he was committed to deliver a shipment of supplies to Detroit. While away it was agreed Amanda would take flight from Campton County and remain with friends in another township.

Damon's lake excursion would take six days. Once it was discovered his daughter had fled the old man would attempt to track her down. Hundreds of volunteers would be mobilized.

Ephraim Brill could ill afford to feud publicly with Damon's father. Endowed with wealth and power Simon Kriel had plenty of local support. Despite overlapping business dealings no love was lost between the pair. Ephraim's accountant's insisted a truce be called. Their perceived amicability contributed toward the well-being of the local economy they argued. Presently, Damon's parents were abroad which suited Ephraim fine. He was aware the day would dawn when someone would attempt to woo his daughter away. Without suspecting who that someone might be – when it was discovered Damon was the suitor he tripled his efforts to keep them apart. Young Kriel and his ilk were vipers. Amanda would be ruined by his infidelities. Memories of Katherine would shatter like glass in wake of such a pairing.

Shadows played upon the stained tablecloth once the dislodged dinnerware had been removed. The young man swallowed hard and addressed his host who remained seated.

"I wish to marry your daughter, Sir. She has accepted my proposal and we hope you might vouchsafe our union with you're blessing."

A deathly silence hung in the air.

Leaning forward the older man slowly rasped, "You must be joking."

Damon held fast, "Your view of me has been tainted by previous quarrels with my father regarding separate matters."

"This is my house!" Brill shouted rising to his feet. "I would have you cast out like a beggar."

"You're daughter is unhappy. We wish to be together."

Ephraim's eyes blazed.

Damon circled the table and drew to within two yards of the wretched man.

"I apologize for my recklessness which may have caused you embarrassment in the past. I've worked hard to remedy my shortcomings. I love Amanda and she feels likewise."

"You'll not have her!" Ephraim bellowed. "That is my testament."

He turned to depart and called over his shoulder, "Consider the matter closed."

"Then we shall elope."

The patriarch stopped in his tracks and swung about.

"Curse you!" he muttered and spat on the floor. "If you attempt to steal my daughter I'll have you hunted down and shot like a rabid dog."

Damon chose not to respond.

"I'll see you're escorted to the stables," Brill muttered.

The young man retrieved his cloak as a hired hand was summoned.

"No need I'll find my way. Fare you well."

The northern periphery of the estate bordered Lake Ontario. Beneath her bluffs whitecaps born of jutting rocks left streams of bubbling residue in their wake. The perturbed waters conveyed meaning to Amanda. Along an incline she observed the massive Brill dwelling framed by a canvas of shimmering stars. Damon was seen approaching the stables and she was intuitively aware of what occurred. She ran to him and they embraced, each acknowledging things would never change.

"Never mind," he whispered. "In eight days we'll be wed."

Acreages of farmland surrounded the estate. With harvest underway dozens of migrant workers resided in nearby shantytowns. Every manner of vessel was seen drifting between New York City and Detroit, by way of the Erie Canal. Influxes of immigrant's from central Europe and Asia were bypassing the crowded coastal cities and journeying further inland.

The limbs of barren trees swayed and leaves crackled underfoot. An autumn chill permeated the air as Amanda reflected on her lover's transformation. Following years of application Damon became captain of a merchant ship. During their youth both attended the same private school. At the time she found him course and frivolous. In retrospect she thought the same of all boys save for brother Peter.

At eighteen Damon was made steward aboard a steamer owned and operated by his father's shipping company. The crew were engaged in transporting hardware and fabrics westward to Michigan and ports of call in Upper Canada. Over time Damon was promoted to second mate aboard a merchant trawler. Three years later he was assigned captain of his own vessel. Each autumn he returned home to spend time with his family.

The Annual Harvest Fair was being celebrated and Ms. Brill found herself drawn to the young man and noticed he'd turned out rather nicely. Fit and trim his dusty hair fell over his right eye like a terrier puppy. His chiselled features were highlighted by a frilly white shirt worn beneath an imported Parisian overcoat. Concealed among the crowd she cast rapid glances in his direction. His companion's were mostly landlocked locals - who like Damon had taken up the trades of their fathers. Being heir to a fortune he'd aroused considerable attention among eligible ladies throughout the district. Having overcome his youthful discrepancies Damon took his responsibilities seriously. On the final day of the Fair he and Amanda spent several hours together, in a secluded spot by the lake. They met there each day when the offer of marriage was proposed.

Towns and villages sprouted up everywhere along the shores of the Great Lakes. Fresh supplies from the east were in constant demand. As a result the Lower Lakes Shipping Lines thrived under Simon Kriel's direction. The seasoned crew serving under his son added greatly to the fleet. Damon proved himself an excellent navigator and intuitive leader. Their vessel was christened the 'Katy' and it's crew would've followed him anywhere. Off-season the men retained a sufficient portion of their salary to survive winter. Toward the end of March work resumed.

With a hired hand observing Amanda she watched her betrothed enter the stables. Mounting a black stallion the rider blew a kiss her way and set off for Buffalo.

Flanked by dark woods the silver trail was bathed in moonlight. Behind swift moving clouds the landscape faded to black, as events of that evening prayed upon the horseman's thoughts.

Eight days.

In just under two hours he arrived alongside the creaking wharves of Buffalo's waterfront. Leaving the stallion secured with a stable master, he strode the docks and noticed the Katy rocking gently at berth. The steam-driven merchant ship was first commissioned by the company in the late 1850's. Having weathered many a storm she'd proved a sturdy vessel. By midnight most of the ten-man crew had assembled. Once midshipman Abe Herman arrived all were accounted for. Illuminated by kerosene lamps they spent several hours assisting a team of longshoremen load cargo. Meantime, Damon scribbled down inventory and made an inspection the engine room and storage compartments.

Their current assignment was routine. With weather patterns in flux, Damon and first-mate Peter Strand monitored the air-pressure by consulting a barometer. They studied prevailing currents to see what might be expected over the coming week. With maps spread on a chart table the 'Katy' departed Buffalo under temperate conditions. Damon managed to sleep for the first time in thirty-six hours.

Next day he gazed through a spyglass at the dark clouds amassed atop one another. Beyond that an inky blackness stretched toward infinity. The wind velocity increased and a massive wave tumbled over the starboard railing. The sky was divided by a jagged streak of lightning, followed by a clasp of thunder.

Whenever foul weather threatened safe passage the usual procedure was to seek shelter along the nearest shore, until the storm abated. Delays cost money, however the Lower Lakes Shipping Line considered the safety of it's crew members first and urged each captain to observe this precaution. Damon decided if a squall impeded their way they would meet the challenge. Unlike the vulnerable sailing vessels of yore - iron steamers such as the one he commandeered held their own against uncertain conditions. The billowing masts of schooners and sailing ships served as fodder for the elements. Despite their durable vessel the Lakes were not to be trifled with, especially this early in the season. Erie could be as treacherous as the North Atlantic so mariners attested.

From the bridge Damon made out the grey walls and turrets of a fortress residing upon a cliff, along the southern shoreline.

"Shall I lean towards the south shore!" helmsman Owen Laird shouted from the wheel.

By now torrential rains had fully engulfed the Katy. The crew awaited the captain's order to steer clear of the furies.

Assisted by a stoker Laird gripped the wheel tighter, "The wind is tipping us lee side captain! It'll be difficult to remain upright if we stay this course!"

"Steer directly into the onslaught we'll slice our way through!" Damon bellowed above a chorus of groans. "Is every hand accounted for?"

"All are within," Strand responded.

"Hold tight a few moments."

"We don't have a few moments!" Laird piped in.

Damon held firm and glanced at the chart spread before him. An instant later the table heaved forward, articles were tossed and a compass and ruler crashed to the cabin floor. The crew grasped at anything solid to retain balance.

"Here's our position!" Damon shouted kneeling and pointing to a spot on the chart. "Six hours east of Detroit. If we turn about now we're certain to go over. The storm is moving towards our point of departure, not our current position. It will pass."

Abe Herman spoke up, "But the gale might last hours captain."

Grasping the wheel Laird shouted, "We need shore shelter now!"

"And risk being upended while we make the turn. Not on your life!" responded the Captain. "Maintain course."

Listening to the exchange first mate Strand stepped forward and said without deliberation, "I recommend we take Owen's advise, Captain. We would capsize just as easily following the course you've chosen."

The crew grunted in affirmation.

"We've been through worse," Damon muttered.

"So we have," Strand responded. "But the winds were mostly spent. This is just beginning."

"The order stands. Stay the course!"

Kriel turned up the collar of his oilskin coat and adjusted his slicker hat. He pressed out the cabin door and felt the full force of the gale. Uncertainty and fear had gripped his seasoned crew. Peter Strand followed the captain on deck and confronted him.

Grasping the rail to avoid being tossed into the froth he shouted, "The crew have families! Are you considering them!"

Gazing into the maelstrom the captain remained silent.

"Three days ago you told me of your pending elopement," his first mate bellowed. "I was happy for you. I fear that day will never come to pass!"

Kriel retained a blank expression.

Strand persisted, "You've never been reckless enough to challenge such a storm. Can it be you're afraid of not returning in time to wed? If those are your thoughts Damon, I assure you you're future with Amanda will survive the extra day it takes to seek safe harbour!"

Turning away the captain struggled towards a row of buckets clattering from hooks.

Every hand was ordered on deck, "Have each take up a bucket and commence baling. We'll toss the spoils back in the face of the demon!"

As the Katy floundered Damon's eyes fixated on the ferocity of waves hurtling over the guardrail. Rain streamed from his hat as he heaved water back at the tempest in vain.

"All hands are on deck save the helmsman," Strand shouted disparagingly.

The path of the storm shifted abruptly. As the crew clamoured for buckets they were sideswiped by an enormous wave.

Someone screamed.

One of the crew toppled overboard and vanished in the swell. Abe Herman gripped the railing with one hand while the rest of him dangled precariously from the port bow. Struggling in his direction Damon grasped the midshipman's wrist. The boat dipped suddenly weakening his grip. The captain lost hold and watched in horror as his crewman plunged into the foaming abyss.

"Captain you have murdered your ship and crew!" Strand shouted.

"Silence!" Damon roared as the steamer righted itself momentarily.

"You selfish bastard," his first mate bellowed.

He turned to the remaining crew and appealed with outstretched arms. "See what your captain has done? Two men gone! We'll soon all be dead!"

He faced his superior, "I hope you're the next to go you son of ..."

At that instant a tsunami-sized wave slammed the starboard side tossing Strand over the rail before he could complete his sentence.

Another wave struck. Then another.

Hearing shouts and cries Damon peered through the hellish black water. The vessel foundered until the Katy went bottoms up.

Swallowed by the foam Kriel recalled Ephraim Brill's curse. Bubble balls ascended in narrow streams as he sought his doomed shipmates. Seconds later his mortal eyes closed forever.

Led to their destruction by an obsessed captain, a mariners bell tolled eleven times. The ritual was echoed with an incantation:

Graveyard women weep and wail
for the doomed crew who serviced Kriel,
benevolent deeds must be performed
to free their souls forevermore...

Word of a ghost spread along the byways and trails winding the lower lakes region. In stockyards, sawmills and farming communities there was talk of a spectre. The apparition had been witnessed by dozens of God-fearing folk not normally given to supernatural flights of fancy. The first sighting was reported by a fisherman and his two sons along the Erie shoreline east of Cleveland. Plying their nets aboard a tiny trawler the promise of a clear day appeared doubtful. Remnants of the previous night's storm lingered and moisture clung to Jimmy Johnson's garments like dew on grass. The morning catch had been a good one. The trough was filled with rainbow trout, perch, and bass. Docking at noon he and the lads secured the trawler and took a half-hour for lunch. The boys reached into their raincoats and pulled out sandwiches and biscuits mother had prepared the night before. Jimmy withdrew his and sat along the pier with his legs dangling over the edge. Seated on either side of their father, the boys commenced to devour lunch in the time it took Jimmy to take a single bite.

"Weather looks ominous lads," he remarked. "One last catch and we're done."

The boys nodded with their mouths full.

It was unusually quiet. Storm warnings had circulated forcing many to await more tolerable conditions. Jimmy's eyes swept the inlet and he caught sight of something on the surface of the water. The dark figure appeared to waver. Turning long enough to bring the sighting to the attention of his boys, the spectre was suddenly very near. Both lads stopped chewing and bore witness to the apparition. Water dripped from it's ragged garments as it stood silent upon the wharf. Strands of seaweed clung to it's frayed vestments. But for the orbs of it's eyes no features were visible beneath a tattered slicker hat. Abruptly, it was gone. For a long moment no one said a word. Instead, they stared at the planks where seaweed and lake water lingered.

"I say we call it a day," Jimmy resolved. "We have a good haul let's go home."

Nodding eagerly the boys clamoured to their feet.

Along that same inlet a short while later a violent storm erupted. Anyone unlucky enough to be on the water would have perished. Jimmy understood this and considered the visitation a warning. Arriving home earlier than usual a quiet prayer was said at supper. Nothing was mentioned to mother regarding the incident.

Several miles from the tiny settlement of Vermilion, Michael Evans and his wife Sarah operated a general store. Two years earlier Sarah had given birth to a baby boy. While the child played out front Michael was busy loading supplies into a wagon. Abruptly, three coarse looking men on horseback veered off the trail with their pistols drawn. Watching from the entrance Sarah dashed out and swept the child into her arms. Michael climbed from the wagon and approached the men. A ridge populated with birch and pine separated the store from the lake. Craggy rock formations were observed.

The bandit leader dismounted and said, "Cover me."

Wiping his face with his sleeve he said, "Who runs this place?"

"That would be me," Michael declared.

The man gestured toward some empty sacks, "I'm gonna follow you inside and watch you fill two bags with liquor and tobacco. Then you're gonna hand over your cash."

He nodded in the direction of Sarah and the child, "Refuse and something bad might happen."

Michael glanced at his wife then at the man, "Follow me."

He grabbed a pair of burlap sacks and entered the store. With a pistol at his back he approached the counter.

"Point me to the money," the outlaw barked.

Michael nodded toward a cash drawer and the thief reached in and pulled out whatever bills and coins were there.

"Now fill the sacks with them supplies and be quick about it."

Outside his confederates maintained watch of their surroundings. One was surveying the ridge and noticed someone or something observing them. He turned to his partner and gestured in that direction. Inexplicably, the thing appeared directly across the dusty byway.

"Can't be ....couldn't have moved that fast!" the outlaw stammered.

Lacerated rags draped the haunt. Beneath a chafe rain hat two yawning eyes were set within a black void. The lower torso remained undefined.

"Del!" the bandit shouted. "You'd best get out here!"

His words faded as the spectre appeared before the highwaymen and their neighing steeds. The panicked animals reared back violently dislodging both riders from their saddles. Gazing up from the dust with stunned expressions they watched their mounts bolt around a bend. Sarah clung to the baby, as one of the raiders scrambled to his feet and reached for his pistol. The outlaw spun about and was hoisted from the ground and propelled with unnatural force toward a stone wall. The other man scuttled for his discarded weapon and took aim at the thing.

Hearing shots the bandit leader charged from the store and felt his skull collide with that of his airborne accomplice hurled in his direction. He staggered backward in a shower of blood and stars but managed to retain his weapon. Taking aim he fired and observed the discharge produced no effect upon the miscreant. Shifting his aim towards the proprietor's wife and child; Michael ran from the store and the weapon was turned on him. About to pull the trigger the raider felt a chill course through him. Conscious long enough to register a ringing bell he collapsed in the dust. Dark clouds moved rapidly from the direction of the lake. In the diminished light the spectre motioned toward a coil of rope in the wagon. Micheal retrieved it as the entity faced the men sprawled along the ground. Before the law was summoned they would need securing. No binds were necessary for the bandit leader. His soul had departed this realm forever.

Abruptly, the apparition was gone.

Over the years similar occurrences were reported and locals were no longer skeptical. Deputies and doctors confirmed sightings. Manifestation's occurred wherever the innocent were at risk. Those who'd encountered the apparition expressed no fear with regards to their well-being. Gathered around kitchen tables they retold tales of the wraith - some were even true.

One story recounted two men who held up a bank in Loraine County, killing a clerk and bystander. They found themselves miles away dividing their bounty about a campfire. The plan was to make it to New York City and lose themselves among the fray. Firelight cast dancing shadows among the trees as their eyes fell upon the apparition. Levelling pistols they fired repeatedly to no avail. In what amounted to seconds they were overcome and strung upside down from separate trees. A day later their bug-ravaged bodies were cut down by loggers who'd come across the unconscious pair. The stolen money was recovered and the killers were turned over to a local Marshal. Still in shock they confessed their crimes. While being led away one kept blathering of an abomination.

Years passed and the entity reappeared time and again.

A storm swept the region and harsh winds pounded the brittle shoreline. Foam lapped the decayed boots of the spectre as it stood upon the water's edge. Raising it's orbs to the advancing onslaught lightning split the sky and Damon Kriel was bound away.

———————

FOURTEEN

Special Agent Theodore Marin of the Chicago Branch Office of the FBI was waiting inside one of O'Hare's bustling terminals as Lee Tondar entered the lobby. Marin was a soft-spoken man Lee had befriended years earlier, while both were assigned watch along the US/Canadian border by their respective agencies. Eventually, the newly created Office of Homeland Security relieved the pair of their duties and both were reassigned. No threats of consequence had been uncovered during their stint. A 'persons of interest' list had been compiled but nothing more. Roughly the same age both shared similar backgrounds, so it was no surprise they interacted well.

Toting a briefcase, the Ohio professor spotted his host and waved with his free hand and approached with his arm extended, "Thanks for seeing me Teddy."

"How was your flight?"

"The same. Where to from here?"

"Follow me."

The pair exited the terminal and a black, four-door Chrysler with tinted windows appeared out of nowhere. As they journeyed downtown Marin remarked, "The Burke family will receive Federal protection until the Evanston woman is apprehended and the nature of her disappearance is made clear."

"Has the family shed any light on the situation?"

"They're in the dark. The last to see Gillian Burke was the father-in-law. It was he who erroneously wound up with her phone. The device was turned over to the FBI and eventually SIGINT, which is when warning signals went up"

"How's the little girl and her father?"

"Worried."

They turned onto West Grand Avenue and entered an underground facility. Stopped by armed guards ID was presented. They departed the vehicle and the pair were scanned. Afterwards, an elevator was accessed and they began a rapid descent. The agent who'd accompanied them disembarked on a separate floor. At a lower-level the two men emerged and proceeded along a well-lit corridor. A security station appeared and Marin leaned into a monitor where his eyeball was scanned. Buzzed into a lush corridor lined with several doors, they drew up before the first where a sentry was posted.

"We're here to visit the Burke family," Marin informed him.

The guard peered at his badge and stepped aside to allow them entry. When they were within Lee observed a tidy, well-maintained living space with an attached kitchen and corridor. A television flickered with the volume low. Before it a girl lay stretched along the carpet doodling on a notepad.

"Hello Samantha," Marin said jovially. "What's ya drawing?"

"Not sure yet," the girl replied. "It started out a desert now it's outer space."

"Looks good!"

He turned to his companion, "This is a friend named Lee. He's a teacher."

The girl glanced up, "I have teachers 'cept it's summer. Won't see them 'till September."

Lee smiled. "Pleased to make your acquaintance, Samantha. You've got a good eye for illustration."

Steven Burke, husband of the missing woman and the girl's father emerged from down the hall. In his late twenties he appeared drawn and tired.

"Howdy Ted," he said approaching the FBI man. "I was working and didn't hear you enter."

Once greetings were exchanged Lee was introduced and they shook hands.

"How are you holding up?" Marin inquired.

"Same as last visit."

"And Tom?"

"He's asleep but may be up by now."

Steven sauntered over to the girl and sat cross-legged on the carpet beside her. Gazing at the drawing he said, "That's terrific sweetie what in heck is it?".

"Outer space."

Marin was about to ask if an interview might be arranged between both Burke men and his colleague. Abruptly, the sound of flushing water emanated from the far end of the hall.

"Dad's up," Steven remarked.

Marin asked if Lee might speak with him, "I know you've both been questioned upside down and sideways - but it won't take long."

"If it's okay with him it's fine by me."

Slippers were heard shuffling along the corridor and Tom Burke entered the living room. Approaching his seventy-first year he appeared quiet robust. When he noticed company he looped his housecoat belt tighter and crossed the floor to greet them.

"How goes it Tom?" Marin asked.

"Hangin' in there."

"Sorry if we've disturbed you."

"It's time I was up."

Introducing Burke senior to his companion Teddy asked if he might spare him a few moments. Tom shrugged and motioned their new guest into the kitchen. Seated across a table from one another Lee inquired how they were coping.

Tom glanced about the space, "As you see we're set up pretty good. This is probably the safest place on earth – or beneath it. It's a shame Sammy has no one but adults around. She ought to be playing in a backyard with friends."

Lee nodded and cleared his throat. "Did Gillian appear anxious when you parted ways at the airport?"

"Not anxious just sad. She'd dropped me off at O'Hare plenty of times and was always cheerful."

"Sad?"

"Sad and distracted. I remember receiving an unusually firm embrace from her before my departure, which was eventually delayed."

"I understand you make frequent trips to Chicago to be with your family. Would you consider your last visit routine? Was Gillian relaxed throughout the course of your stay?"

"She seemed in decent spirits until the morning of our departure."

"Can you elaborate?"

"The four of us spent a rainy Friday evening and most of Saturday together. Gillian was quiet but appeared content. At Sunday brunch she displayed the behavior I referred to. Steven felt it more keenly than I. Gillian had offered to drop me at the airport before heading back to town and her gym. Steve and Sammy had plans to visit a theme park."

Lee referred to his notes, "Having found yourself in possession of Gillian's phone you used the device on two occasions. One was a call to Steven who'd forgotten his own while at the theme park. You then contacted his landline and left a message. Am I correct?"

"Yes...two calls. I left messages both times."

Rising from his chair Lee offered his thanks.

Before departing he asked Sammy's dad if he'd mind joining him at the table. Steven rose from the floor and entered the kitchen. Once he was seated Lee began by asking the same questions he'd posed to his father - minus the airport queries.

"All seemed fine until Sunday morning," the younger Burke responded. "I expressed concern and Gillian assured me everything was okay, she added it was that time of the month."

The FBI had already taken Steven's statements. Lee took a different approach and inquired about Gillian's pastimes. He was informed about the rigorous exercise program she'd immersed herself in over the years.

"We followed a routine," Steven acknowledged. "Gillian took care of Sammy, dressed her, fed her, walked her to school and retrieved her in the afternoon. During weekdays from ten am until two in the afternoon she worked out at the gym – she's a fitness freak. Meantime, I busied myself in the study maintaining deadlines. I gave the FBI the name of my wife's fitness club. They followed up and confirmed most of what I'm telling you."

"Any family associations and recreations?"

"My brother and his wife visit occasionally, otherwise we rarely have company except for dad. Regrettably, we don't interact much with our neighbours except for cordial waves from the driveway. For recreation we go to the movies. In summer we visit Lincoln Park or the harbour. From time to time we eat out. When dad's in town he might spend a Saturday evening with Samantha, allowing Gillian and myself an opportunity to head downtown for a drink and some music. Things were fine until the Sunday of my wife's disappearance."

He lowered his head and remained silent.

"May I ask your brother's name?"

"Carson. He lives in St. Louis not far from dad."

Lee rose and placed his hand on the young man's shoulder, "No more questions son. Thank you."

It was nearly one pm when the professor joined agent Marin by the door leading into the corridor. Bidding Samantha goodbye they thanked her father and Tom and took their leave. As various checkpoints were cleared, they refrained from speaking until they were seated in the rear of the Chrysler they'd arrived in. As the driver made for the airport Lee turned to his companion, "Your assessment of the Burke family was spot on, Ted. They're totally in the dark."

"It's not just my assessment Lee its the Bureau's."

Eventually, the driver drew alongside a curb nearest Lee's departure terminal. As he exited the car Marin followed. Clasping his friend's hand he said, "I'll be in touch if there's news."

"Thanks again Teddy."

Marin reentered the vehicle and departed. Meanwhile, Lee proceeded towards the proper loading gate. Thirty minutes later as his flight gained altitude he pondered the Chicago visit. He peered over the rim of his glasses at the blank pages of his notebook. Abruptly, the vibrator on his phone rumbled. Leaning back he withdrew the device and he peered at caller display. It was the NSA, Director of Operations and deemed urgent.

———————

From behind a leafy evergreen adjacent to the condominium entrance a rapid blur sliced the darkness. Seconds later a pebble the size of a marble struck the door frame. Another let loose with more force leaving a nick in the glass. A middle-aged concierge emerged from the lobby clutching a flashlight. He advanced several steps then paused to take in his surroundings. Stealthily, the stone-thrower crept up from behind and stuck the barrel of a gun into the watchman's spinal cord.

"Utter a sound I shall not hesitate," a voice whispered. "Turn casually about and reenter the lobby."

The guard did as instructed.

Once inside the voice continued, "You shall accompany me in the elevator and we will exit the ninth floor together. My weapon is fitted with a silencer."

Despite his fear the guard kept his wits and they entered the elevator. The doors closed and he noticed his towering escort wore shades, a baseball cap and a black windbreaker. Once they stopped the man said, "Apartment 912 move!"

Straddling the corridor they paused along the right.

The intruder stood to one side of the door and whispered, "Knock. When the occupant responds tell her she has received a telegram."

Following instructions the concierge rapped. Seconds later a female voice called out from behind the peephole, "What is it Gerard?"

"A letter ma'am. "

As the door opened Gerard was thrust inside. The assailant followed and shoved him against a wall, "Quiet or you will leave in a bag."

The startled woman was about to scream when the man lunged forward and clasped a gloved hand over her mouth. "That goes for you too."

He reached into his pocket and tossed a piece of plastic on the floor.

"Into the bathroom both of you!"

Gerard followed the frightened woman down the hall. The intruder frisked the watchman and confiscated his phone. The occupant wore a housecoat over her slip and insisted she had nothing on her person. She was manhandled regardless.

"I'll be close by should you attempt to leave," the stranger informed them.

He shut them in and sprinted toward the entrance. Placing his ear against the door he slipped silently into the corridor. Casually, he made his way towards the emergency stairwell.

Listening for movement outside the bathroom door Gerard emerged after roughly ten minutes confinement. He made a sweep of the unit and returned to find the distraught resident seated on the rim of the bathtub. Informed the intruder had fled Gerard requested use of her phone. Fetching it from the bedroom she passed it over and Gerard entered 911 and spoke into the receiver, "This is Security at Lantern Heights Condominium. There's been an armed breach in one of the units. Please send someone I'll be in the lobby."

Gerard returned the phone and noticed Mrs. Tondar staring at the article their assailant had tossed on the floor. The watchman withdrew a handkerchief, carefully retrieving it he discovered it was a severed security pass. Turning the laminated card over he peered at a photograph. The occupant approached and glanced at the image. Her eyes widened and she gasped.

The professor guided the Volkswagen into it's allocated spot before Sentinel Hall. Glancing in the mirror, he observed his pallid reflection before departing the vehicle. He paused at the foot of the steps and noticed fog had accumulated. The late afternoon air was moist as he laboured up toward the lobby doors. A buzzer sounded and he entered the hall and gazed vacantly at the museum interior.

Leaning into the security booth exchange window Corporal Soo welcomed her boss back. She noticed his melancholy demeanour, "I thought you'd be heading straight home following your trip?"

"That was the plan."

"Is something wrong professor?"

He cleared his throat, "On the flight back from Chicago I received word a close friend was murdered. The young man was once my assistant here at the Institute."

The smile on Sasha's face vanished, "I'm sorry."

Lee nodded solemnly.

"Do the authorities know who's responsible?"

"Evidently not. The body was discovered nearby his vehicle in the underground car-park where he resided. He'd been shot twice."

The security chief remained silent.

Changing topics he said, "I was supposed to meet with Jesse tomorrow. If he's present I'd prefer to speak with him now."

"I'll contact the IRI," Sasha offered.

Pressing an in-house connection she awaited a response, "He doesn't appear to be downstairs?"

The young man had been requested to park behind Hillgram Hall and Sasha studied the appropriate monitor. Focusing on the split-screen she said, "The fog has compromised a number of cameras. Allow me to check on foot, Mr. Carlton may be out for a jog."

"Thank you Sasha."

She donned her jacket and exited the booth. Lee took her place and sat before a row of monitors. Scanning the images he could barely make out his security chief as she entered the courtyard. He rubbed his temples and closed his eyes. News of Stuart's murder kept repeating in his mind and he was concerned for others he'd involved. Sasha and her team were highly trained specialists. Jesse, on the other hand was hastily recruited. Despite his physical prowess it was necessary they discuss this new development.

Sasha found herself peering into an impenetrable fog. She proceeded toward the theatre and glimpsed the blurred form of someone between the Residence and Commons buildings. Thinking it might be Jesse she strode in that direction. Drawing up beneath the glass-enclosed corridor linking both buildings, the area appeared deserted.

Up ahead a male voice chuckled!

The laughter was muffled and the tread of approaching footsteps was heard. Sasha reached for her gun and moved off the path. Listening intently the footfall was in sudden retreat. She advanced toward the playhouse parking lot and noticed it devoid of vehicles and human beings. The yawning chasm of Falls Valley was between herself and town. Starting back she observed words scribbled in chalk upon the Commons Building. Moving closer she read:

WE'LL MEET AGAIN, I KNOW WHERE, I KNOW WHEN
YET I KNOW WE'LL MEET AGAIN SOME STORMY DAY!

Turning rapidly about she surveyed her surroundings. In her haste she hadn't noticed the scrawl. The fog was slowly lifting as she made for Sentinel Hall with her weapon gripped tightly. Remounting the steps, the sound of an approaching automobile was heard and she noticed the faint outline of Jesse's Chevrolet, as it turned onto Abbot Lane. It drew to a sudden standstill, reversed itself, and entered the drive encircling the playhouse. Sasha reentered the Hall and found the professor within the security station gazing at the floor.

"Mr. Carlton just arrived," she reported. "He's parking behind the theatre."

Her boss thanked her and departed the booth.

The security chief hesitated, "Following your meeting professor, I wonder if I might have a word with you. It concerns campus security."

"Of course," he replied. "I'd like to discuss the matter myself. Let's meet in my office once your replacement arrives. My talk with Jesse will have concluded by then."

"Thank you," she replied as he made for the stairwell.

———————————

Doubts continued to plague Jesse Carlton as he secured his vehicle behind Hillgram Hall. He opened the trunk and withdrew several bags containing a variety of bargain basement items. Articles included second-hand leather boots, pullovers, fabrics, sewing materials and accessories. He chose to enter their secret chamber the old fashioned way - through the front door. Striding the courtyard path toward Sentinel Hall, the heavy twin doors unlocked automatically at the top of the steps. Jesse entered the lobby and waved acknowledgement to the Corporal, who nodded back solemnly from within the security station. He strode toward the stairwell and she observed the bags he toted. Inside his quarters he deposited his purchases on top of the bed and noticed 'Legends of the Lakes' still open on the pillow.

A cough was heard from the room next door.

"Jesse?"

"In my quarters," the young man called out.

"Hope I'm not intruding?" queried the professor as he approached.

"Not at all. I was in town choosing materials for the disguise you requested."

"Can you spare a few moments in my office?"

"Certainly."

When Jesse entered he sat opposite the older man and noticed his pale complexion.

"I have some disturbing news," Lee stated outright.

The young man braced himself.

"A close associate of mine was murdered last night in Baltimore. He'd been employed as an encryption analyst with SIGINT."

"I'm sorry."

Lee nodded.

"How did it happen?"

The professor exhaled and explained the body was discovered in a parking garage beneath the victim's building.

"An NSA official informed me as I was returning from Chicago. I notified the father a few hours ago. He lives in Ithaca, New York. The pair were never really close - he took it hard nonetheless."

"Was your friend involved in aspect's of the case we're working on?"

"Yes!" the older man stated unequivocally.

"His name was Stuart Tuppins," Lee resumed. "He was a pupil at this Institute and became my assistant in much the same manner you have - but in a different capacity. Stu was a brilliant communication analyst. Subsequently, he was scooped up by the Signals Intelligence Division. Prior to entering their ranks he'd worked out of this station nearly three years."

The thought occasioned the professor to briefly smile.

"After Stu was transferred we remained in close contact. Dorothy and I would visit as would he. Recently, he revealed something which shed light on the terror file we're investigating. Feeds are relayed to UCOMA outposts by way of SIGINT. You recall me saying portions of those updates were withheld from this station. Stu became aware of the oversight and brought the matter to my attention. Need-to-know aspects are part of national security - but why we were signalled out and not the other stations raised questions. Stuart was assigned to forward updates to all U-stations. 'Feeds' as they're called inform UCOMA personnel what to look for regarding satellite relays, rogue signals, space debris and other data. Stu was able to create a composite rendering of the deleted material and managed to forward me the results. He stuck his neck out now he's dead."

Jesse observed the professor's pained expression and lowered his gaze.

"You should know your own life may be in jeopardy," Lee added sombrely.

Jesse remained unfazed.

"If you wish to withdraw I'll hold nothing against you," Lee reiterated. "You have your whole life to consider. Whoever had Stuart killed is aware of this investigation and those associated with it."

The determined expression on his recruit's face told the professor all he needed to know.

"Thank you son."

Redirecting his thoughts from his loss Jesse said, "Are you able to discuss the Chicago trip and the missing woman?"

"There's been no word from her," Lee offered. "The FBI still has the family in protective custody. There's a charming daughter, a distraught husband and a father-in-law, each concerned about the well-being of their loved one. The latter gentleman is the individual who handed the woman's phone over to the FBI, arousing everyone's suspicion. Her family insists she would never involve herself in anything nefarious. However, they're in the dark. A friend with the Chicago Branch Office has agreed to keep me posted."

It was Lee's turn to pivot. "You mentioned you'd done some shopping?"

"I have," his apprentice replied trying to sound upbeat. "I'm attempting to concoct a disguise out of rags and hand-me-downs."

"Sounds promising."

"If suitable it fits the description of something which haunted this region more than a century ago."

The professor wasn't discouraged in the least.

"I'm still not certain what you expect?" Jesse persisted.

"I'm not certain either," Lee remarked. "We'll know when we see it?"

"Invisible would be nice."

For the first time Lee smiled. His melancholy returned and he withdrew a phone and passed it across the desk.

"This will enable you to establish secure contact with either myself or Corporal Soo. Press number one I respond. Number two informs Sasha you're in touch. Once you arrive in Indiana, it's imperative to remember Penther and his followers are a deadly lot. Strangers are perceived as enemies."

Acknowledging the implications Jesse reiterated his concern, "How will disguising myself quell the inherent danger? It's to my advantage to move about as inconspicuously as possible?"

Lee rubbed the bridge of his nose, "By revealing yourself you place loved ones and the investigation at risk. There are advantages to operating incognito. Adversaries are more likely to reveal information to phantasms. We have little else at our disposal at this late stage."

Jesse nodded skeptically, "I'll work on it.

"I'm sure your choice will be appropriate."

"When do you need to view the results?"

"Tomorrow."

The young man concealed his surprise.

"You'll be departing for Indiana in roughly forty-eight hours," Lee informed him. "Any questions?"

"Several dozen but they can wait."

Lee reached for his phone and contacted the Corporal, inquiring if her replacement had arrived.

"Good," he responded. "I'll see you now."

Jesse rose and the professor glanced up, "I wish I could say there's method to my madness. I'm uncertain myself."

"I'm sorry about your friend."

"Thank you."

As the young man prepared to depart there was a rapping on the door.

"Enter."

The security chief strode in and glared at Jesse.

Puzzled by the abrupt tension Lee remarked, "There's a few matters I need to discuss with the Corporal. Afterwards, I'm going home to my wife. We'll talk in the morning son."

"I'll be here."

Ray Pearson awoke in the musty gloom and realized with sickening clarity he was still a prisoner. Forcing himself into an upright position he glanced about and wondered how long he'd been incarcerated? The dream he'd been having was vivid. It was a Saturday at his sweetheart's apartment. Bored with television she switched it off and they made love instead.

The debilitated lab technician was grateful he could still perceive pleasure.

A sleeping bag was spread along the concrete floor and the pungent air reeked. He adjusted his eyes and observed the faint outlines of objects around him. A ribbon of light was visible beneath the door and he rose unsteadily. It's faint luminosity allowed him to locate the wall switch and he cringed as an overhead bulb flared to life. Glancing about his tiny cell, a grey metal door, secured on the outside featured prominently. Baking soda, tissue, a litter bag and tray were nearby. In the corner was a water jug and some recycled plastic utensils. Once a day a frozen microwaved dinner was brought to him, delivered by thugs posing as plant supervisors. The lukewarm offering was devoured instantly.

The worst of his jailer's was the daytime watchman, a man named Cal Wicker. Spewing derogatory insults regarding Ray's heritage, he'd open the door and kick the food tray inside.

"Give a savage an inch ya take a mile, dontcha."

Afterwards, the lock would catch and his footsteps would recede along the corridor.

The previous day his food was delivered by Wicker's less antagonistic colleague, Samuel Train. He at least made certain the meal was properly heated and would add an apple or banana. At the prisoner's behest Train would remove the waste.

The lump on Ray's skull had regressed following the shipping room assault. Taking stock of his situation he considered a means of escape. A small ventilation grid was embedded along the lower portion of the door. When the stench overwhelmed him he'd place his nostrils up close and suck in gusts of air.

Three thoughts consumed him during his captivity. The first was his sweetheart Gloria Mayorga. Next was finding a way back to her. Lastly, if he managed his escape, he intended to bring the authorities down on those who'd accosted and imprisoned him.

He considered Gloria's likely reaction to his disappearance. Had she alerted the cops?

Moistening his parched lips he moved the sleeping bag closer and switched off the overhead. With his face near the grid he heard the familiar whine of diesel's along the overpass. The telltale sound indicated precisely where he was. He surmised it was dark outside but couldn't be certain? Occasionally, garbled voices echoed along the corridor. Ray could've easily removed the grid with a swift sidekick, however his arm would only extend part way up the opposite side of the door.

Pondering the zealous security measures installed by Jackson Bell, it was clear he'd stumbled on a criminal operation. If the authorities weren't concerned with his well-being he certainly was. The only way out of this dungeon was to take down one of his jailers and escape unseen.

––––––––––––

Breaching the apartment complex posed no serious challenge. His launch point involved a visitor's parking area situated along the rear of the building. Beneath a row of trees, a recycling bin and several automobiles obliterated the view from nosy neighbours. Resident's gained underground parking access via the street and his position was obscured from cameras.

As darkness fell he gazed toward the unit in question. Breaches of this kind were considered routine in his temple days. Slipping on leather gloves he shimmed to a vacant second-story balcony in mere seconds. He'd cased the ten-story Toledo complex the previous evening and established a point of entry. All units were furnished with balconies making the task easier. His target was a female residing on the third floor along the rear. Glancing up he sprang with cat-like agility and gripped the ledge of the overhead balcony. Hoisting himself over the railing he positioned himself alongside a sliding screen door and peered inside. A living room was observed and he heard the sound of running water from the kitchen.

Perfect.

Yanking a ski mask over his features the intruder withdrew a dagger from it's sheath. The screen door was secured and he sliced a straight line along the metal frame. Slipping his wrist through the incision he released a latch-lock. A woman in her forties emerged from the kitchen and froze in her tracks. The stranger stood watching her through the sight holes of a pullover toque. He tossed something at her feet and brought his forefinger to his lips in a gesture of silence. Retreating hastily he slipped over the guardrail and vanished.

––––––––––––

FIFTEEN

In the change room of the gym Jesse frequented he found himself in possession of two phones. One was his own the second had been issued by Lee Tondar. That particular device was encrypted and untraceable; it linked him with both the professor and his security chief. Having been up until the wee hours making amendments to the ghoulish disguise commissioned by the professor, Jesse arrived at the gym early and spent time working out with Danny Owa. For two years the Japanese architect and martial arts practitioner paired himself opposite the muscled Grissim student. Both shared a passion for keeping in shape. At thirty-one Danny was of average height and followed a unique exercise agenda. Specializing in both karate and jujitsu application, he'd been seeking a worthy opponent to spar with. When Jesse arrived in the Falls he enrolled at the gym almost immediately. While giving the bags a thrashing Danny noticed the young man's agility. He inquired if Jesse would be interested in learning some of the finer aspects of martial arts procedure; adding he needed someone with Jesse's ability to enhance his own performance. The young man could hardly refuse. Based on their respective schedules session's lasted an hour and occurred three mornings weekly. Rather than simply jousting full-fledged rounds were the order of the day. Over time Jesse became proficient in the far-Eastern art of hand-to-hand combat. For his part Danny kept his moves honed and benefited greatly from the pairing.

After tousling with the master Jesse headed for the shower. Abruptly, the phone Lee issued him vibrated.

"Yes?"

"If it's not inconvenient I'd like to meet somewhere other than Grissim for our meeting," the familiar voice requested.

"Where do you suggest?"

"Pete's Deli, it's on Rosalee Street."

"I know the place. I'm at the gym and can be there in twenty minutes."

"Fine."

Showering quickly Jesse made for his locker and a fresh change of clothes. He set off on foot and arrived at the eatery a short time later. Lee was sighted in a rear booth and he took the seat opposite his. The older man appeared as forlorn as he'd been the previous day.

"Sorry for moving you about like a chess piece," he murmured.

"Quite alright I was nearby."

The cook hollered from behind the counter, "Something for you my friend?"

"Just orange juice thanks."

Lee withdrew an envelope and pushed it toward his companion.

"After meeting with both you and Sasha last evening I received a frantic phone call from Dorothy. She stated an intruder had gained access into our home by threatening the night watchman. When I arrived I was informed the assailant wore shades and had a cap pulled over his brow. He left a calling card."

The professor indicated the envelope, "Take a look."

Jesse withdrew a single item and observed a severed security pass. Beneath the NSA logo the individual's photograph was highlighted along with a portion of a name.

"That is one half of the National Security Agency pass belonging to my former assistant Stuart Tuppins. Whoever killed him took it and left it on the floor of our apartment in the presence of my wife."

The older man leaned in, "The perpetrator of these crimes is firing warning shots."

Jesse's beverage arrived and they sat in silence. He placed the damaged card in the envelope and handed it back.

"Naturally the police were notified?"

"They were," acknowledged the professor. "I took the liberty of retaining the mutilated card as evidence and consider the incident a breach of national security. I'm taking Dorothy to stay with friends in Cleveland this afternoon. I'll return in the morning and we'll finalize plans for your Indiana sojourn. You can display whatever you've devised to conceal yourself at that time."

As the meeting concluded Jesse was asked if he'd noticed anyone lurking about the campus grounds?"

The recruit shook his head.

"For now I suggest we make use of the tunnel passageway while entering or leaving Control."

The pseudonym had been contrived by Stuart rather than the more cumbersome International Retrieval Installation.

"We need to keep light off ourselves," Lee added.

Was the situation so dire the professor felt obliged to enter his office by way of a tunnel?

"You're certain you wish to do that?"

Lee slid out from his seat, "We're being watched."

With that the meeting was over.

The professor squared up and departed the deli. Observing protocol Jesse took his leave moments later. Lee drove the short distance home to retrieve his wife; meanwhile his protege returned to the gym to fetch his car and started back toward Grissim. He parked behind the theatre and entered the passageway, wondering how the professor would adapt to his own ruling.

The remainder of that day was spent making further adjustments to his disguise. A full-length mirror was propped against his door as the design took shape. If he wasn't so skeptical he might have spooked himself. Tweaking for hours on end, he cut, altered and stripped until his stomach growled in protestation. Other than oatmeal and orange juice he hadn't ingested a thing all day. He entered the kitchen and withdrew pasta and brought water to a boil. Diced vegetables were stirred in along with tomato sauce and Parmesan cheese, and a passable meal was conceived. Once the dishes were rinsed he returned to his room and slipped on the disguise. His creation bore a striking resemblance to the doomed ship's captain imagined in the Kriel story. Tugging back the mask, he yanked the frayed garment's over his shoulders and draped them from a coat rack. The chafed pants were folded and placed aside and he removed the leather boots.

Energizing his laptop he accessed the latest information pertaining to domestic terror in the United States. While reviewing the material his eyelids grew heavy. It was nearly midnight when he succumbed to the sandman. With Captain Kriel hanging from the rack to keep him company, he sprawled along the bed. He'd been asleep roughly twenty minutes when his personal phone chimed. Reaching over he glanced at call-display and noticed it was Emma.

"Hey Ma..."

"Jesse," she said breathlessly. "A stranger entered my apartment moments ago by way of the balcony!"

Hearing her words he sat bolt upright.

"The man wore a ski mask and carried a knife," she continued. "He left the way he entered."

"You're certain he's gone!"

"Yes."

"Are you hurt?"

"No."

"Have you notified the police?"

"They're on the way."

"Are the doors secured?"

"Naturally."

"And the windows?"

"Yes."

The professor's account of Dorothy's ordeal flashed in Jesse's mind.

"Is there anything you remember about the individual?"

"Only that he tossed something on the floor before leaving."

There was stunned silence at Jesse's end.

"What was it?"

"It appears to be part of someone's ID card."

"Can you make out a name?"

"Several letters are missing but what's left says 'uppins' with a double p."

Jesse's brain was racing.

"Mother listen calling the police was the right thing. Naturally, I want you to tell them everything. But please don't mention or show them the severed ID."

Silence registered on the other end. "For heaven's sake Jesse why not?"

"Because I know someone who may be able to identify the intruder. He's an agent with a branch of the government looking into a similar incident."

"But that would be withholding evidence."

Pacing his room Jesse persisted. "It's important Ma. Give them a description of the intruder, but for the time being keep the pass a secret. I'll be at your place at seven am to take you to Gramps. You'll be safe there."

"Gramps!

"Trust me."

"Will you be staying with us?"

"No. I'll be out of town for a few days. Contact your workplace and tell them somethings come up."

Reeling from her son's instructions Emma responded firmly, "I won't mention the card, Jesse. But I expect an explanation regarding all of this."

"Of course," he responded. "You're certain you're okay!"

"I'll be fine I'm not expecting another home invasion this evening."
Jesse heard her doorbell ring.
"I'd better go, Jess. The police are here."
"Check the peephole first. I'll be there at seven sharp."
When his mother signed off Jesse slumped on the bed and threw an arm over his brow. Emma's space had been invaded in a manner identical to that of Dorothy Tondar. Both incident's were inextricably linked. Frustration turned to anger and his gaze fell on the grim disguise draped upon the coat rack. He intended to see his mother safely across the border, then hand the other half of Stuart's pass over to Lee. Seated on the edge of his bed he ran his palm over the foreboding rags. Devoid of uncertainty a sense of mission permeated his being.

Drifting off the scent of lake water entered his nostrils.

A forlorn wind moaned along the Yokum Trail. Above the treetops the moon vanished and reappeared again. Seated on rear deck of his lodge Penther gazed into the murky depths of Rykles Clearing. With their endeavour nearing completion, renewed interest by the FBI increased his paranoia. Special Agent Jake Gill was dead. Due to the proximity of his demise occupants of the lodge were natural suspects. Agents would be swarming over his property like maggots. Until recently the Feds were satisfied he'd disavowed involvement with so-called hate groups and anti-government militia's. When he travelled he claimed it was to visit lawyers or accountants in Fort Wayne and Detroit respectively. Over time the authorities suspended watch, choosing instead to monitor his phone, letters and email. Surveillance would resume in earnest now.

Agent Gill sought a missing colleague and several former Isolationist Army members. Evidently, three remained unaccounted for. It was later revealed he'd taken it upon himself to question both he an Aldo.

The snores of his bodyguard rumbled from the depths of the lodge. The doberman's were whining and Penther observed the empty chow bowls strewn about the ground. Preparations for the final drop-off across the state line were in order. He'd intended to depart that morning, however the trip was delayed on account of his being interviewed regarding Gill's death. He contacted Kristy and informed the pompous middleman, the Bureau had taken a renewed interest in

Rykles Clearing. Inquiries had been made regarding individual's presently installed within the Detroit compound.

Visit's to that city followed a pattern. Aldo would drive his boss to Fort Wayne; once there Penther would catch a city bus to one of several car-rental outlets. Using phony ID provided by Sir a vehicle would be secured. Arriving in Detroit he'd conduct banking transactions at various branches in the suburbs. Afterwards, a meeting with Jackson Bell would occur. Despite Penther's skill at evading tails - keeping below the radar was proving more difficult. Agent Gill likely contacted car rental franchises and interviewed dozens of bank employees. His suspicion's may have been discussed with others before his tragic passing. In order for Electron Era to remain operational these final few days, cash needed to be delivered to Jackson Bell. Last minute amenities were also required. Phones with reprogrammed codes would be issued. Directive's between Besserer and Sir regarding status of the weapon needed to be exchanged.

Penther was fed-up making bank rounds and glad their effort's were nearing completion. Bi-monthly pick-ups and drop-offs had been the life-blood of their venture. For a year he'd been stoking the fiscal fires of their undertaking. Gazing past the slumbering dogs his eyes traced a path among the weeds and dry patches. The fortified bunker seemed a fitting site to host the detonator allowing release of the AC.

The old man would've been proud.

Rising promptly at five-thirty am Jesse showered and dressed. He forged the clandestine tunnel and accessed his vehicle. Guiding it onto Interstate 90 his headlights pierced the darkness for nearly an hour. Daylight appeared by the time he crossed the Toledo city limits. Parking several blocks from his mother's residence he backtracked on foot. Buzzing entry he found Emma inside the third floor unit packed and ready to depart. Moments later they exited the rear door of the complex and arrived at the car in short order. Jesse placed mother's suitcase in the trunk and she entered the passenger side. The rear-view mirror revealed no prying eyes or waiting automobiles.

Considering Emma's ordeal the night before, she appeared more at ease than her son and the drive north went smoothly. Jesse mentioned a similar assault had occurred to a woman in Lantern Falls and implied the two incident's might be more than coincidental. The nameless government agent he'd referred to on the phone only added to the mystery.

As promised Emma handed over the effaced ID card and assured Jesse no utterance of it was made to the police. Due to the early hour only a twenty minute delay was experienced at the Ambassador Bridge. Arriving in Windsor the young man explained to the residence staff, Mr. Carlton's daughter would be spending a week perhaps longer with her father. The woman in charge was on friendly terms with her and had no problem with the arrangement. Having accumulated a backlog of sick days, Emma booked the necessary time off work. Before departing Jesse requested no one be admitted to visit his mother or grandfather, unless he was consulted first. He apologized for the harried circumstances and embraced Emma.

"I'll call each night."

She placed a hand on his cheek and studied his face, "Promise me you'll take care."

"I will," he assured her.

Jesse suggested she say nothing to Gramps regarding the previous evening's encounter.

———————————

Lee Tondar signalled right and swung onto the campus grounds. He entered a driveway and followed it around to the rear of the theatre. His security chief had informed him someone was stalking the Institute grounds. Evidently, the sightings began to occur around the time Jesse Carlton took up residence there. Shunning the thought Lee pressed lightly on the brakes and came to a standstill. The dashboard clock registered 12:30 pm and he realized he was late meeting with his recruit. That morning he and Dorothy shared breakfast with their Cleveland hosts, Minnie and Bud Edsel. The Edsel's had been neighbours back in their Maryland days. Bud was a government bureaucrat while Minnie stayed home to raise three children, who now had kids of their own. As old times were recalled, Lee related the frightful encounter Dorothy experienced inside their home. Their host's were stunned and insisted she remain their guest for as long as she desired. Lee spent the night with his wife in a spare bedroom. Following breakfast Bud left for the office, while Lee remained an extra hour. Bidding Minnie farewell he was escorted to the door by his wife. The pair embraced and kissed each other gently.

"I'll call at bedtime," he whispered before making his departure.

Leaving the car behind Hillgram Hall the professor gripped his briefcase. The restless lake waters reflected the grey rolling skies overhead. A freighter drifted east towards the Erie canal pursued by gulls circling the laden vessel. With a good night's rest under his belt, Lee felt revitalized knowing Dorothy was safe.

At the edge of the parking area he stepped over a guard-rail and disappeared behind the foliage. A granite wall loomed high above his shoulders as he straddled the ridge His pass was withdrawn and he entered the man-made cavern. Faint lighting fixtures revealed moist walls and mouldy crevices. The chamber vanished into shadow and a dim glow was detected up ahead.

A footstep echoed.

"That you Sasha?"

The dank air encumbered him like a veil and a scraping heel was heard .

"Who's there!"

Something moved to his rear and he swung about. Observing nothing he turned again and observed the form of something ominous and imposing materialize from the gloom. The ragged entity bore luminous eyes which glowed within a Stygian face. The towering apparition stood between himself and the tunnel's end.

"That you Jesse?"

No response.

Abruptly the thing advanced.

"Christ!" muttered the spy-chief staggering backward.

"Greetings schoolmaster!" it rasped.

Lee managed to stand his ground.

A hoarse cackle reverberated throughout the labyrinth, "You're late!"

A reticent pause ensued.

"Marvellous!" Lee spouted." Truly magnificent!"

"Do you think so?" Jesse replied in his natural speaking voice.

"I'm overwhelmed..."

Observing the older man through the satin fibres of Kriel's eyes, Lee appeared more invigorated than he'd been during recent encounters. Jesse was relieved no heart attack resulted during the surprise summit.

The professor cleared his throat and gestured toward the steps. He suggested they adjourn upstairs to continue their conversation.

"A cold beer would be nice," Jesse remarked.

"Precisely what I had in mind."

Departing the tunnel and storage room they regrouped in the kitchen. Marvelling at Jesse's creation Lee fetched two cans of beer from the fridge and placed them on the table. The young man tugged back the nondescript face and attached slicker hat, allowing it to drape down his back. He stood with his hands on his knees and drew a deep breath. The dress-rehearsal proved a success. A number of costume adjustment's needed amending in areas related to sight-lines and breathing, otherwise he was able to move about without impediment.

Not knowing where to start Lee motioned the recruit to a chair.

Jesse placed his frayed gloves on the table and sat down. Before Lee could utter a word he was informed of the home invasion which took place in Jesse's mother's apartment. The young man withdrew the mutilated ID card from his rags and watched the blood drain from the professor's face.

"This was left at the scene."

He handed over the missing half of Stuart Tuppins NSA pass, "I requested mother withhold the evidence, insisting it might be of use to someone investigating a similar incident. She hedged but conceded."

Lee turned the laminated plastic over and stared at it solemnly. It was the second time in the last fifteen minutes he was left speechless

"They know you're involved," he finally murmured. "Finding your mother was simply a matter of cross-referencing license plates. Fear is most effective when used against those dearest to us."

Jesse sipped beer and remained silent.

"Where's your mother now?"

"I took her to stay with her father in Windsor."

"I'm sorry Jesse."

The sad irony existing between both men was compelling. Each sought safe-harbour for those who mattered most.

Lee asked his apprentice how the masterful disguise had come about?

"Simply," the young man replied. "Shredded materials sewn onto a thin dark pullover."

Raising part of the fabric he pointed out a variety of mends and alterations.

"About the midriff you'll notice a weathered belt," he indicated a loop bearing several pouches. "Lacerated black pants are worn over dyed long-johns."

"Which are also black," Lee speculated.

"Precisely."

The roll-call continued, "Leather boots cost next to nothing at a used bargain store. Most challenging of all was the mask. Naturally, ventilation is paramount and more than two hundred pinholes are set about the nostril and mouth areas. Silken fibres make up the eyes. An ultra-fine Asian fabric actually absorbs light allowing them to glow in the dark.

"The tunnel bore that out," Lee remarked. "What about the voice?"

Jesse looked thoughtful. "A mixture of New England aristocracy mixed with the harsh vocal timbre of a highwayman."

"I'm not sure I follow?"

Running a hand through his tousled hair Jesse explained, "On the written page my character is silent I had no idea how he might sound. Having settled on the rasp I paired it with the priggish tone of a sanctimonious preacher."

Sweat ran down his back forcing the partially clad recruit to yank the upper portion of his outfit over his broad shoulders. When that was accomplished he reached for his beer and asked if they might discuss Indiana.

"Of course," Lee replied. "There's several items I'd like you to include as part of your arsenal. If you'll follow me."

Rising from the table they entered Control.

"You mentioned your disguise is based upon a ghost story?"

"An oral account transcribed by a local scholar," Jesse asserted. "It concerns the captain of a merchant vessel who returns as a ghost, after having led his crew to their doom navigating a storm. His spirit roams the Lower Lakes undertaking righteous deeds, in hopes of freeing the souls led to their deaths under his stewardship. The captain's name is Damon Kriel."

"Kriel?"

"That's correct."

"Then that shall be your code-name. Do you object?"

Jesse thought for a moment, "As long as Damon doesn't."

"Is Lake Erie part of the setting?"

"Very much. The narrative was first published in the 1930's and subsequently reissued in a recent anthology of ghost stories."

"Do you own a copy?"

"I have the new edition in my quarters You're welcome to it."

"Thank you."

Jesse was guided towards a metal cabinet. The professor accessed the lock and slid open the top drawer. Withdrawing a device the size of a dime he turned it between his fingers.

"This rudimentary item has been utilized in spy fiction for decades. It's hardly a secret. By tossing it on the ground it's chemical content mixes with oxygen, creating plumes of odourless smoke. I retained quantities of these working undercover; they came in handy on more than one occasion. Deception devices or 'dee-dees' as they're called appear low-tech by today's standards. However, they're easily stored and effective should one wish to conceal oneself or distract an adversary. With Penther's dogs prowling about you could do worse."

Jesse considered his limited knowledge of dogs and doberman pincers in particular.

From the same drawer Lee withdrew a transparent mechanism no larger than a match head. "This is a listening device," he stated. "It's an advanced piece of technology developed by a Japanese firm for use in the war on terror. Barely noticeable to the naked eye it has a range of roughly ninety miles using cell tower's for relay. I know of only three agencies with access to these. Most have been denied usage due to privacy right's issues. Those rulings are being contested before an Intelligence review board. Don't ask how I acquired them."

"I won't."

He dropped the article into the young man's palm, "Weightless wouldn't you agree?"

"Can't feel a thing."

"To activate place it between your forefinger and thumb and apply pressure."

Jesse did as instructed.

"Good. It's ready to be placed. Press again and it's ceases recording. If an opportunity to bug Penther's lodgings arises we might learn something. Files indicate he conducts routine sweeps of his home and property. Be selective where such devices are planted."

He removed a sealed jar of white powder along with a zip-lock sandwich bag and placed them on a counter-top surface.

"Looks like cocaine?" Jesse remarked.

"Far more illegal," the professor conceded. "It's actually a concoction of sedatives which could knock out a grizzly bear."

"You're suggesting I defend myself by tossing powder at someone?"

"If it's a hostile animal it may be an option."

The doberman's reentered Jesse's consciousness.

"To address your point more concisely," Lee continued. "The formula works best when administered in food or a beverage. By inserting the substance into a water bowl or sandwich bag containing raw meat, it's debilitating effect is instantaneous. The powder is non-lethal. However, try not to breathe it or get any in your eyes."

"How long does the sleep effect last?"

"An hour possibly longer"

Lee crossed toward a locker along the opposite wall. He unfastened a padlock and beckoned the young man closer. Inside a trio of vests draped from hangers. Retrieving one he passed it to his companion.

"Weightless," the professor remarked. "It's the latest in Kevlar protection. One hardly feels burdened. Drug cartels and rogue states of every description vie desperately to acquire jackets such as these."

"That's encouraging."

Jesse slipped the vest over his upper body and was astonished at it's lightness of being. It fit easily about his robust frame. Physically, he needed to remain unencumbered and agile. Stretching his limbs he strode the length of Control and discovered his movements were not impeded in the least.

"You certain this thing can stop a bullet?"

"High calibre weapons at point-blank range might pose a problem," Lee admitted. "And you're at risk in the head and abdomen areas. However, from a distance your upper-body vitals are protected."

Jesse nodded and handed back the vest.

"It's yours son."

"Thank you I'll work it into the mix."

"You'll be issued an ultra-sensitive recording devise and compact binoculars," the professor added securing the locker and fondling his remote. "

The wall slid aside and they entered his office.

"How long did Kriel await my arrival in the passage?" Lee inquired.

"Perhaps twenty minutes," Jesse responded.

"Your car wasn't behind the theatre?"

"Because I wanted to surprise you. It's parked by the lake."

"Ah."

The pair drew up seats and Lee passed an envelope across the desk.

"Enclosed are the necessary funds you'll need in Indiana. There's a total of fifty twenty-dollar bills, you'll pay cash for everything and retain receipts. This should cover car rental, lodgings, meals and related expenses. Once Penther's movements have been observed and available intelligence gathered - you'll return to Lantern Falls. Four or five days should suffice. Between now and your departure you'll review the flash-drive brief I've included and commit details to memory. At roughly seven tomorrow evening a taxi will be summoned to the Edgewater Drive entrance. You'll instruct the driver to deliver you to a car-rental franchise here in town. From there you'll journey to Ellery approximately sixty miles west of Fort Wayne, Indiana. The sun will have set by the time you reach the Emerald City Motor Motel. It's located along the fringes of town and excepts cash payment. With forged ID you'll register under an assumed name. GPS coordinates are included on the flash-drive. Penther resides at the end of a gravel stretch known as the Yokum Trail. His lodge is on property local's refer to as Rykles Clearing. He's known to townsfolk so you might make subtle inquiries. Be mindful of motion detectors and heat-sensors surrounding the Clearing, and make certain you update me every twenty-four hours."

Lowering his glasses the older man peered over the rim, "Questions?"

"None."

Lee nodded and pointed to a backpack. "There's an assortment of listening devices, dee-dees and several dosages of sleeping powder stored within. The recorder and binoculars are included."

Clutching the Kevlar vest Jesse retrieved the knapsack.

"Have a safe journey and beware of dogs."

Taras was certain Nickolas Dante would come looking for his Candle. Ms. Ellstone's phone had been confiscated making contact impossible - not that she would've responded anyway. Nicky would've been forced to consider one of two outcomes - either Kari had dumped him or some misfortune had occurred. Taras hacked into Ms. Ellstone's devise and discovered it devoid of caller data.

At present the former SIAG sleeper and library researcher was aboard a Boeing 737, winging his way toward Boston in preparation for the drive north. If Kari fled she likely discovered he wasn't who he claimed to be. He'd predicted things would sour and she'd become mired in abandonment. Regardless, Nicholas Dante welcomed her upstate where he appeared considerate for the first few weeks. During a bout of intoxication he may have revealed things he shouldn't have.

Had the SIAG been aware of his new life as a double-agent; the wise-men would've crucified him for leaving them in the dark.

He was his own handler now.

Where the SIAG were concerned he chose to be reckless - with the Face he was a perfect professional.

He'd been meaning to inform Kari he was never a foreign correspondent and there was no book. It was never too late.

Landing at Logan International Airport he retrieved his suitcase and rented an automobile. Two hours later a sign indicated Halton's Cove.

———————

SIXTEEN

Taras drove south with the window down allowing the breeze to ruffle her hair. Pondering Ms. Ellstone's fate, she hoped the girl had taken flight from her false lover. The sheriff in Halton's Cove would've discovered her trussed-up inside her absentee boyfriend's home, the victim of an apparent robbery. If her advice was heeded, Kari would've informed the lawman the house was breached by an intruder with his face concealed. Nicholas Dante was certain to seek her in Cambridge where they first became acquainted. A more likely destination was her parent's estate. Taras intended to conceal herself on the grounds to ensure the young woman's safety. In doing so she hoped to dispatch the treacherous wretch and conclude her assignment.

Stopping along the shoulder Taras withdrew her phone. A search on the family was conducted and she discovered they resided in the posh neighbourhood of Forest Hill Gardens - across from mid-town Manhattan. Scouring the internet she managed to obtain an address. It was revealed in a New York Times gardening supplement highlighting the floral splendours of that prosperous community. Kari would seek sanctuary there. Relying on GPS assistance she arrived in Queens, New York and eventually discovered the address. Casing the Ellstone's opulent mansion properties were wired to fend off trespassers. Despite the precaution Ulsar would have little difficulty avoiding security deterrents.

Taras returned her leased vehicle to a dealership in the city. She squared up and hailed a cab to another rental agency. Going through the motions she drove off in a black Lincoln MKZ, which would meld nicely with the exclusive trappings of Forest Hills, and ensure decent surveillance. Guiding the glitzy car through afternoon traffic she booked a suite at a midtown hotel. Contacting room service and ordered chicken salad and juice. Afterwards, she sprawled along the bed and slept for nine hours. Next day she showered and did laundry in the bathtub. Exercising on the carpeted floor she ate lunch beside the fifth floor window. That evening as the sun began it's descent over the Hudson river, she attired herself appropriately and made her way down to the car-park. She drove off toward the serene grandeur of Forest Hill Gardens and drew the Lincoln alongside the curb a safe distance from the Ellstone residence. Foliage from a spreading tree shielded her vehicle from the glow of a streetlamp and surveillance was initiated. Barring an occasional passing car the neighbourhood was tranquil. An elderly couple strode by with a puppy on a leash. Ten minutes later they reappeared along the opposite sidewalk. Taras was focused upon rooftops, patios, hedgerows and parked cars. If a sniper needed a lair there were no shortages.

During the third hour of her watch a flurry of activity occurred. An unmarked police car drew up before the Ellstone mansion and a young woman was whisked up the walkway by two plainclothesmen. Gathered about the entrance talk with the homeowners ensued - making ripe pickings for a sniper with a scope and a clear shot. Taras avoided detection and was scrutinizing homes opposite the Ellstone residence. She slid beneath the dash as the policemen retreated along a palatial walkway, minus the girl. Meanwhile, the house occupants had withdrawn.

With Kari's whereabouts confirmed Taras maintained watch. By midnight the estate was shrouded in darkness. Her leg muscles were beginning to cramp and she glanced in the rear-view mirror and considered Ulsar. His most formidable asset was eluding detection. SIAG females endured similar training in avoiding obstacles and she decided a walk was in order. Securing the vehicle she crossed the street and heard a neighbour's dog bark.

Wearing a dark pullover, matching slacks and Doc Marten boots, Taras diverted from the sidewalk and sprinted between two homes. Armed with a pair of daggers she moved swiftly toward the rear of Kari's family property. Sticking with concrete walkways to avoid sensors she advanced cautiously. The extended backyard was separated by a hedgerow she breathed deeply.

If Ulsar was present he'd outwitted all obstacles save for the woman riding his coattails.

A scraping sound echoed from the direction of the house; the view was partially obstructed by a garden shed. Taras stuck close to the hedge and advanced in a crouched position. She parted some branches and observed a figure scaling the wall toward a second story balcony. The rope and hooks deployed appeared familiar. If she delayed longer he'd be afforded time to enter. With a dagger between her teeth she bolted across the sod to within kill range. Ulsar heard her approach and spun about in time to witness a woman raise a knife. The blade whizzed by his throat missing him by a hair and he sprang from his perch. Rolling twice on the ground, the knife-thrower charged at him triggering an alarm. Both were in the lurch as flood lights sprang to life and wailing shattered the night.

The SIAG had finally caught up with him - this was bound to complicate matters.

His intended assassin had vanished! With plans to confront Kari scuttled, he sprinted the length of the yard in pursuit of his would-be killer. He dodged an immense garden, a swimming pool, deck chairs and a barbecue. A high fence divided the property from a wooded glen. Ulsar grasped the limb of a nearby tree and hoisted himself among the boughs. He got his bearings and was able to detect which direction his attacker fled. Voices were heard trailing a police dog and the alarms were silenced. With a search underway, he was forced to act quickly and withdrew a semi-automatic. Shimmying the sturdy tree limb he jumped along the opposite side of the fence. Guided by instinct he entered the glen and was promptly tackled about the ankles. Landing on the ground he retained grip of the gun, however he was unable to use it with a dagger at his throat.

"Release the weapon," hissed his opponent.

"A woman," he responded breathlessly. "The wise men are getting wiser."

"You've got five seconds to tell me who controls you?"

"Where shall I begin?" replied her captive. "At least allow... "

As the words left his mouth his elbow flew up striking Taras in the jaw. Tossing her aside he scrambled to his feet and lost grip of the gun. Attempting to retrieve it, she got there first and pointed it at his skull.

"You're fast," he remarked.

Maintaining a bead on him she observed the zippered pockets lining his jacket. His phone might reveal answers.

"Toss your jacket over!" she demanded.

She felt a perplexing familiarity as she glared at him.

With the gun levelled his way Ulsar sighed and did as requested. She caught the jacket mid-air and ordered him to keep his arms raised.

"We're working towards the same end?" he remarked calmly.

Taras released a mirthless laugh while rummaging his jacket. A phone was retrieved and she secured it in an attached belt pouch.

"I'll keep this," she muttered. "You won't be needing it where you're going."

Wavering flashlights zigzagged among the trees. Kristy took advantage of the distraction and lunged at his adversary. Grasping her neck he forced the gun from her grip and whispered, "I'll retrieve my phone then it's forever adieu."

He gripped her belt and convulsed violently as her knee pummelled his groin. Slipping from his grasp she bolted among the trees. Kristy cursed and retrieved his jacket and took off in pursuit. In wake of their encounter several policemen and a leashed dog entered the tiny clearing. Meantime, Taras dodged overhanging limbs following a barely discernible trail. She stumbled over a protruding tree root and rebounded. Ditching the path she found herself ankle deep in a shallow creek.

Had Ulsar been taken into custody?

The outline of several home estates were sighted through the trees.

Abruptly, something splashed behind her.

The sun had set along the outskirts of Ellery, Indiana as Jesse drew up before the Emerald City Motor Motel. He switched off the engine and entered the front office, where a middle-aged woman was seated behind the counter. Giving a false name supported by matching ID, he signed a ledger. Cash was exchanged for four nights occupancy and Jesse was handed a receipt. The attendant moistened her thumb and added up the twenties. Surrounded by plywood walls and Nation Enquirer tabloids, a pair of vending machines were nearby the door. The linoleum floor was uneven and the air reeked of cigarette smoke and perfume. The woman cleared her throat and launched into an oft-recited speech.

"Pop and snacks are available from noon 'till midnight," she nodded toward the machines. "This is a family establishment so no loud music or orgies. Otherwise enjoy."

Jesse smiled as she dropped a room key in his palm. He thanked her and departed the office, retrieving a pair of suitcases from his rented car. Along a battered walkway, he paused before a bright orange door with number 21 attached to it. Inserting the key he peered into the gloom. A switch was discovered and an overhead light sprang to life. Twin beds and an ancient dresser were observed, a bulky television with rabbit ears lay on it's surface. He placed his luggage aside and took a seat on the nearest bed. Bouncing several times he frowned and rose quickly.

The journey from Lantern Falls had been pleasurable and Jesse sang to himself. The Indiana scenery was breathtaking while daylight prevailed. Surrounded by lush farmland interspersed with silver silos and acreages of corn; quaint villages looked as if they'd been canvassed in oil by Renaissance painters. Sparkling lakes and rivers reflected the setting sun as he drove in a westerly direction.

His suitcases were placed on the bed furthest from the door. From one he withdrew pyjamas and bathroom accessories. He showered and changed then searched for a television remote. It was found it in a dresser drawer along with Gidions Bible. The TV provided reception for a single station out of Indianapolis. Viewers were informed temperate conditions would remain in place for coming week.

Earlier that evening Jesse dined at a truck stop and he was stuffed. Sprawled along the bed he reviewed his itinerary. Ellery would be explored first thing in the morning. When it grew dark surveillance would commence at Rykles Clearing.

Moments later the young man was fast asleep.

Sunlight streamed through a crack in the thick brown curtains the following morning. Jesse rose and splashed water on his face; he dressed then departed room 21. His rental was parked beneath a tree at the edge of the lot, rather than before his unit. Setting off for town he sported a work shirt, jeans and runners. He parked nearby a restaurant on Main Street and entered the sleepy establishment. A waitress approached and he ordered toast and coffee and accepted a refill before squaring up. Outside shopkeepers were unlocking their doors. He entered a sporting goods store called Tannenbaum's and perused a row of long-guns. Apart from a lone staffer he was the sole customer.

"May I assist you," the clerk inquired.

"I'm seeking info regarding hunting permits in the region," Jesse replied. "This being a sporting goods outlet I thought I'd try here?"

"I'm not a hunter myself," responded the employee. "There are several gunsmiths in town who could answer that question better than I."

"Can you direct me?"

The young man thought a moment. "Ellery Sports is probably best. They service a lot of game hunters. Their on Fielding Avenue."

"Thanks I'll check it out."

Before departing Jesse said, "A friend used to hunt along a stretch called the Yokum Trail. He mentioned a Clearing?"

"That would be Rykles Clearing," the attendant replied. "My dad used to hunt jackrabbits up there. They closed the place and tossed the landowner in prison for keeping bad company. He was eventually released. No one goes there anymore."

Jesse smiled. "I'll give Ellery Sports a try. Thanks again."

Outside he considered the exchange and received directions to Fielding Avenue. Strolling east he entered a store fronted with a large display window. Seated behind a cash register counter an older couple greeted him with friendly smiles. The woman returned to her crossword, while the man sipped coffee and focused on a newspaper. Jesse browsed long-gun displays and paused before an accessory rack. He picked out a Tovatec penlight and glanced at the price. The proprietor looked up, "Anything I can help you with?"

"Possibly," Jesse replied carrying the penlight to the counter.

"I understand there's some good hunting near a place called Rykles Clearing?"

The woman glanced up from her crossword and frowned. Her partner scratched his chin and pondered the question.

"The place no longer receives commercial game hunters," he replied. "It was shut down several years ago when the landowner went to prison. Following his release he kept the grounds closed off to everyone, including sportsmen who'd patronized his rifle range and hunting trails. Stuff happened to some of the young lads who hung out up there."

"That so?"

"A few started railing against the government calling 'em commies and stuff. William Penther, the property owner was brought up on conspiracy charges and served time. Prosecutors said he was behind an attack on a federal building, but no one could prove it. I'd avoid that neck of the woods. Its a shame 'cause it's dense up there - good for game."

He paused to blow on his coffee, "Several years back a local chap took a bullet in the head in them woods. First it was ruled a suicide, but the trajectory of the missile made that impossible. Then it became a hunting accident but no one else was present at the time of the shooting. So they simply forgot about it."

"Did you know the man?"

"Nope but folks say there was dirt between he and Mr. Penther."

Jesse made a mental note and withdrew his wallet to make the purchase. He thanked the couple and started for the door.

"There's some tourist info on the rack. Help yourself."

"Thanks I will."

Jesse picked out several brochures and departed.

On the sidewalk he withdrew his phone and contacted Emma. He inquired after her and assured her he was fine. Relieved to hear things were stable they chatted for several minutes. Jesse extended greetings to Gramps and promised to touch base the following day.

Jesse's appetite had restored itself and he entered the diner he'd frequented earlier and ordered a BLT and juice. During his walking tour he noticed two taverns within blocks of one another. Deciding to make inquiries at both he finished his meal and left a tip with payment. Gaffer's Inn was first up. The licensed establishment included a bar and offered cheap draft beer. Tables were spread about and patron's tossed darts, played pool or just sat there. Beneath a muted TV screen George Jones lamented from the depths of a Wurlitzer jukebox. A contingent of middle-aged woman sat among the men. Jesse approached the bar and ordered a pint of house ale. He tipped the bartender generously and slid a Chicago tabloid towards himself. Reviewing a column of baseball stats he shook his head. Within earshot of the bartender he muttered, "White Sox foiled. Go figure."

The barman turned to face him, "Money's on Atlanta this season count on it."

"I'll drink to that," agreed the new arrival.

In an attempt to extend the conversation Jesse mentioned he was seeking hunting options in the region.

"A friend suggested Rykles Clearing and said there was an abundance of game. Do you know the place?"

The bartender glanced about the room then stared back, "It's private property off limits to everyone."

It was the third time in as many hours that information had been imparted to him. Evidently, the bartender was uncomfortable with the subject. He said nothing more and strode to the opposite end of the bar.

Jesse finished his beverage and departed the establishment. Arriving at the second watering hole aptly called the Oasis, he entered the restroom and re-emerged moments later. Patrons sat huddled over liquid lunches, while Nashville recording artist's provided a soundtrack. Unlike the former establishment there was no bar so Jesse found an available table. Seated next to him a group of men and women regaled each other with anecdotes triggering near-hysteria among themselves. Opposite them a young man sat alone. Hunkered over a half-empty jug he sported a t-shirt, baseball cap and work boots. His tanned appearance suggested he laboured outdoors.

A waitress appeared and took Jesse's order then returned moments later. He handed her a bill and insisted she keep the change. A patron beckoned and she was gone. Sipping beer he overheard snippets of conversation at the next table. Husbands, wives, workplace and sports made up their agenda. One of the participant's leaned backwards and teetered precariously on the rear legs of his chair. He would've landed on Jesse had he not caught himself in time.

"Sorry 'bout that fella," he remarked.

Jesse said he hadn't noticed a thing.

Taking the initiative he requested direction's to a back road called the Yokum Trail. The man frowned and said maybe one of his friends could help?

"I know the place," intervened the lone gentleman seated nearby. "Need directions?"

"Sure thing."

The labourer rose and drew up a chair and introduced himself as Pete.

Jesse gave a false name and said he had a good memory for directions. When his guest had laid out the best route between town and the trail road, Jesse launched into his hunting trip fiction and said a relation mentioned the ample game in those parts.

Pete frowned, "I had a roofer buddy named Drew were pretty tight for a while. He started hanging around Rykles Clearing with a guy named William Penther. Ever heard of him?"

Jesse said he hadn't.

Hauling back on his glass Pete continued, "Anyway, Drew got involved in some bad shit with this Penther dude. Eventually, he and the rest of 'em got popped by the Feds on a conspiracy rap. The judge tossed the lot of them in prison. After his release Drew came to live with his brother here in town. I was at a red light and noticed him crossing the street. I honked and called to him but he didn't respond. Moving with the flow I lost sight of him."

Pete seemed eager to chat and Jesse was happy to lend an ear.

"Anyway, next I hear is Drew vanishes - no one has heard from him."

Lowering his voice Pete leaned in, "Some say he joined the Klan and this Penther guy is their great wizard or whatever. Perhaps he wanted out and others didn't see it that way."

He shrugged and downed a mouthful of beer.

"Does his brother still live in Ellery?"

"Don't have a clue. I never knew him."

"Was there a last name?"

"Don't know that neither."

Pete could offer little else with regards to Rykles Clearing or William Penther.

Changing topics Jesse asked him about his job as a roofer. Informed the work was seasonal, Pete was currently contracted four days a week at a new subdivision going up south of town. The rest of his time was spent in the bar. The two chatted for half an hour after which time, Jesse politely excused himself. He hailed the waitress and purchased a jug for Pete and thanked him for the directions.

An exit sign pointed the way outdoors and Jesse emerged into sunlight. He returned to his car and stopped at a pizzeria and ordered a small assorted to go. Arriving at the motel shortly after two pm he slept for several hours. As dusk fell he unpacked Kriel's disguise and spread the articles along the bed. The upper body rags and lacerated pants would appear more foreboding when paired with the boots. Jesse decided the legging's were appropriate for someone working in building restoration. Subsequently, his trouser cuffs remained outside the boots when not depicting Kriel. A windbreaker concealed his frayed upper body attire. For all appearances he might have been stripping walls or laying tile. Alterations to the Captain's face, or lack thereof, were were undertaken recently affording better ventilation about the nose and mouth areas.

As night set in Jesse dined on cold pizza washed down with water. Afterwards, he slipped on the Kevlar vest and placed the grim apparel over top - along with the head bearing the slicker hat. He stepped back from the mirror to take in as much form as possible. The boots made him appear taller than his 6'1" frame. Relatively satisfied he drew back the mask and secured keys, fake ID and some bills into a pouch and departed unit 21. Turning the engine over he drew from the motel and drove west along a deserted stretch. The speed limit was observed until a sign indicated the Yokum Trail. The road extended north and came to an end at Rykles Clearing. Jesse made the turn and contemplated where to stash the car once he neared his destination. A rabbit darted across the pavement and vanished among the trees. Abruptly, an open space appeared along his right. The faint outlines of a stable and farmhouse were observed on a strip of grazing land. His headlights illuminated a 'FOR SALE' sign hanging from a fence post.

The clearing faded from view and the paved surface of the road turned to gravel. The sound of crickets intensified and the woods closed in around him. With his attention focused he manoeuvred the twists and bends.

The needle wavered well below the quarter-tank mark. He'd forgotten to refuel and prayed there was enough gas to make it back to town. Further north the remnants of a driveway was observed and he brought the car to a standstill. Shifting into reverse he guided the vehicle into the concealed spot. A dwelling once existed at the end of the weed infested drive; a rusted mailbox confirmed it was no longer there. Jesse killed the engine and tossed his windbreaker on the passenger seat. Despite his ambivalence the disguise felt oddly reassuring here in the wilderness. Exiting the vehicle he tucked his pants into the boots and drew the mask over his face. Mindful of dogs and alarms he gripped the newly purchased penlight and set off for Rykles Clearing.

———————————

Lee contacted his wife at the Edsel's home in Cleveland and found her rested and relaxed. She'd caught up on some reading and found Minnie's companionship reassuring. They chatted for several minutes and Lee said he missed her and promised to call the following evening. Presently, he was downloading information sent to him securely by Brandon DeLong, a longtime associate with the Detroit Police Department. The contents dealt with factories and warehouses; leased or purchased within the greater Detroit area over the past two years. Additional reports highlighted questionable occurrences involving those facilities over the same period. If a weapon of mass destruction was being developed, Lee reasoned a sizable quantity of hydro-electricity would be necessary to advance the undertaking. By the same measure the weapon would need to be assembled within semi-large confines. Lee compiled a dossier on more than a dozen such operations.

On a separate quest he began digging into files detailing the Joint Chiefs of Staff, along with their senior-most advisers - most of whom he knew by reputation. Profiles of the Defence Secretary and his top aides were scrutinized; as were their position's on a range of sensitive issues. He reviewed Senate and Congressional bills, supported or rejected by these same individuals. The list included many leading figures in American politics; each of whom held enough sway to influence America's security agenda.

Plodding through the material was an arduous task. Ultimately, Lee hoped to shed light on the rogue figure he suspected of undermining the nation. He spent hours cross-referencing and double-checking records. Sighing, he switched off the computer and prepared a light meal in the kitchen. He considered his protege and the potentially hazardous situation he'd entered into. Awaiting an update he remained concerned for Jesse's safety.

His study of industrial Detroit resumed, the list was whittled down to three sites where conceivably a WMD might be developed. One entry which caught his eye was a printing firm leasing an entire warehouse. Oddly the building remained empty. Another involved a manufacturer specializing in trinkets for holiday occasions such as Christmas and Halloween. Files indicated the owner had been charged for employing illegals. The offence seemed inconsequential, nevertheless Lee felt compelled to look into it. A third site of interest was a small electronics firm calling itself Electron Era. The plant had been in operation less than a year and maintained roughly a dozen employees. One had gone missing a week earlier and had yet to be accounted for. The worker's girlfriend expressed her concern to the police.

Lee rose from his swivel chair and stifled a cough. He crossed the floor and took a seat before an orbital retrieving monitor. Observing the readings he jotted notes down then sauntered off to bed. The following morning he departed for Detroit.

Wheeling about as her attacker leapt forward, Taras tumbled backwards into the shallow creek with her assailant's hands about her throat. As the life was being chocked from her, she clawed the depths and clasped the slimy surface of a flat stone. Bringing it up full force alongside Ulsar's skull, he let out a moan and his grip loosened. Pushing him aside she reached for her dagger, intending to put an end to the tiresome contest. A bullet whizzed between her and the felled traitor and another struck the bark of a nearby tree. Danger was also present in the form of a canine leading the posse. Taras bolted in the opposite direction leaving her bloodied foe as another shot rang out.

Wiping blood from his head Kristy rose unsteadily and staggered into the brush. His would-be killer had outwitted him at every turn and had possession of his phone. His well-honed skills had been had been irreparably impaired with wine, women and western food. Stumbling through the thicket his head throbbed and body ached. To his rear he heard barking and the voices of his pursuers. Veering off the beaten path he limped in the direction of several blurred structures resembling homes. The windows were mostly dark and he paused to view the layout. He hobbled closely along a wooden fence dividing two properties hoping to evade sensors. Stopping to catch his breath, he found himself at the end of someones driveway in the same neighbourhood. It was still dark and lawns surrounding him glowed by lamplight. From his back pocket he removed tissue and wiped blood and sweat from his head wound. Nobody was watching as he slunk through the shadows toward the car he'd parked, several blocks from the goddamn Ellstone residence.

———————

SEVENTEEN

The disguised operative was aware of his vulnerability. His limited knowledge of alarms and sensors prevented him feeling overly confident. Evidently, Penther had installed security devices along upper regions of the Yokum Trail and Clearing - there was also the small matter of the dobermans. Unlike security apparatuses dogs could scent blood. Overhead, the moon was obscured by clouds leaving the outline of the road concealed. Aiming the penlight, Kriel ducked among trees encircling Penther's property and arrived alongside the Clearing, where the lodge was sighted. Distance was maintained as the ragged figure positioned himself at a safe angle.

Abruptly, the sound of clanging bells and barks erupted. Withdrawing binoculars the watcher focused on the tethered beasts reacting to an occurrence within the lodge. The back door flew open and someone charged on the deck gasping and waving his arms. The alarm was silenced as billows of smoke streamed from the doorway.

"Focus on the task at hand you mindless cockroach!" the man sputtered. "If you've been drinking I'll bust your ass."

"Ain't drunk nothin'," a voice responded. "I was fryin' sausages next thing the pan's on fire."

The arm-waver was sucking in mouthfuls of air. Based on photographs he resembled William Penther. He traipsed a pair of steps onto the grounds and hollered, "Feed the scorched meat to the dogs and open the windows for Christ's sake!"

Emerging from the screen door a second individual appeared.

Kriel withdrew the diminutive recorder and turned the receiver up a notch. The new arrival was a gaunt, dishevelled individual. He strode to the railing and hurled meat toward the ravenous animals. As the snacks were devoured the haggard observer recalled images acknowledging the sausage-thrower as Aldo Dopple.

Penther remounted the steps and stood at the railing as his assistant drew up next to him.

From a distance of roughly hundred meter's the powerful receiver would capture what passed between them.

"We're out of sausages," Aldo remarked. "Want some ham?"

"I'll eat in the morning once you've dropped me off in Fort Wayne," muttered his boss. Facing his subordinate he added, "You'll be in charge until I return tomorrow evening. If the Feds come snooping don't get cocky. Allow them to go about their business. Say nothing understand."

Aldo nodded and stuck a cigarette between his lips.

"And don't pack anything!" the lodge owner continued. "We don't want to give the impression we're hightailing it. You got chores do 'em. Walk the dogs about the Clearing and make certain the security system remains operational."

"How come I don't get to drive you to Detroit?" Dopple argued. "I'm your bodyguard."

"You're trained to be more than an enforcer!" Penther admonished. "It's crucial the property is guarded while I'm away. If the authorities demand entry into the bunker, you tell them I maintain sole access. Got that!"

Aldo nodded acknowledgement and glanced away.

Tangles of dewy leaves reflected the reemerging moon appearing like a thousand glistening eyes. Among the constellation two ghastly orbs gazed unblinkingly from the abundant foliage.

Penther informed his lieutenant he was hitting the sack and reiterated his intention to be on the road by eight next morning. Aldo tossed his cigarette over the railing and said he'd be ready.

Nothing more would be revealed that evening and the onlooker switched off the recorder and turned to depart. A branch snapped beneath his boot and the dogs reacted instantly! Aldo responded by dashing into the lodge and reemerging with a semi-automatic. Penther was at his heels as they hustled down the steps and released the dogs. Grasping both leashes with his left hand Aldo was dragged towards the source of their indignation. He released Boot and watched the doberman sprint across the dark terrain in the direction of the trees.

While this transpired Kriel withdrew deeper in the woods and was able to pick-up his former trail. The snarling beast reached the timberline and hesitated. Moments later Club drew alongside followed by Dopple. Both dog's appeared reticent to enter the thicket. This was puzzling as the two had been groomed in these woods. Probing the underbrush with a laser-scope fixed to the barrel of his gun, Dopple noticed nothing unusual. Along his rear the dog's began to whimper and cower from something they neither saw nor heard. Aldo decided a bear or wolf had riled the pair and re-secured Boot to his leash. Their reigns dug into his flesh as the fearful animal's hastened back toward the lodge. Observing their rapid withdrawal Penther frowned and gazed toward the trees.

Once again the fleeting moon drifted behind lowering clouds. A surge of kinetic energy appeared to propel the wraith from harm's way. In what seemed mere seconds Kriel was back at the car, yanking his face astern in order to breath. Sucking air he withdrew a key and entered the vehicle. The gloves were removed and Jesse wiped the sweat from his neck and brow.

Moments later he was still trembling.

Uncertain if the dog's were responsible for his rattled nerves, Jesse was unable to remember his return to the vehicle. Penther and his sidekick were recalled, along with the branch snapping underfoot - the rest was a blur. Chastising himself Jesse swore to be more observant. If the doberman's had been any closer the outcome might have been different. The matter was further pondered and he decided a jolt of adrenaline likely accelerated his flight.

Donning the windbreaker and cap he tugged the leggings from his boots. Turning the engine over the car inched onto the Yokum Trail and he started back toward the Emerald City Motor Motel.

An hour before the sun rose Taras instructed the cab driver to pull into the service centre along their right. With her hair in a ponytail she stepped from the vehicle and requested he wait. Entering the restroom she sponge-mopped the muddy residue from her damp pullover and slacks. Having rinsed her face she entered an attached convenience store and retrieved tissue. She placed on sunglasses from a rack and peered into a tiny mirror. Adding them to her purchase, she returned to the taxi and entreated the driver to backtrack, expressing a desire to take a second look at a piece of property in Forest Hills. The driver nodded and guided the car in the direction from which they'd just come. While making their way Taras pondered her rented Lincoln. Due to the recent upheaval, the vehicle had likely been impounded as evidence involving a home invasion. The cab turned onto the street where the Ellstone's resided and she noticed her rental had indeed been towed. An unmarked police car was parked before the estate, suggesting the cops had initiated a protective presence over their well-to-do charges. For all Taras knew they might still be combing the wooded glen, for whomever had breached the grounds. Leaning back on the rear seat she wondered again if Ulsar had been taken into custody. While taking flight she'd seen him rise from the creek clasping his head.

The impounded car was of little consequence, there was no paper trail leading back. Registration for the vehicle was made under a fictitious name, with everything paid for in cash.

Ellstone manor receded from view and the taxi departed the ritzy enclave. Merging with Queen's Boulevard Taras felt utterly exhausted. She barely flinched as a police cruiser swept by with it's siren wailing. The Ulsar encounter was considered and she shook her head. The combat skills her opponent displayed were sluggish and his agility greatly diminished – yet he persisted.

Her assignment should have concluded by now!

Requesting the driver drop her off before her hotel he was generously tipped. She entered her suite and ran a bath, tending to a variety of cuts and scrapes sustained in battle. Her clothes were laundered and she hung them to dry along the shower rail. Afterwards, she stretched along the bed and fell fast asleep. Awaking mid-afternoon she splashed cold water on her face. Room-service was contacted and she requested Greek salad and the New York Times. Seated by the window overlooking the East River, she switched on a local news channel and heard no reference to a home invasion in Forest Hills, and was grateful.

Ulsar's phone suddenly entered her mind!

Fetching it from her belt purse Taras discovered the device contained a single item of relevancy. The LCD screen indicated an incoming call registered *after* the phone was in her possession. An Indiana area-code was identified and she returned the call. After three rings a male voice responded. The man sounded bland and peevish.

"You're supposed to be here Kristy!"

Taras hesitated, "Who am I addressing?"

A *click* was heard.

Clearly, hers was not the voice the person expected.

Kristy...?

By revealing a name the individual confirmed a connection existed between himself and someone called Kristy. Perhaps an additional code-name had entered the mix.

Ulsar as Dante as Kristy.

Attired in a summer dress and sandals Taras placed the laundered clothes inside her suitcase. Gazing in the mirror she adjusted her shades and departed the suite. At lobby level she exited the elevator and checked out at the front desk. It was muggy outdoors when she entered the rear seat of a cab. Merging with the flow, the driver was directed towards Madison Avenue and West 52nd Street. Her assignment was proving a costly one. By conducting transactions at a variety of banks, it was possible to withdraw a substantial amount without drawing a large sum from just one. Manhattan was probably the safest place on earth to make withdrawals. Smaller communities harboured suspicion when dealing with strangers and large figures. Retaining the taxi Taras completed transactions at four different branches. Afterwards, the driver was instructed to conduct her to yet another car-rental dealership; delivered to a Hertz agency he tipped his hat at the liberal tip she provided. In a display area Taras acquainted herself with what was available. Subsequently, she drove off with the acquisition and found an internet cafe. Avoiding use of her laptop and phone, she booked a table-top computer. Ice-tea was purchased and she uploaded a map of Indiana and studied it closely. Remaining online she made a print-out and jotted down information. Once she arrived in the Hoosier State she intended to contact the phone company servicing Kristy's phone listing. Naturally, the number she'd contacted would've been deleted - yet it might be possible to recover the person's identity by lodging a harassment complaint.

Forced again to extract information she hoped she wasn't pressing her luck.

Outside the National Security Agency in Fort Meade, Maryland, temperatures soared to a sweltering 28 degrees before it was even noon. Within a conference room on an upper floor soft lighting meshed with panelled walls, lining three sides of the space. Due to the sensitive nature of the meeting about to convene, the panoramic window making up the fourth wall had its blinds shuttered. Framed photographs of infamous spymasters known to no one except practitioners of the trade, lined one wall. In the corridor, uniformed guards stood at attention alongside doors leading into the air-cooled chamber, where a conference table took centre stage.

Around it members of the bipartisan, Intelligence Review Committee were assembled. On one side sat Royston Adams, Director of the Universal Communications Agency (UCOMA). Next to him was Stanton Carter, second in command of Military Intelligence at the Pentagon; along with FBI Assistant Director, Catherine Levine. Across from them Nelson Seymour-Johns, Deputy Director of the CIA was seated. Jeremy Travers of Homeland Security and Ramsay Mays, number two at the Department of Firearms and Tobacco made up the rest.

Each bore a grudging respect for the other even if they didn't always agree. Chatting informally they discussed Olympic site bids, Florida property values and the current heatwave engulfing the Beltway. Rarely venturing into realms of their own agencies, they exercised protocol regarding the circumstances bringing them together.

Awaiting the arrival of Committee Chairman Robert Blakie-Harris, Director of Operations at the National Security Agency; Travers regaled the others of an incident which occurred while piloting his Cessna over the Smoky Mountains of Tennessee. As he got to the juicy part, Blakie-Harris whisked into the room and apologized for being late. Acknowledging his arrival, members expressed greetings and waited for the meeting to come to order.

Dressed impeccably in a Canali suit, beige shirt and polished black shoes, the Director's face and hands were tanned in a manner a Malibu lifeguard would envy. Exuding confidence he sat at the head of the table and placed his briefcase along the surface. A half dozen dossier's were withdrawn and passed around. Participant's browsed the document's then gave their full attention to the Director.

Blakie-Harris cleared his throat and stated frankly, "I've just spent an hour with the Secretary of State and his aides, discussing the problematic file which sits before you."

He adjusted his gold-rimmed glasses and glanced about the table. "First off I want to thank you for taking time from your busy schedules."

The others nodded and allowed him to continue.

"I've looked over each of your recommendation's with regards to the alleged mid-west terror plot - along with the deceased SIAG operative and the emergence of possible successor's. Some believe they're connected. This session will allow you to air those concerns."

He glanced at his notes, "Once the relevant information has been scrutinized by the President and his advisers; a decision will be made as to which course his administration intends to pursue. Our advise will effect that decision."

Committee members noted the 'alleged' reference.

"Everyone at this table has thoughts on how to deal with this latest fulmination to America's security," attested the Chairman. "Some express a more moderate remedy, others take a harsher approach. I might remind the Committee, Amet D'han present ruler of A'biin, has stated publicly any strike against his nation would be interpreted as an act of war. He stresses no threats have been made by his government, or by the SIAG against the United States. He blames rogue US operatives for initiating a climate of fear and hostility between our two countries."

Blakie-Harris glanced at the faces surrounding him, "I'd be interested to know if your thoughts on this matter have changed since your report's were first submitted?"

He turned to Seymour-Johns, "Nelson, lets have your take then move around the table."

Pulling his seat forward the broad-shouldered Deputy Director cleared his throat, "It's my view this 'alleged' threat might be the real deal. The plan could've been advanced by fanatics within the SIAG, who intend to place the blame elsewhere. SIAG moles are entrenched within American society and answer to no one. To carry out such an operation without their leader's knowledge or consent is conceivable. If D'han is truly unaware, he'd be as guilty as the perpetrators, if an attack was staged from within the ranks of his own Intelligence network."

Silence hung over the proceedings as members gazed at their neckties and sipped water.

"It's my position we respond accordingly," he resumed. "First by informing A'biinian officials what our own Intelligence suggests. If they continue doing squat while allowing nut-bars within the SIAG to wreak havoc, I propose we take out one of their principle refineries."

Gauging the effect his words had on those assembled he glanced around.

Seasoned veteran Royston Adams appeared disturbed by the forthrightness of the Deputy Director's comments. Others concealed their thoughts behind frozen stares.

Injecting a bipartisan perspective into the debate Blakie-Harris urged the UCOMA Director to speak.

The congenial spymaster sporting a bow tie and suspenders, adjusted his wire-rim specs and ran a hand through his thinning hair. Despite the high regard his youthful staffers had for their boss they conceded he was a tad bit old-fashioned. He reminded them of American historian Arthur Schlesinger Jr. or a favourite uncle.

"Much as I respect my colleague I disagree whole-hardheartedly with his assessment," Adams stated frankly. "If we continue to provoke these people without proof of complicity we court disaster. I suggest we send a team of respected diplomats and arrange proper dialogue with A'biin's new hierarchy. Naturally, we'll remain vigilant and continue to monitor their Intelligence and military closely. In the interim let us not rush to judgment."

"You seem to think we're discussing Fourth of July firecrackers Royston!" the CIA man shot back. "We're talking about the possible annihilation of an American city."

Stanton Carter piped in, "I share Nelson's view. If we allow these terrorists free reign without pushing back we deserve to be hit."

Adams countered by saying, "Other than the words of a deceased SIAG operative there's no proof of a planned attack. Nothing suggests a plot is being hatched by factions of the SIAG."

Jeremy Travers and Ramsay Mays supported the CIA representative with brief statements. Catherine Levine adopted Royston's position stating, "The fallout would be irreversible if we erred in our judgment."

Noting their views hadn't changed Blakie-Harris reminded them they weren't voting on options.

"That is for the President to decide. I meet with his advisers tomorrow morning and will get back to you once a decision is reached."

Staring at the pensive faces he thanked them and adjourned the meeting.

Jesse awoke to the sound of hissing tires on wet pavement. His phone indicated it was just past seven am. He tossed the blanket aside and recalled the previous night's venture involving Kriel and the dogs. Parting the curtains aside he observed a rain-swept highway beyond the corroded motel sign. Having not eaten in more than twelve hours he decided to grab a bite in town. In the meantime plans would be consolidated for a return visit to Penther's lodge - minus the get-up.

In wake of last night's stakeout he arrived back at the motel and plugged earphones into the tiny recorder. Listening again as Penther and Dopple conversed on the back porch, their dialogue was captured with pristine clarity. Most of the conversation revolved around Penther's planned excursion to Detroit. For his part Aldo would drive his boss as far as Fort Wayne, before turning back to safeguard the lodge. Dopple expressed displeasure at not accompanying Penther the entire way and was roundly reproached. As the recording unravelled,

Jesse discovered some revealing comments made by the lodge owner. At one point Penther reminded his sulking underling not to pack, lest the impression be given they were pulling up stakes. Remarks were also made concerning the bunker and Federal agents.

Jesse withdrew track pants from one of the suitcases and showered. Retrieving his baseball cap and binoculars; he laced up runners and stuffed bottled water and bug repellent into a knapsack. Hoping the hiker guise would suffice, he added a sealed bag of sleeping powder and a listening device in the lining of his windbreaker.

Rainfall eased as he drove to town with the needle on empty. After refuelling he parked outside the same restaurant he'd frequented the day before. Seated by the window he ordered eggs and bacon and watched Ellery come to life. A second coffee was requested before he settled at the cash register. Departing the establishment he purchased a dozen wieners at a convenience store and returned to the car. Driving north amid sparse traffic he recalled Penther's desire to be on the road by eight am. Signalling onto the Yokum Trail, he glanced at the time and noticed it was past nine. Dopple was slated to drive his boss as far as Fort Wayne - an hour's drive. The round-trip would amount to roughly two hours, affording Jesse a window of forty minutes to search the lodge. With the occupant's away it hardly mattered if an alarm was tripped. He intended to neutralize the system, regardless.

The dogs were another matter.

Leaving the car in the same overgrown driveway used the previous evening, he strode north along the shoulder. As he drew nearer the Clearing, he entered the woods and surveyed the lodge through binoculars. The parking area was vacant and he moved into the open, triggering an alarm deliberately. Inside the lodge the dogs reacted and Jesse sprinted toward the rear deck. Mounting the steps, he listened at the door and heard the doberman's scratch wildly on the other side. Avoiding use of the sleeping powder - Jesse had another plan. He withdrew wieners from his backpack and tore the package open. Slamming his elbow through the screen door, he reached down and freed the slip-lock. Several weenies were removed from the package; meanwhile his right foot delivered a blow to the mid-section of the heavier door. It splintered and another kick sent it back on it's hinges. Snarling with rage the doberman's charged through the opening – at that instant Jesse tossed the wieners along the deck. Using the aluminum door as a shield he chucked the remainder of the meat. The dog's took the bait and he dashed indoors and shoved the refrigerator against the entrance, establishing a barricade. He exhaled and peered through a splintered crack and observed the dogs chomping on the prize.

Once the snacks were devoured their attention would revert back to the intruder.

The alarms were unrelenting and Jesse set about locating their source. The digital hardware was discovered inside a kitchen cupboard attached to the wall. Ripping the apparatus from it's moorings he tossed the components on the floor and there was silence.

Having explored the kitchen he moved into the hall and noticed a washroom, two bedrooms and closet along either side. The room to his left was strewn with clothes, magazines and handguns. An unmade bed was littered with crumbs and bubble gum wrappers. Jesse assumed this was Aldo's quarters. The hall closet was stored with an array of camouflaged army fatigues draped on hangers. Jesse frisked the pockets and discovered mostly spent shell casings. Concealed behind the clothes a stash of long guns were mounted on a rack.

The room next to it had it's door secured. Jesse splintered the frame with his shoulder and observed an antiquated bed supported by sturdy hardwood legs. Books lined a tidy bookcase and he noticed they dealt with American history and Law. An ancient dresser stood nearby; rummaging its drawer's nothing of significance was uncovered. In contrast to the pigsty across the hall, Penther's clothes were folded in a precise manner. Shirts and pants were neatly pressed and hung in an orderly fashion within the closet.

He entered a parlour at the end of the hall and peered into the faint light. Similar in style to Penther's quarters - both offered a frontier perspective. An oak table sat before a rustic fireplace, surrounded by matching chairs. A coffee urn and several mugs rested along a counter top. Handcrafted wall murals featured images of wagon trains and buffalo's. Over the fireplace, a pair of crisscrossed Winchester rifles were displayed above the mounted head of a grizzly. With the blinds drawn natural light was in short supply. Jesse scoured several drawers and discovered mostly writing utensils and hunting brochures.

Departing the parlour he decided to give Aldo's quarters a proper going over. He emptied a bag of dirty laundry on the bed and scoured pocket's for anything of relevance. Finding nothing he searched the top dresser drawer and found it stuffed with dirty socks and T-shirts. The one beneath it contained rifle scopes and ammo. A bottom drawer was stored with army surplus catalogues.

If anything was concealed it would be within the fortified bunker.

Jesse made his way back toward the kitchen and peeked between the fridge and pummelled door. Both dog's lay panting along the deck's surface with their eyes focused upon the barricade. Jesse nudged the fridge an inch and they reared up growling. If the carnivorous beast's anticipated more wieners they were out of luck. The entire dozen had been consumed. A bag of dry dog chow was on the counter, however Jesse chose to pillage the refrigerator instead. Two opened tins of wet meat were procured and distributed along the hall. Jesse dismissed the idea of planting a listening devise. With the lodge in shambles Penther would investigate thoroughly.

Once darkness fell Kriel intended to pay a visit.

It was hoped Aldo would be present and inclined to grant an interview. Likely, the sharpshooter had a few questions of his own regarding the general disarray of his master's premises.

The dogs continued to glare at the barricaded entrance. If Jesse departed by the front door he'd be afforded little protection from the rapid beasts. His safest option was the wet chow. The strategy was a reversal of his entrance ploy. He shoved the barricade aside and the beast's stormed past toward the meat strewn along the hall. The fridge was used to reseal the entrance after which, Jesse bolted from the deck and made his way across the Clearing. He paused briefly to glance over his shoulder and heard muffled barks.

Evidently, they were still hungry.

Normally the sights and sounds of a Miami Beach resort would've delighted Carl Kristy. Women dressed sparingly in colourful shorts and bikinis while parading the boardwalk. Waterfront bistros offered exquisite cuisine and provided a splendid view of the ocean. Among the surf and sand a noticeable lack of children was observed. Females who chose to go topless along that stretch were permitted to do so. Such displays were routine among the splendour of the Tangira Resort and Casino.

Massaging the lump on his head received at the hands of his accursed attacker, Kristy felt an unnatural detachment from the paradise surrounding him. With his injuries concealed behind a bandage and sunglasses, tourists cast occasional glances for all the wrong reasons.

Thirty-six hours earlier he'd been engaged among the wooded terrain of Forest Hills. Eluding police he retrieved his vehicle and fled the area, in dire need of pain-killers and a shower. Dehydrated, he slugged back two large cola's at a drive-thru and waited for a nearby Walmart to open. Brushing caked mud and residue from his cloths, he entered the cavernous franchise and purchased new attire. Back at his hotel he showered and slept for twelve hours. Squaring up his bill he drove to JFK and returned the car to a rental affiliate. In lieu of his stolen phone contact was established with 'This way' using a disposable. He informed his former chaperone an incident had occurred and requested to meet privately with Sir. The request was granted and Kristy was instructed to book a flight to Miami. Upon arrival he would take a cab to the Tangira Resort, several miles north of the city. He'd state his name at the front gate and ask directions to Pier 4. Once there he'd be shuttled to a moored yacht called the 'Shelley O'.

Beneath wavering fronds he observed a gathering of lovelies tossing a Frisbee. Sailboats were glimpsed on the horizon gleaming in the Florida sunshine. His meeting was set to commence in twenty minutes. Finding Pier 4 posed no problem - confronting his benefactor with the latest developments might be. Kristy approached the pier and was hailed by a man in a water-taxi. Whisked speedily over the waves towards the anchored yacht, they drew alongside and he observed 'This way' at the guardrail sporting a cap and shades. Motioned toward a rope ladder, Kristy stepped nimbly onto the rungs and scaled the harness. The water-taxi remained as he emerged on deck. 'This way' approached and Kristy was led below. Straddling a narrow passageway, his guide paused before a door and knocked five times in rapid succession. A latch was released and Kristy was ushered within.

As expected his host was seated in the gloom next to a shrouded lamp.

"I hope you're not prone to seasickness Mr. Kristy," gargled the voice. "I take it there's some urgency to this visit?"

Feeling the rhythmic sway beneath his feet Kristy replied, "I felt the matter warranted your attention Sir."

"I'm listening."

"Thirty-six hours ago I was the target of a SIAG assassin," he confessed. "She nearly succeeded in carrying out her assignment."

"She?"

"The woman is a formidable combatant."

As the words left his mouth he felt a surge of pain along the side of his skull.

The Face leaned back, "That would explain the bandage?"

Kristy nodded.

"Where did the encounter occur?"

"New York."

"How did she find you?"

"The SIAG pride themselves on the hunt."

"V tells me you were in contact using a disposable. I assume the woman has your phone?"

"There's nothing of value stored on it."

The apparatus attached to his host's throat crackled.

"Before you depart you'll be issued a secured devise - try not to lose it."

"Thank you I won't."

"It's likely your assailant will seek you again. Make certain she's dispatched this time."

"That may not be easy."

"Allow her to track you and set a trap. Let me know when the matter has been resolved."

"Of course."

Along Kristy's rear his guide cleared his throat and handed him a fresh communication devise. Extending his arm they reentered the passageway.

The Corporal was scheduled to be replaced by Dennis at eight pm. With the professor away, and his apprentice on assignment things were relatively quiet. The absence of students during summer break made for long shifts - meantime the hours wound down slowly. Dennis finally arrived and they conversed awhile beside the lobby museum. Bidding adieu until the following morning Sasha took her leave. She made her way toward the Residence building and entered the coolness of the lobby. Approximately, forty minutes of daylight remained and she decided to jog to town and fetch some grocery items. Climbing four flights she accessed her lodgings and removed her uniform. It was replaced with a sweatshirt, track pants and runners. She looped a purse about her waist and fastened her hair in a ponytail. Descending the stairs her phone vibrated and she paused to respond. Greeted by

Professor Tondar, he mentioned he was home retrieving clothes to deliver to his wife and inquired how things were? Assured all was well, he informed his security chief he intended to spend the night in Cleveland with Dorothy. In the morning he planned to drive to Detroit and meet with a former colleague. She was reminded Jesse was due back at Grissim the following day. The professor would arrive sometime afterwards.

When he signed off Sasha contemplated the return of the prodigal apprentice. She distrusted Jesse Carlton. Within days of his arrival she'd been stalked twice. That fact alone didn't imply guilt, despite his being in near proximity on both accounts.

She picked up her stride and crossed Abbot Lane. Rather than jogging the shoulder of Windover Road, she descended the steps toward a path winding it's way among the fertile sod of Falls Valley. The trail encircled the waterfall and extended towards the opposite side bordering Lantern Falls. Sprinting past some teenagers tossing a football she heard one shout it was time to go. Daylight was rapidly fading and along her right the parking area was vacant. Illuminated by floodlights, the waterfall loomed directly ahead. She paused alongside the cascade and closed her eyes to bask in the spray. A pool gave rise to a mist at the foot of the falls. The haze impaired her vision and she was startled to see the form of someone standing opposite the pool. He appeared to be gazing directly at her and began to circle in her direction. Bolting toward town Sasha caught sight of two words scribbled in white chalk along the pathway:

ALMOST TIME!

Glancing over her shoulder she witnessed no one. Without recourse except to run like hell; her heart pounded as she strained to hear the welcoming sound of traffic. Reaching the steps she dashed up two at a time. At street level the passing vehicles were a welcome sight. She gazed back over the valley and her fear turned to rage. Having endured a brutal relationship in Fort Jackson; a similar evil appeared to be unfolding a thousand miles away. Her former tormentor was dead! Until recently the change of scenery had served her well.

Sasha crossed at a nearby intersection and entered a grocery mart. She purchased pasta, fruit and tea and paid the attendant. Out front she waited until a taxicab was within sight and flagged it. The driver was instructed to drop her off before the Residence Building at Grissim. As they journeyed past Falls Valley she gazed solemnly from the rear seat window. Once Abbot Lane was accessed the cab drew up before her building. Tipping the driver she toted the bag of food items upstairs and reentered her quarters. The door was secured and she drew the blinds tightly shut.

Beneath the sheets Sasha tumbled into a netherworld populated by monsters.

EIGHTEEN

The evening would provide the final act of Jesse's debut in the field. Once more preparations were made to don Kriel's vestment's with the intention of confronting Aldo Dopple. FBI records suggested Penther usually returned from his Detroit excursions between ten and eleven pm. This afforded time to question his bodyguard regarding two point's of inquiry Lee had posed: ONE: Why were several of Penther's closest followers unaccounted for? TWO: Who meets with the militia leader during his frequent sojourns?

Having concluded an unsuccessful search of the lodge Jesse returned to the motel and slept for five hours. As sundown approached he munched on a cheese bagel and banana, purchased in town and washed them down with water. While in Ellery he procured a dozen wieners for use as decoys. Unravelling them they were placed inside the sink with the water running. Holding his nose, Jesse sprinkled sleeping powder into a pair of zip-lock bags. Afterwards, he inserted a half dozen wiener's into each. Sealing both bags he gave them a shake, allowing the content's to marinate. Lee was insistent the formula wasn't harmful to animals and merely provided an hour's rest.

Contact was established with the professor and Jesse brought him up to date. His handler was informed a search of the lodge proved fruitless. Notwithstanding, Kriel planned to re-visit after sundown during Dopple's watch. Jesse mentioned the recording and the references it contained and was reminded to be on his guard.

When he signed off he contacted Emma.

"Where are you Jesse?"

"In a motel room."

"With who?"

"Ma."

"Well...?"

"I can't go into details now but things are OK."

They chatted for several minutes and greetings were exchanged with Gramps. Blowing a kiss into the receiver Jesse reminded his mother they'd talk the next day.

Donning the Kevlar he slid into Kriel's rags. A purse belt was about his waist and the slicker hat and face draped beneath the windbreaker, concealing his upper torso. Departing room 21, he swung the car onto the two-lane stretch and followed the white line. Feeling like a stage actor on opening night; this was to be Kriel's baptism of fire. His first appearance before someone other than the professor needed to be convincing. Aldo Dopple was ruthless killer with a passion for guns. That much was confirmed while rummaging the lodge that morning. Suspected of killing several federal agents; he was a prime suspect in the murder of a black ACLU attorney and his wife. In either case nothing was proven. Prosecutors believed Dopple was responsible for planting explosives in the basement of an IRS building in Memphis at Penther's behest. Had the plot not been thwarted by an undercover agent, the carnage would have claimed many lives. Again no concrete evidence was procured. Instead, the militia leader and several followers were issued minimal sentences.

Drops of rain spattered the windshield and Jesse applied his wipers. Along the way he recited a series of monologues as vocal exercises. The renderings were uttered in a sharp, Anglo-Saxon croak he'd devised back at Control. By repeating the narrative he was able to hone in on the proper timber of Kriel's rasp.

Daylight faded as he signalled onto the Yokum Trail. Guided by his headlights he cruised past the grazing field and stable he'd noted previously. The dim glimmer of a porch light revealed several horses drinking from a trough. The view was cut short by the reemergence of trees. Moment's later he drew to a halt and backed into the concealed driveway. Switching off the engine he remained seated as his eyes adjusted to the dark. The cap and windbreaker were removed and he withdrew the penlight. Outside he inserted the pant cuffs into his boots and pulled the disguise over his features. Donning gloves his transformation into the boat captain's ghost was complete. Thunder rumbled and rain pounded the branches overhead. Taking stock of his surroundings the opaque figure moved among the trees. Having earlier silenced the alarms the trespasser arrived alongside the Clearing. Rain ran in streams from Kriel's hat and a shard of lightning split the sky.

Penther's dwelling flared white in sinister luminosity and light was observed in the kitchen window.

Cautiously the wraith advanced.

Aldo was seated at the kitchen table with one arm hanging limply at his side. His head lolled onto his shoulder as his lighter attempted to reach the cigarette lodged between his lips. He burst into hysterical laughter and grasped a whisky bottle. Glancing about the devastation, he wondered how anyone could gain entry with a pair of doberman's staring them down.

"Useless gobs of spit," he slurred eyeballing the beasts. "Now I gotta take the blame."

The carnage was discovered upon his return from chauffeuring Penther to Fort Wayne. Rather than deal with the crisis Aldo got wasted instead. The rear door of the lodge was splintered; the security system had been ripped from its moorings and the parlour and bedrooms were ransacked. He'd been instructed to keep watch on their compound. If he got drunk he wouldn't feel the beating.

Club and Boot lay stretched and panting along the kitchen floor. Both appeared bewildered as their blithering host conversed with himself.

"Quit starin'!" the sodden killer bellowed as his chin tumbled onto his chest.

Penther abhorred alcohol and would kick his ass whenever he smelled the rancid stench. Aldo brought the bottle to his lips, "Ain't here no-how so screw him."

Coughing up whisky it dripped from his nostrils and sprayed his grimy clothes. He wiped the residue with his sleeve and reached for a nearby rifle. It was target-practice time and he attempted to propel himself to his feet. The struggle was beyond his capacity and he fell backwards muttering incoherent expletives. Without Penther there to slap him around he felt alone and missed the unsmiling son-of-a-bitch.

Abruptly, the dogs jerked and sprang to their feet. Their barks would've awakened the dead as they sprinted toward the barricaded door. Expecting Penther to walk through the shattered entrance Aldo's face was ashen.

"Shit!"

Glancing about he reminded himself, he'd been delivering Penther to Fort Wayne when the destruction occurred. The dogs were scraping the refrigerator barring the way when Aldo realized his boss hadn't arrived at all. Club and Boot would never display hostility towards their greatest provider. Additionally, he would've heard his engine as it drew up outside. Rising unsteadily he ordered the dog's retreat and shoved the fridge into it's rightful place. The alarm system was scooped from the floor and it's crushed component's placed on the counter. The parlour and bedrooms remained in their present state.

Outside the ragged figure ascended the steps and drew up alongside the dangling screen door. A bag of tainted meat was cast along the surface of the deck and the doberman's charged across the threshold, From the doorway entrance the barrel of a rifle emerged. It was driven downwards forcefully, and a blow to Dopple's jaw raised him from the floor and returned him to the kitchen. The intruder entered and Aldo propelled himself backwards on all fours. Illuminated by jolts of lightning, the ghoul's eyes bore into his own and the sharpshooter began to giggle uncontrollably.

Kriel sensed the wretch was armed.

With surprising speed Dopple withdrew a gun from his belt and took aim. A mud-caked boot smashed his wrist and the weapon was sent flying. Aldo's scream was heard by no one, least of all the sleeping doberman's.

"Greetings Mr. Dopple."

"W...what in hell are you!"

"Such impertinence," the creature rasped. "Where's the lodge owner?"

"He ain't here..."

"Then I'll take you."

"Sumbitch!" the militiaman shrieked recoiling along the hall.

The demon advanced with it's hideous eyes. Kicking and thrashing Aldo was thrust skyward by the scruff of his neck and held in a vice grip. Rain dripped from the miscreant's garments; meanwhile Aldo managed to extract a jackknife from his back pocket. The weapon clicked and the thing reacted. Aldo made a slashing motion and missed by an inch. With a wave of the ghoul's wrist the knife was swept from Dopple's grasp.

"Where's Penther!"

"I dunno."

"Liar!"

"H...he goes off and says nothing."

The lodger was slammed forcefully against a wall.

"Furnish answers or you'll dangle from the highest tree!"

"Detroit... he's in Detroit!"

"For what reason?"

"Friends..."

"Certain friends of his have vanished! Where might they be?"

"I dunno."

The bodyguard was pummelled against the wall a second time and the question was repeated.

"Their ex-cons," Aldo cried. "They change their names and drift."

Where were the dogs!

Dopple's feet touched down and he was spun rapidly about. The thing withdrew twine from it's rags and made a slice. As the binds tightened about Aldo's wrists a guttural laugh emitted from the throat of his tormentor.

Moment's ago Aldo was intoxicated beyond reason - he was sober now.

The wraith retrieved the dislodged gun from the floor and levelled it at a fuse-box mounted on the facing wall. Three shots demolished the casing and the lodge was thrust into utter darkness.

From the midst of his shattered world Dopple cursed the entity.

"Shall we depart!" the demon rasped.

Hustled out the door Aldo noticed the dogs sprawled along the deck.

"You killed them you bastard!"

A length of rope held the screen door partially in place. Kriel grasped it and jostled his captive down the steps and onto the grounds.

Spinning him about the demon croaked, "Penther's associates where are they!"

"Who gives a shit!"

Rain fell in torrents creating a veil of mist over the grounds. A solitary tree stood near the middle of the Clearing. Shoved in that direction the militiaman cried, "What in hell...!"

It was clear Aldo had limited knowledge of his master's affairs. What he did know he suppressed.

They arrived beneath an oak tree and Dopple was ordered to kneel. His ankles were shackled with rope and he was hoisted upside down from a sturdy limb.

Across the Clearing the faint whine of a dog was heard. Penther was due back shortly and it was time to depart.

Spitting upon the garments of his persecutor Aldo shouted, "Rot in hell!"

"Your wrist binds have been loosened so you might free yourself Mr. Dopple. Until we meet again!"

Course laughter receded as the downpour intensified. With the exception of the drowsy dog's Aldo's screams went unheard.

———————

Recalling Lee Tondar's fondness for diners, Brandon DeLong escorted his friend to one of Detroit's more celebrated greasy spoons. Greeting his guest outside the 7th Precinct, the broad-shouldered detective was dressed comfortably in corduroys and loafers. With mild temperatures forecast Lee dressed casually and carried his trusty briefcase. Brandon insisted he leave the Volkswagen parked behind the station and they use the detective's enormous '76 Pontiac Bonneville instead. Arriving at the diner they waited several minutes for a booth. Once they were seated, a waitress took their orders and was back with coffee in seconds. Lee withdrew a list of industrial sites he was most keen to visit and passed it to his companion. Despite the trust he maintained for his Detroit colleague, he was able to reveal only what was necessary. Admitting his investigation had to do with a possible terror threat; one of a number on a never-ending watch. It was Brandon who'd provided him with a compilation of suspect industrial sites in and around the greater Detroit area. Following the cross-referencing procedure at Grissim - Lee had whittled the list down to three sites. If nothing panned out he'd return to the extended index.

"Trudy sends her greetings," the detective remarked stirring his coffee.

Lee had met the black couple and their two boys years before.

"The lads must be young men by now?"

DeLong chuckled, "They're both in college."

The two men had been paired together a decade earlier when DeLong served as Detroit liaison, on an investigation involving the illegal transfer of munitions along the Detroit/Windsor corridor. Recalling old times two platters of Eggs Benedict and bacon were spread before them. As they dug in discussion reverted back to the matter at hand.

Ninety minutes later they drew up before their first site of interest. The building was located along an industrial boulevard in the city's east end. At the entrance DeLong pressed a buzzer attached to the name 'Oxymoron Press'. The enterprise was situated within an arch-typical redbrick warehouse with no other firms listed.

A static voice streamed from the intercom, "Yes?"

"Police. We'd like a moment of your time."

There was a pause before they were buzzed through. At the base of a stairwell they were met by an exuberant young man who introduced himself as Morty Lewis. Brandon produced his badge and made introductions. Morty appeared eager to cooperate and led them upstairs. Arriving before an office they were surrounded by an large open area. Amidst the acrid smell of ink, an ancient printing press was on display alongside rolls of unused newsprint.

DeLong inquired about the lack of productivity and Monty informed him he was attempting to inaugurate his project piecemeal. Having acquired the space and printing gear was a miracle in itself. He hoped to publish a weekly newspaper supported by advertisers within two months.

"None of that commie stuff I hope?" DeLong remarked winking at Lee.

"Nope. Pure Americana with a little Trotsky thrown in for good measure," attested the printer.

"Trotsky? Isn't he a hockey player?"

"That's the one," Morty replied.

"So what do you do in the meantime Mr. Lewis?"

"At present I'm attempting to recruit like-minded journalists - who'll work for nothing until the paper establishes itself. Know anyone?"

" Afraid not," DeLong responded.

It was decided Morty was a struggling one-man operator. His guests had a look about and wrapped up the interview by wishing him luck.

The next site was situated uptown in a tough neighbourhood known as a haven for gang-related crime. The firm in question was located in a bland, grey building and called 'Sommers and Co.', a decorations manufacturer churning out trinkets for the dollar-store market. Lee and the detective were admitted into an office strewn with pizza boxes and ashtrays. The stout owner, Horst Sommers switched off the radio and they were offered seats. Before a question was even posed, Horst denied allegations of retaining illegals and blamed a pair of bitter ex-employees. He claimed they presented false ID upon being hired. When it became known they were illegals he fired them.

"My hiring practices are conducted in a compliant manner nowadays," he assured them.

At DeLong's request he and his associate were given a tour of the facility. Strolling a hallway hosting a single washroom, they emerged into a workshop area where a dozen or more Hispanic women sat at paper-cutters and sewing machines. A pair of oscillating fans rotated at opposite ends of the room. Music strained from a tinny radio and the scent of burnt coffee wafted from an urn set upon a card table. It was July and already Halloween novelties were being prepared; orange and black material's littered the tables and floor. The procedure appeared routine. If illegals were involved it wasn't Brandon's concern, he was there on a separate matter. Sommers insisted the complaints against him were lodged by the two fired women. He apologized for previous oversights and added things were being carried out by the book. DeLong thanked him and they found their own way out.

Lee's final priority site was in an industrial region located along Jefferson Avenue East.

Electron Era was a low-tech electronics firm manufacturing digital parts, for inclusion in appliances such as television remotes and play-stations. A missing person's report had been filed with the Detroit P.D. regarding a plant employee named Raymond Pearson. He was last spotted in a corridor by colleagues and a partial investigation had been initiated. Workmates and a girlfriend were interviewed and nothing had turned up since.

The factory was housed within a ground-level, retro-style white brick structure. At one time the facade would've been considered streamlined. Erected during the manufacturing boom of the early 1970s, it now appeared shopworn and neglected. Weeds sprouted between cracks in an attached parking lot and walkway. DeLong brought the Pontiac to a standstill along the curb of Sentra Avenue. The occupant's emerged and strode towards the front entrance and entered a lobby area. They approached the security desk where a uniformed guard sat before a row of monitors. DeLong showed his badge and stated they wished to speak with the person in charge.

"'Bout the missing guy I bet?" the watchman speculated.

DeLong eyeballed him and remained silent.

"I'll ring the supervisor."

"Thanks."

Several moments later a man of average height strode through swinging metal doors nearby a punch-clock. In his mid-to-late thirties he sported a blue shirt, trousers and work boots. Extending his hand he said his name was Jackson Bell. Introductions were made and Bell turned to the guard to let him know he was busy if anyone called. Both visitors were ushered into a broad corridor and guided toward a small, unpretentious office. Gestured toward chairs the pair were invited to make themselves comfortable.

Seated at the desk opposite them Bell said, "I assume you're here to discuss Ray Pearson?"

DeLong nodded and flipped through some notes. "I'd like to clarify a few points and not take too much of your time."

"You're aware the police have already been here," remarked the supervisor.

"I am."

"Then by all means proceed."

Throughout their exchange Lee sat quietly to one side. Listening intently he processed each response.

"In the earlier report," stated the detective. "Ray's lab mates claimed they were with him in the lunchroom but departed in advance. Approximately, ten minutes later he was observed passing before their lab in an agitated state. Is there another exit along that part of the corridor?"

"There's a back door," Bell replied. "It's located in the shipping room beside the loading dock. The incident occurred during lunch while the shipping operator, Mr. Train was taking his break out front. The shipping room remains unlocked at this time, allowing staff to leave product inside the door, rather than clogging the shuttle hatch with trays. Once break concludes the product is retrieved and prepared for shipment. Pearson likely entered the shipping room at this time and departed by the exit door."

"And the shipping attendant saw nothing?"

"That's correct."

"Let's talk about Ray's lab mates," DeLong resumed. "They claim he appeared distracted when they last saw him. This despite the fact he was fine moments before in the lunchroom?"

"So I'm told."

"The police report mentioned the technician's were uncomfortable being interviewed. Why would that be?"

Bell leaned back in his chair, "No one enjoys being interviewed by the police as you well know. Furthermore, there's language barriers. Many of our employees don't speak English."

DeLong nodded, "Can we have a tour?"

"Of course," responded the foreman rising from his seat. "Please follow."

Departing the office they strode toward the far end of the corridor. Along their left Plexiglas walls formed the front portion of each lab. Floor to ceiling partitions separated them. Technicians wearing white smocks were observed through smoky orange glass. Across the hall was the lunchroom where Ray had been with his mates before his disappearance. They entered and DeLong poked about the cupboard and fridge areas, meanwhile Lee made his own observations. Returning to the hallway both washrooms were inspected.

"Did you know the missing worker?" Lee inquired.

"I hired him that's about it," Bell replied. "He's been with us from the start - more than nine months now. Said he'd been employed by a number of firms operating out of this facility. Pearson struck me as the loner type. Regardless, he showed up on time and did the job."

Lee pressed further, "In addition to Ray were others hired who'd previously been employed at this location?"

"Another fellow works here as a watchmen. He contacted me asking if a security position was available. He claimed he'd been employed at this site most his adult life and had the paperwork to prove it. I reviewed his resume and hired him as night guard."

"What's the persons name?"

"Flotsin. Harry Flotsin."

"Do you find it necessary to employ overnight security Mr. Bell?" DeLong queried.

The supervisor stopped in his tracks, "There's been a rash of vandalism, squatters and B&E's plaguing this part of town, detective. They think of it as an abandoned ghetto. Your files bear this out."

Bell allowed his words to settle and the tour resumed.

They passed by Lab C and Lee noticed four technicians staring up at them with blank expressions. Next was Lab D where Pearson served as captain. The faces of those inside were also blank. Arriving before the shipping room DeLong remarked, "Mind if we have a word with the shipper on duty the day of Ray's disappearance. The police never did get his statement."

"Sam Train's the only shipper. You'll recall he wasn't at his post when Pearson departed the building. But be my guest."

Bell accessed entry and they were ushered into an ample space. At the opposite end a door was visible alongside the receiving gate. Boxes and crates were stored on wooden grids. Pausing at his duties a white male of roughly thirty approached.

"Sam this is Detective DeLong and his colleague Lee. They'd like to ask a few questions."

Train hesitated, "If it's about the missing worker I wasn't here when he took off."

The detective quietly responded, "We're aware of that Mr. Train. For the record I'd like to hear where you were at the time?"

"I was out front in the shade drinking coffee and eating a sandwich," Train replied. "Half an hour later I came back inside."

"Did you see Mr. Pearson at any time?"

"Never. I was later told he walked off the job. Mr. Bell asked if I saw anyone leave by way of the shipping room. I didn't."

"Do you know what the missing employee looked like?" Lee asked.

"He's a native guy. I've seen him arrive in the morning and punch in."

The Ohio visitor glanced at Bell, "May we speak with the security man out front?"

"Sure."

Delong thanked the shipper and they departed the space with Bell leading the way.

Their footsteps echoed in the corridor and they reentered the lobby and approached the guard - who'd been monitoring their progress onscreen.

The pair were formally introduced to Cal Wicker. His supervisor asked if he'd mind answering a few questions.

"Why not."

"Thank you," the detective responded. "According to your statement you had no contact with Mr. Pearson on the day of his disappearance?"

"I saw him enter that morning like usual. He punched the time clock and headed for his lab."

"You're certain he didn't depart by way of the lobby at lunchtime?"

"I didn't see him."

"There's an exit door in the corridor," Lee intervened. "Could he have left that way?"

"I was out front having a smoke and could've missed him on the monitor."

The guard glanced at the supervisor.

"I'd like to review the camera footage for the period in question," DeLong resumed.

Bell fielded the request, "As I explained to the police earlier, our system isn't intended to capture images - its costly and unnecessary. Security personnel monitor the site 24/7. That suffices."

DeLong's smile tightened, "Is every part of the interior and exterior under surveillance?"

"Yes," injected the guard. "Each monitor features a four-way split-screen for a total of a dozen cameras inside and out. "

Delong turned to his colleague, "Any questions?"

Lee shook his head.

The detective thanked Bell and the watchman for their time. He handed the supervisor his card and requested he call if anything surfaced.

Departing the building both men entered the vintage Pontiac. Lee glanced at his watch they'd been inside roughly thirty minutes.

"Feel like coffee Brandon?"

"I was about to suggest the same."

Buckling in the detective set off and cast his friend a sidelong glance, "That was interesting wouldn't you agree?"

"Wholeheartedly."

"So how do we proceed?"

"Cautiously."

A moment later the car drew up before Pappas Place. They entered the tiny diner and seated themselves at a table. The cheerful owner greeted them and they ordered coffee.

Brandon stared across at his companion, "Well..."

Pausing as their beverage's were placed before them Lee finally said, "The answers we received appeared contrived. I think their hiding something."

The detective agreed, " Let's not forget the excessive security precautions. All those cameras for a rinky-dink operation like that. The supervisor and guard insisted Pearson departed by the rear door - yet no camera footage exists and no one saw him leave."

"That puzzled me as well," Lee replied. "All the gear and none of it rigged to record?"

"So what's the plan?" DeLong asked.

"I suggest we return to the plant? I'd like to chat with the technicians working in Ray's lab and the one next to it – off premises naturally. They leave work in fifteen minute interval's beginning at four o'clock that gives us time."

The detective exhaled, "You were always thorough."

Ten minutes later he brought the car alongside the curb opposite Electron Era. The supervisor would notice them chatting with Ray's co-workers and perhaps consider it a formality. Parked near a bus stop, they observed the nearly vacant lot attached to the plant across the way, suggesting workers commuted to work via public transit.

"We never inquired about a cellar or basement," Lee remarked gazing at the structure. "The interior dimension's don't seem to jibe with their exterior counterpart."

DeLong was asked if it was possible to acquire a layout of the plant from city archives?

The detective promised to look into it.

At 4 pm technicians from Lab A trickled out the lobby doors. They crossed toward the bus stop and noticed the pair seated within the massive Pontiac. Half an hour later the team servicing Lab C emerged. Departing the vehicle, Lee switched on a tiny recorder in his jacket pocket and approached an aging technician. DeLong hung back while his colleague introduced himself by stating he was assisting police in a missing person's investigation. The gentleman was asked what he'd observed on the day the technician vanished. He stated someone appeared outside Lab C and spoke with their captain. The person was admitted and displayed a ruined digital sheet then quickly departed. A female co-worker joined them and verified his account. Once the Lab D crew emerged, Lee spoke with a pair of Somali gentlemen who worked alongside Ray. He asked if they'd mind repeating their story. One struggled to say they'd been with Ray in the lunch room where he seemed fine. A short while later they noticed him hurrying along the corridor in the direction of the shipping room.

A middle-aged woman who was part of the team spoke up. She reiterated their story in broken English and mentioned Ray had a girlfriend.

"He was good man," she insisted and the others nodded.

Their bus approached and Lee thanked them and parted company.

DeLong observed his friend approach a Lab C technician who chose to wait for a less crowded bus. Introducing himself to the Hispanic woman Lee said, "Someone made an appearance in your lab under a week ago?"

"Si Senor."

"Did he speak with you?"

"Not to me but to our captain."

"Does the captain ride a bus like yourself? "

"Si."

She peered over Lee's shoulder, "If you wish to speak with him he is there"

Lee glanced across the road and witnessed an Asian male emerge from a side entrance of Electron Era. The man strode briskly toward the sidewalk and continued in the opposite direction; before being intercepted by DeLong, who accompanied him back to the car.

Identifying himself as Simon Okawa, the middle-aged worker admitted he was captain of Lab C.

The detective introduced himself and his colleague and asked if he knew why he was being questioned?

"Because of the missing worker?" Okawa responded in good English.

"You were attempting to evade us just now?"

"I've already responded to questions from the police."

"We have more," DeLong asserted. "Ray Pearson in the lab next to your own paid you a visit?"

Okawa ran a hand through his cropped hair, "He showed up over his lunch break and insisted to be let in. Against the rules I allowed him access. He waved a sample of damaged product and suggested my team might be responsible for it's defects. I told him it wasn't our fault. The sample had been ravaged by a process of over-cleansing. He was surprised to discover our lab performed the same function as his own – I was too but let it go. Afterwards, he left in a hurry."

Staring at the inquisitive faces he added, "When I was first questioned I didn't mention his reaction on learning we were both involved in the same cleansing ritual."

"Why do you suppose he reacted in such manner?" Lee asked.

"I don't know."

"So you failed to mention the man's apparent distress to the police?" DeLong probed.

"I didn't want to get involved. Their very strict here and I need the job."

"Is there anything else you didn't mention?"

"That's everything."

DeLong had him jot down his contact number. When a bus drew up Okawa boarded and both men strolled back to the car.

Across the street the day watchman gazed pensively through the glass in their direction.

Back in his 7th Precinct office Brandon closed the door and they discussed their findings.

"I'll obtain a search warrant," he declared.

"I'd hold off the bit," Lee confided. "The investigation must appear routine and precludes involvement of a higher authority until the appropriate time. I trust you like family, Brandon - which is why I implore you to keep today's findings under wrap."

DeLong frowned, "Whatever you're investigating must be concerning.

Hearing no response he added, "Of course I won't mention a thing until I hear from you."

"Thanks."

For several moments his guest stared solemnly into space.

"For heaven's sake Lee what is it?"

Rousing himself his Ohio guest coughed lightly into his fist, "We need to talk with Ray's girlfriend. Can you retrieve her last name and address from the file?"

DeLong was aware his companion had been NSA before his transfer to something independent of that. He remained a government asset of one stripe or another and currently taught history at an Ohio college.

Brilliant cover for a brilliant man.

Gloria Mayorga's file appeared onscreen. Her phone number was scribbled down and DeLong recited her address, "She lives at 1510 Hubert Boulevard, Unit 303."

"Should we call first or just show up?"

"Just show up."

Eventually, they drew alongside a brown-box apartment complex and both approached the entrance. Brandon pressed a button attached to # 303 and a woman's voice crackled through the speaker.

"Who is it?"

"Detective DeLong with Detroit P. D. I'd like a word with you."

"Please say you're not the bearer of bad news...?" the voice quavered.

"I'm not Ms. Mayorga. We're simply filling in some blanks."

A buzzer sounded and they were admitted. Ascending two fights, they knocked lightly on the door and a black woman in her thirties responded. Her attractive features were haloed in an Afro hairstyle and she wore slacks and a yellow t-shirt. She motioned them toward a living room sofa and requested they make themselves comfortable.

"We know you've been interviewed and realize how concerned you must be," the detective offered. "If you wouldn't mind repeating your account one more time."

Seated opposite them Gloria reiterated her statement.

"Six days ago I contacted Ray and received no response. Later I went to his workplace and was informed he'd walked off the job."

"Had the two of you quarrelled?" DeLong asked.

"Not at all."

"The report indicates he stayed overnight with you before he disappeared?"

"Ray often stayed. We'd been discussing his moving in permanently."

Lee cleared his throat and asked if her partner mentioned anything regarding his workplace?"

She considered the question, "He complained about security arrangements. Over the years he'd worked for a number of employers at that location. Most of them folded. Eventually, he was hired there again along with a handful of others. He said the restrictions and cameras were excessive."

Lee glanced at his colleague, "There were no outward signs of stress?"

"None whatsoever just laid-back Ray."

Without asking anything more DeLong thanked their host and handed her a card.

"We appreciate your time Ms. Mayorga. Please call if you hear anything."

Lee switched off the recorder and placed it away.

Escorting them to the door Gloria said, " Do you think he's been harmed?"

"Hopefully he's safe," returned the detective. "We'll keep you updated."

Thanking her again they made their way down to the car.

On the drive back to the station Lee remarked, "Her comments were revealing."

"Really...?"

"The sentiment's Ray expressed to her regarding the unnatural security measures support our own view. Having worked that site forever, he believed the precautions were way over the top based on the work they do. I think it's safe to assume there's more to Electron Era than meets the eye."

Guiding the Pontiac through rush hour traffic, DeLong arrived at the Precinct and swung around behind the building. He dropped Lee off before his own vehicle.

"If anything arises I'll inform you securely."

"Don't forget to forward me a layout of the plant if you're able to? "

"Count on it."

Lee grasped Brandon's hand and they shook.

Clutching his briefcase the professor climbed into the Volkswagen and allowed the engine run.

"Sure you don't want the spare room at my place?" the detective shouted.

"I'm just over an hour from home. Can't thank you enough old friend!"

With that he waved and drove off.

———

NINETEEN

The female voice heard on the phone preyed upon Penther's mind. *'Who am I speaking with...?'*
It was as far as the woman got before he severed connection.

Guiding his rental north along I 75 he glanced in the mirror for signs of a tail.

How Kristy allowed someone access to a secured device was unfathomable! Lines of communication had been compromised. Penther was forced to destroy his own device and reestablish encrypted links with Sir, V, Jackson Bell, Aldo and the fallible Carl Kristy. He wondered what explanation the negligent middleman would have for the unsolicited call?

Repercussions following the death of Agent Gill remained concerning. Naturally, the authorities considered he and Aldo primary suspects. As fate would have it the agent had just departed their lodge before his regrettable demise. No evidence suggested anything other than reckless driving along a winding stretch caused his accident. Aldo had made certain all incriminating evidence was vanquished from the killing site.

Born into poverty among the backwaters of southern Illinois, he'd known Dopple since he was a lad of fourteen. His father earned pocket change labouring as a stable-keeper for a Polish farmer, who permitted the family to reside in a barn. To some degree Aldo's childhood paralleled Penther's - perhaps that's why he'd taken him in. In wake of his mother's passing, Aldo as youngest was raised by his brothers. Being a widower Dopple Sr. became an absentee father. Aldo lived in a series of state-sanctioned orphanages and eventually ran away. Fascinated with guns he heard tell of a rifle-range nearby Ellery, Indiana.

Evidently, they accommodated young men seeking resolve and purpose. He decided to check it out and hitchhiked east. Setting up camp in a field called Rykles Clearing, as nights got cold he was invited to sleep on the floor inside the property owner's lodge. At the time, a fellow named Rog Beasley served as Penther's assistant and bodyguard. Suspected of lying to his boss Beasley abruptly disappeared. The vacancy permitted the illiterate drifter, Aldo Dopple to claim Rog's former quarters.

Under tutelage of his new landlord the youngster developed into an expert marksman. By age seventeen he was able to outgun his mentor and others who'd gravitated to the rural compound. A skilled tracker, Aldo mastered the art of the kill and became the youngest recruit admitted into the ranks of the paramilitary outfit occupying Rykles Clearing. In addition to his duties he became an avid gun collector.

As Penther approached the Detroit city limits he cast repeated glances in the mirror. Scanning his surroundings, he observed the creeping vestiges of humanity advancing over his sacred land. Among the suburban sprawl a road sign indicated the city centre was still miles away. Eager to meet up with Jackson Bell he desired to get things over with. As necessary as these trips were he loathed them. Withdrawals, deposits, rented cars, dodging tails - the whole lot of it. Gazing from the drivers side he noticed a suburban escarpment being erected. Opposite that an enormous mall attached to a vast parking lot blotted out the horizon. The architects of these atrocities would soon find out this was no longer the promised land - it was his land.

Despite the bravado an uneasiness gnawed. The meeting between he and Bell was slated for five pm. Over the next few hours he intended to visit a trio of banks in the suburbs, then make his way downtown. While he drove he considered the lab worker held captive within Electron Era; evidently the police had paid a second visit. Desiring to remain as far from electronics plant as possible, he insisted Bell meet him downtown at Grand Circus Park. He accessed a ramp and delved deeper into a suburban nightmare without sighting any tails. A branch of the Grand American Bank loomed ahead. It was one of several he used to conduct transactions. Further on was Michigan Finance another institution he frequented. Once affairs concluded at a third bank, he stopped for a sandwich and set off to meet with Jackson Bell. Guiding the car through gridlock, he found a parking garage nearby Cadillac Tower and deposited his vehicle. With a briefcase cuffed to his wrist, he lowered the brim of his hat and mixed with the pedestrian flow. Cities made him anxious and his blood pressure rose. It was indecent how rural white folk were forced to fill government coffers, while bankrolling urban expansionism and immigration.

It would soon come to an end.

He paused before the park entrance and feigned browsing a racetrack listing. Foliage from spreading branches overhead sheltered throngs of park goers and vendors from the hot afternoon sun. Scanning his surroundings he witnessed no sign of Bell

"We should have met in an air-conditioned restaurant," remarked a familiar voice.

Penther turned and noticed Jackson Bell pretending to speak into his phone. A briefcase was cuffed to his right wrist similar to himself. They strolled away at a leisurely pace and crossed Woodward Avenue. Reentering the park from the opposite side they found a vacant bench and sat down. The melting-pot of humanity surrounding both men left Penther queasy. He consoled himself with visions of restoring the country to it's frontier glory. The first strike would stem the wave of immigration. A second and third would end the practice entirely.

Bell was aware how touchy his boss could be in an unnatural environment. He guessed this was one of those times.

Penther leaned forward, "Tell me about this latest police visit?"

"Follow-up was inevitable," Bell sighed. "However, before anyone shows up with a search warrant, the cops will have heard from their missing man."

"Do tell?"

The foreman lowered his voice, "Last evening I confronted Pearson and told him his girlfriend would perish, if he refused to tell her he was unable to cope and had fled Detroit. He'd state the relationship was over and he wouldn't be back. Knowing I was deadly serious, Pearson complied and made the call on a disposable Wicker handed him. I figured the police would be listening on her end, or recorded on voice-mail and insisted he keep the message under ten seconds, which he managed to do. Afterwards, the phone was destroyed."

"Is the prisoner still alive?"

"He'll be used as a hostage should anything occur once we depart Electron Era. Afterwards, he'll be disposed of."

The militia leader gazed in the opposite direction, "Confident son-of-a-bitch aren't you?"

"Come on Bill. The guy may have put two and two together - but he's confined; and we managed to stall the cops, indefinitely. I thought you'd be pleased. In a few days we pull up stakes."

An elderly woman tossed bread crumbs on the path and a squadron of pigeons descended. Penther wished he had his rifle.

"What of Besserer how's it between him and the others?"

"No real concerns,' Bell replied. "Wicker can't stomach the guy and the feeling's mutual. Train barely tolerates him. With the clock ticking no one wants to rock the boat. Cooped up in that shit-hole all these months has made everyone shack-wacky. Christ! They even resent the fact I'm able to run outside errands!"

"And Besserer...?"

"The witch-doctor will perish in wake of his own creation as planned."

The briefcase's they carried included final communique's between Besserer and Sir. Resuming their walk Penther noticed an ice-cream vendor. He motioned Bell to follow and they paused beneath an umbrella and ordered two cones. While the woman scooped ice-cream, they unfastened their cuffs and rapidly exchanged briefcases. The transfer was complete before the cones were ready. Penther handed her a bill and they strolled off.

"Eighty hours give or take," Bell mused aloud as he bit into his snack. "The prevailing wind's will dictate the precise moment the weapon is discharged."

Penther tossed his untouched cone in the trash, "I hope the finale is as smooth as your confidence."

Bell reminded his boss the plan was conceived at the top.

As they walked the foreman reiterated their exit strategy.

"Departure from the plant will occur roughly six hours before release of the AC. Besserer will toast his accomplishment by drinking wine laced with strychnine and perish alongside the stockpile. Any incriminating evidence will have been removed from ground zero - except that which points to A'biin. Wicker, Train and myself will head for Indiana and rendezvous with you and Aldo in the bunker. Once our sponsor arrives and the wind's align - we release the poison. Afterwards, we perform our vanishing act."

"If the police show again contact me immediately."

"Of course."

A bit further the militia leader paused, "I'll leave you now, we'll meet in a few days."

Squinting against the sun Penther's longest-serving ally nodded, "I look forward to it."

His boss headed in the direction of Cadillac Tower and paid parking at an automated machine. Driving off with the briefcase on the passenger seat, Penther's wrist was sore as he manoeuvred rush-hour traffic. On Fisher Freeway he accessed I 75 and pondered Bell's assurances. The lodge owner's nerves were shot. What if he were involved in a car accident? With his record the content's in his briefcase would be probed. He glanced in the mirror and signalled into a slower lane. A sports car sped up and practically scraped his rear bumper forcing him to accelerate. Maniacal commuter's closed in on either side - everyone wanted a piece of him! The sound of crunching metal echoed in his skull as he gripped the steering wheel tighter.

Vehicle's continued screaming past at supernatural speeds until the traffic finally eased. Penther's fuel gauge registered under a quarter tank; his throat was dry and hunger pangs rumbled. It was pushing eight pm when a service centre appeared along the right. He swung off the highway and drew up before an available pump. Once the tank was filled he paid the attendant in cash and parked the car. With the briefcase secured to his wrist he sought a restroom. Afterwards, he entered an attached restaurant and took a vacant booth. Browsing a menu he ordered the daily special with coffee. When the meal arrived he ate slowly and sipped his beverage black. He was about to request apple pie and a coffee refill, when his phone vibrated. He glanced at caller display and noticed it was Aldo.

"Yep?"

Dopple was hyper-ventilating on the other end and uttering incoherent gibberish.

"What in hell are you on about!" urged his boss in a harsh whisper.

"I...I been attacked by a demon," Aldo sobbed. "The thing strung me upside down in the Clearing!"

Penther's eyes widened. "Calm down!" he hissed into the receiver. "What happened?"

"It was a demon!"

"What happened!"

"It come looking for you an' I said you were away. I was hung from a tree by my ankles!"

"Where are you now!"

"Inside the lodge. The place is ransacked."

At least Aldo had an excuse for the state of their abode.

"The thing smashed it's way through the back door and ripped apart our security system."

Penther could barely contain his rage, "Stay put I'll be there in under two hours."

The militiaman's face was ashen as he replaced his phone. Fortunately no one was observing him. He skipped the apple pie and left payment on the table. Toting his briefcase he departed the establishment and entered the vehicle. He pressed his head against the steering wheel and struck it repeatedly. When he finally got underway his skull throbbed; his hands were shaking and sweat formed along his brow. He felt like vomiting and rolled down the window. Sucking in mouthfuls of air he considered the litany of bad news. First it was Agent Gill; then the woman on the phone. The cops had visited the electronics plant twice; now Dopple had been assaulted on his own turf.

A hue of orange glowed from the setting sun and he considered Carl Kristy; the call made by the female originated from his device. His phone vibrated causing him to jerk! With one hand on the steering wheel he withdrew it and gazed at the blank display panel.

"Yep?"

Receiving no response he repeated himself. He cursed and tossed the devise on the passenger seat floor. His desolate surroundings offered no consolation. A tree with gnarled limbs appeared in an open field. Dark furrow's stretched like battlefield trenches toward the horizon. Isolated barns and farmhouses appeared occasionally. A pick-up truck whisked by going in the opposite direction otherwise traffic was sparse. Penther glanced in the mirror and noticed circles under his eyes. A pair of headlights bearing down was also observed. Seconds later the vehicle was yards shy of his tail end!

"Go on pass me you bastard!"

Up ahead an off-ramp hove in view. The pursuing SUV swung into the oncoming lane and drew parallel with Penther, who swerved onto the ramp at the last second. His move was anticipated and the SUV braked rapidly and closed in behind. It's tinted windows prevented Penther from determining if there was more than one occupant. They merged onto a county line, and abruptly the SUV pulled ahead and braked sideways blocking access. Penther slammed on his brakes and screeched to a halt several yards from the idling vehicle. Hunkered behind the dashboard with the window down, he reached for his semi-automatic.

"I'm armed you son of a bitch!"

The headlights belonging to the SUV were extinguished and the driver's door opened. A tall figure emerged with his hands raised. Penther recognized his former handler instantly.

"Forgive me my friend," V beckoned. "I bring dire warnings regarding my predecessor Carl Kristy. If you will switch off your lights and engine I shall provide an explanation."

"Wanna talk make a phone call!"

"I attempted that moment's ago but thought better of it. "

Penther's former liaison repeated he was in earnest.

"The situation is serious enough to warrant the presence of our benefactor, who agreed to accompany me. I expect Sir deserves a moment of your time."

"Let him show himself!" Penther bellowed.

The engine and headlights were extinguished and he added, "Have him step out with his hand's raised."

The driver conferred with his companion.

Turning about he said, "We're happy to comply with your request Mr. Penther."

A diesel whined by on the highway and they were alone.

A figure emerged from the opposite side of the SUV with his hands in the air.

"What do you wish to discuss!" the lodge owner hollered.

Gesturing toward the smaller man V lowered his voice, "Allow me to introduce you to Sir. The individual who conceived and bankrolls our endeavour."

Penther noticed the man wore shades in spite of the darkness. Gloves and a fedora added to the mystery.

"We're sorry to have alarmed you Mr. Penther," the stranger gargled.

It sounded as if his larynx was attached to a portable respirator; a more reasonable explanation suggested it was a voice-altering filter.

"You'll recall V's tenure as your handler ended when he was needed to fulfill other obligations. To suffuse the vacancy, Carl Kristy was recruited to carry on V's commendable efforts. A thorough vetting was initiated and it was determined Kristy had no blemishes staining his record. It has since become apparent Mr. Kristy has exploited our fragile enterprise. Funds have gone missing and there have been veiled threats. He's attempted to cast you and your followers in an unflattering light; implying you'll renege on your allegiance and expose our activities. Regardless, I know you and your men remain committed to our cause."

Needing no excuse to despise Kristy the lodge owner hedged, "How did you find me?"

"If you'll allow us to lower our arms I'll explain?" Sir entreated.

Penther nodded and kept a bead on the pair.

"Thank you," acknowledged the smaller man bringing his hands to his side. "V knew you were in Detroit and was aware of the alternate route you traverse on your return to Rykles Clearing."

Penther allowed him to continue.

"At this late stage things might become compromised if measures aren't taken with regards to Carl Kristy."

"What 'things' are you referring to...?"

Sir regarded the militiaman's precaution, "Our warning to the nation's lawmakers that sanctuary will no longer be granted to foreigner's. Those seeking asylum will find America a far more inhospitable place than the wretched hellholes they crawl from."

The words might've been written by Penther.

"Use of your bunker for detonation purposes is greatly appreciated," pursued the mystery man. "Once you and your men claim your most precious possessions and have taken flight, you'll regroup at an undisclosed location – safely below the radar. Preparations for a follow-up strike elsewhere; deploying an alternate deterrent will get underway. However, before anything can be considered Kristy must be silenced."

Sir was again challenged, "So how is it you employ a foreigner?"

Penther nodded towards his assistant who barely flinched.

"I need the expertise and services V provides," responded their paymaster. "He's proficient in matters I'm unable to assume physically."

Convinced of who he claimed to be the militia leader remarked, "So why are we here?"

"I want one of your people to dispatch Kristy."

"Why not allow V the pleasure?"

"Kristy needs to die within Electron Era where your men are stationed. I'll issue him a directive instructing he check up on Detroit. Once he's inside the plant he's yours. Similar to Dr. Besserer's planned demise; strychnine suicide must be the cause of death. You'll be informed when Kristy will arrive."

"The matter falls under Jackson Bell's watch," rejoined Penther. "I'll fill him in."

"Thank you," the voice curdled.

A pause ensued before Sir continued.

"Two million dollars will be transferred into an offshore account made out to you under a fictitious name, following launch of the AC," Sir allowed. "As a token of my sincerity I intend to issue a portion of that sum to you now. I only ask it be stored safely within the bunker, and not in your lodge or the trunk of an automobile."

"You're giving money now?"

"A fraction of it," Sir remarked. "Hopefully, this will assist in what needs to be done as the operation concludes. I take it your people have made plans for exile?"

"We travel light."

"Good."

"So Kristy is disposed of what then?"

"We await word from Besserer signalling readiness of the weapon. Once he's been force fed the same poisonous beverage as his departed countryman; the team departs Electron Era and regroups at the bunker. When the winds comply we launch the payload and watch the world focus upon Detroit."

Mosquitoes swarmed and Penther slapped the side of his face

"A suitcase containing bundles of fifty-dollar bills totalling twenty-five thousand dollars, is in the rear of our vehicle," Sir resumed. "Permit my associate to fetch the cash and we'll be on our way."

Concealing his astonishment Penther allowed V to initiate the transfer. Meanwhile, he retrieved the briefcase and placed it on the ground for Sir to recoup.

"It contains Besserer's final reports," the lodge owner indicated. "Evidently, Kristy won't be passing them along."

"I take it you've had issue with him yourself?"

Penther barely hesitated, "He was careless and perilous! I was contacted by a woman using his encrypted device."

"Really! What did she have to say?"

"I immediately severed connection."

"Interesting..."

Sensing his curiosity the militiaman remarked, "Any idea who she might be?"

"Probably one of Kristy's whores."

Sir changed topics and inquired about Aldo. The lodge owner withheld news of Dopple's recent assault saying, "He provides stellar security at the compound."

The cash was placed on the hood of the Penther's car and V unlocked the suitcase. The militia leader reached in and rolled several bill's between his fingers.

"Twenty-five thousand?" he muttered.

"The rest will be deposited once we've completed our task," Sir reiterated.

Penther secured the suitcase within the trunk of his rented automobile and tucked the key away. Reclaiming the driver's seat he spoke to his benefactor through the open window, "I'll see your request regarding Kristy is carried out. Let me know when he's expected in Detroit."

"We're grateful Mr. Penther."

The car was brought about so it faced the highway and he started away. Ninety minutes later he swung onto the Yokum Trail exhausted from the turn of events. The vehicle had to be driven back to the dealership in Fort Wayne next day. Hopefully, his bodyguard will have recovered enough to follow in the minivan for the return trip. The attack on Aldo preyed upon his mind. Anticipating the ransacked lodge, Penther drew up before their abode and heard the dogs. Exiting the vehicle, he withdrew the suitcase and strode a path toward the bunker. The fortified door was accessed and the loot was stashed within.

Surrounded by woods the trail led back toward the Clearing. With the lodge in view he advanced to face the carnage. Penther allowed a faint smile to crease his lips. He'd met the big cheese and was given the green light to end Kristy's miserable existence.

———————

Robert Blakie-Harris took a seat before members of the Intelligence Review Committee. The Chairman withdrew a file-folder from his briefcase and placed several documents on the conference table. As they circulated, he adjusted his specs and said in a pronounced New England twang, "Catherine, Ramsay, Nelson; Royston, Jeremy and Stanton, thank you for being present."

They glanced up and mumbled, "Director."

"The document in your hands is a summary of a meeting held yesterday between the President's senior security advisers and others, including myself. The brief detailing this committee's recommendations, with regards to the mid-west terror-file was handed to the President's principle secretary."

Anticipation in the room depleted.

CIA Deputy Director Seymour-Johns spoke first, "That's it!"

"For the moment yes."

"Excuse me Bob. Are you saying there's to be no movement on this file?"

"I'm saying the formalities of protocol must prevail, Nelson. I've been assured a special session involving the President and the Joint Chiefs gets underway tomorrow. Within a few days a decision will be made."

Seymour-Johns glanced about the table with an incredulous look on his face.

"We don't have time for the administration to dawdle on a thing like this," he insisted. "We're talking about the lives of millions of Americans. The intelligence obtained suggests a massive strike will occur somewhere in the American heartland. SIAG sleeper's have been activated and a spy in our custody was silenced! It's possible the Russian mob smuggled quantities of plutonium from Siberian stockpiles into SIAG laboratories. Those material's might have found their way into the US to be assembled and detonated. We should point a series of long-range missiles and position an aircraft carrier on high alert in the Mediterranean. By doing so, the ruling elite of A'biin will know they're within our sights should anything happen on American turf."

"If an incident occurs and it wasn't connected to A'biin what then?" cautioned Royston Adams. "Such action would incite an uprising throughout the entire Middle-East."

The CIA man balked. "Those A'biinian bastards are well on their way to completing their effin' nuclear program - if it's not already operational."

Others nodded with the notable exception being FBI counterpart Catherine Levine, "I share Nelson's concerns, Chairman. However, if we're wrong we'd be handing extremist forces in the region a gift-wrapped present."

The UCOMA Director agreed, "Hardliners within A'biin's hierarchy have been cast aside in favour of a more far-sighted leadership - one which encourages dialogue with the west. To jeopardize this would be foolhardy. Diplomacy is crucial at this stage. Meantime, we keep our ear to the ground and remain vigilant along our borders."

Travers of Homeland Security shuffled in his seat.

Taking the cue the Chairman said, "Jeremy your thoughts?"

Leaning forward he said, "I'm grateful for the confidence Royston shows in Homeland's ability - and his appeal for caution. However, I believe he takes a rosy view. Other than a few informants, we have no reliable sources inside A'biin and know virtually nothing. I concur with Nelson."

The Chairman focused on the individual seated next to him, "Stanton?"

"I'm with Nelson," spouted the second in command of Military Intelligence at the Pentagon."

"Ramsay?"

"We should send a strong message to any terrorist organization intent on attacking the US," remarked the upstart from Firearms and Tobacco. "I'm not advocating a Truman-style approach. However, a well-placed smart-bomb aimed at an oil-refinery, or a known terrorist stronghold would give them pause."

The woman widely touted as being the next FBI Director spoke again.

"A delicate balance currently exists. Our differences were always with the hardliners and their unwavering fundamentalist views. Now that they've been driven from the ranks; beefing our presence in the middle-east or staging an outright attack would force Siana to revert to old ways."

Seymour-Johns folded his arms and shook his head.

The Chairman closed his briefcase and rose, "The President will be issued a final report detailing members of this Committee's expressed positions on the matter. You'll be contacted at some point over the next forty-eight hours. Thank you for your input, this session is concluded."

Blakie-Harris strode hurriedly from the room and was met by a host of fawning aids. The remaining attendees slowly rose. A palpable tension was in the air as they filed out the doors.

Following the encounter with Aldo Dopple, Jesse returned to the Emerald City Motor Motel and changed into dry clothes. He packed his suitcases and placed the room key into an office drop-box. It was nearly 2 am when he finally hit the road. Ninety minutes later he crossed the state line and drew up before a Waffle House. Seating himself at the counter, he ordered coffee and recalled the professor was due back from Detroit that evening. His weary operative hoped to get some rest in the interim.

As Jesse neared Lantern Falls he guided the car onto a ramp linking him with Windover Road. Delivering the vehicle to it's 24-hour car-rental base, he retrieved his luggage and entered the office. He passed the keys to an attendant and was issued a receipt. Jesse thanked the man and asked if he'd mind calling a cab. He waited on the sidewalk with the suitcase's flanking him; when one drew up he placed his luggage in the rear seat and climbed inside. Requesting the driver drop him off before Sentinel Hall; it would been hazardous lugging a pair of suitcases along the sloping trail. With baggage in hand he mounted the steps and stood before the lobby entrance. Abruptly, one of the massive doors swung open and Dennis Drake was there to offer assistance. Jesse said he'd manage and they chatted briefly. Afterwards, he crossed the lobby floor and descended the staircase. Once Lee's office was accessed he aimed the remote and entered Control. Inside his quarters Jesse placed the suitcases aside and tumbled into bed.

At roughly six that evening he awoke to find the professor in the kitchen brewing coffee.

"Just the man I wanted to see," Lee remarked cheerfully. "Have a seat I'll fetch us a cup and we'll get caught up."

Retrieving two mugs he said, "Sleep well?"

"Roughly eleven hours," his recruit responded sluggishly.

"I was informed you'd arrived early this morning."

Jesse sat down and a steaming mug appeared before him.

"You sufficiently awake to provide an update on Indiana?" inquired the professor.

"Of course."

As event's were recalled Jesse mentioned the queries made in Ellery; the recorded conversation between Penther and Dopple. He outlined his vain search of the lodge and concluded by detailing Kriel's encounter with Aldo Dopple.

"There are some highlights on the recording which might interest you," he added.

Lee expressed great interest.

His operative continued, "When Dopple was grilled about the whereabouts of Penther's former disciples he held fast. On the recording he's bitter about not being permitted to chauffeur Penther to Fort Wayne. Instead, he's instructed to guard their premises. That part didn't go so well."

Lee considered all this, "I suspect Aldo's out of the loop regarding key aspects of his boss's affairs. Penther is extremely adept at evading FBI watchers as he journeys forth. Rented cars, cash transactions for everything; uses fake ID in the same manner we do. His phone is relayed along a coded frequency SIGINT would find difficult to crack and used sparingly. This suggests he's manipulated by a powerful clandestine figure."

"You think it's our renegade?"

"I wouldn't rule it out."

Jesse backtracked, "Dopple's profile states he's a skilled marksman. He's also a confirmed sociopath, if he's kept in the dark it's for a reason. With Penther elsewhere the kitchen was littered with empty liquor bottles, upended chairs, spilled whisky, upturned ashtrays, guns, ammo! He was well over the rainbow by the time Kriel made his unscheduled appearance."

"I'm sure that brought him back to earth."

"Somewhat."

"Poor bugger."

Jesse grinned and blew on his coffee. "I only wish he'd revealed more. He had every reason to considering how fried he was when company arrived."

"I hope Kriel didn't go too hard on him?"

"It was mostly posturing," Lee was assured. "Aside from allowing Aldo to see the world from a refreshing new viewpoint - no harm was done."

"Lucky for him," rejoined the professor. "Let's consider Dopple a dangerous foot-soldier, but an unlikely key player. More succinctly we find evidence points to Detroit. Your recording along with FBI report's maintain Penther's frequent forays there. My own investigation has turned up suspicious activity in the city as well. All of which has to do with your next assignment."

Lee paused to refill their cups and appeared pensive.

"While driving back from Detroit I received a call from Sasha, who informed me an intruder was caught on camera in the Commons building, roughly a week ago. The breach was discovered during a bi-monthly review of SC visuals. Whenever unauthorized entry is detected during playback the recording stops automatically, allowing the image to be scrutinized. Every building on campus is monitored. Sasha indicated the trespasser's features are mostly out of camera range, but believes he or she, were hunkered in a room facing Sentinel Hall. From there they'd be able to observe comings and goings unobstructed. Your license plates were likely photographed, resulting in your mother's home address being revealed. Whoever paid both she and Dorothy a visit, has access to some sophisticated cross-referencing technology."

Jesse was silent.

Lee got to his feet, "Let's listen to your recording."

____

TWENTY

Once the disc recorded at Rykles Clearing had been reviewed Lee admitted there was plenty of innuendo, but nothing incriminating. Penther was able to convey meaning without revealing a thing; likewise Aldo had been drilled to do the same. Having his cabin bugged and phone tapped most of his adult life, the militia leader had adopted a new vocabulary - one omitting names, dates and times. Lee listened passively as Aldo's burnt-sausage incident unravelled. It was when being chastised by Penther for questioning a directive, that the older man leaned forward and took notice. Their entire exchange was captured clearly - along with the sound of a snapping twig. The dogs erupted instantly and their snarls and growls grew in intensity. Heavy breathing and footsteps echoed as the occupant's of the lodge were summoned to action. Evidently, the dogs stopped short of entering the woods, choosing instead to remain within the boundaries of the Clearing. Jesse acknowledged making it back to his vehicle, but confessed he was unable to recall getting there.

Both he and the professor agreed the most revealing moment was when Penther instructed his subordinate not to pack anything; lest it be construed they planned a hasty departure. Lee considered this a startling piece of intelligence, uncharacteristic of the lodge owner's cautious delivery. The recorded conversation was replayed twice before the pair concluded.

Jesse decided a jog was in order and excused himself. Meanwhile, Lee had a number of UCOMA duties to attend to. He sat before a workstation and began reviewing reams of incoming data. Sliding his roller chair several feet over, he accessed a separate screen with the proper password and squinted at the deluge of incoming messages. Most were routine exchanges between UCOMA personnel, however an encrypted message caught his eye. Posted within the hour, it was from his Chicago colleague Teddy Marin. Lee had texted the FBI agent to inquire about development's regarding Gillian Burke. As Marin's response was transcribed a cloud fell over the proceedings. Lee paused and re-read the message

* CANNOT ASSIST REGARDING WHEREABOUTS OF THE BURKE WOMAN NOR THE STATUS OF HER FAMILY. I AM NO LONGER PRIVY TO THE FILE. THE MATTER IS CLASSIFIED - THEODORE *

There was no reading between the lines. The meaning was as blunt as a dull rock.

Law enforcement agents are often pulled from one file to assist on another - Lee's concern here was the adopted tone. Having worked closely with Teddy, the professor admired him enormously. While in Chicago his full support had been extended. Apparently, he'd succumbed to pressure and was forced not to cooperate. Lee saved the text and placed the matter aside.

Sliding his chair back he resumed scrolling orbiting transmissions.

His phone vibrated and a text from the UCOMA Director appeared. Royston Adams was informing him he'd been in touch with a senior SIGINT official, and was awaiting a response as to why the Grissim station was withheld portions of daily briefs. Adams promised to keep him posted.

The professor continued to feel remorse over Stuart Tuppins passing. He glanced at his old workstation and felt Stu's presence. A week after the young man had been laid to rest in a tiny ceremony Lee attended in Cleveland, his death remained profoundly disturbing.

An onscreen file with Stuart's name attached was uploaded. It was the printout the young man received from a neighbouring UCOMA station just before he died. The document covered the same timeline as when Grissim was receiving deficient briefs. Comparisons underscored several omitted passages. One excluded item informed UCOMA staffer's of an encrypted communique relayed to Evanston, Illinois by way of Siana. The case of Gillian Burke flashed before Lee's eyes. A transcription of the communique by SIGINT analyst's was included. It confirmed her as the likely the recipient of an access signal.

The message could not be viewed as subterfuge - it was a direct communique to an agent in waiting. The relay implied the operative would replace and possibly terminate her predecessor in the field.

Lee tossed his pencil down and rubbed the bridge of his nose.

He contacted security and Dennis Drake responded.

"How are things at your end?"

"Quiet Sir. Nothing on the monitors or on my rounds."

"Contact me if anything arises."

"Will do."

It was almost midnight when Jesse entered the IRI and found the professor asleep with his head on his chest. Light cast by the screen-saver made his skin glow. A series of odd markings were scribbled on paper before him. Lee was assisted to his quarters and into bed. Jesse removed his shoes and placed his phone nearby then withdrew.

Lee's devise shattered the stillness ninety minutes later. Unable to recall returning to his quarters; the phone lay next to his bed with the display screen tinted orange - declaring a Priority 2 call.

"Hello."

"Sorry to rouse you Lee," imparted Blakie-Harris. "It's crucial we meet."

Sitting upright the UCOMA analyst coughed, "Say again?"

"We need to meet! I can't go into anything now; suffice to say your expertise regarding a certain matter is warranted. There's a stalemate here in Maryland between select members of Intel and several senior White House advisers. I need your counsel."

The Director's request was both direct and shrouded in doublespeak.

"When do you wish to meet?"

"Nine am. In light of the inconvenience I'll come to you."

"You'll come to Lantern Falls?"

"It's urgent."

"Of course."

"We'll meet at the Institute."

"Actually, I'd prefer downtown Robert."

"Fine. Where?"

Lee thought for a moment and said, "There's a lunch counter at Saphron's Department Store on Davies Drive."

A reluctant pause followed, "We'll find it. Nine sharp - see you then."

The professor placed the phone aside and sat on the edge of the bed. He vaguely recalled being assisted to his room. Likely, his young colleague was fast asleep within his quarters.

———————

Inside the cubicle referred to as an office Heron focused on the screen before him. A GPS signal was advancing at a snail's pace westward along a tiny stretch of American heartland. On a separate front he pondered Azil Besserer's appearance on some security footage he'd been instructed to analyze. Images highlighted the scientist being smuggled into the Marine Terminal at Jacksonville, Florida. The content had been streamed to Siana by US Customs who demanded an explanation. The wise men were concerned the treacherous microbiologist carried samples of a deadly concoction he claimed to have developed, while in service of the SIAG. As such Heron bore the brunt of their collective fears. The greying analyst had lost two operatives within one week of each other. Both had been stationed for lengthy periods in the United States. The first was murdered; his replacement, a sleeper code-named Ulsar simply vanished. US authorities denied coercion in the first case; claiming the SIAG agent in their custody had been poisoned with strychnine. As fate would have it Ulsar arrived in Jacksonville at precisely the time Besserer was smuggled into the country.

It seemed more than coincidental.

After a month's deliberation the wise men instructed the beleaguered handler to release an assassin. In far-away Illinois Taras was issued a single directive: 'Hunt down Ulsar and terminate his existence'. An exceptional student during her formative years, it was hoped she'd be able to root out the turncoat.

SIAG agent's operating undercover in North America were controlled by Heron. Prior to Ulsar's defection, the wayward sleeper informed his handler he was driving to Florida for a few days sailing. Heron allowed the dubious operative twenty-four hours leverage in order to track him. Abruptly, his signal disappeared several miles west of Jacksonville. If Ulsar was dead the device embedded in his shin would've lain dormant. Instead, the signal vanished entirely, suggesting the tracer had been removed by whomever controlled him. At this stage Taras was directed to seek out and dispatch the former library researcher.

A decade earlier Ulsar's file had landed on Heron's desk. Having never instructed the aspiring operative, his skill at penetrating the most challenging fortifications was renown; making Heron's present task more daunting. He berated himself for having not dealt properly with Ulsar. The warning signs were there! Shuffling continually between Manhattan, Cambridge and upstate Massachusetts, he took off precious time from his cover job. The identity he'd cultivated was placed in jeopardy with the attention he drew. The cautious image fostered among co-workers and neighbours eroded entirely. The reckless Casanova was warned he'd be recalled if further light was cast on him by virtue of his indifference. The former sleeper succumbed to the lure of Western enticement, and grasped at the first straw. Additionally, it became apparent Azil Besserer was working against A'biin's interests, at the behest of the same shadowy figure controlling Ulsar.

———————

Far from the colourful minarets adorning the palatial towers of Siana; the days of living under deep-cover among the suburbs of Chicago would never be forgotten. While her daughter painted watercolours in the backyard, Gillian had been tidying their living room. Upstairs, the child's father was busy at work in his study. Her main concern at the time was finding something the girl's grandfather might enjoy over the coming weekend. Tom Burke was arriving from St. Louis two days hence. Hanging out with his family was all he required; however it was good to have a backup plan.

The sudden vibration of Gillian's phone startled her. Retrieving it she observed the blank display panel. Protocol dictated a double-ring would occur precisely three minutes after contact was established. Responding on cue she discovered her former teacher Heron had texted a secured message from Siana. Familiar with the latest code-configurations she set about transcribing. The message informed her a crisis had occurred and her services were required immediately.

Whenever a SIAG agent blows cover, dies or is recalled; a backup sleeper is given ten days before entering the field as a replacement. The transitional period is necessary in dealing with the emotional upheaval affecting the operative, as he or she prepares to distance themselves for an indefinite period of time. With the current situation, Gillian was allotted only four days preparation before slipping into her other skin. The text informed her a traitor was in play. If circumstances weren't remedied, lives would be lost and global repercussions might ensue. A SIAG operative had been murdered; a sleeper named Ulsar was in line to replace him. Evidently, it was he who'd turned deceiver and she was instructed to destroy the insurgent. The text outlined only the briefest of clues, indicating the rakish sleeper had become involved with a Harvard girl nicknamed 'Candle'.

Gillian replaced her phone and faced the fireplace mantle, where a series of family portraits were displayed. The images documented a life she'd come to cherish. She picked out a photo of Samantha taken on her first birthday; gazing at her giddy features and began to weep. A framed image of Steven was next to it. His face was brimful of hope for the future and she smiled through the tears.

The moment had finally arrived.

Forced to abandon the husband and child she adored, the reality of her predicament seemed unbearable and she wept uncontrollably. Her grief went no further than the drawn curtains of her shattered world.

Exiting the lobby and straddling a broad corridor Samuel Train's footsteps echoed off the Fiberglas along his left. He entered the shipping room and crossed towards a loading dock, making certain the doors were secured. Propped against a nearby wall, he slid aside a sheave of 6' by 4' plywood sheets bound together with twine. Behind the obstruction a solid metal door was revealed. Removing his pass he placed it on a scanner and entered. Once accomplished, the plywood was tugged back into place with attached twine extending beneath the door crack. Train descended a metal stairwell and encountered a passageway leading off in two directions. Turning left he continued toward a pair of secured metal doors. Once entry was accessed a bare light bulb revealed their sleeping quarters and a mess room, fashioned with office partitions along the corridor. A converted storage room was designated as Azil Besserer's quarters. Above a floor drain in an existing washroom a shower had been installed.

A second pair of metal doors sealed off an enclosed atrium.

Train slid his pass along the scanner and entered, pausing short of a hermetically sealed decontamination chamber. The air-tight compartment contained Level A protective suits stored in lockers. For purposes of scrubbing down a shower featured prominently. A short distance away Besserer's lab had been erected. Whenever the microbiologist was assisted they were required to wear Personal Protective Equipment (PPE).

In the middle of the chamber, a circular steel vat had been inserted into an excavated portion of the concrete floor. Hosting a stockpile of polystyrene cubes; the cavity measured eight feet wide and four feet deep. Placed strategically about it's circumference industrial fans stood with their faces tilted skywards. Train considered the months they'd spent filling the vat. He gazed at the content's and shivered. Enough lethal agent was stored within to render the twin cities of Detroit/Windsor a wasteland.

Meantime, Jackson Bell was upstairs in his office conferring with Besserer. Hopefully, the biologist was informing him the weapon was finally operational. His associate Cal Wicker was sleeping. Their revered chief William Penther was point man on the outside, serving as liaison between themselves and the individual funding the operation.

Train shook his head recalling their endeavour. If he wasn't mad already another week in this purgatory would seal the deal. Weary of donning PPE gear day in and day out; nightmares depicting on-site fires or invading hordes of Federal agent's plagued him constantly. Tension between Bell, Wicker and himself had intensified. Cooped up in the dungeon-like environment wrought obvious friction. At least Bell was able to depart the building on supply runs and errands. Train desired nothing more than to be outdoors. If that meant ducking down back roads for the rest of his life - so be it. Following launch of their weapon Penther's paramilitary army would likely swell to unprecedented numbers. Their efforts might even incite civil war, between the monolithic parasite that was the US Government and everyone else. In wake of their attack, Penther's band intended to delve underground and resurface thousands of miles away with a flow of capital and newly forged identities.

Besserer claimed his virulent Anthrax isolate was slow to start multiplying - not an unusual occurrence under conditions ascribed to a foreign continent he added. Burgeoning rapidly enough to remain on schedule the creation of spores was induced. Purification lagged initially before proving successful. As the enhanced Anthrax accumulated; injecting tens of thousands if polystyrene cubes was an arduous process.

Train's thoughts drifted to the poor wretch wasting away in a janitor's room down the hall. Slated to die once they left for Indiana he urged the others to spare him. It hardly mattered when everyone were doomed anyway. Unable to relax he envied Wicker's ability to sleep. Doubts consistently nagged him. None were more pressing than the latest visit by police regarding the missing employee. To hear Jackson Bell tell it the cops were a mere annoyance

That morning Train had been conferring with him in the supervisor office. He was contacted by Wicker in the front lobby, informing him the detective who'd paid a previous visit had returned and requested a word.

This would be their third encounter with local authorities and Train's heart pounded!

Bell departed the office and entered the lobby. Once greetings were exchanged, DeLong informed him the police had intercepted a call made the previous evening to Gloria Mayorga, girlfriend of the missing technician. The gist of the message was conveyed and he stated the caller was Ray Pearson.

Bell shook his head, "At least he's safe."

DeLong shrugged, "Stress and worry - people run from it sometimes."

The detective apologized for any inconvenience bid good day and left.

The foreman glanced at Wicker and a smile formed along his lips.

He returned to the office and found Train anxiously awaiting. Seating himself behind his desk Bell explained what just occurred. He clasped his fingers behind his head savouring the success of his stall tactic.

Despite the supervisor's assurances Train remained uncomfortable. He reentered their quarters downstairs and found Wicker still sleeping. Unable to rest he spent most of that afternoon gazing from the rear door of the shipping room. That evening long after the lab technicians had departed he decided to pay another visit to lobby. He nodded at the night watchman and stood at the plate-glass entrance glancing both ways along Sentra Avenue. A Pontiac was observed parked a short ways up the darkened artery.

"Flotsin."

"Sir."

"Get over here."

Rising from his desk the night guard ambled toward the entrance. Train inquired if he was able to identify the vehicle stationed alongside the curb up the street. Harry glanced in that direction, "It's the same car from last night. It drove by twice. A big ole' Pontiac. They don't don't make 'em like that anymore."

"Why wasn't this reported to Mr. Bell?"

The security guard stammered, "Um ... I think it belongs to someone working night-shift 'round here..."

While Flotsin blathered Train departed the lobby and made for the supervisor's office. Not bothering to knock he entered and found Bell behind the desk scrolling his device.

"Thought you'd like to know that same detective is lurking about outside. His car is parked up the street."

Bell leaned over the desk, "Hope you didn't make a scene."

"I was checking up and noticed the Pontiac. Flotsin said it cruised by twice last night!"

"Why didn't he inform me?"

"He figured the car belonged to someone working nearby. I figure we're being monitored."

"Don't start reciting that paranoid garbage at this late stage."

"Were being observed!" Train shot back.

Bell slammed down his fist, "Get outta here and don't go blubberin' that shit to Wicker and get him riled. I'll bring you both up to date within the next few hours. Until then do your job."

"I am doing my job."

"Get outta here!"

An hour later as Train lay sprawled along his bunk he heard footsteps echoing along the subterranean corridor. Abruptly, the blanket draping the entrance of their quarters parted and Bell entered.

Wicker stirred beneath his sleeping bag, "What gives...?"

Eyeballing Train who glared back the foreman said, "Clean up starts now we depart for Rykles Clearing tomorrow."

Train could hardly believe what he was hearing. Forgetting the animosity between he and Bell, he rose and faked a sucker-punch then threw an arm about his shoulder. Wicker released a whoop and jumped into the fray. The surreal scene resembled the winning goal of a playoff game in overtime. Besserer heard the commotion and pocked his head out the door then withdrew.

Bell cleared his throat,"Once its light we'll meet in the atrium to discuss our exit strategy a final time."

———————

In wake of the call he'd received from the NSA Director of Operations, Lee managed four more hours sleep. Once he'd roused himself he reached for Dorothy and discovered an empty bed. Sitting upright he remembered Control was home for the time being. He longed for a window to determine if it was cloudy or fair outdoors and settled for a radio update. Curious about the meeting slated to take place in town, he tossed a towel about his shoulders and attended to washroom duties. Afterwards, he made coffee and brought up a file he'd prepared for Jesse at his workstation. Downloading it's content's onto a flash-drive, the material detailed Kriel's pending trip to industrial Detroit.

The professor's phone rumbled and he noticed it was a secured text from Brandon DeLong. He wondered if the Chicago detective was withdrawing his support in the same manner Teddy Marin had. He discovered otherwise and learned a phone call had been placed by Ray Pearson to Gloria Mayorga. Police tapped the call and heard Pearson declare he was tired of both her and Detroit and was out of there. Ms. Mayorga was questioned and insisted the voice was Ray's but the words weren't. She stated his dialogue sounded forced and feared he was in danger. Unfortunately, not enough time was afforded to trace the call.

DeLong mentioned he stopped by Electron Era to inform the supervisor of the news. The detective reassured Lee nothing regarding any of this would pass from his lips. Nevertheless, he felt bound to honour Ms. Mayorga's concerns and spent two nights conducting surveillance outside the missing man's workplace. Other than a different watchman nothing was observed.

Lee texted DeLong back and thanked him for the update. He remained concerned their suspicion's might cause those within the plant to bolt. The professor had to remind himself, Electron Era might otherwise be a crystal meth operation or a black market warehouse.

The shower was running in their living quarters as Lee reviewed his notes regarding Kriel's assignment. The case suggested a behind-the-scenes peek at the electronics plant was warranted.

Jesse entered Control toting his coffee mug.

"Sleep well?" Lee inquired.

"Like a bear in winter."

"I vaguely recall being assisted to my room last night, thanks."

"No problem," Jesse replied. "You've been working late."

"The situation would be quite concerning without your help."

The young man blew on his coffee.

"You leave for Detroit this afternoon."

Jesse appeared startled.

"I received a call early this morning from Robert Blakie-Harris, NSA Director of Operations. He requests my input into an undisclosed matter. Whatever it is it must be important, he's meeting me here in Lantern Falls this morning."

"Should we tidy up?"

"Situation being what it is I suggested we avoid Grissim and chose an inauspicious spot downtown."

"Is this meeting place classified?"

"Saphron's Department Store on Davies Drive. They host a superb lunch counter."

Jesse frowned, "You're sure the Director will appreciate such extravagance?"

"Certainly," Lee responded. "There's safety in numbers and the coffee's excellent."

"Does the meeting have any bearing on our case?"

The older man shrugged his shoulders, "I'll let you know if it does. Meantime, let's discuss the Detroit trip. You'll depart this afternoon by Greyhound and rent a vehicle once you arrive. The bus leaves at 4 pm, which gives you time to review the directives I've set down on flash-drive and study the layout. The contents will bring you up to date regarding Electron Era, the electronics plant you'll infiltrate. Once you've reviewed the material I'll answer any questions."

Lee mentioned the assistance he'd received from an old pal servicing the Detroit Police Department, a detective named Brandon DeLong; who divulged the industrial sites they'd visited. He spoke of an interview they'd conducted with the foreman of Electron Era, regarding a missing employee named Ray Pearson. A shipper and security guard were also questioned, as was Ray's girlfriend.

"We were given a tour by the supervisor a man named Jackson Bell," resumed the professor. "Other than a one-page website offering an exterior photograph and little else, nothing is on file regarding the firm. DeLong managed to forward an interior layout of the plant from city archives. It's in my quarters I'll fetch it presently."

Jesse had questions about security. But they could wait until Lee returned from his meeting with the NSA chieftain.

"So Kriel is to penetrate the facility and initiate a search."

"Precisely."

"Do you suppose the local authorities will be alerted an intruder has breached the space?"

"Only if that person is detected."

"I see."

"Until we know what we're dealing with there can be no police, Jesse. I've explained the same to detective DeLong. He's agreed to keep things close to his chest. We don't want anyone hightailing it just yet."

Lee gathered some printouts from off the bench.

"There are obstacles and plenty of cameras," he continued. "You'll need to acquire an access pass somehow. I'll leave that to your discretion."

He glanced at his wristwatch and noticed the meeting with Blakie-Harris was fast approaching.

Snapping his briefcase shut he said, "Gotta go."

Jesse downed the remains of his coffee and nodded.

"I'll be back before noon," Lee called out.

"Hope there's space at the lunch counter."

"Thanks."

The professor entered the storage room and vanished into the netherworld.

Meanwhile, Jesse returned to his quarters and slipped the flash-key into his laptop.

TWENTY-ONE

A jackrabbit scurried across the road and the pungent odour of moist vegetation scented the air. Through night-vision binoculars a view of the Yokum Trail and the lodge was afforded. From his concealed position nothing escaped Kristy's sight-lines; the exception being the bunker, which was obscured by trees and foliage. Beyond this point only dense forest existed. Dopple used to say if someone attempted to penetrate these woods they were no longer around to talk about it.

Shielded by brush and pine on a rising crest, Kristy lay sprawled along a wool blanket roughly two-hundred yards from the lodge. Remaining beyond scent range of the dobermans; he'd forged a wide reconnaissance among the surrounding woods to ensure the best view. The lasers and heat sensors he knew existed about the Clearing were mysteriously dysfunctional. While making his way, he noticed the rear door of the lodge pummelled inward and the screen door hanging from hinges.

The notion Aldo was within prevailed and was confirmed with Penther's arrival. As the dogs anxiously acknowledged their master from within the lodge, the militia leader stepped from a rented automobile. He removed a suitcase from the trunk he started along a path toward the bunker. Moments later he reemerged from the trees and cautiously approached the lodge. Observing the shattered rear door, he bellowed Aldo's name and the bodyguard appeared on the rear deck looking haggard and drawn. Standing on the dry, cracked earth his boss glared at him.

Without the benefit of a listening device Kristy was unable to hear their exchange. Judging from the body-language things didn't look good. Aldo was hastened back inside and the door was slammed silencing the crickets.

Despite Kristy's curiosity it was the SIAG female who consumed his thoughts. Hopefully, the trail he'd left appeared genuine.

Departing Indianapolis early that afternoon he found a sports store in the suburbs. A sleeping bag was purchased along with night-vision binoculars; a camouflaged raincoat rounded out inventory. Quantities of bottled water and fruit were stored in a backpack inside the trunk of his rental. When he arrived in Ellery the supplies were transferred to a taxi; with the driver instructed to drop him off along the upper reaches of the Yokum Trail. It was imperative he arrive at least two hours in advance of Penther's return from Detroit.

The most important item he possessed was nestled beneath his right shoulder. Anyone approaching from the road, woods or Clearing registered in his rifle scope. He pondered the dispatch he'd received from 'This way' on behalf of the Face. In it he was instructed to refrain from terminating the SIAG woman as originally planned. Instead, she was to be taken hostage and secured within the bunker. Once the Face arrived she'd be interrogated by him personally. Secretly relieved Kristy texted his compliance.

He maintained grip on the rifle, regardless.

Around these parts temperatures tended to dip into the low double-digits during the wee small hours of summer. He felt a chill and half-expected the woman to appear. Brief naps were snagged and he sprayed the air with repellent as the mosquitoes began to swarm. Down an incline the lodge remained eerily quiet. He considered the faulty alarms and smashed door. Abruptly, rustling was heard to his rear. Gripping the rifle he scanned the area for signs of someone or something.

The clock mounted above the lime-green milkshake machine indicated 9:05 am. Seated at one end of the lunch counter, Lee Tondar glanced in the facing mirror observing the reflected images of other patrons. Admittedly, there wasn't much intimacy in his choice of a meeting place; however, safety lay in obscurity and he reached for a menu. A man wearing a suit and shades was observed seating himself at the opposite end of the lunch counter. He whispered something into a tiny devise and seconds later the Director, accompanied by a Secret Service man took seats on stools next to Lee's.

The NSA honcho placed his briefcase on the counter, "Sorry for the delay Lee. Detail insist upon reconnaissance."

"You don't travel alone much do you?"

"Protocol. Two agents inside and a waiting driver. It's insane especially for a private person like myself."

"It's not often you visit our community Robert."

"Actually its the first time."

A waitress approached, "Can I help you gentlemen?"

Lee waited for the Director who insisted he go first.

"Bran muffin and coffee please"

"Okee-dokee. And for you?"

Taken back by her forthrightness Blakie-Harris replied in crisp New Englandese, "Is oregano tea on the menu?"

"Just yer' basic Red Rose darlin'."

"That will be fine."

She faced the gentleman seated on his other side, "He with you?".

"Um...he ate earlier."

"No coffee?" she pressed.

"No coffee."

She blinked and scurried off.

"You might have arranged a more appropriate venue Lee!" the Director whispered peevishly.

"I take it your not hungry?"

Ripping a napkin from the dispenser the Director dabbed his forehead and adjusted his specs, "There's not even a booth where we can talk privately."

"It's hard finding intimacy in a town like this," Lee lamented. "Among the more upscale establishments strangers get the eyeball. This was the most secure place I could think of."

The Director frowned, "I'll dine aboard the return flight. The food is actually quite agreeable."

"We should have met there instead."

"Why in blazes didn't we meet at the Institute!"

The spook seated next to the Director glanced over.

"There are security concerns."

The Director looked perplexed, "Have you submitted a report to Royston regarding the matter?"

"I've mentioned it."

Blakie-Harris pressed ahead. "Before I mention the reason for my visit, I received your communique regarding the omitted Grissim brief's and am looking into it."

"Thank you. Any news on Stuart's killer or killers?"

"Mr. Tuppin's was an NSA employee. Naturally, every effort is underway to find out what occurred."

The waitress arrived and placed Lee's coffee and muffin on the counter. An instant later she returned and laid a silver teapot and mug before the Director.

"There ye be gentlemen!" she said and dashed off.

The Director stared at the items.

When he recovered he leaned close to Lee and whispered, "Info retrieved from Stuart's hard-drives reveal he'd been in contact with you. It appears he was concerned about the briefs withheld from Grissim and figured a rogue element was at play."

Lee was about to object to accusation's levelled against his late colleague.

"I know... I know!" the Director intervened. "Before you take issue let me assure you I believe your former associate's suspicions were sound and may have led to his death."

The professor hesitated, "His murder still resonates."

"I understand,"the official responded. "Stuart's observation's highlight the duplicity unravelling within the highest level's of US Intelligence. That's why I'm here. For some time a threat has existed regarding the fate of an unnamed mid-western metropolis. Perhaps you're aware of that fact?"

"I've heard whispers."

"Anyway, if a preventative strike against A'biin occurs it's effects would reverberate globally. Relation's with friend and foe alike would destabilize. Retaliation would be assured."

The two suits who accompanied the Director couldn't have stood out more had they been painted with stripes.

"It's conceivable a plot has been initiated by one of our own," Blakie-Harris resumed. "I've scrutinized every high-level official, each Director and Deputy-Director. The whole thing seems absurd when you consider the quality of people who helm those departments and agencies."

"What do you require of me, Robert?"

With deliberation the Director said, "There are some files I'd like you to review. They represent the views and recommendations of select personnel. Authorities such as the Joint Chiefs and the Secretary of Defence, including their senior-most advisers."

Leaning in he added, "I've gone over every file twice and can't find a thing which would implicate any one of these individuals. In fact I come away with a reinforced view of their loyalty."

The Director pushed his tea aside alerting detail the meeting was over.

"Review the files Lee. See if there's anything I've overlooked. Text me your finding's if there's any."

He withdrew an encased flash-drive from his briefcase and passed it over. Rising from his stool the spooks followed suit.

"I'll await your response."

Lee watched the agent's and their boss retreat through the revolving doors of the department store. Turning the memory-stick between his fingers he placed it in a zippered pocket of his jacket. Payment and a tip were left alongside the bill and he departed the premises to retrieve his Volkswagen.

Breeze surged through the open window as Lee cruised Windover Road in a northbound direction. Along the right Falls Valley bridged the span between town and the Institute. Ahead the broad expanse of Lake Erie formed a sparkling canvas. It felt odd coasting past the familiar campus turnoff of Edgewater Drive. He'd decided not to advertise his presence at Grissim and intended parking elsewhere. Signalling left onto Lakeshore Road, he drove a short distance and drew up in the parking lot attached to the Lighthouse Restaurant. The establishment opened daily at 5 pm – had become a once-a-month ritual for he and Dorothy. Both enjoyed the cuisine and the splendid view the lake provided. Lee hoped to chat with management about renting a parking space on a monthly basis.

Departing the car he took in his quiet surroundings. Aside from an occasional jogger or dog walker, there was little activity at that time of day. Waves lapped the brittle shoreline as Lee casually backtracked along Lakeshore Road; allowing the breeze from the lake to cool his face and ruffle his hair. Strolling toward the rising bluffs and Windover Road, he felt the presence of someone nearby. Abruptly, a muscular arm gripped him about the throat; while another secured his wrists. Wearing a ski-mask the towering assailant dragged his victim toward the waters edge. Lee managed to free an arm and delivered an elbow blow to his attacker's ribs. Recovering quickly, the man brought two interlocked fists down on the base of Lee's neck, and watched him crumple to the ground unconscious. The assailant crossed the road and returned toting a gym bag; rapidly a weight attached to a chain was withdrawn. Lee lay sprawled as the man secured the ballast to his left ankle and applied a padlock. About to cast his prize into the depths, the killer was stuck forcefully along the right temple by the heel of a boot. Crashing to the ground the padlock key landed several feet away. Blood oozed into the fibres of the predator's ski-mask and a stain formed. He glanced up at the liberator and cursed her in a foreign tongue.

Hovering over the felled wretch the lithe security chief held a gun gripped in both hands, "Hands in the air!"

The thug reluctantly followed instructions.

Sasha noticed the professor's shackles and drew the obvious conclusion. The padlock key lay nearby and she took several sidesteps and scooped it from the ground.

'Off with the ski-mask!"

With his arms raised the man got to his knees. Sasha heard her boss moan and turned to face him. It was all the assailant needed as he pitched backward down a recline. Scrambling along the surf he vanished around a curvature of the bluffs.

Sasha swore and turned her attention back to the professor. Kneeling beside him she withdrew a water bottle and moistened a handkerchief. She raised his head gently and sponge-mopped his brow. The bottle was brought to his lips and lids flickered; suddenly his eyes were wide open. The expression on his face was one of confusion. Coughing and wheezing he stared at his security chief and felt a sharp pain in the lower neck region.

"You're safe professor," Sasha whispered.

"What happened?"

"You were attacked."

"Shit."

She inserted the key into the padlock shackled to his ankle and cast the chain aside.

"What in heck is that!"

"It appears someone wanted you in the lake."

"Jesus."

"I don't think he'll return."

"Where are we?"

"Alongside Lakeshore Road."

The professor struggled to sit upright and was assisted by Sasha. He unzipped his jacket pocket and felt for the flash-drive issue by the Director, and found it safely tucked away. He barely recalled the drive along Windover; the Lighthouse parking lot and a leisurely stroll.

"Who accosted me?" he inquired as he was helped to his feet.

"The man wore a ski mask."

Sasha retrieved the shackles, "The ambush was premeditated - the person intended to make you disappear."

Lee's mind was racing.

"Similar incident's have occurred in the vicinity," the professor was reminded. "On campus, in Falls Valley and now here. The man who assailed you may be associated with each of these crimes. I'm just sorry I allowed him to escape."

"Appears to me you saved my life."

Sunlight filtered through overhead branches and Lee took several cautious steps. With Sasha's guidance he gradually stabilized and they started slowly towards the Institute. Dragging the ballast by it's chain as evidence; the security chief closely monitored their surroundings.

"How did you find me?" queried the professor.

"When I'm not on duty I sometimes watch the passing freighters. I was by the water and heard a commotion on my way back. My first reaction was someone's in danger. You can imagine my surprise when I discovered that person was you."

"I'm glad you like passing ships."

The shackles were testament to Sasha's observation the ambush was premeditated.

"Why try to conceal the body?" mused the professor. "Why not leave it there and be done with it?"

"It's a stall tactic," Sasha replied. "When a murder occurs the authorities initiate an immediate search for the killer. If a body is discovered days or weeks later the perpetrator is allotted time to vanish."

Certain the assailant had made himself scarce, Sasha guided the professor up a grassy incline towards the campus courtyard. Withdrawing her phone she alerted Dennis and requested his assistance. He departed Sentinel Hall immediately and met the pair as they approached. Startled to see the professor looking worse for wear, he unburdened Sasha and lent his support to their charge. Mounting the steps gradually they entered the confines of the lobby.

"I'm okay now," the professor muttered breathlessly. "Nothing a few hours rest won't remedy."

The guard glanced at Sasha who remarked, "Let's get him below."

They crossed the floor and slowly made their way downstairs. At the bottom Sasha thanked her colleague and said she'd take it from there.

"What occurred chief?"

"The professor was attacked along Lakeshore Road," she reported. "I'll bring you up to date later. Meanwhile, keep your eyes glued to the monitors."

"Gotcha."

Sasha guided the professor through his office and noticed him sweating profusely.

"Let's get you to your quarters and into bed," she remarked withdrawing her remote. "I'll fetch cold water," she added as the wall glided to one side.

A digital clock indicated 11:07 am.

They entered the narrow passage and Lee shuffled into his quarters and sat along the edge of the bed. Sasha entered a moment later carrying water and administered two painkillers. Afterwards, she examined the area around the professor's lower neck region. A hue of purple had formed and he cringed as she applied moist fabric to the swelling. The injury wasn't extensive, however several days recuperation would likely be required.

Sasha sat opposite him, "How are you faring?"

"Better thanks to you."

The security chief noticed Jesse's quarters were vacant. Abruptly, sounds emitted from the storage room signalling his return. Having embarked upon his morning jog he emerged into the hall and noticed the pair seated in Lee's quarters.

"Am I late for something?"

"Not at all," huffed the professor trying to sound upbeat.

Jesse wiped sweat from his face with his t-shirt and Sasha observed no injury along his right temple. Whoever she struck by the water's edge would've borne a fresh scar. The assailant had been over six feet as was Jesse. It was impossible to imagine the young apprentice attacking his mentor with intent to kill. Despite her suspicions she was aware Jesse admired the professor and the feeling was mutual.

A look of concern clouded Jesse's features,"You alright Lee?"

The older man feigned a smile, "Take a shower and change son. I'll bring you up to date."

Sasha frowned, "You need rest professor."

"I'll only be a few minutes."

A perplexed countenance was displayed on Jesse as he retreated.

"Brief your team about what occurred and about your own encounters," the professor instructed.

"And you?"

"I'll be fine once I've rested."

Sasha insisted she be contacted if anything was needed and departed.

Moment's later Jesse took up her vacated seat.

"Please don't say you fell off a diner stool?"

Lee managed a grin.

His recruit awaited a response and the older man sighed, "I was assaulted by someone wearing a ski mask along Lakeshore Road. I parked by the Lighthouse and was returning to campus when the incident occurred."

Jesse was dumbstruck, "Lets get you to the hospital!"

Waving off the suggestion the professor countered, "I'm alright it's only a bruise."

Anxiously his recruit demanded an account of what transpired.

Lee obliged reluctantly, "I owe my life to Sasha. She happened upon the scene and chased my attacker off before I was dunked."

"Dunked!"

"Apparently, I was about to be fed to the fishes."

"Not funny."

"Not if you're supper."

"You said Sasha *happened* upon the scene?"

"Fortunately for me."

"Go on."

Lee sipped water, "She was off-duty taking in the view by the lake. On her return she witnessed the assault and managed to dislodge the person. While attending me the attacker managed his escape. Sasha believes the incident was premeditated. What bothers me is how this individual was aware of my presence there?"

"You were likely followed."

Lee conceded the point and changed topics. He inquired if his young colleague had reviewed the flash-drive regarding Electron Era."

"I have."

"Any questions?

"Nope. Your brief was thorough."

"Good," the professor acknowledged feeling suddenly exhausted.

Jesse mentioned he'd studied a blueprint of the factory Lee left for him. An exterior photograph of the facility accompanied the document.

"I've devised a plan of entry," Jesse remarked. "I hope to apply it this evening."

"Remember your bus leaves at four pm."

"My things are packed I'll book a cab for three-thirty. Meantime, rest and I'll establish contact at the first opportunity."

"Godspeed Son."

The elder leaned back in bed and drifted off.

Jesse removed his shoes and slipped quietly from the room.

———————————

The disturbance came from behind and Kristy scrambled to his feet. With his eye to the scope, he swung about and held that position for several moments. The rifle was lowered and he raised his binoculars. Gazing along the Yokum Trail he settled upon Penther's dwelling. A sliver of light was visible behind the parlour blinds. The dogs were quiet and it seemed doubtful Aldo would be making his usual rounds.

A rustle was heard and he raised his weapon. The sound came from nearby and may have been a rabbit or squirrel. Like a spectral galleon the crescent moon cast it's pale glow over the wooded terrain. With the toe of his boot he straitened the sleeping bag and heard the hoot of an owl. Getting slowly to his knees he lay on his stomach and resumed a forward position.

"Don't move or say a word," a voice whispered.

Naturally, the woman would have to appear when his rifle was pointed in the opposite direction. He had hoped her arrival might've been scented by the dogs whose growls would've alerted him. It was asking too much.

"Toss your weapon aside and turn about!" the woman hissed.

Placing the rifle down Kristy rolled about and sat upright. He grinned sheepishly while his assassin stared back with expressionless eyes. Above her right shoulder a silver dagger was aimed directly at his heart.

"Farewell," she whispered.

"Hold!" a voice shouted from the trees. Seconds later William Penther emerged with a rifle levelled at the woman's head. In the distance Club and Boot were roused; meanwhile Kristy glared at his would-be executioner. He climbed to his feet, dusted himself and retrieved his rifle. The woman stood motionless with her eyes fixated on him.

"Drop the knife," urged the landowner.

The dogs were fast approaching. Seconds later they stormed through the underbrush dragging leashes in their wake. Penther shouted a command and they reared back. A moment later Aldo charged into the fray armed with an semi-automatic. Instead of witnessing the thing who'd strung him from a tree; he beheld a slender woman in dark clothing with a knife at her feet.

"You certainly know how to draw a crowd Ms...whoever the hell you are?" Kristy remarked.

Receiving no response he addressed the militia leader, "Thanks for the timely intervention, Bill. I've underestimated your instincts."

"Shut up!" the landowner muttered. "And don't call me Bill."

"My we're touchy?"

Penther hollered at his bodyguard, "Grab the dog's leashes!"

Abiding his wishes Dopple mumbled, "What's Kristy doin' here?"

"I intend to find out."

It was Kristy's turn to be perturbed, "Covering your ass is what I'm doing here! You said yourself this place draws federal agent's like a magnet. Well lo and behold!"

Penther spat on the ground, "If you're covering my ass you didn't do so good tonight."

Kristy faced the woman, "That's the third time you've taken me by surprise. That rarely happens."

"You're reckless," uttered the female.

"It's not me with a gun at my head sweetheart."

He approached and struck her face with the back of his hand. Instinctively, the doberman's began muzzling lower portions of her body.

The militia leader allowed Kristy to keep up the pretense, "You know the woman?"

"No," Kristy responded. "Other than the fact she's been trailing me."

He attempted to fuel the lodge owner's paranoia and added, "So tell us which alphabet agency you service, Missy'?"

Watching from the sidelines Dopple appeared puzzled.

"Mind asking Aldo to fetch a pair of handcuffs," Kristy requested. "We'll find out who our guest truly represents?"

Penther nodded at his deputy.

Ogling the female Dopple handed the reigns to his boss and scrambled off to fetch cuffs.

Kristy faced the prisoner, "What's your name!"

"It's whatever you want."

"I can think of some choice ones."

"As can I for you traitor."

"Brave and feisty admirable qualities."

Penther found their dialogue disturbing.

The interrogation resumed and Kristy said, "Why would someone enter into a dire situation unless she'd been instructed to."

More silence as Dopple bounded back up the slope.

Holding the dog's reigns Penther nodded at the woman, "Secure her wrists we'll take her to the lodge."

Aldo's foul breath and yellow teeth distinguished him from the others as the prisoner was cuffed.

"Shall we adjourn?" Kristy prompted.

Leaving his overnight supplies he carried only his weapon and binoculars. Meanwhile, the woman was prodded down the incline by the barrel of Aldo's rifle. When they reached the lodge she mounted the steps and was shoved inside. Penther handed the reigns to Aldo and instructed him to leash the dogs out back. Inside the parlour the lodge owner turned to Kristy, "I'm interested to know more about your relationship with this woman?"

Kristy's grim expression matched the militia leader's own.

"She's a Federal agent!" he reiterated.

The patriot leader grunted.

———————————

TWENTY-TWO

Harry Flotsin laboured nights as a security guard at Electron Era. The word 'laboured' being grossly exaggerated in this instance, as Harry's job required he do nothing. Having 'worked' at that site, on and off for twenty-five years; local authorities had a file on Harry, consisting of mostly of work-related abuse issues. Charges ranged from locking workers outdoors in the dead of winter, to falsely accusing others of alcohol consumption while on duty. In another incident an employee was fired on trumped-up allegations of theft made by the watchman.

The previous evening Detective DeLong uploaded Harry's file from police archives and forwarded it; along with a blueprint of Electron Era to Lee Tondar.

It was 5 am and Harry was seated behind the security desk in the front lobby, listening to the radio. Gazing through the plate-glass entrance facing Detroit's industrial badlands, he tuned into a talk radio channel. Maintaining vigil before a trio of monitors, he felt giddy from the effects of the lengthy shift. He raised the hem of his trousers to ensure his access pass was safely tucked inside his sock. The card allowed entry into the building's main-floor level and was kept apart from other pocket articles. A key chain dangled from Harry's significant waist making his approach sound like sleigh bells.

Aside from staring at monitors Harry's most important task was to remain blissfully unaware. The shipping room included a loading dock and rear exit; none of which were imaged on Harry's monitors – nor was a lower basement level. If something occurred he need only punch a code on his phone and management would respond. Each of the desk monitor's displayed four-way split-screen panels, for a total of a dozen images. One frame might highlight the labs, while another featured the corridor from various angles.

Supermarket tabloids and pop cans lay strewn about Harry's desk. Engaging in social media activity was forbidden while on duty. His supervisor believed such endeavours were counter-productive to security protocol.

Shift change was less than an hour away and the watchman considered his daytime counterpart. Cal Wicker was about as engaging as a cockroach and just as creepy. His only attribute was the fact he was never late for work. At precisely six am he'd arrive and give an obligatory grunt, before stifling any conversation Harry might initiate. Curiously, Wicker never entered or exited by way of the lobby doors. The same was true of the supervisor and another manager. The point was raised on one occasion and Harry was told to mind his business.

A rig rumbled along Sentra Avenue with it's headlights piercing the darkness. The shift had been a snooze-fest like all the rest - the way Harry preferred it. Abruptly, frame three on monitor two conked out. The image highlighted a parking area along the right side of the building. Other frames remained operational and he tapped the screen to no avail. Harry decided to stroll outdoors for a peek at the dysfunctional camera. The initiative afforded an opportunity for him to gaze upon his new acquisition - a Jaguar XF. The streamlined vehicle had been purchased a month ago and numerous trips to the parking lot ensued. Earlier that evening Harry discovered pigeon turd on the car's sparkling chassis. He withdrew a handkerchief and wiped the offensive stain away and replaced the rag in his watchman's jacket. Afterwards, he polished the hubcaps though no grime accumulated since the last shine an hour before.

It had been roughly ten months since he'd been hired by the current tenant. The arrangement was part of a year-long contract he expected would be renewed indefinitely. Having worked security for every fly-by-night operator who'd leased the space, he figured no one knew the job better than he.

"These clowns need me," he muttered. "I validate the lot of 'em."

Harry was making more money now then ever. Nearly four times the amount his last posting offered - which explained the Jaguar. He assumed his employer's were engaged in some kind of funny business; whatever that might be he didn't want to know. Following each shift he handed the company phone to his replacement; who passed it back when he returned for work twelve hours later. Occasionally, Jackson Bell would inform him he was departing the premises on an errand and Harry would watch his taillights swerve onto Sentra Avenue and vanish.

Harry's loafers echoed off concrete and Plexiglas as he shuffled the corridor. He drew alongside a grey metal door and pushed the bar-latch forward. A light breeze brushed his face and ruffled his hair. To avoid triggering the system, he'd taken the precaution of silencing the alarm attached to that exit. Above the door a lighting fixture should've illuminated automatically. Harry glanced up he noticed the bulb had been removed. Withdrawing a flashlight he crossed the threshold and aimed the beam at his shiny convertible. A sliver of orange crested the horizon. Several yards distant he noticed a mangled security camera lying on the pavement. He approached the devise and the door closed of it's own accord behind him From the surrounding gloom his ears were assailed by an insidious laugh. He froze as two arms gripped his collar and shuttled his three-hundred-pound bulk, a foot and a half from the ground. The flashlight fell from Harry's grasp and his gaze fell upon a twisted mouth set within a ghoulish face. White eyes blazed beneath a tattered rain hat and rags of dark matter. The overall impression was one of decay.

The walls of Electron Era provided more than adequate sound insulation as he struggled to free himself.

"The master-pass Mr. Flotsin I'll have it."

"W...what?"

"The master-pass give it!"

"You know my n...name...?"

The horrible eyes bore into Harry and his stuttering turned to a whine, "I got cash, credit cards...take my wallet."

Beads of sweat fell as he gave up the struggle and went limp. A tattered glove ripped the key-ring from his waist and he was dropped to the pavement like a sack of potatoes. Scrutinizing the keys the ghoul rasped, "Your pockets empty them and remove your shoes."

Seated cross-legged on the pavement Harry blathered incoherently. He emptied his pockets and struggled with his loafers. The ragged figure studied each article. To Harry's dismay his key ring was placed inside the folds of it's wretched garments. His phone was also retained.

The horrid gaze eyes caught sight of something concealed in Harry's left sock. Reaching down it pulled on the fabric. "A pass! Liar!"

Harry's quaking arms fell limply to his side in a gesture of defeat.

"Speak!"

"I...I forgot it was there."

"What purpose does it serve!"

"It accesses the front and side doors."

"Who employs you!"

"Mr. Bell...," uttered the security guard.

"What are your duties!".

Harry had to think about that one.

"Speak!"

"I keep lookout for unauthorized persons - thieves, rummies, squatters."

"You keep a shoddy watch, Sir."

The entity loomed while the hapless watchman snivelled, "I know nothing 'bout what goes on below."

Below.

"Could be a distillery I wouldn't know..." his voice trailed off.

The intruder was silent as Harry withdrew the handkerchief he'd used to wipe bird shit off his car. Honking into the folds he stuffed it back in his pocket.

"I do twelve hour shifts seven nights a week. One year contract..."

In the distance a diesel whined along an overpass.

"Your paymaster shall learn of your betrayal," the ghoul rasped. "Go to! Run ya rogue! HA, HA, HA, HA!"

A dog barked and another responded.

Harry stuffed his belonging's in his pockets, grabbed his shoes and staggered off toward the Jaguar. Retrieving a spare key from beneath the passenger seat, he hightailed it and heard the thing's closing remarks delivered to his retreating backside, "Ha, Ha, Ha, Ha!"

Penther's gaze shifted between the trio of faces occupying his front parlour. He squinted through the blinds and noticed his pale reflection cast against the inky darkness. Prior to coming across Kristy and the woman, he'd temporarily shored up the damage inflicted on his rear door. The security system was beyond repair. None of it mattered now that he and the lads were set to depart Rykles Clearing for good. Having resided on this land most of his life; it was hard for Penther to fathom leaving it. For years patriot's found their way to his door to train in the company of other like-minded souls, rallying against a corrupt, money-gouging government. The rifle range and hunting trails offered solace to scores of frustrated young men.

With society's dregs creeping ever closer an opportunity had been afforded Penther; one which allowed incisive action. The stench of encroaching civilization was spreading like wildfire. As with any war sacrifices are made. Abandoning his beloved property was Penther's ultimate offering. Handed down to him by Strom Rykles - the old man's memory guided his every move. Rykles would've understood the necessity of pulling up stakes; for their war was just and ongoing No longer would America be viewed as a land of freedom and opportunity; instead it would be known as a place of fear and dread. The tide of immigration would be stymied in wake of their attacks. Penther and his militia would continue to thrive elsewhere, financed by their sympathetic backer.

As Kristy so knowingly implied the woman was likely a government operative observing their movement's. Once Sir arrived she' be passed to him.

SMACK!

The sound of a hand striking flesh interrupted Penther's meditation.

"Contact your superiors and tell them the occupant's of this property will take action if further harassed!" Kristy shouted.

Shackled upright to a support beam the woman remained silent.

Aware of who she truly represented Kristy was talking double-speak. Meanwhile, Aldo was seated with his arms draped over the back of a folding chair leering at the hostage.

Kristy motioned the lodge owner into the hall and lowered his voice, "When you mentioned the FBI had paid another visit a warning signal went up. Too much is at stake, which is why I kept vigil outside."

"You think I'm stupid," the militia-leader asserted.

It appeared to Penther his supposed colleague was conducting a bogus interrogation. The woman had been slapped around a few times - none too forcefully. His questions were hardly probing and he seemed to be speaking subliminally. Penther suspected a connection existed between the two.

Present circumstances made it difficult for Kristy to convey meaning to the prisoner. There was something about the woman he was unable to put his finger on. Apart from her being a SIAG operative, her eyes suggested familiarity. If they were afforded a moment alone he might gain insight.

Penther wondered if she was the female who contacted him using Kristy's device.

"You made a phone call to me!" he asserted.

"No," she lied.

His eyes narrowed.

Staring back she said, "People know where I am and will come looking."

"We'll be gone by then," Kristy interjected. "Answer the question."

Taras remained silent.

On the sidelines Aldo sat grinning like an ape.

"So who's she with!" Penther demanded.

"She won't say," Kristy admitted. "I assume FBI."

"You would know wouldn't you," insinuated the lodge owner.

Kristy bristled, "When I arrived here the rear door was smashed, your pooches were drugged, the security system was in tatters and Dopple had been assailed."

"I'm wondering if you had a hand in that!" spoke Penther accusingly.

Keeping his anger in check Kristy remained composed, "I simply wanted to make certain Rykles Clearing wasn't compromised."

The lodge owner grunted and turned away.

Kristy watched his departure and said to Aldo, "Watch her."

The bodyguard nodded.

Intending to confront the militia leader and reestablish a chain of command Kristy followed him.

Meantime, Dopple rose from his chair and circled the restrained woman. Standing to her rear he gagged her mouth with a rag. He came around to face her as she struggled against the cuffs ripping into her wrists and ankles. Without taking his serpentine eyes from her his thin lips curled to reveal a lecherous grin.

On the rear deck Kristy gripped the lodge owner by the wrist, "What exactly were you insinuating in there?"

Staring back with dead eyes Penther said, "Get your hand off me."

Kristy stood firm.

From his camouflaged vest Penther withdrew a gun. "I said get your hand off me or I'll splatter your brains over these grounds."

The guest released his grip.

"Your girlfriend contacted me using your phone," Penther asserted. "Perhaps its you who should be chained and interrogated?"

"I have no idea what your on about."

"So you say."

A muffled shout was heard from the parlour.

Lunging through the kitchen and down the hall, the lodge owner was followed closely by Kristy. When they entered they saw the woman's sweater pulled above her breasts; meanwhile her tormentor was licking the side of her face. Penther gripped his gun by the barrel and charged across the floor. He grasped Aldo by the hair and pried him from the female. As he was pistol-whipped about the head, Kristy adjusted the prisoner's sweater and removed the gag. Lashed to the support beam she gasped for air.

"I'll fetch water," he said.

As Aldo was being thrashed Penther shouted, "So the authorities walk in and you're raping one of their own you dumb shit! Want it to end here!"

As he cowered the side of Dopple's face looked like raspberry jam.

"Get outta here!" Penther bellowed kicking the stricken bodyguard.

In a pathetic pantomime Aldo rose and staggered from the parlour. The militiaman turned and saw the female staring at him with an expression as impassive as his own. In the same instant his phone vibrated and Jackson Bell's code registered.

"Ya!"

Kristy reentered carrying water and a facecloth. He brought a glass to the woman's lips and wiped her forehead with moist fabric. He glanced over at Penther and noticed his expressionless features had brightened somewhat.

"When?" the lodge owner responded into the receiver. "Good, we'll be waiting inside the bunker. Make certain your not followed."

On the other end Bell signed off.

Kristy determined the Airborne Cataclysm was ready for deployment and Penther's compatriots planned on returning to the Clearing.

The militia leader replaced his phone, "Guess you know what that was about?"

"Judging from your response I'd say you've been informed our operation in Detroit has concluded."

Penther was amused by the 'our operation' part.

The corridor within Electron Era was barely visible in the dim glow of the night lights. Kriel allowed the door leading to the parking lot close silently, and noticed a camera mounted on the ceiling. The ragged figure hastened alongside a Plexiglas wall shielding several empty labs. Having reviewed a blueprint of the building the shipping room was sought. A pair of doors were observed at the end of the hall and the watchman's pass was removed. The scanner required card access and the plastic was inserted. Failing to unlock the intruder stepped back and smashed both doors open with it's boot. A dark space beckoned and Kriel withdrew the pen-light and entered. It's beam cut a trajectory toward the rear wall where boxes were stacked at random. The wraith pried several open and noticed most were filled with sawdust or empty. Tools and accessories lay on a nearby workbench. Crates of cleansing solvent's were stored on wooden skids, and a rear door was situated beside the loading dock.

A rat scurried between the Stygian figure's boots and disappeared in the gloom. Allowing it free reign Kriel noticed several sheets of bound plywood propped against the right wall. Sliding the bundle aside a door was revealed. No light was divulged along the bottom crack and a strand of twine was observed. Attached to the base of the plywood, it trailed beneath the door. Presumably, the twine allowed the concealment to be pulled back in place upon entry.

To gain access a code needed to be entered on a keypad. Kriel took cover behind a stack of crates and waited for someone to emerge. Twenty minutes later shoes were heard ascending a metal stairwell. Kriel slipped from cover and wedged himself alongside the door frame. A bar latch was applied and when the door opened, a wrist emerged to grip the plywood veil. Kriel's boot kept the door ajar as a man appeared. Gripped by the collar he was whisked across the threshold. The individual struggled until a knee delved into his gut stilling his efforts. A doorstop was sought and the person's flashlight lay nearby. Reaching over the inert body his torch would serve that purpose. The felled man was dragged toward the hiding place Kriel occupied earlier and two lengths of twine were sliced. Binding the man's wrists and ankles, the intruder ripped a shred of fabric from it's upper garment and gagged the prisoner. Scouring the man's pocket's a pass and phone were confiscated. The doorstop was removed and the grim figure descended the stairwell.

Hunkered before his computer, Lee zeroed in on a singular name beside a tiny asterisk on a reference page. It was a name he recognized instantly. Most officials serving America's Intelligence institutions were aware of Richard Valamar. The ruthless asset had worked on behalf of several Federal agencies over the years.

Valamar fled Cuba with his mother and an older brother after decades of rule by Fidel Castro. They settled in Miami they were supported by members of the Cuban exile community. His mother found work as a radio station receptionist in the Liberty City section of town. When elder brother Carlos left home at nineteen for an overseas sojourn, Richard was devastated. Each month he'd receive a post from Carlos until the letters abruptly ceased. Shortly thereafter he was contacted by a mysterious caller who related the appalling news Carlos had been murdered in Siana, A'biin. Details of his death were vague and Richard demanded proof. Confirmation arrived a week later in the form of two grizzly photographs, depicting his brother's swollen face and blank stare, as he lay in a filthy doorway with three bullets in his chest.

From that point Richard Valamar was never the same. An intense period of self-discipline and training followed as he mastered the art of deception. According to the anonymous caller, Carlos had been running guns to rebels along the A'biinian frontier and keeping one step ahead of the SIAG. Richard blamed his brother's murder on that clandestine organization and swore to do everything to destabilize the regime supporting it.

Lee's research indicated Valamar replaced his late brother as an asset in A'biin. Retaining ties to US Intelligence he learned to read, write and speak the language while living among locals. He sought out frustrated students who desired A'biin pursue a more western-style democracy. Once their confidence was gained, he proceeded to indoctrinate them as potential informers, spies and even assassins. Staging covert operations, Valamar made preparations to flee the country as the SIAG closed in.

Tension between Washington and Siana was at an all-time low, when one of A'biin's more progressive civil servant's; the Minister of Foreign Affairs was assassinated. He'd been driving through a busy marketplace in the capital city, when rapid gunfire erupted killing the minister instantly. Moment's later the assassin - a young man recruited by Valamar, stood next to the bullet-ridden car smiling at onlookers. Tossing an AK 47 to the pavement he withdrew a pistol and blew his brains out. Conspiracy theories abounded as to who was behind the attack. Both the SIAG and US Intelligence turned their collective gaze stateside.

On the heels of this setback a task force on Mideast relations convened. Entrusted with investigating several American spy agencies; the committee's worst fears were realized. Evidence suggested the assassination was initiated by an American official and carried out by a fanatic.

As Valamar sailed for America at the behest of his anonymous handler; ongoing investigation revealed the Cuban dissident was responsible for a series of strikes along the A'biinian border. Targets included military installations and several government-sanctioned farms. More than two-thousand acres of crops had been destroyed by fire.

Arriving back in the US, Valamar was taken into custody on a tip provided by the SIAG. He stood before a tribunal consisting of Mideast and American task force members. UCOMA chieftain Royston Adams proved to be one of Valamar's harshest critics. He urged member's not to extradite the former asset; rather he should be placed in solitary confinement until he revealed what was known about the A'biinian border strikes and killings. Unwilling to yield to A'biin's demands for extradition, the tribunal decided Valamar would be interred within a clandestine facility in Texas on terrorist charges. When his transfer occurred, four US Marshal's escorted the prisoner in leg-irons and handcuffs in an armoured vehicle. As they drove to their destination the driver and his front seat partner were shot at point-blank range. Their bodies were left off a deserted Texas highway by their rear-compartment betrayers. Moment's later a second vehicle appeared to retrieve Valamar and his liberators.

Having solidified a lucrative deal with Juan Pulido, the notorious Mexican drug-lord; Royston Adams was in a position to offer the corrupt US Marshal's plenty of cash and further employment, to ensure they were on the detail escorting Valamar between prisons. Once their assignment concluded the pair would continue servicing Adams. Their final detail was escorting Azil Besserer across the Atlantic, where both perished in a Jacksonville firefight.

The reference Lee uncovered indicated a meeting between Royston Adams and Richard Valamar occurred *after* the latter's escape. Admittedly, Lee hadn't scrutinized Adams file as thoroughly as others, however he couldn't imagine his friend being the zealot they sought. The notion he would plot against his own countrymen was inconceivable. No one championed restraint to the degree Adams had. His views ran counter to the knee-jerk mindset which prevailed among the beltway elite.

Over the ensuing hours, Lee meticulously reviewed everything attached to Adams file and uncovered nothing which might further incriminate the UCOMA boss. If he access to the Director's financial records, he might learn if sizable sums of money had been outsourced for purposes unknown. Robert Blakie-Harris could be of assistance on that front. Stifling a cough Lee churned the matter over in his head. It seemed like a bad dream.

With his vision blurring he switched off the computer and refilled his glass in the kitchen. Entering his quarters he downed his meds and wondered when Jesse would establish contact? They agreed he'd touch base only after Kriel had penetrated the electronics plant. If Lee initiated communication the distraction might alert others within Electron Era.

He massaged his neck and recalled a picnic Royston Adams arranged at his West Virginia estate, in honour of he and Dorothy's thirtieth wedding anniversary. While in the cross-hairs of political rival's the Director's defence of him was also recollected.

Lee swore to review the disturbing reference again before he drifted off to never-land.

———————————

TWENTY-THREE

Descending to an altitude of 30,000 feet the Bombardier Challenger cruised gracefully above the Sierra Madre mountains of northern Mexico. Misty forests and grey canyons extended south through Sonora into the northernmost regions of Sinaloa, where the plane was scheduled to land at a tiny airbase outside of Alamos. The colonial mining town was situated in the foothills and catered mostly to tourists, due to it's attractive setting and centuries-old Spanish architecture. Heavy rains had arrived early that year followed by a high-pressure system, initiating an early summer season.

Apart from the pilot Royston Adams was sole occupant aboard the aircraft. Slated to meet privately with Juan Pulido (meaning 'polished' or 'refined'); the leader of the Culiacan drug cartel was most often referred to as El Pido. His operation was Mexico's largest and most notorious drug trafficking enterprise. To say he'd prospered over the years was an understatement; Pulido made the Forbes billionaire list two years running. His cartel had infiltrated both the Mexican government and the military. Presently, he was able to add a top-ranking US Intelligence figure to his list of associates.

With the arrest of the cartel's former chieftain, Alejandro Zamora by the Mexican Navy; the capture was made possible with Intelligence provided by the US Drug Enforcement Agency. Pulido seized control of the cartel and consolidated power, by deploying gangs to engage in widespread violence along the northern border towns. Having eliminated the competition, Polido's success made him the most wanted drug trafficker on both sides of the border within a relatively short time.

It was the third such meeting between Adams and Pulido in Alamos, where the drug lord established a money-laundering scheme involving several regional logging companies. Adams recalled their first conference taking place in the very hacienda Juan Pulido was born in thirty-six years earlier. The single-room shack had supported both parent's and seven siblings. Ironically, the picturesque region was birthplace to many cartel leaders who'd become multi-millionaires, despite the prospect of dying a violent death. The base of El Pido's operation was considered the gateway to Mexico's 'golden triangle' - a remote and mountainous intersection of Sinaloa, Durango, and Chihuahua. There among lush green surroundings opium and marijuana had been harvested for generations.

Under former cartel leader Zamora, a tunnelled drug route had been established beneath the border town of Nogales, sixty-five miles south of Tucson, Arizona. The clandestine crossing propelled the cartel to unprecedented heights, before it was raided by the Drug Enforcement Agency on the US side. Alerted by UCOMA Director Adams, the DEA was issued the appropriate satellite data. The underground route had served the cartel successfully for five years. Tens of millions of dollars were reaped from the transfer of cocaine and marijuana alone. Additional shipment's of meth and unrefined heroin were funnelled through to various US partners for a piece of the pie. The contraband was distributed proportionally among US criminal organizations, who found their way into markets throughout Canada and parts of Europe. With the collapse of the Nogales route, Pulido desperately sought a new point of entry into the United States.

As a source for the drug lord's predicament, Royston Adams initiated contact under an assumed name. Pulido was informed he was a ranking US intelligence official in a position to reestablish an alternate route. The way would enable a cross-border flow of goods unimpeded by satellite images or border patrols. In return for salvaging the cartel's annual multi-million dollar enterprise, Adams insisted upon ten percent of all profits. Over the course of eighteen months that sum amounted to tens of millions of dollars deposited safely into a Cayman Island account.

Initially, a meeting was arranged with the drug baron in the shade of his birthplace hacienda. A battalion of Pulido's snipers were stationed behind every tree. Over the course of an hour Adams outlined his offer - namely an opportunity for the cartel to function free of eye-in-the-sky detection and border guards, at a specific point along the Sonora corridor west of Nogales.

Assigned the name 'Felt' because of the fedora he wore, Adams said without use of a voice synthesizer; it was within his power to substitute routine satellite images while contraband was being transferred across the border. Nothing would be exposed to any authority except a wall and dry canyons. In the hours leading up to a transfer, Adams would personally monitor the crossing both ways via satellite. He could alert runners of approaching helicopters or ground patrols, affording time to abort. By securing their investment a follow-up could be undertaken.

During that first meeting El Pido leaned back and cleared his throat, "Tell me Mr. Felt which agency is it you represent?"

"I'm not at liberty to say," the UCOMA Director responded.

The drug czar considered this, "Please continue."

"As you're aware Mr. Pulido, hundreds of miles of mountainous desert stretch along the Sonora/Arizona corridor. The length makes it impossible to patrol diligently around the clock. Stealth chopper's hosting platoons of US border guards, crisscross isolated stretches of the frontier every 24-hours. That leaves ample time for a transfer to occur. Desolate crossings such as the one I propose are monitored almost entirely by satellite."

"And the wall?"

"You'll deploy utility vehicles equipped with twin bucket lifts, such as those attached to telephone and cable trucks. One bucket contains a runner the other contraband. The items are received at a given point over the top of the wall, by your people on the Arizona end. Once the product is loaded into a waiting SUV, it makes a twenty-minute journey to Interstate19 and onto it's destination. The transfer must be precisely timed and coordinated on both sides."

"We're used to tunnels," Pulido stated frankly.

"So is the Drug Enforcement Agency and US Customs. It's what they look for, especially around Nogales. Since the 1990's, nearly one hundred underground passageways of various lengths have been uncovered along the stretch separating Nogales from it's US counterpart. Patrol's zero in on them but remain comparatively lax when it comes to desolate overland routes. The border relies mostly on satellite observation and wall protection. If a deal is struck you're ensured a window of opportunity at various intervals."

"Your proposal sounds like a perfect set-up for an ambush," Pulido responded. "Why should I trust you?"

"Because you need what I have to offer and I need the capital you can provide."

Without a second option Pulido considered a trial run. Throughout his life he'd taken chances - it was that time again.

The Culiacan drug czar leaned forward, "We will set a date for a trial crossing at your proposed location. I'll have men on the Arizona end co-ordinate with both yourself and the Mexican side along a scrambled frequency. You will communicate using a device I provide. If things proceed accordingly we will establish a second meeting, whereby means of payment shall be discussed along with a schedule of crossings."

It was Adams turn to sit back.

"Sounds fair to me Mr. Pulido. The test run will cost you nothing. However, our accord can exist only so long as I'm paid in advance of each transfer. And I'll require an invoice for quantities of contraband exported across the line. For instance if 840 pounds of cocaine is transported - it's value to American consumers is worth approximately 6.5 million. A more modest example would be the $400.00 you charge your US associate's for a pound of cannabis. Such an exchange would yield me forty dollars rebate. Finally, payment for each transfer is to be deposited into an offshore account."

The American focused squarely on Pulido, "Do you accept these terms?"

The cartel kingpin remained silent then smiled, "If I agree and discover I've been betrayed, there is no place on earth you'll be safe."

"I'm already risking everything."

"Shall we arrange a trial run then?"

"By all means."

A date was set and they shook hands. Three weeks later the first overland transfer was successfully undertaken. Shortly thereafter a second meeting took place at Alamos, where banking arrangements and transfer times were established.

The above event's transpired fifteen months earlier. As the final phase of Adams elaborate undertaking neared fruition; without El Pido's input the operation would have never been possible. Since forging their alliance nary an eyebrow had been raised. There were no attempts to interrupt the supply chain at their clandestine crossing. Having concluded his third encounter with Pulido, the UCOMA Director flew directly to Fort Wayne, Indiana to meet with Richard Valamar.

For the better part of eleven hours the GPS tracer pinpointing Taras remained stationary. If she was sleeping it was a long nap. At least she wasn't dead, not yet anyway - her tracker implant would have ceased emitting had that occurred. Perhaps she was observing her target from a fixed position? Heron found it frustrating being unable to touch base with his operative. Ironically, it was he who implemented the no-contact policy. With a traitor on the loose the risk was too great. Satellite coordinates indicated her position was among the wilds of central Indiana. Her stationary status implied she might be held captive.

Heron's thoughts were interrupted when his desk phone rang. It was the second call he'd received that morning from the wise men. They'd been following his operative's progress with growing alarm. Heron placed his tea aside and picked up the receiver.

"There's been no movement!" a curt voice informed him.

"I'm aware of that."

"Eleven hours is a long time?"

"I agree," Heron responded. "She may be observing the target from a concealed position."

"If that were so some movement would occur."

"Not if she were up close."

"Or being held against her will."

"Allow me a few more hours. Her signal is still transmitting."

There was a pause, "Two hours."

"I'm grateful."

Heron's eyes never averted from his agent's signal as he replaced the receiver.

The device planted in each SIAG operative includes a self-destruct mechanism. It can be accessed by the host or triggered by means of satellite relay. Once activated a toxic poison is released into the carrier's bloodstream killing them instantly. If it was decided her mission was compromised this would be his former pupil's fate. Entering her code onto his secured devise, Heron's thumb lingered over the contact button. He refrained from asserting pressure and muttered, "Two hours."

———————

On the outskirts of Fort Wayne a black SUV drew to a standstill in the parking lot attached to the Sheppard Inn Hotel. Stepping from behind the wheel, the driver paused to rub his swollen temple then circled the vehicle. Sliding the panel door aside, an older gentleman sporting a fedora and clutching a briefcase emerged from the rear seat. The driver removed two suitcases, scanned their surroundings and escorted his passenger toward the hotel lobby. At the front desk, he booked a double-bedroom suite for a single night under assumed names. Issued an access card accommodating Suite 512; the pair entered and the smaller man claimed the larger bedroom. He placed his suitcase and jacket aside and withdrew a laptop.

Seating himself along the bed Royston Adams recalled meeting his right-hand man. Before Richard Valamar there had been an older brother. Recruited by Adams as a ground asset, Carlos Valamar was posted to Siana, where he learned the language and assimilated himself into the student population. Diligently, he set about converting young people to agitate against the regime. At the time A'biin's ruling directorate was comprised of mostly fundamentalist hardliners. Anti-government rebels assembled by Carlos began conducting raids on munition stockpiles and crop fields. Meantime, UCOMA's inaugural Director remained in contact with Carlos - after his role as handler was turned over to another Intelligence official. Subsequently, unauthorized directive's benefiting Adams agenda continued.

Following several months in the field the Director decided Carlos was a risk. Fearing the SIAG were onto his asset he hired a gunman. It was at this point the elder brother's letters stopped arriving, and Richard Valamar became ripe pickings for his sibling's handler. Initiating contact Adams followed up with photo's depicting Carlos lifeless body. He insisted his brother died at the hands of the SIAG, and offered consolation and financial support to the grieving mother. It was arranged Richard would take up where his brother left off. In a short time he exceeded all expectations.

It was sad the elder sibling had to die, however the SIAG would have killed him anyway. The hired gun simply got there first.

Taking over the operation established by his late sibling, Richard began devising plans aimed at further destabilization of A'biin's infrastructure. Under Adam's tutelage a modest flow of cash, along with caches of automatic weapons and explosives were supplied to his band of marauding saboteurs. Richard was effective rallying others to the cause.

As had occurred with the elder sibling, the SIAG eventually got wind of Richard's activities and he was abruptly recalled. The container ship he boarded docked in New York and Valamar was promptly arrested, and taken into custody. Stunned by the arrest, Adams discovered Homeland Security had been tipped off by an overseas source. Facing crimes of sabotage and murder against the smaller nation, A'biinian officials insisted Valamar be extradited. With Richard integral to his master plan Adams devised a way to prevent the transfer. Thus the Texas escape while en route to prison.

UCOMA had been created in response to advancements in satellite technology. By becoming it's first Director Adams retained access to NSA resources - while remaining at arm's length from the parent enterprise. With Valamar acting as lieutenant a plan was formalized and things got underway. Persons of A'biinian extraction were sought. Professionals who didn't give a damn about God or country - who'd risk everything for asylum and the financial benefit's Adams could provide. The first to accept was Dr. Azil Besserer. Rumoured to have developed an anthrax-laden weapon within SIAG laboratories; the disgraced scientist had been charged with selling state secret's. With outside help he escaped prison and fled the country with a flask containing the lethal extract. The SIAG eventually tracked him down and instead of proceeding with his execution, the biologist was instructed to manufacture further quantities of the deadly concoction on behalf of the state - without compensation naturally. Under round-the-clock surveillance, the arrangement lasted several months until Besserer managed yet another escape.

Royston Adams bore connections throughout the continental underworld. Following the doctor's second escape he was discovered hiding in Veenendaal, Holland. A meeting was arranged between Valamar and the exiled microbiologist to discuss money. An offer was made of monthly instalment's totalling one million dollars. Payment would be deposited into a Swiss account on the last day of each month. The proposition was accepted and Besserer was committed to the project until the weapon was fully realized. Assembly would be undertaken within a clandestine base in the American mid-west. It took Azil all of ten seconds to climb aboard and he was smuggled into the US one month later; as the first stages of Adams plot got underway.

Making certain the effectiveness of Besserer's weapon was verified, the UCOMA Director reviewed the relevant documentation contained within NSA files. The results bore witness to it's potency. Adams also learned a deceased colleague, working alongside Besserer actually discovered the bacterial isolate. The weapon was capable of inflicting mass casualties, while affording no material carnage. With Besserer both a weapons-maker and conspirator were rolled into one. This would do nicely in implicating A'biin.

A SIAG agent had been taken into US custody following a Maryland sting operation. Requisitioning access to the prisoner's phone devise Adams plundered it's data banks. Information enabled him to lure the operative's replacement into the open. A directive was issued stating his predecessor's cover had been blown. The message instructed the receiver to await the arrival of Azil Besserer, as he was smuggled into the US by way of Jacksonville. All that remained was to see if the ruse would draw the newly-minted SIAG operative from the shadows.

On the opposite side of the Atlantic a pair of burly men attired in sailor outfits, appeared at Besserer's door in Veenendaal. Escorting him overland to Lisbon, safe passage to America had been prearranged aboard an antiquated container ship leased through underworld contacts. With instructions to kill the traitorous microbiologist, ULSAR made a textbook entry into the waiting arms of Royston Adams in the ensuing Jacksonville firefight.

A rapping at the bedroom door interrupted the Director's musings. "Yes."

"It's eleven pm Sir I'll retire now," Valamar related.

"Very well Richard tomorrow's a busy day."

Tethered upright to a support beam the woman appeared unconscious. Kristy hadn't forgotten their encounter in Queen's, nor his confiscated phone. A feeling of recognition persisted? The sensation initially struck him during their struggle behind the Ellstone residence.

With the psychotic sharpshooter licking wounds inflicted on him by his master, Kristy suspected the militia leader was a sadistic cold-blooded cretin - now he knew for certain. Dopple deserved an extended thrashing; it was the severity of the beating which caused even him to wince.

Kristy gazed at the woman's motionless form and considered her damaged beauty. His so-called interrogation before the others hadn't been very convincing. He knew too well who she was and why she was there. His contention she was a federal agent had helped prolong her life. Sir's request she be kept alive was welcome – but alive for how long? Kristy peered through the blinds and noticed the sun rise above the treetops. Abruptly, his phone vibrated and the screen indicated the Face beckoned.

"Sir."

In contrast to previous phone contact there was no exaggerated vocal effect. Instead, the voice spoke in an unaffected manner.

"Two questions?" the caller announced. "Are you at the Clearing and has your would-be assassin been detained?"

Affirmation greeted both queries and Kristy conveniently omitted Penther's participation in the woman's capture.

"Is she secured in the bunker?"

"Yes," Kristy lied.

"No doubt you've heard our Detroit undertaking has concluded?"

"Penther informed me."

"I'll be arriving at Rykles Clearing sometime over the next thirty-six hours," confirmed his boss. "Once I've questioned the female we'll oversee the final stage of our operation."

"Understood."

"Meantime, you'll depart for Detroit. You have the pass and entry-codes necessary to access Electron Era. Besserer will waiting for you to deliver him to a private airfield outside of town, where he expects to catch a flight to Zurich. Once you've laced the doctor's champagne glass with drops of strychnine, you'll toast his remarkable achievement."

"But..."

"Besserer trusts you Carl," the Face added reassuringly. "After all these months he still recalls how you both awoke with fierce migraine's in a Jacksonville safe-house. It's imperative the doctor is discovered within the facility where his weapon was assembled. Once this is carried out you'll return to Rykles Clearing."

There was silence at Kristy's end. Finally he said, "Why can't Bell or one of the others attend to the matter - they're on site?"

"Besserer can't stomach the others let alone join them in a toast. He'll be happy to raise a glass in your company and expects to depart Electron Era with you."

Kristy was livid, "I've never been inside the bloody place!"

"I'll text you a layout of the plant. The lower-level is accessed via the shipping room. You'll interact with Besserer then depart. The others will have already left for Indiana."

Tension was palpable at either end.

"Right..." sighed the blighted operative.

"Very well then. I'll await your presence at the bunker once you've undertaken the initiative."

Kristy signed off and spat out curses in two languages.

The directive was a ploy to get him inside ground zero - where Bell and his thugs would be waiting to administer the aforementioned poison to he and Besserer. It would be revealed the bodies of two

A'biinian suicide conspirators; deploying a biological weapon were discovered at the launch site.

Kristy's intent was on preventing the strike. This could only be achieved by remaining nearby the bunker where detonation was to occur.

His loyalty to A'biin throughout the years had wavered. It had been his good fortune to live abroad for much of his adult life. Regardless, his allegiance remained with the homeland.

Kristy reached out and touched the face of his would-be assassin. In her quest to dispatch him she was simply following directives. Tossing his jacket over his shoulder he strode reluctantly toward the back porch.

"Looking for me?" Penther uttered as he stood at the bottom of the steps stroking the dogs.

"I'm required in Detroit," Kristy stated solemnly. "I need to borrow the minivan. I'll return it this evening."

Penther tossed him keys, "Take the Econoline back of the bunker."

"I wouldn't leave Dopple alone with the woman. Sir expect to chat with her."

"He won't touch her unless I say so."

Kristy reentered the lodge and looked in on the female. Earlier, he'd suspected her of faking unconsciousness - he was less certain now. Departing by the front entrance, he followed a path to the bunker and guided the rusty van onto the Yokum Trail.

Aldo was crouched behind the bunker on a rickety bench. A bloody rag was pressed to his head and a pail of water and bandages lay at his feet. The lodge-owner rounded the corner and bid him to follow. Dopple's face was scarred with cuts and bruises. He rubbed an eye with his sleeve unable to look at his boss.

"Gimme a hand getting the prisoner to the bunker," Penther muttered.

"You gonna beat me some more?"

"If you accost her I will."

Dopple struggled to his feet and trailed him toward the lodge. As they entered Penther removed a key and approached the woman. He crouched to unlock the cuffs shackling her ankles to the pole, and repeated the procedure with her wrists. She fell forward and he caught her and laid her along the carpet on her back.

"We'll carry her through the kitchen and onto the grounds."

Penther clasped her wrists and Aldo took her ankles. Despite her lightness of being the victim's limpness suggested she was truly unconscious. Part way along the hall they paused to allow Aldo a better grip.

"Have your gun ready in the event she comes to," Penther urged.

As the transfer resumed, the woman suddenly thrust her weight forward and drove a well-aimed boot into the wrist of Dopple's trigger hand. A second kick caught him in the groin and he doubled over. Penther went for his chest-revolver but never reached it. With her boots planted firmly on the floor she wheeled about and grabbed his wrists. Thrusting him over her shoulder, backwards at a bone-crunching angle, the militia-leader screamed in agony as he landed on top of his bodyguard. Out back the doberman's strained at their leashes. Aldo shoved his moaning boss to one side and retrieved a gun with his good hand. Levelling it unsteadily he discovered the woman had bolted. Penther struggled to rise without use of his arms and slid down the wall.

"The bitch took off!" his assistant bellowed.

Writhing in his skin Penther hissed through his teeth, "Get her!"

Dopple leapt to his feet and charged onto the rear deck. The tethered beasts were snarling in wake of the fleeing woman. Suppressing his injuries Aldo dashed onto the grounds. His wrist throbbed and he was sweating profusely. Penther would kill him if he failed to capture the whore. He unhitched the dogs and gripped their leashes. Allowing them to lead the female's path of flight was quickly determined. She was headed south towards civilization.

"Hell with takin' her alive," Aldo muttered.

Plenty of daylight remained as the doberman's sniffed the air. Dopple's fierce eyes fixated on a newly minted trail leading deep into the thicket. Shouting a command they set off in pursuit.

———————

TWENTY-FOUR

Descending into the netherworld of Electron Era, the intruder entered a shadowy corridor branching in two directions. Utilizing the shipping room overhead as a reference point, the route to his right was chosen first. Through silken-fibres of the drowned sailor's eyes Kriel observed a metal door along the right. A ventilation grid was inserted at it's base and a crack was evident beneath the door. Card-access wasn't required, rather a keyhole was centred on the doorknob. The wraith crouched and listened at the grid. From within laboured breathing was heard.

An instant later shuffling resounded, "You there Train?"

The wraith remained silent.

"I need water and a trash bag."

Believing the individual to be Ray Pearson the intruder twisted the knob and found it secured.

"Who's there!" the prisoner demanded.

Kriel leaned in, "I might beg the same question?"

"Ray Pearson – who in hell are you?"

"This is a rescue," a course voice responded with less than it's usual compass.

Kriel withdrew keys appropriated from the person in the shipping room. Applying each - the third key caught the doorknob turned. Light from the corridor flooded the dark confines and the prisoner staggered backward shielding his eyes.

"I've heard those keys lots," Ray stammered. "You're not here to free me."

The figure glanced about the squalid quarters, "Hush Mr. Pearson, these were acquired from one of your jailers."

Ray lunged at the figure and was tossed forcefully aside. The door closed and the felled lab technician noticed the outline of something large and undefined. Kriel withdrew a penlight and focused it on the sprawled man. "Do you know where you are!"

Ray blinked and said he was within Electron Era but was uncertain where.

"I'm familiar with the sound of diesel trucks in the distance," he added.

"Are you able to move about?"

"Where?"

"Out of here!"

"Lead the way."

The fetid odour was none to subtle. Normally, Ray would have felt humiliated, however he no longer noticed.

The stranger extended an arm, "Come."

Ray griped hold of a gloved hand and was hoisted to his feet. His guest opened the door and peered into the corridor. Motioned to follow they entered the dank passageway. Ray glanced both ways then turned to face his liberator. He staggered backwards and swallowed hard. Before him loomed a hollow-eyed miscreant draped in rags.

"Follow," the thing rasped.

Ray appeared reticent until footsteps were heard. He was pushed back inside the cell and the door closed from within. Running a hand through his tousled hair the footfall resounded. Meanwhile, his ghoulish companion listened attentively.

"It's Wicker," Ray whispered. "One of my jailers I know the walk."

Footsteps drew along the opposite side of the door. The person appeared apprehensive and decided against entering. The pervasive odour may have been a factor.

"He's looking for the guy you borrowed the keys from," Ray speculated.

Wicker's steps retreated and were eventually heard clambering up the stairwell.

"We'll follow," the wraith proclaimed.

"These men are armed."

"Which is why you'll remain behind me unless I say otherwise!" the intruder croaked.

They emerged into the passageway a second time and converged at the foot of the stairwell. Part way up the figure paused and whispered, "I'll issue you the gun confiscated from your jailer. Once we enter the shipping area you'll remain concealed until I return. Understood?"

Ray acknowledged the request and was handed the weapon.

"Do you know how to use it?"

"Aim and pull the trigger?"

The spook grunted and they continued their ascent.

On the landing Kriel listened at the door then pushed the bar latch forward. They entered the space and made their way several yards before pausing. Concealed behind a skid stacked with boxes a man lay trussed up and unconscious.

"Samuel Train!" the lab technician muttered.

The fact it wasn't Cal Wicker was Ray's only regret. Unlike the foreman the daytime watchman displayed no remorse regarding the Ray's predicament and even threatened his life.

"There's room for you to hunker here," rasped his liberator. "If the prisoner comes to keep the gun on him until my return."

With that the ghoul vanished.

Departing the shipping room Kriel made his way along the main floor corridor.

Cal Wicker was in the front lobby and discovered his night watchman counterpart absent.

He reentered the dimly lit passageway and noticed the faint outline of something approaching. A feeling of dread overwhelmed him and he withdrew a silencer-affixed, semi-automatic. Attempting to still his trembling grip he took aim. The intruder was a dozen yards distant when he got off two rounds. The thing appeared to blur and avoided both projectiles. Before Wicker got off a third shot he was thrust into the air and tossed forcefully against a concrete wall. Everything went black and he was relieved of his weapon. Gripped by his ankle the quiescent militiaman was dragged along the corridor like a sack of road salt.

Someone entered the shipping room and Ray peered between boxes. The ghoul was observed dragging something in it's wake. Seconds later it hovered over him.

"This one shall keep the other company," the voice grated.

The latest to succumb was none other than Cal Wicker! The man who'd given Ray so much grief during his incarceration. He gripped Wicker's limp arms and hoisted him alongside his confederate. The ragman withdrew twine and sliced off two lengths and bound Wicker's wrists and ankles securely. Afterwards, it ripped fabric from Wicker's jacket and used it as a gag.

"What are you...?" Ray inquired.

"Not relevant."

"I suppose..."

Silence ensued before Ray's redeemer spoke again,"When were you taken hostage?"

Ray pondered the question.

"Speak!"

"I'm not certain perhaps a week ago?"

"Why were you abducted?"

"I ran across some irregularities."

"Did you confront your employers?"

"They confronted me once I discovered product never leaves these premises."

The ragged figure pointed to the men lying at Ray's feet, "What of them?"

"They were here prior to my being hired," Ray responded. "Train is a foreman. The guy you just delivered is daytime watchman."

"Are there others?"

"Jackson Bell. He's the plant supervisor and the one who hired us technicians. These two answer to him."

"Is he on site frequently?"

"He makes his presence known," Ray replied. "When he's indisposed these guys make the rounds. Bell's office is across from the labs."

Ray was instructed to watch over both men. His frightful liberator intended to seek Bell out within the lower depths.

"Do you have stamina enough Mr. Pearson?"

Mr. Pearson' stank to high heaven and desired a shower more than anything. Freed from his confines he needed to indulge this one necessity.

Ray nodded.

He was reminded to keep the gun levelled on the pair if they came around.

"Don't leave until I return," rasped the entity.

Seconds later the door leading below was accessed. Ray glanced at his sleeping charges and considered the irony of his situation. Grateful to have been freed he wondered by whom or what? Perhaps it was a dream and he was still confined below. The pair at his feet looked as though they'd received a severe thrashing and would be out awhile. Ray needed to sponge-bathe himself and decided he could pull it off inside of three minutes. The washroom was just down the hall. In defiance of his rescuer's request he made for the exit.

———————————

Not knowing what to expect on the second trip below; the subterranean labyrinth would yield answers. Kriel followed the passage not previously taken and went left along the corridor. Ray had identified two men and their supervisor; however there might be others. Striding the hallway the wraith slowed as a pair of metal doors obstructed passage. The confiscated pass allowed bar-latch release. Greater illumination was provided on the other side. The corridor extended roughly thirty yards and came to an end before a second pair of doors. Along the left makeshift quarters were erected; partition's formed a mess room where a card table sat flush against a wall, with chairs strewn about it. A microwave and refrigerator - with a radio perched up top was nearby. Next door Kriel parted aside blanket and entered a barracks-style bunkhouse. The space was equipped with a trio of cots containing linens and pillows. A dresser and trunk were observed, along with a coffee table hosting a variety of hunting magazines. A pre-existing washroom was situated further along the corridor. The room next to it appeared to be a storage facility. Unlike the washroom its door was secured. Across the way a shelving-unit was stocked with non-perishable food items.

A final set of metal doors required the pass.

———————————

Cal Wicker stirred and felt cold concrete beneath his clothing. His mouth was gagged and his wrists and ankles were shackled. He recalled the foreboding sight of something emerging from the gloom in the corridor and remembered firing his weapon. He forced his throbbing bones into an upright position and was startled to discover Sam Train, lying unconscious beside him. He nudged the heel of his shoe against Train's leg in an attempt to stir him. As consciousness returned Train's eyes grew wide at the realization of his predicament. He clutched his aching gut and noticed Wicker similarly bound. Last thing he recalled was departing the lower-level and being overwhelmed by a nightmare. The incident occurred after receiving word they were leaving the plant. Train contemplated this frightening turn while his partner struggled to free himself. The twine bit into Wickers flesh as his nimble fingers reeled and writhed. Making swift progress, he managed to loosen the bonds enough to free one hand then the other. Ripping the gag from his mouth he breathed deeply and cursed. He undid his ankle binds and freed his compatriot's wrists. Once his own ankles were unshackled Train tore the gag from his mouth and rose to his feet. They were in the shipping room. Someone or something had assailed them.

"What the...?"

Wicker shushed him and spoke softly, "If we're gonna get outta this we gotta deal with whatever is laying siege."

Train remained silent.

"Do you remember what hit you?" Wicker probed.

"Other than it's eyes I recall nothing."

Wicker's shoulder and neck agonized, "I went looking for you and noticed that prick Flotsin away from his post. I entered the corridor and I saw it. Things blurred and I got off two rounds. That's all I know."

At the mention of gunshots they reached for their chest-holsters and discovered their sidearms missing. Train thrust a hand in his pocket's and discovered his keys, pass and phone were gone as well. Wicker retained everything except his gun and phone.

"There's box-cutters on the workbench," he muttered. "They'll serve as weapons until we can get downstairs to the armaments stash."

Wicker rose and limped towards the bench where a pair of box knives were retrieved. He gave one to his mate and retrieved a flashlight, "Let's make a quick search."

Before they could explore the dim recesses, Train pointed toward the displaced plywood obstruction along the wall.

"Whoever assaulted us penetrated the lower-level," he whispered. "It waited then attacked."

Wicker nodded.

"I'll go below and get guns. Bell and I will root out who's down there. Meantime, you keep watch up here."

"Did you strike the thing when you fired at it?" Train pressed.

"I hope so."

Wicker withdrew his pass and descended the stairwell leaving his colleague as sentry.

A suitable hiding spot was obtained and Train hunkered among the shadows.

Ray spent several minutes in the washroom sponge-mopping with soap, hot water and paper towels. Carrying a flashlight in one hand, and a gun in the other he returned to the shipping room. The torch beam guided the way to where his charges lay and his heart stopped! Twine and fabric lay strewn about the concrete floor!

Had the ghoul returned to claim the prisoners?

With growing alarm he steadied the flashlight and scanned his surroundings.

"Hello Ray..."

The voice emitted from an obscured recess.

"Tell me about the person who left Wicker and myself trussed up and worse for wear?"

Ray held his breath and remained silent.

"Was it you or do you have an ally?"

The question went unanswered.

"I feel I've been treated unjustly Ray. After all I responsible for keeping your sorry ass alive during captivity."

The native American recognized Samuel Train's voice.

"I see you clearly," Train warned. "You're armed! The gun your holding looks a lot like mine. Wonder how you acquired it?"

Ray calmly responded, "I was released from that shit-hole downstairs and given the weapon for protection."

"Protection! Your gonna need it."

Ray gripped the weapon tighter.

"The others wanted you dead," Train resumed. "I kept you alive and this is my reward!"

Ray peered into the gloom, "You were more considerate than the rest but you're one of them."

"Come and get me Ray."

Jackson Bell steadied himself atop a sturdy ladder two floors up. He was within the atrium attaching explosive charges around the periphery of the ceiling. The procedure would enable that portion of the roof to implode. Meantime, gas-fuelled flames would ignite within the pit below, inducing a melt-down of polystyrene encasing the lethal spores. Industrial fans would propel the deadly strain skywards through the exposed roof.

As Bell laboured he cussed his two associate's who were nowhere to be found.

Meanwhile, Cal Wicker hastened along the subterranean passage in the direction of their quarters. With his phone appropriated he was unable to alert Jackson Bell. Flinging the blanket aside, he entered their bunk room and approached the weapon's cache next to Bell's cot. He withdrew an AK 47 and shoved a Smith & Wesson 45 in his chest-holster. Rounds of ammo were stuffed into his pockets and he reentered the corridor. Deciding Train could take care of himself, he headed for the atrium to seek Bell. Together they would destroy whatever infringed upon their doomsday dwelling.

———————

Only moments before the haggard intruder stood before double doors at the end of the passage applying a pass. A click resounded and a lair of moderate proportions was revealed. The figure advanced cautiously and heard the sound of laboured breathing and unravelling tape from above. A fluorescent lighting fixture dimly illuminated the chamber and nearby pit. The vat was surrounded by fans with their propellers tilted upwards. Kriel noticed the cavity stockpiled with polystyrene cubes. A ladder extended toward the ceiling where someone laboured in shadow.

Along Kriel's right stood an enclosed Fibreglass chamber. Peering through the transparency, hazmat suits and a shower stall were observed. Directions bore an image of skull and crossbones.

Several yards distant a second chamber appeared. It was a solitary laboratory and looked more foreboding than the ones upstairs. A freezer was within alongside a workbench and stools.

It was assumed the individual working overhead was Jackson Bell. Surrounded by four grey walls extending two floors up he appeared thoroughly engaged.

The atrium doors were suddenly accessed and someone entered.

The wraith remained obscured in shadow.

"You in here Bell!"

The man carried an automatic rifle.

Kriel circled the lab and vanished within and noticed Wicker through the transparency. He was supposed to be upstairs under Pearson's watch. Once again the technician's fate was brought to bear.

"You deaf Bell!" his compatriot hollered.

Glancing over his shoulder the supervisor's response echoed, "You're supposed to be helping me rig these charges. Thought you wanted outta this hole!"

"We got company," Wicker informed him.

"Don't tell me the cops are back!"

"I don't think it's cops."

"Good!" returned the supervisor. "Maybe Penther stopped in to witness our handiwork?""

"It ain't Penther neither."

"Then who!"

"Train and I were attacked by something on ground level. I think it's down here."

Bell placed a package of explosives aside and immediately began his descent.

Wicker was inspecting the area surrounding the pit. He entered the decontamination chamber and noticed nothing unusual. His companion reached the halfway point on the ladder as Wicker approached the lab. Abruptly, it imploded sending shards of tempered glass raining down upon Wicker - who was brought to his knees by something formidable.

Bell touched down and withdrew his gun levelling it at whatever was on Wicker. Unable to fire lest he struck his co-conspirator, he moved closer and was stunned to see a spectre hovering over his felled compatriot. It smashed his rifle and Bell took aim a second time. Abruptly, Wicker's limp body was thrust upright as a shield against incoming projectiles.

"You fear the gun...," Bell muttered as he advanced toward the entity.

He glanced about rapidly for possible confederates; as he did the thing cast it's burden aside and lunged forward with astonishing speed. Bell's weapon discharged and the target appeared to blur. Reeling backwards the supervisor toppled into the pit. His features registered shock as he lay motionless along the surface of the stockpile. With his gun out of reach he stared up at the abhorrent eyes gazing silently down upon him.

The intruder tarried briefly to observe Bell's impact on the contents of the pit. The horror etched upon the supervisor's face belied the fact that nothing occurred.

During the altercation Cal Wicker took flight.

In the corridor the vengeful conspirator withdrew the gun from his chest-holder and staggered toward Besserer's sanctuary. He pounded the door and a groggy voice responded. Once the latch clicked Wicker forced his way inside. The door slammed shut and he quickly secured it.

The biologist was appalled, "What is the meaning of this violation!"

Wicker responded by pressing the gun to Besserer's temple, "Back off kebab eater."

With the scientist cowering Wicker listened with his ear to the door. He opened it slightly and peered into the corridor.

"I have a hostage," he bellowed. "Bar my way and he dies!"

A consistent hum of hydro-electricity was his only response.

"Hell with this," he murmured.

Wicker opened the door and shoved the reluctant microbiologist across the threshold.

"Move up the hall *away* from the atrium!," the militiaman commanded. "Make a wrong turn and I'll take your head off."

Besserer was frantic, "Where are Bell and Train? Who are you talking to!"

"Shut up!"

Using his hostage as a shield they straddled backwards along the hall towards the outer passageway.

Besserer screamed as something manifested in the funeral darkness before them. Wicker fired twice and holes appeared in the atrium doors.

A shuffle echoed behind them.

The biologist hit the deck as Wicker turned and fired at nothing.

When the terrorist swung about again the thing stood before him. Disbelief registered as he was raised a foot from the ground in a choke hold. He was unconscious before he hit the floor.

The thing turned it's ghastly eyes upon the microbiologist.

"I'm a prisoner - a hostage!" Besserer pleaded. "These men have held me against my will!"

"We shall see," the thing grated.

Besserer was dragged to his feet and shoved toward his quarters. Within it's confines he shivered as the abomination glared from the passage.

"Attempt to leave and you will perish."

The door slammed and Besserer rapidly secured it. Bowing his head he wept into his sleeve.

TWENTY-FIVE

In the dim light of the shipping room Ray Pearson sought to determine Samuel Train's place of concealment.

"I'm unarmed Ray," the voice resumed. "You have my gun."

"Then reveal yourself,"

Ray considered the other man and wondered if Wicker had yet to regain consciousness.

"Was it you who attacked us Ray?" the voice persisted.

"No."

"Then who? And how did you get my gun?"

"I said it was given to me."

"By whom?"

"It doesn't matter."

"Let me guess you summoned your native kin and they conjured a shaman to free you?"

"Something like that."

The response was greeted in silence.

"The police have been contacted," Ray lied.

Again no answer.

An object struck the floor and reverberated across the cluttered void. As Ray turned he was body-slammed against a row of crates. The gun was still in his grip and he was able to drive the butt end down on the head of his assailant. Train reeled and Ray landed an uppercut on his jaw, which sent him forcefully backwards. Moving in he levelled the weapon between his former jailer's eyes.

Still smarting from the earlier blow to his gut Train muttered, "Let's not get carried away!"

Weak from hunger Ray responded feebly, "Your friends got carried away. It was they..."

As the words left his mouth Train's boot drove into Ray's ankle. The lab captain buckled unable to maintain grasp of the gun. Train scuttled for the weapon and snagged it several feet from where Ray fell.

Glaring at the fallen worker Train hissed, "I outta blow your brains all over this room red man! Instead I'll leave you to the whims of Wicker."

Ray bit down on his collar in an effort to stymie the pain caused by his fractured ankle. The conspirator got to his feet and leered over stricken employee, "I've got business below Mr. Pearson. See ya later."

Dragged agonizingly towards the lower-level door kept ajar with cardboard placed by Wicker, the lab worker was unconscious as he was deposited along the stairwell stoop.

No need to secure him, Train thought.

Hastening down the stairs with his retrieved weapon he sought his two compatriots.

———

Accessing reentry into the atrium the grim figure stole towards the pit where Jackson Bell lay sprawled. The supervisor hadn't budged for fear of disrupting the metabolism of the cubes making up his mattress.

The intruder considered Ray Pearson and strode purposefully from the chamber. In the corridor Wicker was observed rising unsteadily. Kriel had taken precaution of smashing his rifle and ravaging his handgun. The terrorist fumbled for his pass as the thing loomed. Grasped by the scruff of his neck the pass fell away. Within the atrium Bell heard his compatriot's cries as he was dragged toward the bunk room.

Shoved into a folding chair Wicker glared up at the abomination.

"You have an ally?" the thing rasped.

"I have many allies."

The wraith stuck a match and lit a candle.

"Indeed, one of them lies within the pit.

Wicker glanced away.

"You appear helpless without a weapon at your disposal Mr. Wicker?"

The militiaman spat on the floor.

In the flickering light weird patterns danced upon the facial abyss of the miscreant. Wicker was certain it was grinning insidiously. The Stygian eyes made his blood run cold.

"Our job here is done bogeyman," the prisoner sneered. "We've left a calling card and plan to take back what's ours."

The wraith's silence underscored the gravity of the moment. From within it's rags a spool of twine was withdrawn. Pulling it taut a slice was cut and Wicker's wrist's were bound. A length was thrust about his neck below the Adam's apple. Pressure was exerted and the noose tightened.

"What is being harvested within the pit Mr. Wicker?"

There was no response and the twine tightened drawing blood.

"Fare thee well," the demon croaked. "Ha, ha, ha, ha, ha, ha...!"

"Stop!" Wicker screamed.

Tension eased and the terrorist gasped for air. Coughing he sputtered, "S..strains of enhanced anthrax are contained in polystyrene shells. Once the insulation melts the strain is propelled upward by fans. The nigger Besserer created it."

"When is it to be released?"

The prisoner was silent.

"How much of the area will be affected?"

Again nothing.

"Speak!

A thin smile formed along Wicker's lips, "Business will be slow around these parts for awhile."

"Naturally, your people will have vacated the premises before the poison is released," the interrogator surmised. "The weapon will be detonated from a point other than the launch site. Where!"

The prisoner made no response.

His neck was grasped and the noose tightened, "These quarters shall be the last thing you witness. Adieu!"

"The detonation site is in Indiana!"

"Where exactly?"

"Off the beaten track."

"Where!"

"A place called Rykles Clearing."

Seconds passed before the wraith spoke again.

"When is it to be deployed?"

"Depending on the prevailing winds any minute now," Wicker lied.

Glaring up at his tormentor he added, "Despite the masquerade you're too late!"

"Liar! Neither you nor your associates would be within a hundred miles of this place were that so!"

Wicker leaned back, "I got nothing more to say."

"We shall see."

Kriel withdrew twine to secure the prisoner's ankles. At that instant Wicker bolted for the corridor with his hands tethered. He noticed his pass on the floor and rushed forward. An object landed nearby and the corridor filled instantly with smoke.

Opposite the outer passageway doors Samuel Train drew to a standstill. Without a pass to gain entry the obstruction became fodder for his gun. Bullets shattered the door lock and he entered the smoke-filled domain and heard footsteps charging toward him.

"Who's there...?" he shouted.

Engulfed in plumes of smoke the onrush continued. Likely, it was the same thing who'd accosted he and Wicker at ground-level. Firing into the swirling billows a groan was heard. Train peered through the haze and observed a form sprawled along the concrete surface of the floor. In the diminished light the figure appeared familiar. Advancing cautiously he noticed the features belonged to Cal Wicker! He crouched next to the body and observed the bound wrists. Two slugs had entered his chest killing him instantly.

Train retrieved the pass and cursed out loud. Having unknowingly taken his partner's life, he vowed their uninvited guest would pay dearly.

He made for the atrium. Along the way he stopped before Besserer's door and pounded.

"It's Train!"

"Who?" cried the frightened occupant.

"Train," he shouted. "Open up."

"Are y...you alone?"

"Ya!"

The door latch clicked and Train entered.

Besserer backed away, "I heard shots! Did you kill it?"

"What occurred down here!" Train demanded.

"I was sleeping a...and Wicker showed up at my door. I let him in and he put a gun to my head and ordered me into the hall. We made our way towards the outer passageway and were confronted by a demon. The thing accosted Wicker and I was forced in here and threatened."

"Was Bell present throughout any of this?"

"No."

Train recalled the supervisor saying he'd be mounting charges in the atrium. His mind was racing; they were probably dealing with the feds. Whatever was wreaking havoc was neither demon or goblin. Train heard it breathing during his own assault upstairs.

The first order of business was to find Jackson Bell. Together they would become the hunters and dispatch the intruder. Once the threat was eliminated Penther would be informed.

Without mentioning Wicker's demise the biologist was told to stay put.

"Don't leave me," the defector pleaded.

Train slipped out the door and made for the atrium. He gained entry using Wicker's pass and called out Bell's name. Shards of glass littered the floor nearby the lab. He approached the pit and his blood ran cold. Along the surface of the stockpile lay the sprawled form of Jackson Bell! He appeared paralyzed and his expression bore a look of mortal terror. Attempting to convey meaning his eyes were fixated above Train's shoulder.

The foreman considered ways to extract the supervisor without damaging the contents of the pit. Having been second-guessed by Bell for the better part of a dozen years; he took an almost perverse delight in his helplessness. The man had an answer for everything except dealing with crisis. Train returned with a broom and extended the stick end toward the supervisor to grasp onto. Instead, he heard a garbled utterance escape Bell's lips.

"Above...!"

Train glanced up and witnessed the same appalling entity he'd glimpsed earlier. It's dreadful eyes bore into him from part way up a ladder. Before he could get a shot off the thing was on him. Struggling alongside the perimeter of the pit Train was unable to free his upper limbs. The thing grasped his throat; however a reserve of strength afforded Train to liberate an arm and deliver a blow. Retaining his weapon he scrambled to his feet and remarked breathlessly, "You're pretty solid for a ghoul."

The thing approached.

Train steadied himself and pulled the trigger. A click was heard and he cursed the empty clip. Tossing the gun aside he dove forward and locked his arms about the weathered boots of the entity. He managed to bring it down and followed-up with a second blow.

"That's for Wicker," he muttered.

His advantage was short-lived and he was tossed effortlessly aside. As the frightful thing loomed Train backed away on all fours. He attempted to rise but was rendered unconscious with a single blow to the skull.

Kriel gazed in the pit and noticed a wet stain had formed inches below the supervisor's belt buckle. His accomplice was grasped by an ankle and dragged from the chamber. They approached the biologist's quarters and Wicker's lifeless body, was observed at the end of the passage. Kriel dispensed with his load and strode forth. Retrieving the dead man he was deposited on a cot inside their barracks. The blanket used as a doorway partition was ripped away and draped over the body. Kriel returned to the motionless figure sprawled nearby Besserer's quarters and pounded the door.

Believing it was Train the occupant responded.

Besserer screamed and shrank back as the door yielded and Train was dragged within.

"The weapon is bogus!" the doctor pleaded.

"Stand aside!" rasped the demon.

Train was spread along the floor and his wrists and ankles were bound a second time.

Besserer was spun about on his heels and secured in a similar fashion. Between sobs he kept repeating the weapon was a hoax.

"I was abducted and forced to labour for these terrorists! No lives were ever at risk...!"

The door slammed and the entity withdrew.

Three priorities remained: The explosives had to be disengaged, Ray Pearson needed to be found; and contact with his handler regarding the anthrax plot outlined by Cal Wicker would be established

The explosives came first.

Heron cradled his teacup and watched the steam rise in swirls. Seated before his desktop monitor he remained focused on the motionless signal emitting from Indiana. As he prepared to establish contact with the wise men; he was aware his period of grace was up. Abruptly, the signal belonging to his operative advanced ever so slightly. Honing in on the relay he wondered if his agent had moved of her own accord.

At least she's alive!

There was no way to determine her physical or mental well-being with a Global Positioning Signal. Heron glanced at the phone and considered the wise men two levels below. Focusing on his agent's position he attempted to determine her present course. The ratio of speed as determined by the relay suggested Taras was on foot. The line denoting her coordinates remained in motion before coming to a stop.

Heron fixated on the screen and held his breath. Abruptly, the signal resumed its irregular pattern.

A moment later his desk phone rang.

"Sir?"

"There can be no further delay," the wise man insisted. "Your agent is likely in the hands of Ulsar and whoever controls him."

"I was about to inform you there's been movement."

"When?"

"Moments ago I need time to determine her course against the satellite reading. Her signal suggests she's on foot."

Silence registered at the other end.

"If Taras is in a vehicle," Heron resumed. "The pattern of her GPS would register a consistent line - not the hare-brained trail I'm observing."

The signal came to a sudden stop - an observation Heron neglected to pass to his superior.

"You're certain about this?" the wise man inquired.

"Yes."

"If her signal remains stationary for any length of time I want to know."

"Of course."

The spy-master replaced the receiver and focused on the screen. Once again his agent's signal advanced.

"Good girl," he whispered.

———————

Mist hovered over trails penetrating the woods surrounding Rykles Clearing. Relishing pursuit of the prey the doberman's crisscrossed each other's path. The nearest dwelling was several kilometres south of the lodge. Aldo listened intently and shouted a command as Club and Boot fell back. Pumped up and frantic as a result of the woman's aborted transfer, Dopple vowed to track the bitch down and feed her to the dogs. First he'd have some fun with her himself.

He considered Penther's helplessness. Hopefully, he downed painkillers while awaiting news of the whore who'd mangled his limbs. When the current business concluded Aldo intended to chauffeur his boss into Ellery, where his injuries could be doctored.

If the female had been under Aldo's watch none of this would've occurred. She would've been dealt with accordingly. He cursed Penther for admonishing him a beating in front of the witch.

"Bastard," murmured the bodyguard. "A wench strung up all ready and they wanna talk!"

Reigning in the reluctant beasts they aired their grievances with a display of whines and whimpers. Secured to a tree unwillingly they stretched reluctantly along the damp earth.

"I'll feed your sorry asses when I'm back," Aldo muttered resuming the hunt alone.

Crouched behind a protruding boulder Taras massaged her bleeding ankles and wrists with moist leaves. A weapon needed to be fashioned to stave off the dogs and their overseer. Other than twigs and pebbles nothing presented itself. The frenzied barking had been stilled; however, the notion someone was near persisted.

Once again Ulsar had given her the slip.

Referred to as Kristy by the others he bore the distinction of having a trio of pseudonyms. The upper limbs of lodge owner Penther had been neutralized. For the time being he posed no threat. The twisted psycho Dopple who'd raped her was presently on her trail.

Staggering through the woods Taras held her pain in check. Beneath a leafy oak she crouched and sprang up, grasping a lower branch. Exhaling, she hoisted herself further upwards and buttressed herself along a sturdy perch. The foliage offered concealment and an observation platform. Her only recourse was to take down the hunter as he passed below.

A stench of dirty laundry and gum reached her nostrils.

"Ain't you the bitch monkey," a voice echoed.

Aldo's contorted features glared up at her from below.

"You happen to know a rotting slime decked out in rags? I got a score to settle with him as well."

Panting audibly he began his ascent.

Taras climbed higher while Aldo groped at her ankles.

"Thought you fooled me didn't ya?"

If Taras jumped serious damage would likely occur.

Aldo withdrew the dagger he'd confiscated back at the lodge and stuck it between his teeth,

"Remember this?" he garbled. "You're gonna make like a sow while I do the carving."

She noticed his rifle upright against a tree below.

"Go on," he taunted. "I dare ya?"

Twisting her body she administered a swift kick to the side of Aldo's head. The demented hunter teetered and grasped a nearby limb retaining balance. Thrusting her left hand down Taras attempted to snatch the dagger from Dopple's mouth. He gripped the weapon and drove the blade through the palm of her hand. Uttering a cry she brought the sole of her boot down upon his clinging fingers. He dangled precariously as she delivered a second blow to his skull with the heel of her boot. The force sent Aldo spiralling towards solid ground twenty feet below.

In quiet agony she gazed at her pierced flesh, then at the motionless figure sprawled along the forest floor. A painful descent ensued and reached the limb nearest the ground. Gripping it with her good hand, she lowered herself and staggered backwards. Getting her bearings, she tore leaves from an overhanging bough and applied them to her bleeding hand. Fabric from her cuffs was ripped away and wrapped about the injury.

Limping toward the crumpled form of her assailant, she noticed the reversed position of his head in relation to the rest of his body. His neck was broken and his nose in the dirt - the rest of him faced heaven. Retrieving her dagger she tottered towards his rifle upright against a tree. The weapon would serve double-duty as a crutch until something more suitable was obtained.

TWENTY-SIX

Kriel reentered the chamber bypassing the enormous fans encircling the pit. Cables were taped to the floor and trailed toward a silver console attached to the stockpiled cavity. The intruder's heels reverberated off concrete and a continual hum prevailed. The lighting fixture cast angular designs about the space. The reverse ends of cables ran alongside the ladder towards the shadows overhead.

A leather boot mounted the first rung and Kriel ascended. The wraith continued scaling past ground level where once a floor existed. The top of the ladder was set roughly two feet beneath the summit. It was here Jackson Bell abandoned his explosives to deal with unforeseen events below. Kriel gazed from on high and observed the supervisor lying motionless in a polystyrene pantomime.

A single package of explosive charges had been attached at the nearest juncture. Fastened with electrical tape; four bundles would have raised the roof. While his compatriot's chased ghosts Bell had been awaiting their assistance. Focused on the bundle Kriel placed a gloved palm firmly down on it's surface. Exerting pressure the cable was yanked from it's moorings and slithered to the floor below.

Descending rapidly Kriel vaulted between fans, in the direction of the console attached to the pit. Cables were gripped by their ends in a similar manner and ripped from their bearings.

From the pit Bell witnessed his set-up being systematically dismantled. The effort he and his fellow patriot's invested nearly a year assembling was forsaken. Words formed but no sound emerged.

Departing the atrium, Kriel searched their living-quarters and discovered a stash of automatic weapons. The tattered figure cast a final glance at the shroud covering Wicker and hastened toward the outer corridor. At the bottom of the stairwell a leg was observed, dangling from the top landing. Ray Pearson lay unconscious with a swollen and bloodied ankle visible beneath torn jeans. The wound was either a fracture or an outright break. Kriel retrieved bottled water from the shipping room and crouched next to the victim. Applying moist fabric to Ray's brow, the process was repeated and he came around and groaned in agony. The sound rebounded within the stairwell; paramedics would be necessary if he were to be moved.

Ray observed the grim mascot looming over him.

"Your leg is fractured!" the thing rasped.

"I know it," stammered the plant worker.

He attempted to shift his weight but the motion caused excruciating pain.

"You need medical attention," his liberator stated bluntly. "You shall receive it in due course. Are there remedies stored within the building to help alleviate pain?"

Ray responded haltingly and stated pain-killers were kept in a first-aid kit inside Lab D.

"It's behind the d...door as you enter."

The wraith returned moments later with pills and a lab coat. As convulsions rattled Ray's shattered ankle the coat was folded and placed beneath his head. The ghoulish medic dispensed three tablets and brought water to Ray's parched lips.

"Swallow while I administer one pill at a time."

Once the process was completed the injured man settled back.

"Any attempt to move you now would prove unwise Mr. Pearson."

Ray nodded.

"The people who abducted you have been contained until the authorities arrive. Allow the medicine to take effect I shall return shortly."

With those words the entity vanished.

Traversing the ground floor corridor in the direction of the lobby, Kriel was intent upon updating his handler. An orange hue crested the horizon beyond the plate-glass lobby entrance. Perspiration glistened on Jesse's brow as he drew back the facial disguise and breathed in deeply. A pause ensued before he withdrew a phone from a belt pouch and entered a code.

Seconds later Lee Tondar's voice carried across the miles.

"It's me," Jesse uttered in his natural speaking voice.

"You're safe!"

"So far."

The professor allowed him to speak.

"The perpetrators at this end have been restrained," Jesse informed him. "Four in all - a microbiologist is among them. There was one casualty erroneously killed by a fellow conspirator."

"Four!" the professor repeated. "Go on."

"Having been locked inside a cellar room, Ray Pearson turned up worse for wear but alive. One of the plotters revealed their plan, was to allow a concoction of lethal anthrax to enter the air above Detroit. They'd regroup at Rykles Clearing and await the prevailing winds, intending to launch the extract sometime over the next thirty-six hours."

Lee coughed at the other end.

"Your research proved accurate professor," Jesse remarked. "The detonation site is Rykles Clearing - which suggests either the lodge or bunker?"

"I'll wager the bunker."

"That's my guess."

"Anything else?"

Jesse mentioned the weapon lay within a restructured chamber inside the lower-level of Electron Era.

"Dosages of Anthrax injected into polystyrene cubes are stored inside a vat," the young man related. "The intent is to melt their casings and propel the spores upwards through a blasted-out portion of the ceiling. I was able to disengage cables from the ceiling explosives and toxic pit. However, a threat may still exist?"

"You have Detective DeLong's private number?" Lee urged.

"I do."

"Establish immediate contact and inform him of the situation. I'll be leaving for Rykles Clearing. A personal matter needs to be dealt with. I'll keep you posted."

His recruit was stunned, "With respect Lee you're supposed to be recuperating."

"I'm fine now."

"Then allow me to join you I'm familiar with the place. My work here in Detroit is finished."

"I need you to remain where you are," Lee insisted. "You're to observe the arrival of DeLong and the Feds – from a distance naturally. They'll be accompanied by a C.D.C. bio-terrorism unit. Once they arrive you'll return to Abbot Lane and await further instructions."

"But ..."

"I have to go!" a ping echoed and the connection was severed.

Beyond the doorway entrance a diesel rumbled along Sentra Avenue.

Jesse yanked the face back into place and departed the lobby. Striding the corridor he returned to the stairwell landing.

"Have the pills quelled the pain!"

There was an edge to the grating voice Ray hadn't recognized earlier. He attributed it to abandoning his post.

"The pain has eased so long as I'm still," Ray responded.

"Help will arrive."

Wrinkles formed on the technician's brow, "Who shall I say freed me?"

"Tell them what you will."

"Do you have a name?"

"Make one up."

A smile formed along the corners of Ray's mouth, "Thanks."

"My pleasure Mr. Pearson. Here's wishing you a speedy recovery!"

With that the thing was gone.

In the corridor Kriel entered a number linked to Branden DeLong.

A groggy voice responded, "Lee...?"

"No a mutual friend."

The detective sighed, "Why not allow Lee to speak for himself?"

"He'll explain later," the caller rasped. "I've been instructed to inform you a terrorist cell, engaged in biological weaponry has been detained. One has expired - mistakenly shot by a confederate. Among the living is a microbiologist."

DeLong sputtered,"Who in blazes is ...!"

"An innocent man held captive needs medical attention."

"Where!" urged DeLong.

"Within the lower-level of Electron Era a place you're familiar with."

The detective tossed his blanket aside, "Is Lee at the scene!"

"Once the biological threat is neutralized and those within the plant are in custody, you will hear from him."

"How do I know this isn't a set-up?"

The connection terminated abruptly.

Placing the devise back in his rags Kriel departed the facility by way of the parking lot. Dawn was breaking and responders would soon converge at that location. Perhaps two minutes remained to seek concealment. Tugging back the captain's spectral features, Jesse allowed the material to drape down and pulled the hem of his pants over his boots. He glanced either way and crossed the street, to retrieve the windbreaker he'd stashed twenty-four hours earlier. Drawing himself among the shadows behind a neighbouring warehouse he waited.

Once DeLong and the C.D.C. team arrived he was bound for Indiana.

Jackson Bell attempted to relax his muscles atop the bed of polystyrene cubes. He cursed the atrocity who'd placed him in such dire circumstances. His fate and those of his brothers-in-arms were doomed. He'd watched helplessly as the miscreant severed connection to the generator and ripped cables from the console. Everything was devised to act in synchronicity; now the alignments were subverted.

Bell gauged the distance between himself and the atrium floor. He attempted to propel himself toward the edge of the pit, but froze as the polystyrene grated beneath his weight.

An alarm suddenly clamoured at ground level. Footsteps bounded overhead in the direction of the shipping room. Gradually, voices were heard emitting from the lower-level passageway. Bell's heart sank at the realization the authorities had penetrated their lair. Sequestered like moles for months on end; as they prepared to depart company arrives.

Charges were applied to the atrium doors and Bell no longer cared about the hazardous stockpile. He reached in his pocket and fumbled for a lighter. The wick flickered to life and he manoeuvred himself into a seated position and removed his denim shirt.

A task force barged into the atrium attired in PPF gear and swept the room with automatic rifles. Bell flicked the lighter and ignited his crumpled shirt.

A tactical squad member shouted, "Extinguish the lighter and toss the fabric here!"

"Why would I want to do that?" the terrorist answered reproachfully.

The militiaman considered William Penther - a man he truly loved. Three years Bell's senior; the patriot leader was like a father. The former supervisor remained proud of their righteous struggle.

As the unit surrounded the pit Bell calmly remarked, "I'm behind the eight ball - but have you for company."

"Over here Sir!" hailed a sniper.

A senior officer entered the chamber accompanied by DeLong in a hazmat suit.

The detective noticed the shirtless man clutching burning fabric and reacted instinctively. The content's of the pit needed to be contained.

"Give the word Sir!" a squad member shouted as the fiery shirt was tossed onto the cubes.

"Hold!" DeLong shouted.

Noting the terrorist's weight was supported by the payload he bellowed instructions to fetch water. Sliding on his stomach onto the surface of the pit, DeLong inched cautiously toward the burning fabric and cast the material beyond the point of danger.

"Extinguish it!" he shouted.

The detective ran his protected hand gently over the surface of the affected cubes. Those tarnished with black singes harboured superficial burns. Another ten seconds the results might have been different. Aside from a pungent scent of burnt polystyrene, no toxic odours were detected by C.D.C. observers.

Seated upright a foot away Jackson Bell closed his eyes as if it were all a bad dream.

"Your rights will be read once we're out of this hole," DeLong muttered.

Members of the detail kept their weapons fixed on the target. Bell put up no resistance as he was harnessed with rope and hoisted cautiously from the pit. Assisted slowly from the vat, the detective was informed Ray Pearson had been transported to a waiting ambulance. Presently, a search of the entire facility was underway.

Bell was cuffed and read his rights then led away.

Jesse's rented car lay among a labyrinth of warehouses and factories several blocks away. It resided behind an abandoned auto-body shop, with access to an artery leading from the industrial no-man's land. He scaled several fences along an extended alleyway and finally arrived at the vehicle. If the cops were to pull him over, he'd produce fake ID and say he managed a metal band seeking warehouse rehearsal space. It was a confrontation he hoped to avoid.

The arrival of the Feds accompanied by DeLong was an impressive sight. From Jesse's vantage point, he observed a squadron of emergency vehicles descend upon the electronics plant. From the opposite direction a stealth black vehicle the size of a bus appeared. It braked and a platoon of snipers wearing hazmat gear; accompanied by a bio-hazard unit spilled from the rear doors. A team circled the exterior of the facility effectively guaranteeing it. A plainclothes policeman Jesse assumed was DeLong, was guided by an official into the bus. Moments later he emerged, having been administered a protective anthrax antidote and assisted into PPF garb.

In the grey light they advanced toward the lobby entrance. C.D.C. experts accessed the doors and an alarm sounded. Given the go-signal an assault team stormed the doors as if they'd landed at Normandy.

Over the professor's objections his recruit prepared to depart for Rykles Clearing. With federal agent's and C.D.C. experts on hand, the anthrax threat would hopefully be neutralized. Starting the engine Jesse slowly pulled away, careful to avoid the circus along Sentra Avenue.

Twenty minutes later he was on the Interstate bound for central Indiana.

Parking in his usual spot Sean Drummond stepped from the car and marvelled at the stillness of the morning. Fog blanketed the lake and hovered over the grounds attached the Grissim Institute. He preferred arriving several minutes before his shift commenced, affording time to breathe the air while taking in the splendour of Lake Erie. This morning his sightseeing prospects were on hold; with the inclement driving conditions he'd arrived in time to relieve his superior officer. Mounting the steps, he strode purposefully through the lobby and observed his boss scrutinizing monitors in wake of a rash of security breaches. Sean admired Corporal Soo's leadership; he believed she'd taken appropriate measures and implemented proper precautions. The young sentinel hoped it would be his privilege to command his own detail someday.

"Howdy Chief," he announced cheerfully.

Sasha glanced up, "Morning Sean, barely noticed your arrival with all the fog."

"I took it real slow along Windover Road," he acknowledged.

"Been quiet here," she informed him. "The professor's still recuperating from the Lakeshore incident. I kept my notes brief."

Drummond entered their narrow quarters and made for the Gatorade in the fridge.

"I gather nothing further has occurred during your rounds?" probed his boss.

She was referring to an entry Sean recorded two nights earlier. He'd been patrolling the area around the School of Journalism building; when an outburst of laughter emitted. It sounded as if it came from the courtyard and he sprinted in that direction. Sighting no one he initiated a search then returned the station, where he remained glued to monitors.

"Nothing," he reported.

Avoiding Falls Valley was one thing; however the campus was Sasha's jurisdiction. Dutifully, she toured it's boundaries several times over the course of each watch and requested her staff do the same.

"I'm happy to accompany you to Residence if you like?" Drummond offered.

"Thanks Sean I'm good."

Footsteps echoed from the stairwell and the professor appeared. He sported a windbreaker, corduroy trousers and hiking boots. Adjusting a shoulder bag he strode in their direction.

Sasha slid the panel aside, "Should you not be resting Professor?"

"I'm fine Corporal," he responded. "I'll be gone a day possibly longer."

He coughed lightly.

"Jesse's due back later today," he added. "When he arrives tell him I'll be in touch."

"And the effects from the assault?" persisted his security chief.

"My injuries aren't life-threatening. I replaced the old bandages and slept like a baby."

He glanced at the antique clock, "I've called a cab to take me to Roams Airfield - a private airstrip east of town. Kindly inform me when it appears onscreen?"

The Corporal's gaze shifted to the monitors, "There's plenty of fog."

Sean weighed in, "I drove up from town Sir. It's slow going out there."

"I'll remind the driver to take precautions," the professor responded somewhat curtly.

A vehicle emerged from the grey swirl onscreen.

"Your cab's here Professor," Sasha informed him.

The revived spymaster paused to check his wallet, "I'll be in touch."

He departed the lobby and entered the rear of the cab. Seconds later it's taillights vanished.

Sasha sighed. "Guess I'll mosey on home."

She slipped on her jacket and reached for her flashlight.

"You'll be alright?" Sean inquired again.

"Positive," she replied. "See you this evening."

Exiting the booth she made for the lobby doors. Outside, the fog obliterated Abbot Lane and and most campus structures. Sasha considered the professor's departure and was concerned. If something unforeseen were to happen she would hold herself personally responsible.

Her flashlight offered sparse illumination as she descended the steps onto Abbot Lane. She cut a swath through the haze, toward the courtyard path with her senses alert.

Early morning's along the south shore of Erie are often fogbound. It was thicker than usual that day. The lowering sky hunkered like a grey sheet above the surface of the lake. It's effects engulfed the bluffs and lingered along the coastline.

Casting occasional glances over her shoulder Sasha arrived safely at the Residence building. She entered the lobby and took the stairs to the fourth floor. Listening with her ear to the door, she entered her quarters and secured the lock. With her flashlight energized and the lights extinguished, she unbuckled her holster and carried the gun into the bathroom. Undressing, she entered the shower and allowed the warm flow of water to massage her tensed muscles. Afterwards, she donned a bathrobe and towel-dried her hair. Inserting a teabag into her cup she boiled water in the microwave. Approaching the window, she parted the blinds and noticed the fog slowly dissipating. Across the way the vague outline of Sentinel Hall was visible.

Sasha recalled meeting the professor's wife. It was a charity function held among the artifacts gracing the lobby museum a fortnight ago. Dorothy Tondar proved to be a charming, cultured woman whom she took an immediate liking to.

Overcome with drowsiness, Sasha placed her tea aside and crossed towards the permanently reclined pull-out couch. She fetched her pyjamas from the closet and recoiled. Scrawled along the side of her suitcase were the words:

DARLING SASHA
    WE'RE BOUND TO ROAM ETERNITY TOGETHER
    PERMIT ME TO SEND YOU THERE
      I'M RIGHT BEHIND

She brought a hand to her mouth and stifled a cry. Someone had breached her space! Gripping her gun she backed away and surveyed every inch of the tiny dwelling.

———————

TWENTY-SEVEN

Kristy had no intention of going to Detroit. If the Face thought he'd fall for such a ploy he was as stupid as he looked. Did the wee man truly believe he'd hightail it to ground-zero, kill a rogue biologist only to be murdered himself - all while a Weapon of Mass Destruction was about to be deployed! He would meet again with the Face that was certain; however this time he intended to take him out. Likely, his own life would be forfeited during the confrontation.

Seated in a roadhouse bar, Kristy stared into an empty whisky glass considering options. He intended to inform the Face of evidence he had stored on disc. Content's highlighted Sir's synthesized dialogue outlining what was being constructed within Electron Era. Technology existed which rendered the true timbre of a subject's voice - regardless of vocal disguises. The recordings related aspect's of the pending biological strike on Detroit, narrated by none other than Sir himself. Three copies of the disc were distributed to Kristy acquaintances unknown to one another. Enough incriminating evidence was available to send the Face to prison for ten lifetimes. If Kristy wasn't heard from for a period lasting ten days the recordings were to be turned over to the FBI.

Unfortunately, there were no incriminating discs. Meetings between he and the Face were held in different locations; where he was frisked by 'This way' with a hand-held sensor.

Kristy tugged gently at a loose tooth attached to his lower gum. It gave way and he flipped the enamel lid open with his thumbnail. The cavity cradled a minuscule recorder fashioned by SIAG specialist's more than a decade ago. Able to evade most sensor-based technology; it's one drawback was when it was put to the test the devise proved dysfunctional. The Face wouldn't know that, however. He'd inspect the tiny contraption and likely conclude it was the real deal and have it tested. With the seed planted Kristy hoped to live a little bit longer. Once 'This way' was removed from the equation the Face would be next. A phone call would inform the Feds of the intended plot regarding Detroit. It was a win-win scenario provided the Face didn't just shoot him outright.

Kristy tossed a second whisky back and ordered a third. He left forty dollars for a thirty dollar tab and strode out to the parking lot and the rundown van. The liquor added momentum to what needed to be done. Behind the wheel he withdrew a semi-automatic and placed it on the passenger seat and drove off. The forty minute drive afforded time to finalize plans regarding the arrival of the Face at Rykles Clearing.

During his forced recruitment nine months earlier, Kristy had been drugged alongside Azil Besserer and detained in a Jacksonville safe-house. His desired presence at Electron Era, was to place him in proximity with his former countryman as the curtain came down.

Along his right a road sign indicated the Yokum Trail.

The tiny aircraft touched down along a narrow strip of runway on the fringes of Ellery, Indiana. Departing the plane, Lee Tondar entered a taxi he'd contacted in advance and gave the driver instructions. The Yokum Trail lay four kilometres east of their position. The driver knew the location and mentioned he hadn't had a fare up that way in some time. Lee determined the flight from Lantern Falls had taken roughly forty minutes. Two hours had elapsed since Jesse informed him of events unravelling in Detroit. His report confirmed the bunker on Penther's land was to be used as the detonation site for a biological WMD. Royston Adams was certain to be on hand.

As the cab journeyed forth civilization appeared to retreat. They signalled onto an isolated stretch and wound their way through a densely wooded area. A pasture and farmhouse were glimpsed briefly and the pavement segued to gravel. Surrounded once more by trees, a light drizzle persisted as the wiper's slapped rhythmically. Lee peered out the front windshield and observed a grey ribbon of sky visible above the treetops. A sign indicated the end of the road was a mile ahead; The passenger tapped the driver's shoulder and informed him he'd handle the last lap on foot.

"Sure you want to do that?"

"I need the exercise."

The driver shrugged and drew to a halt. Both agreed on a forty dollar flat-rate from the airfield. Lee clamoured from the rear seat and handed the driver two twenty's and a ten. He requested a card lest his services were required again.

The driver tipped his hat, "Ask for Gerry if I'm not on duty someone will be."

"Thanks."

Gerry waited until his passenger was safely to one side of the road then swung about and drove south. His taillights faded and Lee faced the opposite direction. Aside from crickets there was utter stillness. Hopefully, the alarms Kriel silenced remained disabled. Reaching into his shoulder bag he produced a bag of laced dog biscuits. The idea of running wasn't appealing, however he would do so if he had to.

Royston Adams involvement in a plot which would claim tens of thousands of lives seemed unfathomable. Lee was determined to confront his former friend and patron. Unfortunately, evidence against the Director linked their investigation inextricably to Adams. It suggested the UCOMA chieftain, aided by Valamar smuggled Dr. Besserer into America. A compound was established and a weapon was devised. To enable the front and muddy the waters, a cell of domestic terrorists were recruited. Engaging diverse allegiances Adams was able to cover his trail.

But to what end?

Drizzle turned to rain and pelted the overhead branches. Lee dodged puddles and veered off the Yokum Trail; and heard the distant barks. The hiker clutched the biscuit bag tighter and came at last to the Clearing, where a single van was parked nearby the lodge. Evidently, Adams had yet to arrive. Remaining concealed among the foliage, Lee arrived at a position offering a view of the bunker. A vehicle was heard on the Yokum Trail and he parted aside some branches. A dilapidated van was observed drawing up alongside Penther's vehicle.

The driver allowed his engine to idle and waited.

A shower of raindrops roused Taras from a brief siesta. Her muscles reacted painfully as she sat upright. Nearby, the death-stare in her assailant's one visible eye repulsed her, as he lay twisted along the ground. Struggling to rise she grasped the tree with the perched rifle. Her wounded palm felt as if it were on fire. Recalling the farmhouse, she gripped the rifle and limped in a southbound direction. With the dogs silent she paused to apply moist leaves to her wounds. The cuffs used to secure her as a prisoner, caused her limbs to throb and mosquitoes vied for her flesh.

Whoever was pulling Ulsar's strings remained a mystery. The cabin dwellers he'd allied himself with appeared to be American dissidents. Detroit was referenced frequently and she pondered it's significance. A phone conversation took place between Ulsar/Kristy and someone he addressed as Sir. The dialogue appeared strained and Kristy informed the lodge owner he was bound for Detroit.

The previous evening, Taras had been let off at the foot of the Yokum Trail by a friendly rig driver. They'd chatted briefly in an Ellery diner, and she mentioned her hiking companions were awaiting her arrival a ways up the road. The trucker was headed that direction and offered a lift. Twenty minutes later she thanked him and disembarked. Coursing the roughly four-mile stretch she arrived at Rykles Clearing shortly after sundown.

Two of her abductor's were out of commission - one permanently. Meantime, her target was bound for Detroit but slated to return. Her injuries needed attention before infection set in. When she reached the farmhouse she'd cleanse her wounds.

Kristy had departed by the time Taras made good her escape. Twice now he'd given her the slip. During his chat with the unidentified caller he sounded rebuffed. Was he playing both sides? It would explain his being at odds with the wise men back home.

Experiencing 'bouts of dizziness Taras pressed ahead. Sucking in air she blew on her palm and shook it forcefully. Motion gives a false impression pain is being exorcised.

The farmhouse must be nearby!

Roughly ninety minutes elapsed before Taras felt a breeze caress her perspiring features. Between the trees an open space was observed. Straddling the border of a pasture she glanced at the twin-story home across the way. It stood against a backdrop of pine and spruce. A stable was in the meadow and an ancient automobile was propped on bricks in the drive. Along her right wound the Yokum Trail.

The thought of a terrified homeowner, reacting to a bloodied woman creeping from the woods made her frown. Abruptly, barks were heard from within the abode. If the place was unoccupied she'd enter and secure the animal in a separate room. She'd clean her wounds, rinse her face then depart. If someone was home she'd rely upon their good graces.

A pair of drainage ditches ran the width of the pasture along either side of the road. Forging the nearest Taras lurched off in the direction of the driveway. Unable to stand she gripped a roadside mailbox as the barking resumed. Intent on appealing to the homeowner's better nature, things started spinning. The rifle fell from her grasp and she slid along the incline of the ditch.

————————

Kristy tapped the gun in his shoulder-holster and looked straight ahead. Parked beside the lodge owner's preferred minivan, he spent several minutes idling in the driver's seat of the less glamorous vehicle. His sudden return would raise questions. He was supposed to be in Detroit dispatching Besserer.

In the neighbouring woods Penther watched him closely. Disabled from the waist up, he sat upright against a tree awaiting Kristy's next move. Wracked with pain and sweating profusely, the militia-leader wondered what was keeping Aldo. The bitch who'd impaired him would be dealt with severely. Swallowing several more painkillers he stroked his ruptured shoulders gently.

Kristy departed the van and noticed shattered rear door partially open. Drops of blood were visible along the deck and on the ground. He withdrew his gun and entered the kitchen. Straddling the hallway he made for the parlour and discovered the woman gone. Signs of a struggle were apparent and Kristy followed the trail outdoors - unaware he was being observed. The moist earth revealed a trodden path led in a southerly direction; shoe prints and dog tracks were evident. A faint course persisted the opposite way. Kristy followed the busier trail and found himself deep in the thicket. A commotion kicked up by Club and Boot, found the pair tugging rigorously on reigns fastened to a tree.

Kristy ignored the dogs and noticed the trail broken by a protruding boulder. Blood stains were visible along it's surface. Gradually, he came across a tiny glen and observed the form of someone stretched upon the ground. He advanced and found himself staring at the lifeless body of Aldo Dopple. His neck was contorted at an unnatural angle and he lay there twisted. Leaves were strewn about the corpse and Kristy scanned the limbs overhead. Their broken disarray suggested Aldo struggled among the boughs, and either slipped or was tossed from the tree.

He considered the lodge owner and recalled the divergent trail.

Anxious to find the woman he maintained a southbound course. Without food or shelter how far could she go? There was only the lodge and...*the farmhouse!*

He'd passed it dozen's of times while journeying to and from Rykles Clearing. It lay a few kilometres south of his position.

In under forty minutes Kristy drew up alongside the meadow. The house and stable were clearly visible. To his right the Yokum Trail linked the highway with Rykles Clearing.

The drizzle continued and he strode toward the road. Serving as flood deterrents, a pair of ditches ran the width of the pasture on either side. Gazing along the nearest trench he noticed a mailbox with a sign affixed to it. Beneath it lay the female partway submerged in the ditch. Kristy rushed to her aid and found she was still breathing. Lacerations were observed about her face and wrists and a gash was visible on her left palm. Withdrawing tissue he placed it over the hand injury and raised her using both arms. Soaked with trench water and perspiration her feverish head lopped to one side.

The old familiarity resurfaced as if Ulsar had known the woman in a previous lifetime.

He tapped her cheeks repeatedly and withdrew a whisky flask from his jacket. Bringing it to her nostrils he received no response. He splashed drops on her lips and she slowly stirred.

"Pardon the application," her liberator whispered.

The woman sputtered and peered at him, "I...I knew I'd get you..."

"Dear lady 'tis I who got you."

His tone became serious, "You're at a disadvantage."

Taras released an arduous moan and nodded.

His plan was to get her into the farmhouse.

Gripping her about the waist he said, "Lets see if we're offered shelter."

Stringy, damp hair hung over her features as she took an uncertain step. Her resilience was telling as they made their way up the drive.

With her arm about Kristy's shoulder he muttered, "A dozen more yards..."

The sound of an approaching automobile was heard from the direction of the highway.

Kristy leaned in, "We have company.

In a strained voice Taras urged, "The flask give me the flask."

———————

Lush Indiana farmland yielded to strands of pine, spruce and birch flanking the SUV. Inside the UCOMA Director and his chauffeur Richard Valamar drove in silence. The whitewashed sky provided no end to rain as they journeyed toward Ellery, Indiana. Having spent the night in a hotel along the fringes of Fort Wayne, they'd been on the road roughly an hour.

The backseat passenger shuffled uncomfortably, "Feels more like ten years than two."

"What feels like ten years Sir?"

"Our operation! What else if there Richard?"

"Nothing I suppose."

Allowing the driver to share in his musings Royston Adams continued, "Once Besserer and Kristy were acquired things fell rapidly into place. Both establish a clear link to A'biin. Their remains will be discovered by the Feds at ground zero. Meanwhile, their female counterpart shall turn up dead at the detonation site at Rykles Clearing. What could be more incriminating!"

Valamar rubbed his sore temple and nodded from the driver's seat. He'd been assailed by a security guard as her charge was about to be cast into Lake Erie. Sir was less than amused to hear the Ohio professor survived the attempt.

The driver felt an ill-wind stirring. Having retrieved his boss from Fort Wayne's International Airport following his Mexico stopover, Valamar experienced several misgivings. The benevolence Sir projected remained intact; however deadly overtones were attached to his every syllable. The cavalier manner with which he discussed dispatching the militiamen assisting their endeavour was unsettling.

"You have William Penther," resumed the backseat passenger. "He and his tax-evading malcontents insist America's immigration policy will reverse itself as a result of their contributions. Hopefully, he's proved correct."

Sir was speaking mostly to himself now.

"He and his delusional super patriot's provided our campaign remarkable momentum," the Director ruminated. "Once the AC is launched Penther and his team shall be relieved of duty."

Valamar spoke over his shoulder, "What is required of me at Rykles Clearing?"

Adams considered the question, "First remove the bicycle from the rear of the vehicle. Once the Detroit team arrives I will join them, along with Penther in the bunker to determine weather patterns over northern Michigan. Once conditions align the weapon will be released. With that accomplished you'll be summoned to partake in the celebration. Instead of champagne you'll bring the AK 47 and dispose of the others. Once the weapon is wiped clean of fingerprints you'll slip it into the hands of deceased female terrorist."

"Why the bicycle?"

Adams hesitated, "The authorities will zero in on Rykles Clearing. Aware of what Penther drives; they'll assume he intended to cycle to a nearby airfield and vanish. The woman would've prevented that from occurring."

The driver's puzzled expression was observed in the mirror and Adams returned his gaze to the window.

"It's procedure for me to accompany you into a potentially hazardous situation," Valamar cautioned. "Under the circumstances protocol should be observed?"

"Thank you for your concern Richard," replied the passenger. "You and the rifle will be summoned in good order. Meantime, you'll wait in the van while I assure the others I remain their humble servant."

The previous night at the Shepard Inn Hotel while Valamar lay sleeping, Adams attached an explosive device to the underbelly of their SUV. Cruising the highway that morning the Director had the tiny remote tucked inside his jacket pocket.

Dark clouds threatened more rain during this final phase of their journey. Time dragged like a month of Sunday's for Adams. It was imperative he be back in Maryland by that evening to cover his ass.

Sir concluded his narrative, "Mr. Penther is aware of our approximate arrival time. The woman is secured in the bunker which only he has access to. The funds I provide him with entitle me to the entry code should anything unforeseen occur. Penther assured me he'd be at my side for the duration of our stay. I protested insisting the bunker establishes relay coordinates; allowing the final stage of our operation to proceed. Were he to suffer a stroke or another calamity our undertaking would be forfeit. Penther scoffed and stated he was in excellent health. Eventually, he conceded and texted me the code securely."

Adams fell silent again.

Everyone associated with the undertaking needed to be vanquished once the AC was released. The aftermath would reveal several domestic terrorists, recruited by a cell of SIAG firebrands; responsible for the catastrophic tragedy.

Adams could then refocus on dispensing with Lee Tondar and whoever was assisting him.

The trio of plant workers slated to rejoin Penther and his unhinged assistant at the bunker; would find Sir awaiting their return. Following interrogation of the female prisoner, she'd be forced to ingest strychnine; making it appear she'd taken her own life. Afterwards, the team would witness Sir enter a coded frequency on his laptop - allowing release of the AC. The signal would target the Detroit stockpile, triggering gas-fires and delivering the payload above the city. Valamar would then be summoned to dispatch the other conspirators.

The two would return to the van and Adams would state he needed to pee. From a safe distance the remote would be accessed deploying the bomb beneath Valamar.

With the operation under wraps, the Director intended to retrieve the bike and peddle to the highway. From there a brief cycle would take him to an airfield east of Ellery - where a private plane had been booked in advance for the return journey. It would be the pilot's final flight.

An hour later Adams would be home in bed.

Back in real time Valamar continued to navigate the Yokum Trail. Around a sharp bend a farmhouse hove in view and two figures were sighted in the drive. One supported the other and both appeared startled by their arrival.

"Bring the van to a stop!" instructed the backseat passenger.

Valamar responded instantly.

"Turn length-wise," his boss urged. "Then get out and greet the pair in a friendly manner."

"It's Kristy for Christ's sake!"

"I'm aware of that," Adams responded. "He should be in Detroit."

Valamar swung the vehicle sideways and undid his seat belt.

"Remove the bike from the van and place it nearby as an offering."

The chauffeur looked perplexed and opened the door.

"The woman is likely Kristy's intended assassin," Adams asserted. "We'll finish her task."

Hunkered among the trees Penther wondered what had become of Aldo. To quell the pain the militia-leader worked up saliva to consume more painkillers. Club and Boot were affixed to a stationary position. Kristy had been observed entering the woods on Dopple's trail. For the first time in his adult life Penther found himself without a weapon. He figured the woman would circle back and only had time to grab the pills. In his haste he'd forsaken his gun and phone.

Sir was expected to arrive shortly.

Once the AC was discharged he and the lads were supposed to delve underground for a spell. The day should have been one of celebration!

Unable to remain idle any longer Penther crisscrossed his arms and gripped both shoulders. He staggered off toward the dogs who scented his approach and grew even more riled.

TWENTY-EIGHT

Kristy had his eyes fixed upon the tinted windows of the SUV. With a gun gripped in his right hand, he maintained support of the feverish woman with his left arm and shoulder. To his rear the farmhouse appeared deserted except for the dog. His original intent had been to find the woman and confront the Face. It now appeared the confrontation had come to him.

Their observer's must have found the scene amusing as Kristy stood in the rain propping up his half-dead assassin. The woman swept clumps of matted hair from her face and tried to focus on what was occurring. Her rescuer adjusted his body to accommodate her weight and breathed deeply. The driver's door opened and 'This way' emerged. A bandage was visible on his right temple and his features displayed benevolence. Paying close attention Kristy was aware the terrorist asset concealed an assortment of weapons.

V gestured with empty hands and strolled towards the rear doors of SUV.

"An ambulance is expected to retrieve this woman any moment now," Kristy lied. "Get back in the van and drift."

Valamar improvised. "It is good to see you too Carl. I'm simply removing a bicycle which will allow you to peddle into Ellery; rent a vehicle and depart for Detroit to complete your assignment."

"I won't be going to Detroit," Kristy responded. "However, there is something I wish to discuss with your boss. Tell him I'll meet him at the lodge in an hour."

'This way' shrugged and reached for the rear door of the van.

"Back away!" Kristy warned.

"I'm merely retrieving the bicycle."

"I told you that won't be necessary!"

The side door of the SUV slid to one side and Kristy swung his weapon in that direction. The woman tensed and glanced about for the rifle she'd taken from her late stalker.

A languid voice sounded as someone exited the van, "I wasn't expecting to find you here Mr. Kristy."

Emerging from the rear seat a diminutive white male ambled out, sporting a fedora and an overcoat. In deference to the woman he removed his hat revealing a round face topped with thin wisps of hair. In a cordial manner he remarked, "I won't be speaking through any audio rigmarole, Carl. The precaution is no longer necessary."

Kristy remained silent.

The Face resumed, "Over the past nine months you must have viewed my demands as somewhat erratic."

"Never thought much about it," Kristy responded.

His former boss smiled and shifted his gaze to the woman, "I take it the person clinging to your arm is the same individual sent by the SIAG to be rid of you?"

He allowed the words to marinate, "She has a flair for the job. I hope our arrival hasn't interrupted anything."

The quip was greeted with more silence.

'This way' recommenced withdrawing the bicycle.

Kristy swung his weapon on him with laser-like rapidity, "Stand back!"

Valamar's hands were fastened on the bike frame as the twelve-speed was removed. Kristy's eyes darted between both men, meanwhile V leaned the bicycle against the mailbox post and took his place to the rear of his boss.

"Why are you not in Detroit carrying out your directive Carl?" the little man requested. "Your absence throws a proverbial wrench into the works."

Kristy responded calmly, "And allow you to dispose of me alongside the likes of Besserer."

"You're instinctive," his former handler acknowledged. "Jackson Bell and the others have been taxed with numerous responsibilities; including arranging your demise."

Kristy decided to play his hand.

"You should know something Mr. Face."

Adams frowned at the reference.

"Our meetings were recorded. The content of those encounter's have been transferred in their entirety onto four discs - one of which I retain. The others were turned over to acquaintances unknown to each other. An agreement was forged between myself and those recipients, that should I fail to contact them within one week's time; the disks are to be delivered to their respective FBI Branch Offices. The content's deal explicitly with Electron Era and the transfer payments, necessary to fund the terror agenda you've mounted. Your voice features predominately.

Adams and his lieutenant stared ahead silently.

"You're aware 'Sir' the Bureau employs state-of-the-art vocal enhancement technology," Kristy resumed. "Your natural speaking voice will emerge clearly and you'll be revealed for what you are."

A smile spread across Adams face.

"Naturally, this is a fabrication since you were thoroughly scanned by V before entering into any conference involving myself."

'This way' tensed as Kristy raised his left arm over the woman's head and placed his forefinger and thumb in his mouth. The lowercase tooth was removed and he tossed it forward and watched it land at the feet of both men.

"SIAG arsenal," Kristy remarked. "Scanners used by V were ineffective against the shell protecting this device. The cavity encasing the minuscule recorder is a blend of stealth properties, created by Soviet scientists in the late 1980s. The SIAG acquired them via black market contacts. As a highly placed spook you've no doubt heard of their existence?"

The Face sniffed, "A thorough scan was conducted on you by the surgeon who removed the tracer from your ankle. It included a probe of your dentures. I assure you nothing was uncovered."

"Failure to detect the device is testament to it's effectiveness," Kristy replied.

The Face motioned his assistant to fetch the improbable article. Scooping it up he passed it over and the Director studied it.

While this transpired the woman allowed her arm to fall limply to her side. Valamar observed her and placed his right hand in his jacket.

The Face glanced up from the tooth, "Your lady friend appears unwell. You should treat your women better?"

Kristy allowed the taunt to pass.

"I'll have this item analyzed," the Director added placing the article in his pocket.

"Please do."

The woman nudged Kristy placing him on alert.

"I wish to speak with your companion," the Face asserted. "I suggest you allow her to talk and urge you to put down your weapon."

Kristy reminded him he was at a disadvantage.

Abruptly, the woman bolted for the woods alongside the farmhouse. Kristy was on her heels, as Valamar removed his weapon and steadied his aim. He missed the target with a first volley and followed in pursuit.

It was apparent to Kristy the shots were being levelled at the woman. Alarmed by the 'recording' fiction, the Face would've preferred looking into the matter before killing him.

The female scuttled among the trees and Valamar took aim. Kristy strayed into the line of fire and was struck in the head. Tumbling into the undergrowth he was dead before he hit the ground. His dislodged gun landed several feet from the woman. Taras retrieved it as the shooter advanced and Valamar dove for cover. Seconds later a barrage of bullets whizzed over his head.

Scrambling further into the thicket she heard the older man shout, "We only wish to talk."

A shot kicked up the dirt an inch from where she stood.

Whisky and Adrenalin kicked in and Taras doubled her resolve.

About to fire again Valamar's boss shouted, "Let her go!"

"What!"

"She's not going anywhere," Adams called out. "We'll catch up with her later Right now we have an appointment to keep."

The Director gazed at the motionless form by the ditch and summoned his lieutenant. Valamar was pacing backwards with both hands gripped on his weapon. Covered in mud and grime he scanned for movement among the trees. His expression registered frustration as he drew alongside Adams.

"Place Kristy's remains in the rear of the SUV Richard. We'll dispose of it at the bunker."

V scowled and strode off to fetch the body. Gripping Kristy's cold wrists he was dragged through the ditch toward the vehicle. A dozen yards away the Director smiled and raised the rear latch.

When the transfer concluded Valamar wiped his bloodied hands, "You should have allowed me to take the woman out."

"Don't concern yourself.."

A blanket was tossed over the body and Adams slammed the latch down.

"Shall we depart for the lodge?"

Returning to their respective seats Valamar started the engine.

"Hold it I need to pee!" intervened his passenger.

Adams slid the door aside and straddled toward the ditch. As his business was conducted he glanced back at the van. Valamar noticed him in the mirror and saw him remove a tiny device from his jacket. Aware of what it was he scrambled to grip the door handle as the van exploded. Two pairs of tires left the pavement and dropped down in virtually the same position. Engulfed in flame the rising sparks were extinguished by the drizzle.

From a safe distance Adams gazed at the scorched hull of the van. Turning rapidly he strode toward the bicycle. The pungent stench of burning rubber mingled with the smell of gasoline and singed metal. From somewhere nearby a neighing horse was heard and a dog barked. Fortunately, no one witnessed the fiery disturbance. Adams glanced around for signs of the woman and noticed only trees. Mopping his brow, he gripped the bicycle handlebars and placed his right leg over the crossbar. He hadn't cycled since university and the challenge would likely prove taxing. Asserting his balance he left the carnage behind and peddled toward Rykles Clearing.

The wise-men were aware of the path Taras was carving among the Indiana woodlands. Her trail extended for several kilometres over a period of more than three hours. Once her GPS presence resumed Heron breathed easier. The wise men were still inclined to believe his agent had compromised herself. The sluggish movement of her signal implied she was on foot. Due to her proximity among turncoats and dubious Intelligence figures, she would likely be targeted by her own superiors. With the push of a button an orbital relay would terminate her existence. The custom was accepted by all SIAG field operatives as a preventative necessity.

Abruptly her signal vanished!

Heron blinked and leaned forward. Her motionless status was one thing; however if her signal ceased emitting it meant the host was either dead or submerged underwater. For nearly forty minutes he maintained vigil. Finally, her indicator flashed to life and Heron released a breath of air and waited for motion.

The phone call he was expecting never came. Perhaps the wise-men were granting their handler and operative the benefit of the doubt. As bureaucrat's none had served in the field for decades. More was at stake than merely taking out a rogue opportunist. SIAG analyst's had determined a terror threat existed within the US, with possible links to A'biinian extremists.

Heron sipped tea and wondered if Ulsar had been enticed or forced to work for an American renegade. Evidently, a high-alert was in effect among US Intelligence agencies regarding one of their own.

The handler watched his operative's signal stagnate once again and conceived a dozen reasons which would cause delay. Having served in the field himself he was aware of the intangibles. Stationed multiple level's beneath the earth Heron would given anything to be alongside his charge. He was weary of responding to men who desired peace, but preached hostility and suspicion. For years the West had extended an olive branch; with the rise of D'han the gesture was being cautiously reciprocated. Moderate dialogue and the appearance of a progressive policy offered a ray of hope. Good intentions were never on the minds of certain people, however. Entrenched in past doctrines these individuals continue to plot in the shadows.

Awake for more than forty-eight hours Heron found it difficult to relax. The desk phone shook him back to reality.

The fields along that stretch of Indiana highway retreated in deference to the driver's single-minded haste. Since his departure from Detroit four hours earlier the drizzle had turned to a scattering of showers. Jesse's rented car manoeuvred the shimmering surface of the pavement handily. A windbreaker concealed the rags clinging to his body and he felt the light weight of the face along his back. Straining the speed limit he continued southwest in the direction of Ellery, Indiana. A little over a week had passed since he'd departed the region.

Drowsy from white lines and slapping wipers, Jesse stretched his right arm along the passenger backrest. On his previous visit he found himself in the grip of what could only be described as a form of kinetic energy. From the instant the branch snapped underfoot; until he reached safety from the pursuing doberman's - a presence was ostensible. Once the ghoulish attire was removed the sensation dissipated.

Fortunately, events in Detroit tilted in Kriel's favour. The factory blueprints provided by the professor along with an element of surprise benefited their crusade. Lee's decision not to allow Kriel to participate at Rykles Clearing rankled the young man. It was understood Kriel would handle physical aspects attached to the case. Detonation site for the poisonous stockpile resided in the bunker; Lee insisted on being there to confront the perpetrator.

Likely a private aircraft was retained to deliver him to the tiny airstrip near Ellery. From there transport to the Clearing could be obtained. Lee mentioned unravelling some startling information, which couldn't be revealed over the phone. As the miles flew by, Jesse couldn't shake the notion his friend was headed into a dire situation .

A sign indicated the Yokum Trail was ahead.

His experience in the Motor City was decidedly different from the bewildering sensation, which propelled him through these woods. In Detroit he was fearless and alert – a feeling unlike anything he'd ever experienced. From the moment he encountered the night watchman; until the arrival of the Feds and the C.D.C he felt empowered. Steroid ingestion could never have replicated the overwhelming lightness of being and duty. The symbiotic fusion of otherworldly tenure seemed fully realized in Detroit. Hopefully, it would prevail at Rykles Clearing.

Enhanced Anthrax.

The words were uttered by Cal Wicker to describe the WMD concocted within the frightful chamber. It was hoped the cables Kriel severed would prevent it's intended design.

Was it possible a signal could override the attachments and trigger release of the weapon!

Were such a horrific scenario to occur it would be broadcast over the airwaves. So far nothing had been reported. Keeping tabs on news reports Jesse maintained faith in the bio-terror unit deployed to Sentra Avenue.

A dilapidated billboard sign whizzed by along Jesse's left and he signalled onto the Yokum Trail. Proceeding north along the winding route he slowed considerably. Rounding a bend he slammed down hard on the breaks! A dozen yards distant a burning vehicle blocked the way. Heat waves rippled and steam emitted from it's charred hull. Thoughts of the professor flashed and Jesse grasped his door handle. He sprang from the driver's seat and got to within six feet of the wreck before being forced back. Raising his jacket to shield himself from the heat, the stench made his eyes water. To get closer he would need to wait until the burning petrol subsided.

Jesse needed to determine if an oncoming vehicle caused the wreck. He leapt on the hood of his rental and viewed the smouldering ruin from on high. It appeared to be a single van and nothing more. By its simmering condition the incident likely occurred sometime over the past hour. The van stood upright on molten axles and melted tires. It spanned the width of the road between two drainage moats, preventing access. Jesse jumped from the car hood and held his breath against the tepid stench. It was impossible to determine if one or more individuals had perished. His calls to Lee had gone unanswered.

The young man decided the truth lay at the end of the Yokum Trail. The bunker and Clearing would reveal if the professor was among the carnage burning before him.

Passage around the charred vehicle was impossible on four wheels. Jesse recalled a nearby farmhouse where a bicycle might be 'borrowed'.

A dog barked and the sound of a neighing steed was heard.

A mount!

Jesse had become a proficient horseback rider while growing up. Saturday sojourns to the stables west of Toledo were routine. The pastime continued until he embarked upon his continental wanderings following high school graduation.

He returned to the car and brought it about until he faced the opposite direction. Applying his foot lightly he advanced around a nearby bend. Both ditches tapered off and he sought a place to stash the vehicle. No abandoned driveways were encountered, however a brown willow patch stretched along his right. He got out to survey the depth of the swamp beneath the towering weeds. The ground was reasonably solid and the water rose to the top of his ankles. Returning to the car Jesse backed slowly among the weeds. The mowed-down willows rose before him like stanchion soldiers.

Tossing his windbreaker on the passenger seat, he pushed the door open and parted aside the rushes. The shins of his boots were soaked as he emerged from the bog and strode around the bend. Stopping shy of the simmering wreck he heard distant thunder. The turbulence raised the ire of the nearby dog and stable animals. Drawing the disguise over his features he stuffed the frayed cuffs in his boots and slipped on tattered gloves. Adrenaline coursed his sinews as he skirted the wreck and forged a trench. A short way off stood the farmhouse. His attention was drawn to a stable a dozen meters from the homestead. Along the drive a rusted station wagon sat on blocks. Within the dwelling a single light burned. With the exception of the dog the place appeared deserted.

The clad figure observed an elderly gentleman emerge from the entrance. He appeared to be in his mid-eighties and looked as though he'd just been awakened. Kriel withdrew among the shadows and noticed a hound dog alongside the old man.

"Told you 'twerent nothin' but thunder Farley," the old timer remarked drowsily.

He withdrew a hearing-aid from his shirt pocket and inserted it in his right ear.

"Wayne and Janet aren't due back 'till the day after tomorrow, so you might as well quit yer yabberin'."

The gentleman glanced towards the Yokum Trail, "Lord Thunderin' Jesus somebody ought to get their muffler repaired. Them fumes reek to high heaven."

Farley barked and the man leaned over to pet him. He glanced around a second time then coaxed the pooch back in the house.

Kriel pondered the old timer's words. Wayne and Janet might have been homeowners destined to return later - unless it was they who were victims of the accident? The elderly gent was likely a parent or relation. Being mostly deaf he appeared to have slept through the resulting car wreck or mistaken it for thunder. The destruction was obscured from their sight lines by the curvature of the road, and the dense woods running alongside the property.

Withdrawing deeper among the trees, Kriel circled the home and came to a position nearest the stable. Dashing over a section of open field he drew alongside the entrance. His presence startled the animals and triggered Farley's response from within the house. Hopefully, the old fella wasn't dragged outdoors to witness a scarecrow ripping off one of his horses.

The skies suddenly opened and rivers of rain ran from Kriel's slicker hat. He entered the stable and observed several stalls lining a wall. A total of four horses were within. The inclement weather gave them cause to ruckus and kick up the dirt. Their frayed guest offered further incentive. Kriel moved towards the nearest stall and reached over the gate. An attempt was made to pet a brown steed and it retreated instantly. Dressed as he was one could hardly blame the poor beast. Speaking in hushed tones he moved to the next stall and came upon a black and white pony. It gazed at him and shook it's mane. An older mount occupied the compartment next to the pony. Like the first it wheezed and quickly backed away. In the stall furthest from the entrance a black mare neighed to beat all hell.

"Hey gorgeous no need to get riled."

The creature was more receptive than the others. Perhaps a jaunt up to the Clearing would be welcomed.

Kriel returned to the entrance and glanced toward the farmhouse. The downpour continued and he strode back to the stall and engaged the mare with soothing words. Stroking her fine mane she nuzzled the face of their featureless visitor.

The sky was dusky and there was little time to become acquainted. Blankets, saddles and bridles hung along a facing wall. Retrieving one of each the intruder returned to the stall.

"How's about a night ride girl? I promise to return you safely."

The mare appeared to nod and Kriel took it as a yes. Her gentleman caller unlatched the gate and held it open allowing release. She steadied herself while Kriel applied the blanket, bridle and saddle. Rain pelted the tin roof lulling the other beasts into a trance-like state.

"There's a girl shall we take that ride?"

Led from the stable she reared back as her escort surveyed their surroundings. Guiding the mare across the pasture, the view from the house was obstructed by the stable. Drawing alongside the bordering woods, Kriel stood astride the mount and placed his right boot in the stirrup. He swung into the saddle and the horse bucked slightly rearwards.

"Easy gal."

Stirring the reigns the mare was coaxed gently forward. Both horse and rider paced the timberline and merged with the Yokum Trail facing north. Farley's barking let up and the farmhouse lights had been extinguished. Glancing over his shoulder the horseman considered the charred wreck lying out of his sight-lines. By now the downpour would have eradicated the fumes.

Kriel vigorously shook the reigns and they bolted forward. Crouched over her velvet neck the mare charged over the landscape like a prevailing wind. The rider's garments fluttered behind like strip-rags from a fan. Night air streamed through silken threads of the horseman's eyes. The image would've presented a chilling sight had anyone observed it. They finally slowed and drew to a standstill.

The rider leaned over and whispered, "You move like a hurricane."

The mare snorted and scraped gravel.

"Hurricane...I like that, " mused the rider. "So it shall be."

Hurricane pranced on the spot and their route receded into darkness. Jagged shards of lightning split the sky illuminating both the road and surrounding woods.

Staring directly ahead the rider leaned forward, "Let's make tracks."

Thunder clashed as Hurricane reared up and bolted forward. Despite their haste the rider sensed a nearby presence.

Taras heard the explosion rock the ground beneath her feet. The sound came from the direction of the road where she and Ulsar were confronted by two men. As bullets whizzed about her she fled into the woods, and witnessed Ulsar being struck down. In a gesture of affiliation he managed to toss his gun her way.

Her sorrow weighed heavily as a result of his shivery. She recalled an evening long ago and closed her eyes. A young man had been admitted to her chamber and blissful passion was exchanged. A child resulted and the rest faded to black. While being assisted from the ditch, she noticed in her rescuer's eyes and smile that of her young lover. The same was briefly observed during their encounter in Queens.

The effects of the whisky had worn off and the flask lay with her departed colleague. Despite her exhaustion Taras willed herself to carry on. The sky grew dark and the stench of burning fuel reached her nostrils. Fresh bindings and water remained the priority. Armed with Ulsar's gun, her only recourse was to follow the shoulder of the road toward the cabin. With the owner waylaid and his henchman dead the odds were better. If she could determine the enemy her assignment might not have been in vain.

Without a compass the overcast sky prevented her from reading the stars. The best way to maintain bearings was to remain close by the road. Her mind replayed Ulsar's death repeatedly and she recalled the unspoken recognition in his eyes. He had saved her and she clung to him and drank his whisky.

Her hand throbbed and she felt faint. If infection hadn't already set in it soon would.

Along her rear around a bend in the road something approached. The sound grew in intensity and she scrambled among the brush. Sheet lightening ignited the way as a horse and rider rounded the curve. Like a demon from Hades the beast reared up and paced back and forth. Taras held her breath aware the creature sensed her presence; she suspected the rider did as well. The excruciating pain prevented her from crawling deeper into the thicket.

The mount bestrode the side of the road and gradually disappeared from view. Taras wiped her feverish brow and strained to listen. When she looked up again a ghastly spherical-eyed spectre glowered down upon her.

"An odd place to seek refuge Madam!" it rasped. "Especially under such inclement conditions."

Taras shivered and remained silent. Conditioned to hold fear at bay the application somehow failed her.

The Stygian figure dismounted and stepped forward.

"Why are you here!" it grated.

The wraith and hellish landscape suggested Taras had bridged the afterlife.

"Very well," the rider grunted. "Here's hoping you outlive this night."

The horseman remounted and the woman spoke, "I ran into trouble."

"Were you involved in the wreck littering the road!" the thing croaked.

"I was threatened by two men and managed to escape."

"How did they appear!"

Taras was hesitant, "One tall...the other small and stout."

Fortunately neither description matched Lee Tondar.

"And you chose to trod this path?"

Barely able to speak the woman could only nod.

"Without treatment you will perish!" the rider admonished. "Shelter and bindings are available at the end of the road. If you wish transport there we can accommodate."

"Thank you."

Taras suspected the horseman was disguised and in league with Penther, and those who'd murdered Ulsar. The rider reached down and the woman grasped hold of a frayed gauntlet. Gripped about the waist she was raised sidesaddle. As their course resumed the rider's arms clasped the reigns flanking her along either side. With her good hand fastened to the saddle horn she heard an exhaled breath above her shoulder. Whoever she shared the saddle with was mortal. Approaching the cabin she felt certain dread.

At the appropriate moment she would take action.

TWENTY-NINE

The horseman was aware of bends furnished by the road as Rykles Clearing loomed. Lightening illuminated the winding stretch with the feverish woman slumped sidelong in the saddle. Hurricane slowed to a trot and the rider leaned in. Among tangles of dripping hair the woman's strained breathing was heard. Beyond a final curvature the lodge would be sighted.

The sudden appearance of a bicycle taillight among the trees piqued the horseman's curiosity. Kriel dismounted and held the wayfaring stranger securely; guiding the trio toward a concealed twelve-speed bicycle. The rider considered who it belonged to? It was too far from the airstrip for Lee to make the journey. Cautiously, the horseman remounted and guided the mare toward a cluster of trees somewhat nearer the lodge. Leaning over to adjust the stirrup, the rider was driven from the mount by the blunt efficiency of the woman's elbow. Leaping from the saddle she staggered towards the sanctuary of the woods. Hurricane reared into position and Kriel swung into the saddle. They patrolled the timberline and the rider allowed the doomed woman her moment. The horseman was more intent on investigating the lodge and bunker to determine Lee Tondar's fate.

The mare was secured to a tree and soothing words were whispered.

A moment later the rider was gone.

The UCOMA Director's voice reverberated within the fortified confines of the bunker. Meanwhile, Lee Tondar struggled with the cuffs securing his wrists to the back of a folding chair. His efforts elicited a coughing fit resulting in a build-up of mucus which nearly choked him.

Royston Adams sighed as he sat before a laptop receiver. "Imagine! The seasoned spy led inevitably to his doom."

Allowing the words to settle he added, "I see you still suffer from those chronic chest ailments. You could've chosen retirement. I would have green-lit the request immediately."

Adams rose and strode to a position directly behind the restrained prisoner. He had stopped short of gagging him hoping they might converse. Awaiting the arrival of Penther and the others, the Director postulated on his plans for a better world. He was hardly surprised at Lee's diligence in uncovering the detonation site among the wilds of Indiana; what did surprise him was how little time it took. He never imagined the aging analyst to come waltzing up to the door as the weapon was about to be launched.

Adams appeared poised and confident. Despite the posturing the Director harboured nagging doubts as the plot drew to a close. Penther and his clan were missing in action. Kristy had defied a crucial directive, with regards to terminating Azil Besserer at ground zero. Their celebratory Strychnine-laced champagne toast would've contributed conclusive evidence of SIAG involvement. The Director remained confident Jackson Bell had prevented Besserer from ever leaving Electron Era.

Perhaps the Detroit team were awaiting Kristy's arrival!

If that were so they'd be waiting a long time.

The Director attempted repeated contact with both Penther and Bell to no avail.

On a positive note the charred remains of a SIAG sleeper agent would be discovered in a burnt-out van nearby the detonation site. Kristy would be found alongside notorious mercenary Richard Valamar. As for the escaped woman she was three-quarters dead already. The authorities would recover yet another expired SIAG operative nearby the point of detonation.

Where the hell was Penther!

The question seared into Adams brain like a laser. The militia leader and his sidekick were instructed to await his presence in the bunker. The twenty-five thousand dollar advance issued to Penther was intended to implicate him. Authorities would interpret it as payment by the SIAG.

Adams stashed the bicycle he'd arrived on along the dead-end of the Yokum Trail. Following the path he happened upon Lee Tondar observing the bunker. The Grissim professor was on his hit list and Adams crept up stealthily and placed a gun to Lee's head. With the acquired code, he accessed the bunker and hustled the frail station-chief within. Lee's weapon was confiscated and he was cuffed to the chair and pistol-whipped. Between coughing bouts he informed the Director, accounts had been left with several sources implicating Adams as mastermind of the planned Detroit strike. His recruitment of domestic terrorists and a rogue SIAG microbiologist were also detailed.

"Your intent was to construct a weapon and deploy it over a populated area," Lee imparted. "The expectation was to incite a war of retribution against A'biin."

Adams eyes narrowed, "That's the second time today someone's said they'd left information with unnamed sources. Care to know what happened to the first?"

No answer was forthcoming and Adams sniffed, "Let's just say he no longer walks the earth. His remains will be found nearby this bomb shelter as will yours."

Lee was informed he'd live long enough to witness launch of the chemical weapon. A few extra moments would be allotted as radio report's describing the occurrence trickled in. Once the account was verified the professor would be commissioned to that spy agency in the sky.

Adams laptop receiver was linked to a low-orbital satellite. He returned to the keyboard and entered a code. The digits granted access to a selected frequency. Once the winds complied he'd press 'enter' and the payload would ignite; allowing the exposed anthrax spores to drift skywards through a rooftop opening.

"Why such a heinous act, Royston?"

"I'm a patriot!" the UCOMA honcho declared.

"While you and the other Chamberlain's were busy lifting embargo's and extending treaties, I assumed the role of a soft-bellied liberal plotting the initiative you're about to witness. Seymore-Johns and his cream-puffs are mere posers, who cow-tow before the same weak-kneed elites you serve. Despite outward appearances A'biin remains in the hands of extremists - whose intent is to ravage our economy and reduce the US to third-world status. That won't occur under my watch."

"So you intend to reign terror upon your own people?"

Adams sighed. "You need to think like the enemy Lee. Targeting an industrial centre like Detroit will be perceived as a strategic blow by the Pentagon. Think of the twin towers."

Lee looked him in the eye. "You believe the authorities won't thoroughly investigate an attack of this magnitude?"

"Within hours they'll determine whose responsible and retaliate instantly."

Lee was silent.

"Detroit's infrastructure won't suffer," Adams added reassuringly. "Buildings, streets, homes remain intact."

The prisoner cast down his eyes and shook his head.

"No comment Professor? I kept the gag from your mouth for a reason."

"Did Stuart Tuppins have to die?"

"Of course he did he was passing sensitive information to you. You would've followed up on encrypted directives regarding the activated SAIG sleeper in Evanston. The NSA would've been alerted, creating an unnecessary stir among the Intel community. Naturally, I wasn't seeking attention. Mr. Tuppins sealed his fate all by himself."

"He was doing his duty."

"Your right from your side I'm right from mine."

Lee glanced up, "You'll have the death of thousands on your conscious and be forever vilified once the truth emerges. There will be no strike. A'biin won't be held responsible – you will be. Think about it Royston. It's not too late to reconsider."

Twisting the top off a clear vile of liquid Adams calmly remarked, "The administration will conclude other US cities are targets. As the body count rises swift retaliation is assured."

"You've defended me Royston, allow me to extend the same to you and we'll leave here together," Lee urged.

"I leave this place alone!" the Director responded heatedly. "Once America regains its rightful place in the order of things, folks will know I played a part in maintaining that integrity."

He poured the vile of poison into a plastic cup.

"It took a bleeding heart like yourself to allow people to view me sympathetically. With your support it appeared I was beyond reproach. I never shared your marshmallow sentiments. Instead, I lobbied to make certain you were transferred to a remote station. Your opinion carries weight along the beltway - so it wasn't easy. Covertly, I aroused suspicions insisting your views were alarmingly soft on terrorism. Shortly thereafter you were bound for Lantern Falls. It was yours truly who undermined you. While you tread water along the Erie shoreline I was able to conduct my affairs, knowing you'd been marginalized. I see now with sickening clarity I was only partially correct."

Adams stirred the beverage, "There's another reason why the gag was kept from your mouth."

His voice lost its congeniality, "Know what's in this cup?"

Lee had a good idea.

"It pays to be a ranking official when it comes to acquiring certain concoctions," resumed the Director. "I assure you the end will come swiftly. Thanks to Botulinum Toxic you'll be found dead of unknown causes here inside the bunker. With talk of renegades and traitors folks will wonder why you were on site? Rumours of a rogue have been persistent. Your printed accusations will be viewed as deception and the authorities will indite you posthumously. Its you who'll be vilified."

While Adams rambled Lee pondered his helplessness. He should have accepted Kriel's assistance. His apprentice sensed danger and urged him not to act alone. Lee believed he could bring Adams around, never suspecting how far gone he truly was.

The Director placed the deadly potion temporarily aside and focused on his laptop.

"Others are expected, however they'll miss the countdown. Consider yourself privileged."

A radar map of the Great Lakes was uploaded. The forecast indicated mild conditions with a negative wind velocity. A light drizzle was expected throughout the greater Detroit/Windsor area. Adams reached across the desk and switched on a radio. Finding the clearest reception he turned to Lee, "Once the code is entered the strain will be released. Afterwards, we'll listen to the media response and drink a toast."

Leaping about the legs of their damaged master the doberman's muzzled the cuffs of his pants. Penther kept them at bay so his limb's weren't further strained. At his command the beasts charged among the thicket in search of Aldo. They paused to sniff the earth and gradually his scent became apparent. Maintaining a southerly course they pursued an obscure trail, meanwhile Penther laboured behind allowing their barks to guide the way. Drizzle penetrated the leafy canopy overhead as Rykles Rock came in view. Embedded in the earth, the massive boulder was named in honour of Strom Rykles by Strom himself.

The dogs sniffed the forest floor about the rock; raising their snouts they dashed further among the trees. Penther's wrists and shoulders screamed agony and he paused to ingest more painkillers. Up ahead the barks and growls were replaced by whimpers. Advancing cautiously, the militia leader entered a tiny clearing and beheld Aldo on his back at a horrific angle. His legs extended unnaturally to one side; likewise his swollen neck was craned about entirely. The death-stare in his one visible eye registered shock. Penther knelt slowly and placed a wrist on the body and lowered his head. A glimmer caught his eye and he rose and moved toward the object. Lying on the ground was the woman's blood-stained dagger. He grimaced as he bent to retrieve it. Wiping the bloody residue on his cuffs he determined Aldo's rifle had been confiscated.

Kristy would've come across the body and continued pursuit of the female. Struggling to sheath the knife into a belt loop; Penther desired nothing more than to confront the bitch. In addition to his own misfortune, she'd been responsible for taking the life of his bodyguard. He would feed her to the dogs and offer Kristy for dessert.

Observing the strewn foliage he determined Dopple tumbled headlong from the tree. The woman scaled the boughs; in the ensuing struggle Also was dislodged and broke his neck.

A key-ring was unfastened from dead man's belt and his pockets were frisked. Cigarettes were tossed and a half-bottle of perks were retained. The cogent painkiller was a godsend. Penther stood upright and glanced at his fallen compatriot and a seething hatred welled. Whimpers turned to snarls as his pets glanced along a southerly course with their snouts raised.

Certain Kristy and the female were in league he shouted at the doberman's, "Hunt them down and leave them for me. I'll feed you their remains!"

The dogs vamoosed and Penther turned from the corpse lying at his feet. The body would be buried later. The famished beast's were granted wide berth as he withdrew the knife. The pills kicked in and he gripped the weapon firmly. The doberman's surged ahead intending to flank the prey, meanwhile their master smelled blood.

Kriel entered the darkened Clearing on foot. Making for the lodge no sign of the dogs were apparent. Taking precaution a stone was tossed on the rear deck and only crickets responded. Evidently, the doberman's weren't serving duty. The rear door had yet to be mended and no light was within. Thunder rumbled as the clad figure mounted the deck and moved silently. At the doorway, a splintered 2 by 4 was kicked aside and Kriel breached the threshold. The kitchen table lay on it's side and a trail of blood led from the hallway. The wraith entered the parlour and observed duck tape and rope, alongside two pairs of handcuffs chained to a pillar. Dry blood was smeared along the edges of both cuffs. Thinking it might be Lee's the ragged intruder returned to the deck and discovered the trail vanquished by rain. In the distance dogs were heard. Vaulting the railing the figure made for the trees. Hurricane was retrieved and they ventured onto the Yokum Trail. The doberman's might lead to the endangered professor. Kriel stirred the reigns and the mare leapt forward. The road was as black as the rider's garment's and gave way before the thundering mare. The dogs were nearby and abruptly Hurricane reared back. A man's voice echoed among the trees.

Treading the woods the horseman advanced cautiously.

———————————

Taras heard the approaching doberman's and the voice commanding them. Evidently, the lodge owner was no longer writhing on the cabin floor. Despite his injuries he'd been able to track her down. Lamenting loss of her dagger she was grateful for the rifle.

A rustling was heard and both doberman's emerged from the trees. Their salivating tongues and white fangs glistened in the dark.

"Stand down!" a male voice hollered.

Panting heavily William Penther stumbled from the thicket. Drenched with sweat he locked eyes with the woman while gripping her dagger. Levelling the gun in his direction Taras faced a triple threat while stalling the inevitable.

"Good boys," huffed the landowner without taking his eyes from the female. "Now back off!"

The dogs paced restlessly while the hunter spoke.

"Five quick thrusts and it's over. One in the heart for Aldo and four for my twisted limbs."

With the gun aimed at his head, Taras noticed the dogs distracted by something beyond their line of vision. Summoning all her strength she lunged forward and grasped Penther about the waist. Uprooted, the dagger slipped from his grasp. They hit the ground and the pistol Taras held fell. The dogs were whimpering and backing away as the presence approached. Oblivious to their fears the woman had Penther by the throat. Connecting his boot to her bleeding shin she let out a moan. About to administer a second blow she drove her knee into his groin. Twisting about she struck him with her good fist and watched him reel backwards and land in the dirt. The dagger lay inches away and both scrambled. Penther was nearest.

The night air was shattered by the sound of a neighing steed. The startled dogs cowered as Taras kicked the dagger from her opponent's grasp. Penther's attention lay elsewhere as he beheld the ominous sight above the woman's shoulder. Astride a black mare an abomination glowered down on them with ovulated eyes. The militiaman recalled Aldo being set upon by a demon. The doberman's avoided the skull-crushing hooves as a grating laugh resounded. Something was tossed along the earth and the dog's rushed forward scenting the fragrance. Moments later the pair lay motionless.

Liberated a second time by the entity the woman stared wide-eyed as the scene unravelled.

The rider dismounted and retrieved the knife and gun. It's abhorrent eyes fixed upon Penther and the hunter stammered, "W...what in hell are you?"

"The older gentleman where is he!" rasped the horseman.

"Haven't a clue what you're on about."

With sudden fury Penther was gripped by the collar and thrust skyward. He groaned as the fabric bore into his throbbing shoulders and avoided the miscreant's gaze.

"The gentleman!" the thing repeated.

"I don't know!"

Believing the reference regarded Sir, the militiaman pivoted the question, "My assistant was murdered by this bitch!."

Penther was cast aside and moaned as he hit the ground. Throughout the exchange the woman remained motionless. She watched the thing remove twine from it's rags and use her dagger to cut strips for use as binds. The impaired hunter was dragged by his ankle and shackled to a tree in a seated position. His wrists and ankles were bound and a gag was produced. Penther shouted he needed painkillers for his injuries.

"Their in my jacket!"

Having observed the inert nature of his mangled limbs the horseman fished out a pill bottle. The perks remained in militia leader's back pocket.

"How many!"

"Several."

With water unavailable the thing dispensed three tablets into the palm of it's rotted gauntlet and administered them. The pills dissolved in Penther's mouth and the demon rasped, "You're not averse to sharing your medicine with someone who requires it as badly as yourself."

The militiaman made no response and looked away. Meanwhile, the female was passed three tablets and the bottle was tossed alongside the prisoner.

Aware the horseman wasn't in league with her enemies. Taras wondered who or what it was?

The rider approached, "You rewarded my assistance by lashing out and taking flight?"

Responding feebly she nodded at the lodge owner, "I believed you were with them. They held me prisoner in a cabin and I escaped. I thought you were taking me back."

"They?"

"There's was another."

"The person you dispatched?"

"He tried to kill me."

The horseman noticed her scarred wrists and recalled the blood-stained handcuffs in the lodge.

"Why were you taken hostage?"

"I was investigating someone's disappearance."

"Did you witness the arrival of an older gentleman?"

"Just the two men in the van."

No reference of Ulsar was made.

"I heard an explosion and kept going," she resumed. "Then you arrived and offered assistance."

Her answer's were as vague as they'd been on the first occasion.

Hurricane's mane shimmered in the forest night and the rider drew alongside and whispered in her ear.

Kriel slipped the blanket from beneath the mare's saddle and returned to the woman. Placed about her shoulder's she was assisted upright against a tree.

"I'll seek water and aid," her redeemer croaked. "Remain awake! If you slumber or attempt flight you shall perish."

The woman was shivering as the horseman remounted and vanished.

————————

Despite the bunker's fortification Royston Adams heard the distant barks. Having typed the detonator code linked to a low-orbital satellite; pressure need only be applied to the 'enter' key - and a seismic shift in US foreign policy would occur. The dogs gave him pause; Penther and his band of rednecks may have simply been delayed.

The barks ceased and Adams focused upon the bunker door. A security monitor highlighted the area surrounding the shelter from various angles.

Cuffed to a chair Lee felt helpless.

"Perhaps we'll have company after all," Adams muttered.

The professor suppressed a coughing bout while struggling to free his wrists. The Director glanced at him and shook his head. The shelter door was deliberately left ajar and his attention remained focused upon the entrance. Abruptly, Lee charged forth like a threatened rhino with the chair attached to his stooped body. He collided with Adams and sent him reeling backwards and his head struck the corner of a filing cabinet. Losing consciousness the Director slid toward the bunker floor. Lee reclined over his motionless shoulder, attempting to grip the gun beneath his body without success. With his arms bound to the backrest of a chair, the restriction prevented him from scouring for the key to free himself and delete the deadly transmission. The Director began to stir and Lee noticed a gash beneath his right temple. The gun needed to be retrieved quickly. Adams groaned and Lee nudged him onto his side where the gun lay exposed. If not for the cuffs he could've snagged the weapon and reversed the situation. Alas, it was not to be and the Director came slowly around. Lee thrust his outstretched fingers through the backrest in a final attempt to grasp the gun. Adams eyes opened and awareness registered. He brought his hand to his head and glanced at his bloodied fingers. Releasing a stream of profanities, he struggled to his feet and administered several kicks to his former colleague's guts. He retrieved his gun glared menacingly at the choking figure at his feet.

"You came close."

He applied a handkerchief to his gash and glanced toward the bunker door.

"No further delays. You'll witness my existential wake-up call then bid this world adieu!"

Poison was Adams choice of dispensing with the meddlesome station chief. The gun was for the others. He hovered over the laptop and brought a forefinger to the keyboard.

Sprawled along the floor Lee pleaded, "The innocent Royston...!"

"Three, two, one...blast off!" Adams chimed as the signal was entered.

He reached over and boosted the radio volume. Seconds passed...then minutes.

Interspersed with commercials regular programming continued and still no breaking story. An on-air host was discussing increased tourism the US was currently enjoying.

Lee observed the Director's clenched fists and white knuckles.

He spun the tuner from one station to the next and still no word. The effects of the AC would've trickled in by now.

"Hellfire and damnation!" Adams thundered as his fist slammed the desk surface. "A delay...a mere delay!"

Aware the cables had been severed at the Detroit facility Lee thought it best to withhold the information.

"What in hell!" the Director bellowed.

He turned and glowered at the prisoner, "I've got more pressing matters than force-feeding you the beverage. They'll assume you were shot by one of your co-conspirators. You can witness my handiwork from heaven or that other place."

Lee closed his eyes as the gun was retrieved from off the desk.

Rustling was heard and the bunker door swung wide open. Shifting his gaze Adams stared at the obstruction blocking the outside world. The presence caused his face to pale and the gun veered from Lee toward the door.

"This is a joke!" Adams uttered disbelievingly.

The intruder remained silent.

Lightening illuminated the wooded landscape behind the ghoul. A shot rang out and the creature jerked and advanced. A second shot was avoided. The Director aimed a third time and the weapon was slapped from his fingers. Gripped by the throat he was cast violently aside and the thing turned toward the trussed figure crouched nearby. Kriel was oblivious to the five-inch blade Adams produced from a body-sheath. As he prepared to thrust Lee contorted his body in such a fashion, he was able to retrieve the gun. He fired in the Director's general direction and Adams staggered sideways and fell across the desk. The laptop was uprooted along with Lee's intended drink. The radio was airing a beer commercial when the Director's eyes closed forever. Lee released a gust of air and allowed the gun to slip from his grasp.

Yanking the disguise rapidly back Jesse assisted him to an upright position, "Are you alright Lee!"

"I'm fine," he sighed. "And you?"

"The Kevlar is quite effective."

"Wait till you see the shiner on your chest."

"I did feel a little pressure."

"I'm grateful the bullet struck your vest and not somewhere unprotected."

The older man got his bearings and nodded toward the dead man, "Frisk his body for keys will you son."

The Director's jacket was rummaged and two phones were withdrawn - one belonged to Lee. Plundering his trousers some keys were found.

"One of these should fit the cuffs," Jesse affirmed.

Once the proper key was inserted the professor's arms fell away and he cringed. Massaging his wrists the blood began to gradually flow.

"Your breathing sounds irregular," Jesse remarked.

"It's cumbersome moving about with a chair attached to one's ass," replied the other.

The younger man was scouring the shelter for blankets and water. He found several bottles and tossed them into a burlap sack along with a woollen shawl. From from the shelter door he peered into the gloom and wondered how Hurricane was coping. His first priority was to see Lee and the woman received immediate medical attention. Penther could be attended to in prison. Being a deep-cover operation they could hardly call 911. The professor would need to engage his contacts. Clean-up could proceed along lines deployed at Electron Era handled discreetly by professionals.

Once Lee had taken a tentative stride Jesse urged they depart. The professor was requested to establish contact with his sources and arrange an airlift be given the proper coordinates.

Replacing the disguise Kriel glanced about the bunker a final time.

Lee stood gazing at the fallen UCOMA Director.

He turned to his recruit and said softly, "Thank you."

"The citizens of Detroit should thank you!" the wraith grated .

"Then we're even."

His operative peered from the entrance and motioned the older man forward.

Lee withdrew a flashlight, "I take it Detective DeLong responded to your request once contacted?"

"Almost immediately," the entity confirmed.

His handler hesitated, "I'm grateful you chose to disobey my directive about coming here."

There was no response as they traversed the nighttime forest slowly.

"You'll bring me up to date I hope?" Lee persisted

"I will once you and the others have been tended to."

"Others?"

"Two of them. Both in dire need of medical attention?"

"Who!"

"William Penther for one. His upper limb's have been ruptured. I took the liberty of securing him. The second individual is a feverish woman. She won't survive unless she gets to a hospital.

"A woman?"

"According to Penther she's responsible for killing Aldo Dopple and inflicting the militiaman's injuries."

"Where are they?"

"Along the trail road. In your condition you won't make it on foot. However, help is at hand and she's a beauty."

"Another woman!" Lee exclaimed. "This is a covert operation."

"Indeed."

They came to a standstill and the guide rasped, "A moment."

The opaque agent vanished among the trees and reemerged guiding a black mare. The beast shook its mane and pranced in a possible greeting.

"She's christened Hurricane."

Lee was stunned, "How in the world was this acquired!"

"A long story. I'll inform you later."

"You expect me to ride her!"

"I do."

From behind the clouds the moon emerged as Lee was assisted into the saddle. Kriel mounted up behind and gripping the reigns gave a nudge. Departing by way of the Clearing they merged onto the Yokum Trail. Lee grasped the saddle horn as they surged forward. Moments later the mare reared back and they came to a halt.

Lee removed his phone, "I'll summon an airlift and request a detonation team scrutinize the bunker and Adams laptop."

"Adams? You mean Royston Adams!"

"Correct."

The name was frequently referenced. The horseman had no idea it was the UCOMA Director confronted in the bunker?"

Contact was established and Lee spoke with Robert Blakie-Harris. He gave their precise coordinates and urged a medical airlift be sent immediately. A detonation expert was also requested and the NSA honcho agreed to both. He stated an additional airlift bearing a team of Special Agent's would be deployed to sweep the area for possible collaborators. Informed of Royston Adams duplicity, the Director of Operations fell silent. Lee indicated Rykles Clearing was linked directly to the operation being dismantled in Detroit, and stated a detailed report would be forthcoming.

Kriel dismounted and guided Lee and the mount through the thicket.

Gripped about the waist the aging spymaster was assisted from the saddle

"They're up ahead," rasped his agent.

CHAPTER

THIRTY

The professor gazed upon the two incapacitated antagonists and a pair of sprawled dogs. The woman was wrapped in a course blanket, with her features concealed by lengths of matted hair dangling from her lowered head. The horseman took her pulse and tapped her cheeks repeatedly until her eyelids fluttered.

"She's alive," Kriel announced

The professor drew alongside the slumbering militiaman and he was requested to diagnose Penther's condition. His bulging shoulders and swollen wrists were clearly obvious.

Kriel applied damp linen to the woman's perspiring brow.

"She's fading."

Water was produced and several drops moistened her parched lips. Gradually, she was able to swallow and Kriel placed the shawl behind her head and administered several tempered sips.

Rising from a crouch the horseman glanced overhead; meanwhile Lee withdrew his phone to check on the status of the airlift.

"An air-ambulance is on it's way from the Air-Reserve Base in Cass County," he reported after signing off. "It's expected to arrive above the Yokum Trail within minutes. A second aircraft carrying a tactical squad will land in Rykles Clearing."

While the professor spoke the militia leader listened with his eyes closed.

"I'm not certain the width of the road will accommodate the chopper," Lee speculated. "They may resort to using a lift."

Intent on guiding the woman to the landing site Kriel assisted her carefully to her feet. The professor was tapping Penther's face urging him to awaken.

"This entire area will be swarming with Federal agents," Lee remarked. "Once we're in flight I suggest you return the horse. When this is over I'll forward money and our appreciation to it's owners. Meantime, retrieve your vehicle and head for home I'll contact you from the hospital."

Lee's attempt to resuscitate the militiaman was unsuccessful. In order to transport him to the pick-up site he undid his ankle binds and left his wrists secured. While this occurred, the female was swept into the arms of the tattered horseman - who requested Lee to accompany them to the roadside. Kriel would return for the militia leader.

A dry spot was found along the Yokum Trail and Lee adjusted the blanket about the woman's shoulders. The clad figure glanced about their surroundings and hastened off to retrieve the lodge owner. Sidestepping the slumbering dogs Kriel noticed their master was gone! His ankle binds had been undone so Lee could escort Penther to the roadside. It was assumed the militiaman was in no condition to hightail it. With the lodge and bunker compromised. Where could he go?

Kriel returned and relayed the news to the professor.

"The ankle cuffs!" Lee muttered. "Shit!"

"You were distracted by my request to accompany myself and the lady to the road," Kriel acknowledged. "I'll find Penther – or the authorities will."

The wraith hesitated, "I neglected to mention an explosion occurred involving a single vehicle south of our position. The occupant's would've perished instantly. Passage either way along the Yokum Trial is obstructed. The horse was borrowed from a nearby stable."

Lee wondered who the passenger or passenger's might've been? A forensics team would need to investigate.

In the funeral darkness the professor appeared older. The storm had run its course and a damp mist lingered. A helicopter was heard approaching from the west; withdrawing his flashlight Lee waved it back and forth. He turned to the haggard escort, "I'll keep tabs on the woman's condition en route to the hospital. See if you can track Penther. If he's apprehended text me his coordinates and I'll see he's rounded up pronto. Lastly, avoid being observed by federal agent's on the ground. There might be questions."

Lee laid a hand gently on wraith's rags and a smile formed.

"Make certain you're tended to with due diligence!" his recruit grated.

Floodlights ignited the Yokum Trail and the airlift appeared overhead. Descending slowly there was room enough on either side of the road. It touched down and the rotating propellers stirred up a whirlwind of dust. The fuselage door whisked aside and medical personnel assisted the beleaguered pair inside. Meantime, a platoon of helmeted tacticians disembarked.

Concealed among the trees Kriel observed the transfer. A team of special agent's departed the aircraft and proceeded south along the Yokum Trail. The airlift made it's ascent and disappeared above the treetops. Kriel spun on boot heels and made directly for Hurricane. Drawing alongside the mare, it appeared the disturbance hadn't ruffled her in the least. The doberman's slept and a vibrant moon emerged. It's light filtered through branches as the pair made their way. Dense foliage prevented the horseman from mounting. Abruptly, the mare bucked as something foul was scented. Withdrawing the penlight, Kriel advanced and came upon Aldo Dopple lying at an improbable angle. Flies buzzed about the corpse.

The rider spoke soothingly to his companion and they pressed on. Perhaps the doberman's could be enticed to scent their master's whereabouts? The pair backtracked and arrived at the spot where the doberman's were starting to come around. Kriel withdrew several unlaced biscuit's from a pouch and dispersed them. Boot rose unsteadily and rolled the food about with his paw. He glanced about tentatively then wolfed down the snacks. His mate came around gradually and the procedure repeated itself. Kriel allowed both free reign and watched as they veered among the trees along an easterly course.

Their master's first priority would be to free up his wrists and seek refuge in a remote hideaway.

As the dogs charged forth the horseman followed.

Racked with pain Penther staggered towards the boulder named in honour of his adoptive father. He dropped to his knees and felt the cold surface against his perspiring features. Recalling the water and shawl looted from his bunker; he wondered how the bogeyman gained entry? Struggling to retrieve the perks from his back pocket he swallowed two. Guns and ammo were essential if he was to survive the woods north of the Clearing. Supplies from the bunker were also needed. With his wrists bound he struggled to keep balance. Distant barks were heard, indicating Club and Boot had awakened from their drug-induced stupor. The militiaman hoped they weren't pursued by the horseman. If so he'd bid the doberman's turn on the rotting ghoul and devour it. The paramilitary drill had been instilled in the beast's should government forces invade the sanctity of his compound.

Moonlight pierced the leafy domain as the bunker hove in view. Parting aside branches he noticed the door ajar. The hum of a stealth chopper was faintly heard approaching. It's likely destination was the Clearing. Penther's adrenaline was pumped as he hastened toward the bunker entrance. Upon entry he was stunned to find his patron lying lifeless on the floor! An exit wound revealed Sir had been shot through the chest at close range. Penther cursed himself for granting the dead man coded access.

The chopper drew closer and Penther placed his tethered hand's inside a desk drawer. His fingers grasped a knife handle and it was transferred to the desktop surface. Gripping it tightly he sliced the wrist restraints along the blade, until they fell away. Rapidly, he crossed the room and fiddled with a padlock attached to a metal cabinet. Reaching inside he withdrew an assault rifle, rounds of ammo and a blanket. He stored beef jerky and bottled water in a backpack. Last but not least, he retrieved the suitcase containing the money advanced to him by his late patron. His limb's throbbed mightily as he grasped the door handle and stumbled outdoors.

Avoiding the sight lines of the overhead aircraft Penther made his getaway.

———————

The rider tugged back on the mare's reigns and glanced toward the Clearing. A second aircraft was making it's descent. Within it's hull a team of Special Agent's attired in assault regalia prepared to disembark.

Damn!

The dogs had given up the chase and Hurricane stopped short of the Clearing.

Avoid being observed by troops on the ground.

The professor's word's underscored the horseman's dilemma. The militiaman was nearby, however Kriel was unable to do a thing about it. The aircraft touched down the horseman's pursuit was terminated. Penther would be left to ground forces. Hurricane was brought about and they set off toward the stable alongside the Yokum Trail.

Sunrise was in less than an hour.

Intent on returning the mare safely; the car would be retrieved and a hasty departure would follow.

Flourishing the Yokum Trail in the direction of the farmhouse, it was just a matter of time before the wreck blocking that stretch was inspected by a forensic detail.

Abruptly, voices were heard around a bend and a trio of armed agent's appeared on foot. They beheld the mounted apparition and raised their automatic weapons instantly. The mare slowly advanced and the horseman gazed down the barrels of their guns. Drawing to a standstill the rider leaned over and whispered, "Wait in the woods for my signal."

The entity dismounted and moon-glow reflected in it's spherical eyes. One of the trio turned his rifle on the mare as it vanished among the trees. The agent-in-charge prevented him from firing.

"Identify yourself!" he shouted.

"Captain Kriel at your service!"

"Captain of what?"

"The good ship Katy! Finest vessel to sail the lakes."

The agent nodded, "I haven't noticed a body of water about. Where is this 'vessel'?"

"Beneath the rolling whitecaps of Erie!"

The leader frowned, "I'd like you to speak with a higher authority. Perhaps some logic can be made from this."

The horseman was silent.

"Cuff him," the officer ordered. "We'll escort him to command."

Lunging forward the thing gripped the spokesman's rifle and spun him about like a marionette. A frayed sleeve was about his throat and the wraith issued a guttural command, "Tell the lad and lass to toss their weapons or you'll be broken in two!."

"Y...you heard him!"

The hapless agent felt the grip loosen about his neck.

Once the rifles were cast down they were instructed to step backwards. The would-be horse shooter reached for a sidearm and Kriel levelled his superior's rifle at his face.

"Tell your man to behave or I'll take off his head!" the Stygian figure croaked.

"Do as he says!".

The man reluctantly tossed his handgun and glared at the entity.

The horseman requested the female redirect the beam of her flashlight. Meanwhile, the ranking officer kicked back in an attempt to topple the ghoul and his hothead underling charged forward. Kriel delivered a series of bone-shattering blows and sent the pair to the land of cotton-tailed bunnies. The agent left standing scrambled for her weapon and aimed it at the creature.

"Back away!" she shouted in a wavering voice.

The horseman's eyes fixated upon her and the rifle fell from her grasp.

"Your confederates will sleep awhile," the brittle voice cautioned. "You shall be found secured but safe."

Harnessed to a tree with twine the woman observed her unconscious colleagues, as they were dragged toward the side of the road. The horseman whistled and the mare trotted into view.

Remounting, the spectre raised a gauntlet and nodded courteously toward the bound agent. Daylight streamed through the trees and the horseman bolted. Around a bend the stable and house appeared. Forging a ditch they crossed the dewy grass. The twitter of birds were heard and Farley was fortunately silent. As they drew near the stable Hurricane appeared reluctant to part company. Her companion felt a similar reticence. Kriel relied heavily upon his new found friend during their brief time together. Drawing alongside the shed the rider dismounted. Tugging back the disguise Jesse breathed in deeply. He removed his gloves and ran a hand along Hurricane's shimmering mane. Guiding her toward her stall she protested with an indignant snort and put up resistance.

"Steady girl you're home now."

Following the events of the past several hours the mare couldn't abide remaining behind. She bucked rearward and held defiantly to the spot. Against a backdrop of the rising sun Jesse decided a smooth getaway might be difficult.

Leaning in he whispered, "Your owners will worry if you're not here to greet them."

Gradually, the mare accepted the inevitable and simply stood there. Jesse removed her saddle and bridal and hung them from hooks. The gate swung inward and Hurricane reentered her stall and turned slowly about. Jesse placed his palm on her snout and both were silent. In the stalls next door the neighbours stirred, but were otherwise placid. Quiet words were uttered and Jesse whispered goodbye.

An outburst of barks emitted from the farmhouse.

"Farley..." the trespasser sighed.

The door of the homestead slammed and Jesse peered from the stable door. He witnessed the hound straining at the leash dragging the old timer in his direction. Farley was intent on discovering what the hubbub in the stable was all about. As the gentleman hobbled to keep up, Jesse made a dash for the trees. An inspection of the stable ensued and Farley reemerged and peed on the wall. Guided back toward the farmhouse his tail wagged furiously. Watching from the woods Jesse wiped perspiration from his brow.

With the Feds combing the area north of his position he remained safely obscured. His car lay south of the wreck affording leeway to make a quick departure. Drawing the disguise over his face, Kriel forged the ditch and noticed a 'For Sale' sign hanging from a mailbox post. Lee mentioned extending thanks to the mare's owner and the number was committed to memory. An oily stench persisted around the calamity that once was an SUV. Arriving at the willow patch the veiled figure plunged headlong through the swampy mire. The rented vehicle lay undisturbed and a phone was withdrawn from Kriel's rags. To prevent the carrier's position from being tracked the devise was tossed into the quagmire. In the driver's seat the disguise was retired and he removed his gloves. Slipping on the windbreaker Jesse pulled the cuffs from his boots. The engine responded and he shifted into reverse and pressed lightly on the peddle. The car was guided onto the Yokum Trail and he rolled down the window and listened intently. Other than rustling leaves nothing was heard and Jesse drove south toward the highway.

A thought suddenly struck him!

If a roadblock were erected where the Yokum Trail intersects with the highway, he'd be detained and questioned. Astride Hurricane such obstacles were of little consequence. As the highway hove in view he eased up on the peddle. Fortunately, no obstruction barred the way. The driver considered Lee Tondar's well-being and pondered Penther's whereabouts. At the stop sign he signalled left and allowed an eighteen-wheeler to pass.

Gazing in the rear-view mirror Jesse watched the Yokum Trail recede

———————————

Dorothy Tondar was first to receive a phone call regarding her husband's status. The caller identified himself as Robert Blakie-Harris, Director of Operations at the National Security Agency. The name was unfamiliar.

The Director stated Lee had been admitted to Fairview Hospital after being airlifted from a field assignment.

"He insisted on being flown to the Cleveland facility to be near you," he added. "During the return flight Lee was placed on a respirator."

"What happened!" the stricken woman pleaded.

The official hesitated, "According to the attending physician your husband's symptom's are the result of an ongoing lung-related malady Mrs. Tondar."

"Will he survive!" Dorothy asked frantically.

"That has yet to be determined."

Allowing her time to breath the caller quietly added, "I can have a driver pick you up and deliver you to your husband's side?

Dorothy thanked him and said she'd find her way there. She replaced the phone and stared at the floor.

Minnie Wren overheard her guest's alarmed response and strode in from another room.

"Everything alright Dot.?"

"I don't think so," she responded. "The person stated he was a national security official. He said Lee fell ill while on assignment and implied it might be fatal."

Dorothy brought a hand to her quivering lips, "He's been airlifted to Fairview Hospital here in town."

Minnie fetched tissue and guided her friend to the couch.

"I need to be with him," the distraught woman murmured.

Her host was already in motion, "I'll grab my purse and car keys and be right with you."

"Thank you."

A field assignment implied her husband had been somewhere other than Lantern Falls. Lee hadn't worked away from home in years. He was a History professor at a prestigious college in northern Ohio. She recalled the home invasion. Whatever danger her husband encountered, it was real enough for him to arrange sanctuary for her out of town. Lee rarely discussed work-related matters. Aside from academic responsibilities, Dorothy was aware he was occasionally outsourced to the government. Uncertain what that entailed she would ask questions later. Right now she needed to be there. Grateful for the kindness shown to her by her friend she waited by the door.

"We'll be there in a jiff, " Minnie assured her as they strode toward the car.

The overcast sky merged with Lake Erie to form a grey canvas.

———————————

Corporal Soo was typing up a summary report detailing the appearance of person's unknown; both on and off the Institute grounds. She glanced at the clock and realized it was time to make a final turn about the campus. Her boss's abrupt departure followed an attempt upon his life; meanwhile his apprentice was on assignment.

Jesse Carlton

Having personally vetted the young man Sasha uncovered no criminal background. He was as he appeared to be: focused, thoughtful, athletic even attractive. Imbued with these qualities why would such an individual tilt toward evil - if he was indeed the perpetrator? Clearly another person had made the attempt on the professor's life. Was collusion was a factor? Aside from her security team no one was at liberty to roam the grounds with impunity?

Having downloaded the report Sasha donned a raincoat and adjusted her holster. She inspected the gun clip and exited the lobby doors which sealed automatically. Across the way the buildings dissolved into fog. Descending the steps her phone chimed and a blank screen was revealed.

"Corporal Soo?"

"Whose inquiring?"

The caller stated his name was Robert Blakie-Harris, Director of Operations at the NSA.

"I'm calling to inform you Lee Tondar is in a Cleveland hospital. He's been airlifted from Indiana where he was engaged. I've been informed by his physician his condition is quite critical."

Sasha steadied herself against the railing.

"I've been in touch with both Lee and his wife," resumed the official. "He's able to communicate and requested both you and Mr. Carlton join him at Fairview Hospital. His wife Dorothy will be there to receive you."

Startled by the apparent seriousness of the professor's condition Sasha replied, "I'll secure transportation and leave for Cleveland within the next thirty minutes. Mr. Carlton is on assignment. He was due to return yesterday I've received no word."

"In that case go alone," the Director instructed. "I'll see what can be learned of Mr. Carlton's whereabouts. Meantime, the matter remains classified?"

"Understood..." she responded haltingly as the Director signed off.

Wisps of fog swirled as Sasha made her way down the steps. She berated herself for not insisting the professor receive proper medical attention following his assault. Had she done so this wouldn't have occurred. Instead she allowed him to proceed into a hazardous situation.

She crossed Abbot Lane and withdrew her flashlight. Once her rounds were complete she'd meet briefly with her replacement. A cab would be summoned to deliver her to the bus depot downtown. Cleveland was under an hour's drive from Lantern Falls and buses ran frequently between both stops.

Her cellphone beckoned.

"It's me chief," Dennis informed her. "I'm inching through town at a snail's pace. The fog is making the drive difficult. I'll be a few minutes late. Sorry"

"I'm doing a final go-round Dennis. Drive safely."

"Will do."

Replacing the phone she traversed the courtyard path and paused beneath the corridor bridging the Residence and Commons buildings. She was tempted to dash up to her room for fresh clothes but rejected the idea.

"Hello Sasha..."

The voice behind her sounded familiar.

A hand gripped her wrist as she reached for her gun. She struggled as the assailant wrestled the weapon away and secured her hands behind her back with cuffs.

"Surprise!" her stalker whispered."

She recognized the voice and froze.

Thrust into an alcove alongside the Commons building she was horrified to discover who her assailant was.

———————

THIRTY-ONE

The fog made it difficult to discern the white line along the middle of Windover Road. Guiding the vehicle closer to the right shoulder the journey from Indiana had been taxing. Fuelled by coffee and sunflower seeds Jesse managed to stave off exhaustion. Signalling onto Edgewater Drive it felt like week's since he'd been home.

Home...

Without a cellphone he was at a disadvantage and wondered if Lee attempted contact? He swung onto Abbot Lane and his headlight's cut swaths through the fogbound campus. In the foreground loomed the murky outline of Sentinel Hall.

A male voice was heard and Jessie lowered the window. It came from the cluster of buildings to his left. Braking lightly he brought the vehicle to the curb, before the School of Journalism and switched off the engine. A second outburst emitted - this time it was a female. A stalker had been reported and there was Lee's attack. Jesse removed his jacket and adjusted his pant cuffs and gloves. He pulled the disguise over his face and departed the vehicle. Stealing across Abbot Lane, the stealth figure accessed the path leading toward the Commons building; where the sounds originated. Kriel swept along and heard an alarmed shout. In a shadowy recess, Corporal Soo was noticed backing away with her arms secured behind her back. The person confronting her was obscured.

"You died!" she bellowed.

In a detached manner her attacker responded, "I'm delighted you thought so. Had I not staged my own death I would've been prevented from witnessing your own."

Blended with the surroundings the spectre advanced.

The stranger brought a gleaming machete to his victim's throat.

"It wasn't me blown to bits in the boating accident on Ridgewood Bay," her assailant confessed. "A vagrant acquaintance aspired to helm a powerboat like mine. I needed a substitute and allowed the poor sod to take my vessel for a pleasure excursion. Prior to his departure, I had him sport my marina attire and concealed my wallet and cigarettes in the boat. A powerful device I'd obtained on the black market was rigged to explode after thirty minutes. The bomb components dissolve in water. When the pieces were finally recovered, the authorities deemed fuel leakage and a lit cigarette caused the explosion. The body parts were determined to be my own. On that day Daniel Sommers was born."

With the machete at her throat the killer rambled on. Sasha stalled for time and prayed for an opportunity to retaliate.

"H...how could you function!"

"Before I died I withdrew my savings and placed them in a separate account under Mr. Sommers name," replied her tormentor. "Rebuilding a new life kept me occupied. Essentially, you became the focus. I've been in this forsaken place more than a month watching and waiting. The dissolute shoreline provides a suitable setting for our storybook ending."

"You don't have to do this Brian."

"Brian's dead – its Daniel remember! You should never have abandoned me Sasha! Your rejection didn't sit well at all. You attained officer status and cast me aside like a disposable diaper. See how fate smiles on you now, bitch. You could've shared my inherited wealth instead of facing death along the desolate fringes of the world. I'm glad I died to savour this moment!"

He leaned closer and Sasha prepared to thrust her right knee into his groin. When he keeled over, she'd do the same to his face then run like hell.

The blade of the machete caressed her neck and blood trickled down her flesh.

The stalker raised his arm to strike and a brittle voice resounded.

"There dwells but one resurrection upon these shores 'tis the good ship's captain!"

An appalling laugh followed as the perpetrator found himself confronted by a decayed corpse. The machete was slapped effortlessly aside and the assailant grasped by the throat. Struggling to free himself he fixated on the rotting creature's eyes and went limp. Sasha staggered backwards and gazed in awe as her tormentor was hurled against the brick wall.

The spectre turned its countenance upon the security chief and grated, "Chivalry has it's rewards when those as fair as yourself are to be defended , madam."

A vehicle was heard entering the campus grounds. Sasha shouted and the car braked.

"Commons Building!" she bellowed.

Sasha turned again and the thing was gone.

Through billows of fog Dennis hollered, "Corporal!"

"Over here!"

Sasha focused on the form strewn along the pavement. Leaning over she threw up. Dennis rounded the corner with his sidearm drawn and noticed the displaced machete. His gaze fell upon the sprawled figure lying nearby his superior officer.

"You alright Chief!"

Sasha turned and displayed her secured wrist's and nodded toward the felled stalker. "Frisk him will you Dennis. See if you can find a key to match these cuffs."

The guard squatted alongside the unconscious form and keys were withdrawn. Once the proper one was inserted the cuffs clattered to the pavement. Sasha massaged her wrists and peered into the vaporous abyss.

"What was it!" she murmured.

"What was what chief?" Dennis asked as he rifled the man's pockets for ID.

"Sorry I'm still rattled."

Sasha intended to update her staff at a more opportune time. Right now she needed to remain calm.

"No identification," the guard confirmed. "The gun tucked in his belt looks a lot like your own."

"It was confiscated."

The brawny guard handed it back and eyed the tiny wound on Sasha's neck.

"How were you able to render this whack-job unconscious with your hand's bound?"

"Secure his wrist's I'll explain later."

Following instructions the sentry applied the cuff's formally worn by his superior.

"What's his condition?" Sasha inquired.

"With a bleeding lump like the one he's got he'll be out awhile. Likely, he's suffered a concussion."

Sasha nodded, "I'll summon an ambulance and the police. Stay with him until they arrive."

"Got you boss."

She turned toward him, "Your appearance was timely Dennis."

"I only wish I'd been here sooner."

Probing her surroundings Sasha started back toward Sentinel Hall. She established contact with the Lantern Falls Police Department on an existing frequency. Identifying herself she outlined the situation to the official on duty. He agreed to send officers and paramedics to the Grissim campus.

"The prisoner will be escorted to the Rose Danelli Health Center," she was informed. "An officer will remain until the patient's condition is determined. The crime scene will be investigated and you'll be interviewed and kept updated."

Sasha thanked the official and called Dennis to relay the news, "Keep watch on things until they arrive."

"Will do boss."

Dennis placed his phone away and knelt over the inanimate figure sprawled at his feet. He conducted a brief inspection of the head injury and determined the culprit struck a solid surface with considerable force.

Meantime, Sasha recalled her liberator's words, *'Chivalry has it's rewards...Madam.'*

Had she been able to speak she would have agreed.

Arriving at the foot of the steps leading up to the Hall, she was startled by the sound of an approaching automobile. From the haze enveloping Abbot Lane an unfamiliar vehicle emerged. Sasha hedged as it swung into a parking space. Her hand was on her holster as the driver emerged.

"Sasha!"

Jesse Carlton's voice was recognized and she responded, "I barely noticed your approach with the fog."

Aware of how traumatized she must have felt, Jesse had to appear oblivious to event's which unfurled within the campus shadows.

"How's things Corporal?"

Sasha's mind was as clouded as her surroundings. She'd been harshly judgmental of the young man addressing her based on an unfounded notion.

Noting her apparent distress the young man remarked, "Allow me to accompany you inside."

"If you wish."

She observed his dishevelled appearance and tousled hair.

"Where's your own vehicle?" she inquired.

"Behind the Lighthouse along with the professor's."

"The professor!" she exclaimed.

With everything that transpired she'd forgotten her charge's dire predicament. Recounting Blakie-Harris's phone call, she stated the professor had taken ill while on assignment.

"Due to a preexisting condition he may not recover," she added.

Jesse was stunned, "Where is he!"

"Fairview Hospital in Cleveland."

"I can be there in under an hour."

"We're both requested to attend," Sasha interjected. "His wife Dorothy is expecting us. I'll have Dennis keep an eye on things here."

"Fine," Jesse replied. "When you're ready we'll use my rental."

"I'm ready."

When she was in the car Jesse asked, "Did Blakie-Harris specify if Lee was conscious?"

"He's able to communicate that's all I know."

The driver reacquainted himself with the murky road conditions.

Their thoughts were interrupted by emergency vehicles entering the Institute grounds. Sirens wailed and Sasha turned to her colleague, "Something occurred in the courtyard before your arrival Jesse."

She informed him she'd been making the rounds when a voice called her by name. It belonged to someone from her past. Outlining the sordid details, Sasha said her stalker admitted to staging his own death in order to terrorize her. She glanced away and her body trembled.

Hearing her perspective Jesse urged her to continue, "What happened to the assailant?"

"I was about to taste the blade when something intervened."

"Dennis?"

"The fog must have contributed to the other-worldliness of the thing. It possessed unnatural strength, felled my attacker then vanished. Moments later Dennis arrived."

Cruising south on Windover Jesse signalled onto an overleaf and they began the journey east.

"You sure you want to make the trip?" he inquired.

"I'm fine."

They drove some distance in silence.

Sasha withdrew her phone and contacted the sentry.

"Yes chief?"

"Quick update Dennis. Something off-campus requires my immediate attention. I observed emergency vehicles arriving - how are things proceeding?"

Dennis assured her the prisoner's transfer was being properly conducted and inquired about her status?

"I'm a bit better now and will be in touch," she said before signing off.

She turned to Jesse, "Did you notice anyone or anything when you entered the campus grounds?"

"Only you at the foot of the steps and the fog."

Sasha closed her eyes,"The fog...?"

As the miles accumulated Jesse recalled the beating Lee sustained at the hands Royston Adams inside the bunker.

The professor's fragility as he boarded the airlift still haunted him.

———————————

A grey mist lingered as the black limo emerged from the heavily fortified car-park beneath NSA headquarters in Fort Meade. In the rear seat, the Director of Operations peered through tinted glass at the morning traffic. He inserted a flash-drive into his laptop; adjusted an earphone and listened as Lee Tondar prepared to give a recorded update forwarded to him twenty minutes earlier.

In addition to the driver a pair of operatives sat opposite him. Within minutes the limo arrived before a guarded entrance along Maryland's Friendship Annex Airport, and were waved through. As the occupant's prepared to transfer aboard an Agency jet, Robert Blakie-Harris emerged and strode briskly towards the streamlined aircraft. Accompanied by both agents they settled into the traveller's compartment. One conferred with the pilot and clearance protocols were observed. The Director buckled in and removed the laptop, while a flight attendant entered to check on seat-belts. When she departed he adjusted his earphone and listened as Lee's narrative was set to commence. Blakie-Harris noted the station chief's apparent exhaustion. The report had been filed en route from Rykles Clearing to Cleveland, by way of Lafayette, Indiana.

The recording began thus:

"This is a partial account of an investigation conducted by yours truly Lee Tondar; with the aid of my recruit. This individual's services as an asset were financed from a reserve fund I had set aside. Having reviewed evidence based on statement's made by a SIAG operative, prior to his untimely demise in US custody - the outline of a plot emerged. Due to health concerns I was prevented from following up on some of the more challenging aspect's afforded the case. This is where my recruit came in. Possessed of uncanny physical attributes, his intellectual curiosity served me well on more than one occasion. Thoroughly vetted he endured an unusually harsh recruitment exam. He's proved as invaluable to me as Stuart Tuppins was - which says something."

Lee detailed the investigation by acknowledging the deceptive measures, put in place to conceal the perpetrator's crimes.

"As a result of this individual's unimpeachable character he remained above suspicion."

Lee hesitated, "It's difficult to believe our colleague and friend being guilty of orchestrating such a plot. I could never have fathomed Royston embroiling himself in such monumental betrayal. Once events in Detroit were linked to the Indiana compound; and infamous absconder, Azil Besserer was smuggled in from exile; it became apparent a WMD was being devised."

The Director heard the muted drone of a helicopter above Lee's voice.

"Others were enlisted," the professor continued. "Notably William Penther and several of his militant insurgents. They were an integral part of the endeavour."

The name resonated with the Director.

A coughing spell interrupted Lee's account and an airlift attendant urged him to place the recorder aside. Acknowledging her request, Lee reiterated faith in his recruit and in his security chief, Sasha Soo. If both agreed it was his wish they maintain the Grissim station jointly.

"Their combined efforts would ensure the outpost is effectively sustained."

With that the recording concluded.

Blakie-Harris drew a breath and placed the earphone away. Members of his entourage looked up and quickly glanced away. He had hoped Lee would've expanded on the female who'd boarded the airlift in his company. Crucial intelligence could be gleaned from a SIAG sleeper. When she regained consciousness he planned to interrogate her.

On the minus side her chances of survival were less than Lee's.

The Director considered who might've funded Adams demented ambition. He was aware Rykles Clearing once hosted scores of rabid anti-government extremists. Penther remained a prime suspect in the unsolved murders of two FBI agents. Blakie-Harris decided to wait until the fats were known.

The Director's phone chimed and Lee greeted him.

"Were you able to review my brief?" he inquired.

"Affirmative," the Director replied. "I'm stunned!"

"As am I."

Blakie-Harris asked about hospital accommodation's and how Lee was faring?

"The meds make me drowsy and the nurse is a drill sergeant," the patient responded.

The Director inquired about the woman who'd accompanied him as far as Lafayette.

"She was discovered alongside the Yokum Trail in a dire way."

Evidently, Lee refused to be offloaded in Lafayette and insisted on being transported to Cleveland to be near his wife. Blakie-Harris made the call allowing him to be flown to the destination of his choice.

The professor indicated he was compiling a report intended for the Director's eyes only.

Once the call ended Blakie-Harris sat perfectly still and began humming a discordant note. Whenever, stress clouded his judgment he practised this style of meditation. Devoting five minutes to utter calm he found his thinking improved greatly. As the jet hurtled toward Lafayette, he removed his shoes and crossed his legs. Seated like Buddha he continued humming. Detail were familiar with the ritual and pretended not to notice.

Reality intruded when the Director's phone vibrated. Jason Redford his point man in Maryland beckoned.

"Yes Jay."

"Sir, our people in Lafayette forwarded three photos of the female patient. They were taken while her life-support apparatus was removed in midst of her transfer to ER. Two frontal images and one profile."

"Match confirmation?"

"Enhancement confirms it's the Evanston woman."

The news was greeted in silence. The Director had correctly identified the 'sleeper' whose family remained sequestered in protective custody in Chicago.

Redford continued, "The Lafayette team are sending a hair sample for DNA examination. I'll get those results off to you as soon as we have them."

"We're entering Lafayette airspace now Jay we'll talk later."

The Director contacted his agent-in-charge at the hospital.

"Ronnie, I've spoken with Jay Redford at HQ. The woman's likeness matches Gillian Burke. Has she regained consciousness?"

"Still unresponsive Sir."

"Have a female agent remain with her. If hair sample's match I'll contact Chicago and inform her family - and arrange for them to be reunited. Otherwise, I'll join you shortly."

A government helicopter was waiting as the jet touched down. Several armed guards were present and drew to attention. The Director emerged carrying his briefcase and scrambled beneath the rotating propellers. The aircraft rapidly ascended and swung off in the direction of the hospital. Moments later they hovered over a marked X on the landing pad atop the facility. Procedure was exchanged between a rooftop controller and the pilot, as he made a cautious descent. The two agent's leaped to the tarmac followed by the Director. Passing through emergency doors, they established clearance and were admitted.

Guided by his detail Blakie-Harris strode the hospital corridor.

Heron was closely monitoring the GPS signal depicting his agent. Her position had been stationary for more than an hour. Taras was now on the move again at an increased rate of speed, suggesting she was being transported by air. Superimposed over an onscreen map of Indiana; the controller followed his agent's flight-path, indicating the signal was moving in the general direction of Lafayette. Visual relay was provided via an orbiting satellite and Heron locked onto her position. Her signal slowed and gradually hovered above a fixed position.

An airlift!

The map was replaced by a grainy black and white image. Heron made adjustments to enhance the resolution, however it was still snowy. Once the feed steadied a large structure revealed a glowing "H" indicating a hospital. The aircraft made a slow decent and coordinates registered at the bottom of the screen. The fuzzy image witnessed medical personnel leaping down from the aircraft, burdened with a stretcher. Intravenous equipment guided by staff rushed alongside as the patient was wheeled into the building.

She's alive!

It was apparent Taras had been seriously injured, which explained her motionless signal. Transported to a Lafayette medical facility; interrogation was certain if she recovered sufficiently. She had nothing to offer. Her directive was singular - seek out and dispatch a deceiver. The target aligned himself with a highly-placed rogue within US intelligence. Naturally, the situation was of concern to both A'biin and the US.

Heron conceived a plan. In exchange for a pair of suspected US spies languishing in a Siana prison - Taras would be released. He intended to discuss the matter with a senior NSA official.

Ninety minutes later a second helicopter appeared above the Lafayette hospital. Heron enlarged the frame and noticed the images of government officials disembarking. The NSA Director of Operations was among them. He'd dealt with Robert Blakie-Harris in the past. He hoped the Director was receptive to his offering.

Blakie-Harris felt his phone vibrate and slipped from the hospital room occupied by Gillian Burke. The call was from Jayson Redford at Maryland HQ

"The hair sample extracted from the Burke woman match one's found on her hairbrush in Evanston."

"Good work Jay "

The Director reestablished contact with the agent-in-charge of securing Rykles Clearing.

"Any further updates?"

"Experts verify the bunker detonator was rendered inoperative as a result of damage inflicted upon it at ground zero. Severed cables at the source would've deterred an incoming trigger signal, Sir."

The official added a positive identification of Royston Adams had been confirmed. He'd expired in the bunker the result of a single handgun projectile.

"A second fatality was discovered in the nearby woods," he continued.

"He's been identified as Aldo Dopple; a militant white supremacist associated with William Penther. A third and fourth recovery have yet to be identified. Their charred remains are being extracted from a burned out vehicle along the Yokum Trail."

"And William Penther?"

"Possibly one of the victim's in the wreck," the agent responded. "Forensics will conduct a study."

"Keep me posted."

Contact was established with the Chicago branch office of the FBI; who were informed Gillian Burke had been found alive, in serious but stable condition. Blakie-Harris passed along instructions for the family to be airlifted to the Lafayette hospital.

His phone vibrated yet again.

Fort Meade was claiming they'd received a scrambled message expressly for Director of Operations.

"The signal was transmitted from SIAG HQ in Siana," the staffer related. "Analysts determine it belongs to an official named Heron. He wishes to confer with you only."

Blakie-Harris had last spoken with the reputable SIAG controller months before. They'd negotiated the exchange of an American asset imprisoned in A'biin on charges of espionage. With input from Heron, the matter was resolved to their mutual satisfaction. The SIAG veteran was viewed as a moderate by US intelligence.

"Put the call through," Blakie-Harris responded.

A voice in heavily accented English finally spoke, "I trust our conversation is being monitored?"

"Naturally, by both my people and your own," the other replied.

"It's of no consequence, " Heron reasoned. "What I have to say should be heard not only by yourself but by your political masters."

"I'll make that determination," sighed the Director of Operations "What concerns you Heron?"

"We've negotiated successfully in the past so let us be direct."

"If it serves our mutual interests."

Clearing his throat the SIAG controller stated, "You have in your custody one of our operatives; a female code-named Taras. I wish to offer an exchange; one of your political prisoners in return for her."

Silence greeted the request and Heron continued.

"Taras was instructed to dispatch a SIAG defector referred to as Ulsar. It's our contention this traitor betrayed his country for personal gain. It's believed Ulsar was recruited to work on behalf of a US Intelligence figure. Ulsar's predecessor was approached, but refused to be swayed. Attempting to flee the country, he was taken into US custody and died shortly thereafter under mysterious circumstances. Perhaps you recall the incident? It hindered progress between our two nations and lingers still. I believe Ulsar was somehow lured by this same renegade. It's speculation of course, however it's possible our turncoat is working alongside an American provocateur, in an attempt to increase hostilities."

Blakie-Harris played along knowing his counterpart spoke the truth.

"And who do you suppose this deceptive American figure might be?"

"That I do not know"

"Then how can you be certain your dubious agent is involved with this person. He may simply have taken a liking to our American lifestyle."

Heron smiled and pressed his ear to the phone. The American was a circumspect man.

"Ulsar's profile suggests he's a pathological liar who harbours personal gratification and profit above all," confirmed the SIAG analyst. "How these ambition's went unnoticed before his assignment in America commenced is beyond me. I was not engaged with him during his formative years. Nor was I asked to vet or pass judgment on his recruitment into the ranks. I do know he possesses a series of remarkable skills, which would benefit anyone offering large sums of money."

Blakie-Harris allowed the chips to fall where they may. Unbeknownst to Heron, the turncoat referred to was likely dead. The Ulsar reference remained compelling, however.

"Thank you for voicing your concerns," the Director finally said. "Your observation's will be looked into. The exchange you propose might prove difficult, as the woman in question is currently under investigation. Our people are presently unravelling evidence which may or may not bear out your assertions. We'll discuss the matter furth... "

"I'm aware our operative is at a medical facility in Lafayette, Indiana," Heron intervened. "Might I inquire as to her condition?"

"She's stable," the NSA honcho responded. "I'll leave it at that and get back to you. Until then keep our discussion close to your chest. Agreed?"

"Agreed."

Blakie-Harris signed off and established immediate contact with Lee Tondar. The ailing station chief was able to respond from Fairview intensive care in Cleveland.

"It's been at least ten minutes since we last spoke Robert what's up?"

"Very funny how are you feeling?"

"Dorothy's here she just stepped out to the ladies room?"

"Are others present?"

"Jesse Carlton and Corporal Soo are on their way. Where are you calling from?"

"Lafayette. I'm outside Gillian Burke's hospital room.

"Is she who we suspected she was?"

"Everything's a match."

"How's her condition?"

"She'll be laid up awhile, however she's slowly coming around. Her family is being airlifted to be with her."

"No doubt you're anxious to hear what she has to say, if anything?"

"It's my job."

The Director paused, "Lee there are a few pieces that don't add..."

"Robert, I'm attempting to chronicle the events as we speak. The notes are for your benefit but you keep calling."

"Do you know anything of a SIAG sleeper code-named Ulsar?"

"No, but I'll wager the lady might have insights. Allow her to recover before you inquire."

"Thanks..."

A female agent emerged from Mrs. Burke's room and strode toward Blakie-Harris.

"She's regained consciousness Sir."

Lee overheard the words, "That's your cue Robert. Go easy with her."

"Stay alive Lee. I'll be in touch."

THIRTY-TWO

Blakie-Harris found himself banished to the hospital corridor after the attending physician requested he leave the room. The Director had attempted to converse with his patient, who lay wired to an array of intravenous devices. Their exchange was brief. Her single utterance was laboured and delivered incoherently, *"Ulsar killed by the road... an American and subordinate... "*

The rest was indecipherable.

Ulsar...

The code-name Heron made reference to.

As for ' American and subordinate' perhaps Penther and one of his follower's were responsible for Ulsar's death? Possibly even Adams himself! It was a lead worth pursuing.

Granted permission by hospital staff to set-up shop in a cramped office attached to the reception area, the Director re-established contact with Heron.

"You'll be happy to know your operative has regained consciousness," he related. "When questioned she was heavily sedated and her response was garbled. The physician on duty requested I speak with her later. The good news is she'll make it."

An inward sigh registered on part of the SIAG analyst.

"When she comes to she'll likely contract amnesia?" the Director speculated.

"That sometimes occurs," Heron replied. "In any event she has nothing to offer. Her mission was singular it's now concluded."

"Naturally, I must believe this because you say so."

"It is the truth."

"She mentioned the name Ulsar."

"In what context?"

Blakie-Harris repeated the patient's halting rumination.

"Thought provoking," Heron remarked. "Have you recovered the men she refers to?"

The Director exhaled, "An AWOL Intelligence chief surfaced - one of our own. He was killed during a raid in rural Indiana. Oddly your female operative happened to be close by."

"What of Ulsar?"

"'*Ulsar killed...*' according to your agent."

"By an American..."

"Could be anyone," the Director cautioned. "The expired official I refer to was involved with a sordid lot - anti-government extremists, assassins and your own accommodating microbiologist, Azil Besserer."

The name made Heron wince. The biologist would be dealt with severely once extradition arrangements were undertaken.

"Two unidentified bodies were discovered in a burnt-out vehicle at that location," resumed the Director. "Their identities are unknown. Currently, our forensic people are attempting to determine who they are. In order to identify Ulsar's remains you'll need to forward his dental records. I'll put you through to Forensics so a transfer can be arranged."

"What are your plans for Taras?"

"For now she'll remain in custody."

"Are you suggesting an exchange won't be possible?"

"I'm suggesting one might be arranged, once the woman recovers and I've had a chance to speak with her."

The Director placed the receiver to his other ear, "I'm prepared to accept the reasoning behind your agent being in America. So here's my offer - once she's well enough and we've chatted; I'll hand her back in return for the two American translator's rotting in an A'biinian prison cell."

"I beg your pardon?"

"You heard me I refer to the linguist's accused of being American spies. Having committed no offence, they were led off at gunpoint by agents of the SAIG. For more than a year the State Department has attempted to negotiate their release to no avail."

"You're suggesting a two for one trade?" Heron asserted.

"Besserer's extradition is also guaranteed. We'll even arrange for Gillian Burke's husband and child to resettle with their beloved family member, if they so desire."

The notion was greeted with silence.

"Naturally, we'll need assurances her family would be provided for," cautioned the Director. "That's four for two."

"I rarely have much say in these matters," Heron conceded.

"But you hold sway. These linguist's are educators not spies."

"So you claim."

"Consider the offer Heron. Discuss the matter with your superiors and get back to me."

The SIAG spymaster felt a willingness to cooperate, "I'll be in touch Director."

———

Sasha was grateful for the company even if that company lay curled asleep in the rear seat of a rented automobile. Events of the past several hours had proved overwhelming. Unable to shake off the ordeal involving her assailant; once she was back in Lantern Falls the police would be personally updated. References to her frayed liberator would be omitted for the time being. Instead, they could ponder the fact her attacker died a year earlier in a boating incident in South Carolina.

The clouds broke and rays of sunlight glistened as the curvature of Lake Erie was followed. Jesse had found himself nodding and Sasha offered to take over driving duties. With his knees scrunched in the rear seat, an occasional snort assured the driver her passenger was still alive. Jesse's worn attire was observed in the mirror. Hopefully, he had a change of clothes stored in the trunk. If not she would insist they stop and find something suitable.

Brian Winsmore...

Her past was supposed to be past. The posting at Grissim had been therapeutic. How her tormentor staged his own death and managed to track her down was unsettling. All because she rejected the physical and emotional abuses heaped on her in South Carolina.

On the heels of that was the Director's call informing her of the professor's condition.

A Cleveland city limits sign whizzed by. Sasha punched Fairview Hospital onto GPS and the location was highlighted. Gridlock was no obstacle this late in the morning which suited her fine.

She called Jesse's name over her shoulder. It was time he changed into something approaching civilized.

"Yep," he muttered.

"We're entering downtown Cleveland. If it's all the same to you I'd like to pull over so you can sort out your wardrobe. We'll be at the hospital soon."

Sprawled along the back seat the young man ran a hand through his hair and swallowed hard. Rising to a seated position he leaned forward and squinted through the front windshield.

"Have you locked onto GPS?"

Yes

Leaning back he peered outside.

"We're on Lakeside East?"

"Correct."

"That puts us several blocks away. Stay the course when we come to East 9th' hang a right and we're there.

"Got it."

Jesse rubbed his eyes, "How long was I out?"

"Roughly forty minutes."

"Any word on Lee?"

"Nothing."

Jesse again recalled his mentor's drawn features as he boarded the airlift in Indiana.

"About fresh clothes," Sasha remarked. " Is there anything in the trunk?"

He glanced at his mud-caked boots and the hems hanging from beneath his windbreaker.

"Did you crawl from a foxhole?" the driver inquired.

"The professor suggested I dress down for my last excursion."

"You succeeded."

"The turn-off is just ahead," Jesse indicated.

Across from the hospital a service-station was sighted.

"About clothes?" Sasha reiterated.

"I have pressed jeans and a sweatshirt in the trunk. There's a pair of runners as well."

Sasha made a left turn and drew alongside a self-service pump and Jesse was handed the keys.

"While I refuel you change in the car."

He nodded and stepped out to retrieve his items from the trunk. Still in uniform, Sasha squeezed gas into the tank and paid the attendant. She returned to the car and found Jesse properly attired behind the wheel.

"The nap helped," he said through the open window.

Sasha nodded and entered the passenger side. Her companion started the engine and they drew up to the intersection. When the lights flashed green he signalled into the hospital parking area. A ticket was withdrawn from an automated machine and he tucked it away. Once a space was obtained, Sasha straitened her uniform and Jesse ran a comb through his hair. The weather was balmy as they strode toward the main entrance. At the information desk an older gentlemen greeted them.

Jesse cleared his throat, "We're here to visit a patient by the name of Lee Tondar. He was admitted early this morning."

The information was retrieved onscreen and the attendant glanced up, "Mr. Tondar has indeed been admitted. However, you'll need to provide identification in order to visit him."

"Understood," Jesse responded reaching for his wallet.

Sasha withdrew ID while her companion passed over a laminated UCOMA card. The document's were observed and the gentleman indicated a log book, "If you'll sign in I'll be happy to escort you."

Once their names were entered, a female concierge relieved the gentleman and they departed the building. A parking area reserved for staff was traversed and their guide remarked, "We could've taken an indoor route but this way is quicker."

He paused momentarily, "Your friend must be a VIP. We don't usually have armed guards stationed outside hospital rooms."

Jesse nodded and Sasha made no reply.

They entered a side entrance and moved along a narrow corridor towards a staff elevator. The doors parted and their guide accessed the seventh-floor. They were received by two men attired in suits. Jesse thanked their escort and the carriage began its descent. One of the agent's extended his hand and introduced himself and his partner. Apparently, they were expected.

"I believe the patient is with a doctor at the moment"" remarked the spokesman. "I'll need to see photo ID before we proceed."

"Of course," Sasha replied handing hers over.

Jesse fumbled a second time for his wallet and the agent glanced at their images.

"Thank you Corporal and you Mr. Carlton," he said dutifully.

Their ID was passed back and the agent withdrew a phone and confirmed clearance protocols were in order. They were motioned to follow and passed through a pair of swinging doors, where medical personnel were observed. Sasha caught sight of Dorothy Tondar, in the company of a woman who appeared to be consoling her. Guided toward a nurses station the new arrival's were introduced. Dorothy overheard and turned with a startled expression.

"Over here!" she beckoned.

Before either could respond a doctor emerged from a hospital room.

"Mrs. Tondar would you step inside - alone if you don't mind."

She glanced at her friend then at Jesse and Sasha.

"I'll join you presently," she said in a faltering voice.

———————————

The family of the woman found in rural Indiana braced themselves as the airlift prepared it's descent onto a heliport atop the Lafayette hospital. The husband, daughter and father-in-law were whisked across the tarmac and led to the room where Gillian Burke lay. Meeting them partway, her physician Dr. Bower explained the patient had suffered severe exposure, dehydration and infection from a pierced hand.

"Gillian appears to be experiencing a loss of memory," he added. "She's groggy due to the medication so it's too early to tell. We should know the extent of her amnesia over the next forty-eight hours."

The doctor smiled at the girl clutching a pad and coloured markers. He turned to her dad, "There's someone who wishes to speak with you before you visit the patient."

They were led along the corridor and introduced to Robert Blakie-Harris. The NSA Director of Operations was outside the room reserved for Mrs. Burke. Offering condolences he said their loved one was in good hands and her recovery was assured.

He addressed Steven Burke directly, "There are a few formalities we'll need to discuss."

The girl was tugging at her father's sleeve anxious to see her mother. Guided into the patient's room the family observed the motionless form of their beloved family member, as she lay attached to a series of tubes. Steven and Samantha approached the bed rail followed by Tom Burke. Blinds were shuttered to prevent sunlight interfering with the patient's rest. Faint light radiated from a lamp on an end table. IV tubes hung from a galley along the opposite side of the bed. Dr. Bower prepared to depart and nodded at the nurse who was damp-mopping the patient's brow.

"Gillian is coping well but she's exhausted," the woman informed them. "We thought she'd contracted pneumonia but she managed to avoid it. The patient has been administered pain medication to ease the discomfort caused by a series of lacerations."

"Lacerations!" Steve said alarmingly "What caused them?"

"Apart for her hand wound we believe the cuts were inflicted by branches and tree limbs, while she'd been in motion."

"She was running from something!"

The distraught father was drawn aside. Choosing her words carefully the nurse whispered, "Mr. Burke it appears your wife was shackled about the wrists and ankles. Her left-hand palm was penetrated by a sharp object. Evidently, she escaped from whoever was responsible which resulted in the lacerations."

Steven Burke stood there stunned.

The others were out of hearing range. He noticed Sammy's tears as she leaned in close to the bed-rail. The girl stroked her mother's hair while the nurse made an inspection of IV gauges. Satisfied with the levels she remarked, "I'll leave you folks alone. If Gillian awakens I'll be outside."

Steven returned to his wife's bedside and placed an arm around his daughter's shoulder. Tom stood quietly by and they focused upon the woman, who'd vanished from their lives for nearly a month. A pair of chairs were along the wall. Steven gestured in that direction and suggested Sammy and Tom make themselves comfortable.

"Then you won't have a seat dad?"

"You're thoughtful," replied her father. "I have to step outside and speak with one of the gentlemen. You stay with Tom and keep mom company. I'll be back shortly."

"Okay."

Her father smiled.

"You don't mind do you dad?"

"Of course not," the older man responded. "We'll be fine."

Steven cast a sidelong glance at his wife and departed the room.

Blakie-Harris was busy working his phones inside the makeshift office - when a member of his detail poked his head in.

"Mr. Burke is here to see you Sir."

"Good. Show him in and see that were not disturbed."

The door was held open and Steven Burke entered and was offered a seat opposite a cluttered desk. The NSA man switched off his phone and inquired with noticeable concern, "How is your wife fairing, Mr. Burke?"

"Please call me Steven," his guest responded. "According to the nurse Gillian's exhausted and unaware of our presence."

The Director nodded, "She awoke briefly while you and your family were en route. After a few words she went out like a light."

"What in hell happened!" Steven said raising his voice. "The nurse mentioned lacerations, bondage wounds and an improbable escape. How did she end up like this and why all the security!"

An agent poked his head inside and was waved off by the Director who calmly remarked, "That is why I desired to speak with you Mr. Bur...I mean Steven. We need to discuss what we know and don't know."

Allowing his words to settle Blakie-Harris resumed, "Does the name 'Ulsar' mean anything?"

"No should it?"

"It may be of relevance?" the Director replied. "Your wife is what people in the business of national security refer to as a 'sleeper'. Someone who resides in a given country for an extended period of time, under an assumed name and identity."

Steven leaned forward and listened incredulously as his host unravelled a tale as bizarre as any he'd heard. He spoke of foreign operative's trained from early childhood and taking on new lives in different parts of the world - in his wife's case America. Gillian, he insisted was a SIAG agent servicing the Intelligence division of A'biin.

"We believe she was recently accessed and was undertaking an assign .."

A rapping at the door intervened.

Visibly upset the Director hollered, "What!"

The same sentry appeared, "Apologies Sir. But you gave instructions to be notified if Mrs. Burke came to. Apparently she has."

Steven rose instantly and made for the door. Blakie-Harris nodded to allow him to pass unimpeded.

The Director focused on another aspect of the case and contacted the head of ground forces at Rykles Clearing.

"Have the two bodies in the wreck been identified?".

"Not yet Sir. Their remains were transferred to a lab in Fort Wayne. Analysts are burrowing into dental regions and matching them against what we have on file."

"Keep me posted," he said and signed off.

Twenty minutes later Jason Redford was in touch.

"We've received a match on both counts from Fort Wayne," he reported. "Analysis confirms one of the victims is Richard Valamar; a Cuban mercenary from Miami. He'd been recruited as an asset by Royston Adams while he was still NSA. Valamar disappeared eighteen months ago, while en route to a government holding facility in Texas. Two US Marshals were found dead at the scene."

Blakie-Harris recalled the incident.

"Our Israeli cousins were helpful in forwarding his dental records," Redford added.

"The second individual is identified as Nickolas Dante," he continued. "Dante arrived from Bucharest, Romania as part of an exchange program more than a decade ago. Until recently he was employed as a research assistant within the New York Public Library system. The dental examination conducted match Dante's. His file states he'd been arrested in an altercation with some college boys in a Manhattan nightclub four years ago. He was admitted to the hospital with a broken jaw. "

"Thank you Jay."

"Sir."

Things appeared to be moving forward. It now looked as though Ulsar and Nickolas Dante might be one and the same.

Ulsar killed by the road... an American and subordinate...

Gillian Burke may have witnessed both murders at the hands of either William Penther or Royston Adams.

Transfer arrangement's regarding the pair of detained US 'educators' had been set in motion - along with Azil Bersserer's extradition. Heron received authorization from the wise men, allowing the American linguists to be exchanged in return for their ailing operative. Darren McJohn and Rose Freeling had been working as translators in two different Siana night schools. Arrested on suspicion of espionage, they were now free to return stateside in a swap for Gillian Burke and her family.

Once the former Illinois housewife had recovered sufficiently and was home in A'biin, she would report for duty as an instructor, within the temple she'd graduated from as a young woman. Along with her husband and daughter, they were to be ensconced within a small but comfortable home nearby the temple. Steven Burke would continue to write features for both online and print media. Samantha would resume her education at a private English school for girls. Her buddy Tom would remain in St. Louis to negotiate sale of the family's Evanston home. Blakie-Harris cleared the way for him to be flown to the shores of the Black Sea at Christmas - and to spend ten days at their home each summer. The arrangement would last indefinitely.

Heron was afforded leverage to green-light a straight-forward exchange of political prisoners with the US State Department.

Revelations implicating Azil Besserer's involvement in the failed attempt came as no surprise. The biologist-for-hire was discovered cowering in a room inside the facility, where his bogus weapon was developed. Maintaining his innocence, he insisted no American lives were endangered and pleaded unsuccessfully with US authorities not to be extradited.

Heron discovered the burned out van discovered in rural Indiana, had been rigged with an explosive device acquired by UCOMA chief Royston Adams. More shockingly he learned the remains of their agent Ulsar, was one of a pair removed from the decimated vehicle.

Had the plot succeeded the involvement of two SIAG agents, along with Besserer would've placed the blame solely on A'biin. During prisoner exchange discussions, Heron was informed the conspiracy had been financed inadvertently, with drug cartel money originating out of Mexico. Allegedly, an arrangement worth tens of millions of dollars existed between Royston Adams and cartel leader Juan Pulido. News of Adams death drove a spike through the heart of the cartel.

Seated alone inside his cramped cubicle Heron stretched his arms and glanced at his watch. He switched off the computer and retrieved his teacup. The cold, bitter taste was good. Placing the cup aside he slipped out the door thinking of bed.

––––––––––––––

It had become a tale of two hospitals. Three if you included the Rose Danelli Health Center in Lantern Falls - where Sasha's assailant lay unconscious. The security chief and her companion were in a waiting area inside Cleveland's Fairview Hospital; when the door to Lee's room opened and Dorothy Tondar emerged with the doctor. He strode off in a separate direction and Dorothy approached the woman who'd been comforting her.

"I'll be remaining here Minnie," she said. "I'll call the moment I know something. Thank you so much for your kindness and support."

She kissed her friend on the cheek and watched as she was escorted to the elevator by one of the suits. Turning to her guest's she strode in their direction. The pair noticed her solemn expression and rose to embrace her separately.

"How is he?" Jesse asked.

"Alive," Dorothy replied haltingly.

Sasha thought how difficult it must be to keep up a pretense of graciousness at such a time.

"I'm glad you both could make it," Dorothy remarked as they were guided toward Lee's room. "Incidentally, that was Minnie Wren who just departed. She's been at my side since I received word of Lee's condition. I've been staying with her and her husband temporarily. I would have made introductions but my thoughts are in disarray."

They drew up before Lee's door and she turned to them, "He can talk but the doctor advises rest."

"How serious is it!" Jesse pressed.

Her eyes lowered and they were motioned within. Expecting the worst both visitors were startled to see the professor seated upright in bed with his back propped against pillows. An oxygen mask covered the lower part of his face and he sat scribbling on a pad. They entered and his eyes flashed recognition. Dorothy frowned as her husband brought his hand up and lowered the mask.

"It's only for a few minutes promise," Lee insisted.

His security chief spoke first, "How goes it professor?"

"We're not on campus Sasha please call me Lee."

"Lee."

Smiling at them he stifled a cough, "Damn mask. They're trying to bump me off by smothering me."

A smile formed on his recruit's lips as he focused on his mentor who appeared noticeably frail.

"Dot would you inform the nurse I need to keep the mask off for a brief spell. There are some urgent matters which need discussing."

"I'll see what I can do," responded his wife.

Before departing she turned to the others. "I have to attend the ladies room. See he doesn't overdo it."

She smiled softly at her husband and closed the door behind her.

Lee placed his notes aside and switched off the oxygen.

"Is that wise?" Sasha inquired.

"Why waste good air?"

Jesse requested a no-holds-barred update.

"I'll give Robert Blakie-Harris credit," the professor admitted. "He implied I might not survive the next few days. Apparently, my physician supports his assertion.'"

Sasha brought a hand to her mouth.

"The doctor informed Dorothy and myself of the situation. I didn't wish to repeat it in her presence a second time."

The security chief sat down and Jesse placed his hand on her shoulder, "What's the diagnosis?"

"An ongoing case of obstructive pulmonary disease coupled with a collapsing lung," Lee replied. "Evidently, I have less than forty-eight hours."

The nurse reentered the room, "l see you've managed without me Mr. Tondar mask or no."

She crossed toward the oxygen tank and studied the gauges before taking Lee's pulse.

"I'm having a rather important huddle with my team nurse. I'll keep it as brief as possible."

She frowned and tilted her head, "Ten minutes."

"Thank you."

When the nurse departed Lee breathed deeply and winced.

"Since I'll no longer be manning the IRI at Grissim it's my hope you'll consider jointly replacing me. If you choose to accept I'll inform Blakie-Harris. He supports me in this matter and is aware of your qualifications. Once a new UCOMA Director has been appointed you'll be hearing from that individual. I've left detailed notes,"

Unaware of what the job fully entailed it was difficult to respond immediately to the professor's request.

"You're capable of operating the station Sasha. By combining your Intelligence training and Communication skills, you can enlighten Jesse in matters of signal detection and satellite tracking. In return Jesse will impart an understanding of our task in the field. I have little doubt his gifts will be required again where the safety of others are concerned.

"Should you avow this challenge you would each be employed in the capacity of school administrators in name only. Sasha, would undergo a transfer from Special Forces to UCOMA. Blakie-Harris will make the transition as smooth as possible. I'd also encourage you to vacate the dormitory and take up residency within my former quarters. With regard to your present status; the member under your command with the lengthiest service record will assume command until further notice."

As his listener's strove to keep up Lee concluded his narration.

"Regardless of who becomes UCOMA Director you'll respond solely to Robert Blakie-Harris; he becomes your handler. You'll be informed of salaries and benefits in due course."

Allowing the professor and Jesse time alone, Sasha rose and excused herself stating she'd look in on Dorothy. Before departing she placed a hand on the professor's wrist.

"It's been a privilege to serve you, Lee. The honour of accepting the new posting is all mine."

The patient smiled.

Sasha departed and walked solemnly along the corridor. She withdrew her phone; accessed contact and waited for Dennis to respond.

"How's things boss?"

"Uncertain. What about at your end?"

"Pretty quiet here."

"Any news from the Lantern Falls Health Centre?"

"I received a call from the stationed officer. Your assailant will survive his concussion. He remains unconscious and will be there several days. Afterwards, he's to be transferred to the city jail pending trial."

"I'll touch base with the police chief and explain I was called away," Sasha replied.

"Copy that."

"Over the coming days our team will sit down for a chat."

"There's been lot's going on," replied the guard.

"To say the least."

The phone was replaced and she looked in on Dorothy.

Within the professor's hospital room Jesse watched him retrieve a digital recorder from the bed table. With only the two present Lee said, "I received this update an hour ago and I'm still reeling. A copy has been forwarded to Blakie-Harris."

Jessie leaned in as the recording commenced:

Howdy Lee - Brendon DeLong here I hope your recovery proceeds smoothly? This recording originates from the depths of the manufacturing plant known as Electron Era. I have some startling news to impart. Once I heard from your colleague who confirmed this location as the launch site for a WMD; the Office of Homeland Security were immediately contacted along with the C.D.C. Utilizing an emergency task force and a team of hazmat responders, the lower-level of the electronics plant was penetrated. Participant's were inoculated and attired in PPE's. Ray Pearson was discovered alive, and the body of one of the perpetrators was found. Another was recovered alive atop a stockpile thought to be toxic. The hazardous properties were stored in a crater filled with polystyrene cubes. As the individual was raised from the cavity two significant events occurred: One - the pit was deemed harmless by C.D.C experts who deployed state-of-the-art technology. The substance found in the cubes was water. Secondly - two men were recovered inside a storeroom. The most talkative claimed to be a Dr. Besserer. He ranted about being coerced into working for terrorists. His accusations extended to the man in his company. Besserer insists no US citizens or neighbouring Canadians were at risk from his bogus weapon, which he claims was intentionally dysfunctional. His plan was to pull the wool over the eyes of the men he says abducted and threatened him. To appease his captors he created an environment, where it appeared a biological WMD was being assembled. The doctor states emphatically he has no access to anthrax. Evidently, his client believed otherwise - a notion Besserer likely encouraged. To avoid extradition he claims to have information he's willing to bargain with.

Samuel Train, the man discovered alongside the doctor spoke nary a word throughout Besserer's admission of innocence.

I've removed my hazmat gear and can safely say I suffer no apparent side-effects. C.D.C officials insist none will surface. Whoever pulled the strings behind this operation should have inspected the launch site personally. Any knowledgeable law enforcement official would have recognized the unpractical aspects of the weapon. A fact overlooked by the clueless terrorist's undertaking the project.

This is a preliminary report a more concise effort is forthcoming. Take good care my friend.

The professor glanced at Jesse who appeared stunned.

"You mean it was all for naught!"' the young man declared. "The endangered lives including family members!"

"I was surprised too," Lee admitted. "However, it wasn't for naught son. Had someone truly been equipped with the raw materials; a deadly incident might have occurred. Fortunately, it turned out to be a greedy biologist with neither the wherewithal - nor ingredient's needed to assemble such a devise. He deceived his compatriot militiamen accomplices and his employer, based on obsolete information. Something similar could arise which might not prove false. If it does we're better prepared.

The recruit cast his eyes to the floor and shook his head.

Lee mentioned William Penther and stated a landing party at Rykles Clearing found no trace of the militia leader."

The young man frowned, "I figured what of the woman?"

"She's recovering in a Lafayette hospital."

Drawing his chair nearer Jesse made a confession, "Kriel was confronted by a trio of special agents along the Yokum Trail."

"I wouldn't concern yourself," Lee replied. "Your new handler has plenty of experience in covert espionage. If he hasn't put two and two together with regards to Kriel he soon will. I assure you our secret will remain his secret. He's a firm believer in cloak and dagger subterfuge. Both he and Sasha will discover your other self."

The patient coughed into his balled fist.

Jesse rose, "You need to replace the oxygen mask."

The professor beckoned him nearer and whispered, "Those who witnessed the dead ship's captain will be ignored, laughed at or acknowledged as first-rate storytellers. I'll wager his ghost will eventually return."

Voices were heard in the hall.

Throughout the debriefing Jesse was uncertain whether to reiterate his claim of otherworldly encroachment, whenever Kriel's rags were donned. He decided the matter would have zero-effect on restoring his ailing friend's health and refrained from bringing the matter up.

Abruptly, the nurse entered accompanied by Dorothy Tondar.

Bending close to his mentor Jesse posed a final question, "Just wondering if you had anything to do with retaining those purse-snatchers following dinner that first evening?"

Lee looked perplexed, "I'd forgotten about that! I had to make certain you were up to scratch before you agreed to enter into harm's way. The purse thieves were part of a Special Op's team who owed me a favour. They paid a sore price. Say nothing to Dorothy she'd never forgive me."

"Your secret's safe," Jesse whispered. "Thank you for injecting my life with principle. I'm keen to take up the new posting."

Lee took the young man's hand, "Both Sasha and yourself will learn from each other."

The nurse interjected, "Mrs. Tondar will remain with her husband. Perhaps you and your lady friend would care to visit our cafeteria."

THIRTY-THREE

Lee died at 6.05 the following morning. The monitor flat-lined while Dorothy; alongside his two colleagues flanked the mute woman. An attending physician had made frequent overnight visit's. Occasionally, Dorothy would place a hand on her husband's chest and offer a silent prayer. Whenever, grief overwhelmed her Sasha offered a comforting arm and solace. With the coming of daylight the sombre trio gazed a final time at Lee Tondar. Sasha guided the widow towards a seat in the waiting area, while Jesse fetched water.

The previous morning as the young pair were en route to the hospital, Lee appeared chipper in the company of his dutiful wife. He removed his oxygen mask and pointed toward some notes lying on the bed table.

"Those are for you Dot," he remarked. "They include instructions regarding cremation rituals at the parlour we chose." He paused to catch his breath, "I've notified hospital staff my remains are to be transferred to the Emerson Funeral Home in Lantern Falls. The paperwork and payment has been delivered. Also included are notes addressed to Sasha and Jesse. Their names appear at the top of the relevant pages."

Dorothy retrieved the documents and slipped on reading glasses. Written in Lee's tidy handwriting were seven sheets. Her name was on top of four; the rest were devoted to his young colleagues. She folded the papers and tucked them in her purse. Focusing on her husband, he gazed back silently and smiled. Dorothy leaned over and kissed him on the lips gently. The brightness in his eyes reminded her of the day they'd met.

"I love you," said the man she'd married a half-century earlier.

In the waiting area the doctor who'd attended her husband arrived carrying a clipboard. He offered condolences and handed Dorothy several forms outlining the causes of death. She rubbed her eyes and thanked him. When he departed she said to her companions, "I need to freshen up in the ladies room."

Five minutes later she rejoined the pair and asked if they'd mind dropping her off at Minnie's.

"Of course not," Jesse replied.

"You'll be staying with your friend?" Sasha queried

"For the time being," replied the widow. "Once I've made funeral arrangements I intend to return to Lantern Falls."

A clock indicated 7:15 am as the trio strode towards the elevators. They departed the ground floor and made for the parking lot, where Jesse held the rear door open allowing their solemn passenger inside. He squared up at an automated machine and returned to the car.

"You've both been so kind," Dorothy remarked once they were underway.

"We're family," Jesse said from behind the wheel. "And you're to call if there's anything you require."

The widow reached into her purse and removed a sheaf of papers, "Lee gave me these."

She peeled off the pages addressed to herself and handed the rest to Sasha.

"Your names are up top."

Dorothy indicated left at the next intersection and they entered a residential area.

"This is the street where I'm staying," she related.

They drew alongside a tidy bungalow with a garden out front. Jesse stepped out and opened the rear door, extending a hand to Mrs. Tondar. Sasha emerged from the front and noticed a woman scurrying down the driveway. She joined them and embraced Dorothy.

"I'm so sorry."

Words of consolation followed before the widow turned to her young companions.

"Minnie meet Jesse and Sasha - they're valued friends of both Lee's and mine. Without the three of you this ordeal would have been unbearable."

Greetings were exchanged and Sasha remarked, "Dorothy told us how generous you've been."

It was evident Minnie hadn't slept much.

"Dot's an angel," she sighed. "She's done the same for others countless times."

Following a round of farewell embraces Dorothy informed her escorts, she'd be in touch once funeral arrangements were finalized. Sasha reminded her she was available to assist in any way. Back inside the car they waved and drew from the curb. Merging with traffic they continued towards Highway 80.

As the vehicle was guided onto a westbound ramp its occupant's were silent. Much had transpired over the past seventy-two hours - it took time to process.

Sasha broke the silence, "I'll drive if you like?"

"I found a second wind," Jesse replied. "Thanks anyway.

He cast a sidelong glance and noticed Sasha's windy hair reflecting the morning sun. In sharp contrast a diesel whined by belching plumes of black exhaust. To their immediate right the surface of Lake Erie shimmered.

"You hungry?" Jesse asked.

"A snack would be nice."

West of Cleveland they pulled into a service centre with an attached diner. A booth was secured next to a crew of highway workers devouring breakfast. Jesse scoured the menu while Sasha reached into her jacket for the notes given to her by Mrs. Tondar. A waitress arrived and Jesse requested a toasted western with coffee. His companion ordered tea and a muffin.

Once they were alone Sasha glanced across the table, "I'm glad we agreed not to mention my assault to Lee. He'd been through enough."

"I concur."

"I'm still dumbstruck by his request," she added.

"An understatement to be sure," Jesse affirmed. "You've trained for years I'm a novice."

"The professor seemed to think otherwise."

Jesse looked thoughtful, "Confronted by certain realities I realize now the necessity of everything he stood for."

"You're being modest."

"When Lee was absent you busied yourself observing sky readings and reviewing Intelligence feeds," Jesse insisted. "All while maintaining heightened security - how's that for modest!"

Sasha smiled and allowed the matter to drop.

When their orders arrived she stirred her tea and recalled Jesse's muddied boots and the frayed hems dangling beneath his windbreaker. His appearance implied work of an unusual nature. She returned to Lee's notes and browsed the pages with her name attached. Most dealt with technical matters. On the final page Jesse's name appeared and she passed the sheet to him. Three lines were scribbled.

40 Shopton Drive,
Larchmount County Line north of Hwy 80.
Contact: Mr. Herbert

The address was in the vicinity of Lantern Falls and sounded familiar.

"Shopton Drive," Jesse mused. "I think it can be accessed from the highway."

He asked Sasha if she'd mind accompanying him, "It'll involve a slight detour, but might prove interesting being Lee's last written entry."

His companion was curious and happy to oblige.

Jesse remained a trifle skeptical with regards to working alongside his female colleague. Until recently interaction with Sasha had been strained at best. Perhaps things would change in light of the venture which lay ahead.

He finished his sandwich and noticed Sasha peering over the rim of her teacup.

"Ready to go?" she said.

"You haven't touched your muffin?"

"I'll take it with me."

An ATM machine at the hospital provided Jesse with ready cash. They made their way to check-out where he paid and left a tip. Outside, Sasha withdrew sunglasses and they reentered the car. Breeze streamed through the open windows as they continued their westward journey. Jesse indicated they'd arrive at the Larchmount County Line in roughly forty minutes. With the wind in her hair Sasha reached over and switched on the radio. Big Bill Broonzy was picking country blues on NPR. The song provided an appropriate soundtrack as the scenery flew by and she nodded off.

Jesse's voice penetrated her consciousness, "Were nearing the turnoff!"

She woke with a start, "Huh...?"

"Turnoff's ahead," he repeated.

"Right."

An anchorwoman recited the news at the top of the hour. Nothing was mentioned regarding events in Indiana or Detroit. Jesse noted the omissions and remained perturbed by what unravelled at both locations. It was fortuitous the twin cities were never endangered. Regardless, the affair hastened the professor's condition and was responsible for placing others at risk. Lee once mentioned a Government's first priority is to prevent widespread panic among the populace. This jibed with the lack of report in the media.

A sign indicated the Larchmount County Line.

Jesse guided the car onto a northbound ramp and recalled Shopton Drive was up ahead.

Traffic was sparse as they gazed at the pastoral setting around them. Sunlit meadows gave way to strands of pine and cedar. Moments later they signalled west onto Shopton Drive. Jesse glanced from side to side repeating the address Lee had scribbled down. Cruising past several homes he slowed to a crawl and observed a row of mailboxes. Proceeding slowly they came to a second cluster displaying the number's 44 and 42.

They were close.

The car laboured up an incline and Jesse brought it to a stop at the summit. In the distance, the turrets of Sentinel Hall were sighted alongside her sister buildings. Beyond that Lake Erie glistened beneath a clear blue sky. To their immediate right a hand-crafted sign stood next to an extended driveway. Engraved in brown cedar, bright yellow words welcomed visitor's to Herbert Stables.

"Of course!" Jesse declared. "The stables."

Sasha cast a sidelong glance, "You know this place?"

"I did some horseback riding back home, when I arrived at Grissin I hoped to continue. Someone mentioned Hebert Stables so I had a look. The local is surrounded by woods offering pristine trails and routes along the Erie shoreline."

He backed the car up, "This occurred during my freshman year. Due to a lack of funds I stuck to jogging."

They turned into the driveway and Jesse recalled an office further ahead in an old brownstone. Along their right a lush pasture stretched towards the distant trees. Jesse parked in a spot reserved for visitors and switched off the engine. Stables were visible in a fenced-off area. On an acre of dry grass a hired-hand sprinkled manure. An office sign was attached to a door at the side of the house.

"Ready to inquire?" Sasha remarked.

"I suppose so."

"Would you like me to accompany you?"

"That would be nice."

They entered the office and a middle-aged gentleman behind the counter nodded in their direction. He was concluding transaction's with a young couple who'd arranged riding sessions.

"This Saturday at nine?" confirmed the woman.

Saturday morning it is," the owner replied.

When the couple departed the man smiled, "How may I help you folks?"

Jesse cleared his throat, "Are you Mr. Herbert?"

"I am indeed."

"I'm Jesse Carlton."

He nodded toward his partner, "My friend's name is Sasha."

The young man hesitated, "We were wondering why your address appeared on a piece of paper I have in my possession?"

Creases formed on the stable owner's brow.

Jesse awkwardly explained, "A person close to us recently passed away."

"I'm sorry."

"Yes...well this individual left me your name and address."

Jesse withdrew the document and laid on the counter.

Mr. Herbert appeared perplexed, "That's the right address alri..."

He paused mid-sentence and a look of realization crossed his features, "Would you repeat your name?"

"Jesse Carlton with a C."

"Any ID?"

The young man passed him his driver's license.

The stable owner smiled and handed it back, "If you'll follow me."

He made his way around the end of the counter and paused, "I forgot something."

Retracing his steps he unlocked a drawer and retrieved an envelope.

Afterwards, he rejoined the pair with his hand extended, "Might as well make this formal, I'm Herman Herbert."

Jesse responded in kind as did Sasha. They followed him out the door and rounded a corner scurrying to keep up.

Their guide shouted at the hired man, "Take over behind the counter Lenny. I'll be a few minutes."

The man nodded and placed aside his shovel.

In the distance a trio of riders were seen galloping across the field towards a trail set among the trees.

"You appear busy," Jesse remarked.

"Seven days a week," replied Herman. "The business has been in the family for several generations. Bred and trained horses most of that time."

They drew alongside the stables and approached the one most distant.

"This hosts a single stall," he informed the pair. "It was erected in the event we were burdened with a noisy animal. Restless mount's often need to be apart from the others. It has a calming effect on the agitated animal and prevents it's mate's from becoming riled."

Jesse was motioned closer, "As of now this stable is yours ".

"Mine!"

Mr. Herbert produced a key and unfastened a padlock attached to the gate and the young man's eyes widened.

"Hurricane!"

Kicking up dirt the animal arched her neck towards his outstretched hand.

"She seems pleased to see you," remarked the stable owner.

Jesse's face was radiant as he stroked her velvet mane. While this unfurled Sasha stood off to one side.

"I take it her name is Hurricane?" the owner pressed.

"That's correct."

Exchanging cheerful glances the uniformed woman smiled.

Jesse pet the mare and whispered, "Atta girl."

He turned to the stable master, "How in the world did she wind up here?"

Offering him the envelope Mr. Herbert stated, "Two men arrived early this morning hauling a horse- trailer. They handed me this letter and placed the animal in my trust. I was instructed to make certain she was stabled and maintained. She's available to you on and off this property whenever you desire. Financial considerations have been provided indefinitely. In conclusion, this wonderful creature is all yours. The content's of the letter will explain everything."

The recipient glanced at the envelope then at Sasha. He was handed a key by the stable owner.

"This allows access to your stable - and so you know the grounds are routinely monitored. I live on the premises and keep a spare. The men who delivered your prize suggested you may not arrive for days. I'm delighted you showed so promptly."

Herman Herbert sighed and stroked the mare, "I'd best return to the office. You're welcome to stay as long as you wish "

He started away and Jesse turned to face Hurricane, "So what about these new digs!"

Sasha stood at the entrance observing the pair.

The new owner glanced over his shoulder and urged her to draw nearer, "She's quite friendly."

"I haven't been around many horses," she responded, "She'll sense my reticence."

"She likes you already I can tell.'"

Sasha approached reluctantly and placed her hand along the creature's sleek neck as if it were a bedspread. Warming to the touch she whispered, "Her coat is so fine."

The mare craned it's neck and snorted.

"She says thanks."

Sasha chuckled, "Hurricane you say?"

"Yep. I needed a name quick."

"She's fast?"

"For certain!"

Venturing into the sunlight Jesse tore open the envelope and perused it's contents. A typewritten message indicated the horse had been purchased on behalf of Jesse Carlton, by the late Lee Tondar, in appreciation of a job well done. The document went on to state all provisions had been accounted for until the animal's eventual demise; whereupon burial procedures would be observed at the owner's behest.

The letter was drafted and signed by Robert Blakie-Harris.

Jesse folded the note and placed it away. He repeated the gist of the message to Sasha.

Taking a deep breath the young man experienced a tidal-wave of exhaustion.

"We'd best be going," he murmured.

Hurricane was stroked and Jesse bid adieu, "When I return we'll hit the trails."

Securing the gate they retraced their steps. Along the way, Jesse poked his head in the office door and thanked Mr. Herbert. The stable owner waved and said the pleasure was his.

Sasha was waiting in the passenger seat. Jesse entered and guided the car towards Shopton Drive.

"I can't believe Lee arranged all of this in the short time he had left," he remarked.

His companion weighed in, "No doubt the Director of Operations had a hand in arranging the professor's request."

The driver nodded.

Windover Road loomed and fresh water was scented. Along their right, the granite crest above Falls Valley extended toward the bluffs. Jesse made the turn and marvelled at how close the stables were in proximity to Sentinel Hall. He intended to purchase a bicycle and make the distance by way of the valley.

He signalled into the campus grounds and Sasha resolved not to give sway to the past. Her attacker was under observation and awaiting trial. Once details of murder and assault were added to his staged death, he was looking at an eternity behind bars.

As for her spectral Savior she had her own ideas.

They swung onto Abbot Lane and the familiar sight of Sentinel Hall greeted them.

"I'll walk you to the Residence Building," Jesse offered.

"That's kind of you," Sasha responded. "I'd prefer it if you'd accompany me along the path surrounding the Hall. It would be nice to view the lake."

"Sure thing."

They parked out front and stepped into the sunlight. Jesse reminded himself to return the car to the dealership the following morning. Afterwards, he'd retrieve his own from behind the Lighthouse and make arrangements with Dorothy Tondar regarding Lee's VW.

Seagulls reeled overhead as Sasha stood facing the courtyard. Her companion could only imagine what was going through her mind.

"Let's take that walk," he gently coaxed.

They strode casually along the path and stared across the water towards the Canadian side. In the shadow of the grey fortress Sasha took in a mouthful of lake air and exhaled.

It felt good.

A mile or so out Jesse noticed an antiquated merchant ship drifting towards the horizon. The vessel was similar to those featured in paintings displayed in Sentinel Hall's storied museum. During seasonal months replicas sailed the lower-lakes from one end to the other. Enthusiast's converged along waterfront's lining Erie and Lake Ontario. They navigated the Welland Canal as mariners did, more than a century before in celebration of their regional heritage.

Jesse witnessed the facsimile and wondered why Sasha hadn't noticed? She would have mentioned the sighting had it been observed. When he inquired she acknowledged she could see the masts of sailboats - the rest was mist.

"I don't think I'll be returning to the Residence Building."

The statement caught Jesse off guard

"Lee offered me his quarters."

"Indeed he did."

"I like to think I left dorm rooms behind years ago," she insisted.

"Of course," agreed her companion a little too eagerly.

Faced with the prospect of living alone within the bowls of an ancient fortress Jesse welcomed the company.

Sasha placed her hand in his, "Let's take a moment to remember the professor."

Overlooking the water she closed her eyes.

The merchant ship was now a vague outline and Jesse observed a ragged figure on deck.

A moment later the vessel dissolved into mist.

———————————

www.ingramcontent.com/pod-product-compliance
Lightning Source LLC
Chambersburg PA
CBHW070305310726

48976CB00005B/1586